NU-EVERMORE

by Peter Magliocco
(C) 2002

Peter Magliocco (signature)

National Library of Canada Cataloguing in Publication

Magliocco, Peter, 1948-
    Nu-evermore / Peter Magliocco.
ISBN 1-55369-891-6
    I. Title.
PS3613.A37N8 2002   813'.6   C2002-903950-9

TRAFFORD

This book was published *on-demand* in cooperation with Trafford Publishing.
On-demand publishing is a unique process and service of making a book available for retail sale to the public taking advantage of on-demand manufacturing and Internet marketing.
On-demand publishing includes promotions, retail sales, manufacturing, order fulfilment, accounting and collecting royalties on behalf of the author.

Suite 6E, 2333 Government St., Victoria, B.C. V8T 4P4, CANADA
Phone   250-383-6864   Toll-free   1-888-232-4444 (Canada & US)
Fax   250-383-6804   E-mail   sales@trafford.com
Web site   www.trafford.com   TRAFFORD PUBLISHING IS A DIVISION OF TRAFFORD HOLDINGS LTD.
Trafford Catalogue #02-0704   www.trafford.com/robots/02-0704.html

10   9   8   7   6   5   4   3   2

NU-EVERMORE

by Peter Magliocco   (C) 2001

Part 1

Bravura, Christina

1.

It felt like he'd fallen from a distant black hole in space where gravity did not exist and the laws of nature did not apply, except for those of the unseen space satellite watchers above all ...

Stumbling down a blind alley, Macon wondered how much time was left to make the deal. The digital prostitute had steered him wrong – into a dead end, clearly. She'd given him the address of a supposedly wealthy patron living in the finest apartments Amsterdam boasted, and Macon had gone hoping to sell some good-quality Euro-hemp. Instead, he found two men waiting for him: the kind of burly and solemn types his practiced eye immediately associated with the C.I.D., or other U.S. government military men.

It was with a flayed conscience that he went there in the first place, for Raul Macon was sick. Nursing a perennial cold in drizzly October wasn't enough. He was also sick of the deals and the rotten compromise of being an indentured servant to Tito, his erstwhile mentor and owner of four hotels scattered around Central Station, hub of incoming traffic.

Jari was one of the working girls who sometimes hung around the bar of The Amstoy (Tito's largest hotel, where Macon also worked.) She definitely had screwed Macon up. Sending him to the *haute couture* apartments where he could have been royally busted, or worse. Had she knowingly set him up? It was something that plagued Macon the moment he suspected he was in certain double-trouble.

"Are you Jari's friend?"

Macon wasn't sure who the voice belonged to. Both of his receptionists looked American, and his suspicion was immediately alarming. They looked thirtyish, with the manicured jowls of office-types who read and completed endless forms, between karate lessons and target practice. Raul feared they might be cyberclones. How Tito would have relished this moment!

Macon mumbled something about having the wrong address. He was not sure he – or they – had the right Jari in mind either.

The swarthiest one of this stout twosome suggested Raul Macon sit down. The man identified himself as Rolf-something, "American businessman." Macon felt a familiar queasiness – *the sickness* – rise up inside him, pushing aside dregs of buried memories.

"This shouldn't be much of an inconvenience," the swarthiest man said. "Jari said you might help us –"

Macon felt the foil-covered bag of Euro-hemp inside his left coat pocket burning a hole into his side. Too close to his ulcer, the bag acted like a radioactive touchstone. Macon wanted to puke on the carpet, to upset propriety.

"Listen, old fellow," said the other man, with an English lilt unbefitting his rough-hewn features. "You're wondering who we are, and we're wondering who you are. All we need is –"

"Some information," his partner interjected, smiling and offering Macon a Dutch cigar while simultaneously checking a joy-buzzer in his palm the size of a 20th century beeper.

The heavy-set conveyor of hemp refused, unable to subdue a large sigh. "I work at The Amstoy. You know that place? Tito's my employer. Is this a trans-terrestrial espionage intercourse?"

Was he talking too much? The others nodded, the fake English one returning to the sofa where a mixed drink awaited him. "We're gauging you, sport."

"Mind if I leave?" Macon asked the large swarthy man, who stood intimidatingly before the doorway.

"You're not really interested in us, then?"

"Not in the least. I hate to be rude, but I've got other appointments."

"Jari said you might be more cooperative ..."

Macon made a face-mask of chagrin. "I don't think I can provide you gentlemen with what in hell escapes me."

The pair laughed, almost simultaneously. Angel-ectoplasm was released into the air, which produced a pleasant uplifting effect Macon ignored. Soul-less bastards, he thought. Raul Macon was an old Army man, true, but these birds had no jurisdiction over him now. The Government couldn't touch him for holding – it was too "open" in Amsterdam, he believed -- but automatic responses from past encounters had Macon uneasy. Times kept changing.

"You know," the swarthy man said quietly, "G.I.s get in trouble here. They come away with the wrong souvenirs."

Macon stopped. "You lookin' for G.I.s, or buried treasure?"

"We'll tell you what we're looking for." Rolf-something closed the door, trying to smile nonchalantly. "Wouldn't some unearthed treasure interest *you*?"

Well hell this is all fucked up, Macon thought. *Here I come hoping to score on two Dutch dudes, and I got Old Glory's global cops tryin' to bribe me. This must be rich.*

"I don't know a fuckin' thing about Jari," he finally responded, disdaining the paper guilders thrust under his nose.

"How about Gaylen Tomasi?" the dark man said, confronting Macon in the lethal-seeming way these men found natural. Though the name surprised him, Raul kept his bridling temper on idle. Suddenly he gave an abrupt, mocking laugh.

"Man, you C.I.D. or C.I.A.? ... I should call the Dutch cops on you impostors --"

"They already know we're here," the same man smiled, with relish.

"Well. Don't show me any badge, man – or any metal." Be straight, he told himself. "I don't know any Gaylen whoever, okay? Who is the guy?"

"An Army deserter who might be collaborating with terrorist groups in Western Europe," the man on the sofa replied "How's that?"

"Fantastic," Macon said. The name rang a bell, like an old alias from long ago. "But I don't know him, never heard of him. Maybe Jari does, but I don't."

The two agents exchanged looks, almost friendly now. They were nearly twins in their ruddy beefiness and overly barbered heads ... Someone was trying to make a killing, they maintained, and Macon "had better be careful as careful could be," unquote.

Now Raul Macon had more of a mission than any ever foisted on him, and he rued this fact ambivalently. There was more "information" on him that could cause problems if broached to the wrong people. Back at The Amstoy bar, Raul was knocking back trepidation with several shots of Geneva gin.

It was friggin' inevitable, he told himself. He knew it was bound to happen all along, but another part of his piebald psyche kept willing to bury it in the amnesia of daily living.

Merde, he told himself. It was his favorite phrase (picked up from a French tourist Macon let fondle his knee before kicking the bugger into the street), yet he wasn't sure if it meant God or Hell.

That porcine king of bartenders, Hull-E., was standing behind the bar in his behemoth fashion. Panting, he smelled of booze sweated out, and with a cocked eye behind bifocals watched his quasi-employee. "You want another?"

"No, thanks, Hull-E."

Hull-E. grunted dourly, with some conviction, and blinked back smoke above his steel rims. "Raulie! ... The hell you don't."

"Then hit me, beautiful man."

It was their ritual – quiet but corrosive – though Macon never usually got blown away. It was 4:30 in the afternoon and his errands weren't finished. Tito would have Raul's ass basted in acid. "Shit. Keep an eye on me, Hull-E.," a voice said in his brain, and the way he glanced at the suspendered fat man drinking also. But nothing finally rebounded from Macon's lips.

"Where you been, Raulie?"

"Makin' my rounds ... Takin' care of business – " A wave of disgust prompted him to dry his lips with a callused forefinger. "You seen T.K., Hull-E.?"

"He's around."

Son-oh-bitch. Hull-E. was pouring out another, matching him round for round. That tacky old man was a drinking machine. Raul Macon felt like shit – looked it squared by a high number – and wanted to get himself obliterated. "T.K., look out wherever you are ..." But he knew he should be blaming Jari, that sorry excuse for a digital harlot.

The Amstoy hotel was located along Canal Street, the street of low-tech whores. It catered mostly to the tourist trade, and wasn't the sort of hotel where prostitutes took their johns to consummate business. (One or two favored prostitutes – such as Jari – were allowed to drink at the bar and leave with a prospective custormer.) It was one of three hotels around the Oudevoorburgwal that Macon worked in. All three were quite old and

forbidding-looking, and owned by the entrepreneur Tito, who had a finger in everything. Well into the 21st Century.

If T.K. Keller was around, Raul Macon was going to kick his hempiness, just for general principles. He left the bar in a careening state, nearly knocking over somebody's beer bottle. The early evening patrons from the street started to filter in, and the bar was no longer crazy. Only Raul felt like it.

T.K. Keller sat in the cramped apartment and tried to watch a T.V. pulsating like a giant bug's digital eye in the corner. There was a Dutch program on and he didn't understand the language. He stared bleakly on anyway, waiting for a re-run of *Gunsmoke of World War III,* a news show, that was supposed to follow.

In the interstices of his mind, T.K. was a lost soul in bankrupt Valhalla. He knew Raul Macon's girlfriend, Karin, didn't like him relaxing zombie-style in her sacrosanct but tacky living room, which he littered with peanut shells and cigarette butts, riding out the crest of another high (to him only the obverse shadow of The Big Downer). Karin was a digital slut anyway (she had to be, making it with Macon), one with the face of – yes, thought T.K. – a *ferret.* She didn't understand his "ways," and Macon was trying to get T.K. quartered again in The Amstoy's rotting attic, where once he nearly died from bad hallucinations, thanks to poisoned crystal drops.

T.K. hated that creaking closet, where he slept in a sleeping bag on the floor. He sensed that a murder or something diabolical had occurred there.

But now before the T.V., young T.K. nodded off, sinking comfortably into the doilied sofa chair smelling of musty odors and domestic abuse. His mind was like a tape recorder playing blank tape. The troubling fluctuations of the hemp high – here unbearably pleasurable, there excruciatingly scary – had left him, and he gratefully succumbed to the encroachment of sleep.

"T.K., get your ass in gear," he heard Macon's rasping voice commanding him. "Hull-E says you didn't help with the chores today. What's your fuckin' story?"

The chores. T.K. could hardly suppress a laugh, yet he knew Macon was seriously mad. He yawned, shaking his head, buying time.

Karin was there too, petulantly studying him, trying to decide if he was high or down. It was a strangely hypocritical business all right. As long as the lurid realities of life went on outside her domicile, there was no problem. But bring it inside and she was like a shrew possessed of unquenchable fury.

"I want to talk to you, T.K. --"

T.K. Keller slumped back, smiling inanely.

"I hear you."

"You were at the Maradisa all day -- "

"So what?"

He uttered the words with slow difficulty, and they hung on his lips like some primordial curse.

"There ain't no guilders in the kitty ..."

T.K. implied that he failed to "score," but Raul Macon was shaking his head, smoking and belligerently hovering above. "Tito's gonna have the royal ass, T.K. And it's not my problem what he does to your forever-teenage asshole."

"I swear it, Macon ... Nothing came up."

"We're having a problem here, T.K. You understand that? We're having some might big fucking hassles -- " He slapped off the T.V. with a sudden viciousness, nearly knocking it over. "You don't understand the score, you greasy bastard."

"I'm sorry, man."

"You're sorry? You're fucking sorry. You don't do a goddamn thing but diddle your pecker all day."

"Raul," came Karin's admonishing voice from the kitchen.

"Nobody learns here. *No-*body fucking learns here."

Raul Macon sat down on the sofa, cursing like the soldier he once was. They made a strange pair all right, and Macon resented having to be T.K.'s overseer and whatnot. But that was what Tito wanted, and Tito ruled.

So Macon sighed, a rumpled ex-linebacker gone to seed, drowning in this world of popular corruption, wondering how he was successfully going to interrogate this skinny wimp without getting bullshit. Raul smoothed over his blue rayon sweater and absently tapped a hand to his knee.

"I got a job for you, T.K."

"What's that?"

Macon paused, finally blurting it out: "I want you scouting around for a dude named *Gaylen Tom-a-si,* who's gonna cop some superhemp." Macon squinted with wistful perseverance through blue traces of smoke. "That name ring your bell?"

"Naw, it doesn't," replied Keller, now visibly nonplussed. "Who is he?"

"I'm gonna tell you," Macon said, lowering his voice, listening to Karin's cooking sounds from the kitchen. *"Later."*

After that the burly veteran with the receding yellow hairline grunted and walked away.

... He knew that Tito would be slightly incensed if he discovered his foreman was wasting precious time tracking down some mysterious character the C.I.D. (?) wanted. Macon was enough incensed himself, and considered just forgetting the whole business, or telling the C.I.D. twins to go replicate themselves with a branding iron.

But for some reason unknown to himself, Macon was afraid. He hadn't encountered a nebulous fear like this since his Army days, and it accounted for his exacerbated behavior towards T.K. and Karin. Now this worried him extravagantly, and as Macon ambled purposefully along Canal Street toward Jari's "office," he debated just how to deal with the incorrigible witch.

"I'll steal all her candied prophylactics," he muttered angrily.

Meanwhile, Jari the digital courtesan -- inside her cramped picture window cubicle overlooking the canal -- was engaged in giving a lumpy German tourist less than his money's worth. The flaccid devil could hardly achieve the state known as erection (not to mention what supposedly followed), since his member was painfully attached to a digital device known as *The Happy Hooker's Palm Pilot.* O, it was an unsavory sight indeed, and finally the man collapsed, his impotence due to Jari's skilled manhandling. On the floor he mewled an incomprehensible lament nearby Jari's velvet-covered bed.

"Jari? Jari ...?"

It was about then that Raul Macon was reddening his knuckles on the ancient oak door, not caring how *flagrante delicto* things were behind it. Jari slipped on her robe and told her prostrate customer to get his pants on. The distraught German (believing secret space police had come for him, thanks to the strong Geneva he'd consumed) began to gyrate from invisible electric shocks.

"Mein Gott!" he screamed, proclaiming his innocence, which is impotence no doubt justified.

Jari opened the door a crack, keeping the chain on.

"Raul, I have a customer --"

"Shoo him out of there, honey. I got matters to discuss."

Still floundering, the pot-bellied German managed to slip his suit pants on, so Jari admitted her hulking visitor inside without further ado.

"What's so damn important at a time like this?"

"You know damn well what's so important," huffed Macon, looking disgustedly at the john writhing pathetically on the floor. "Jesus Christ, mister. Let me kick your ass out."

"Let him alone, Raul. He's going --"

"Frustrated again, no doubt, by your cyber-wizardry. Honey-bitch, you're in the wrong business."

She squeezed the paper guilders in her robe pocket. "They never get it back," she winked campily, "and they get a taste of being really downloaded."

Looking embarrassed and bedraggled, the German managed to find his hat and pull on his overcoat. His head bent and scrunched like a turtle within his shoulders, he immediately hobbled out without even a farewell glance at his lovely tormentor, and Macon stepped gingerly aside.

"You did it again," Raul marveled, slamming the door so that the picture window rattled nearby the large and upright computer-console in the corner, a machine resembling an old-fashioned automobile's smog-exhaust checker. "He didn't stay for a smog-check or tune-up, did he?"

"He paid well, dear baby."

"Tito should be glad, then. Except he paints a different picture about your activity around here."

"What does he say, Raul?"

"He says you better ante up or they're gonna find your pretty buns in the can."

"You can't scare me, Raul."

"I wouldn't want to try, honey. I'm just relaying his unedited message. He's fit to be tied, and so am I."

"What's your problem?"

Macon sighed, knowing she was difficult. He sat down on a sofa chair in the far corner and propped his Spanish boots on the settee. With thoughtful slowness he lit a cigar, watching Jari slip into her slippers and comb out her long blonde hair before the bureau mirror. She was a Hans Holbein Eve, no question. Older than he was by a good ten years, however, and the tight wrinkles he noticed advertised her as used goods, Tito inspected.

Macon didn't give a damn. If he was going to get shot over this mess, tough titty. He'd take the Eve with him.

"I checked out this Tomasi dude cold, like I was told, but there was no score. Turns out he's hot property."

Jari kept attending to her make-up, applying fresh orange lipstick. "What does that mean, Raulie?"

"It means I was in the right place at the wrong time, or vice versa, hell if I know." Slowly he exhaled smoke, feeling like a man exhumed for the occasion.

"Raul, you sound tired."

"I'm straighter then you are. By God, my head is together, woman."

"Sure, Raul."

"*Okay.* Okay, then. Was this Tomasi dude a trick of yours, or did I portray him in another lifetime?"

"That's right, darling. That's how I learned he wanted a connection -- a deep one."

"When was this?"

Jari screwed up her features, comb frozen in mid-air, pained by the intellectual effort required of her. "Last Tuesday night, I think." She placed the comb back atop the bureau. "Raul? What's the matter?"

"Some finks don't trust him, I told you. They could make the market blacker around here in a way you wouldn't like." He spat out a cigar flake and closed his eyes. *Lying* to him. Women were all the same. Profiteers above and under the skin. He felt queasy again, his ulcer acting up. He asked Jari for a glass of wine.

"You can't seem to get it straight that *I'm serious* about all this."

"I know that, man."

She handed him a greasy mug filled with mote-speckled Moselle. He sipped carefully, eyes half-masted, listening to the busy traffic sounds outside. The street was a freaking circus every night after 7:30, and Macon dreaded going back out to elbow his way home again. Through a curtain crack he caught fleeting glimpses of hard-looking male faces prowling outside, waiting for Jari's curtain to open again. Waiting for her to resume the provocative pose she always affected before the window, sitting languidly in her fishnet stockings and open blouse (with a flesh-colored bra) showing plenty of what men treasured most. What a sweet bullshit act, Macon believed.

And her room: so utterly cramped with female things, it gorged his senses. Everything reeked of perfumes and incense, and Macon pictured her cooking-up hemp in here, or living on white cyber-crystal. The bright velvet red and pink colors of the curtains made the place resemble a depraved doll's house known only on some outlawed internet.

It was too much, of course. Amid the quaint bureau, coffee table, narrow bed and assorted junk, Macon felt claustrophobic and cold. Like everything else, the room was part of an old building stuck too close to other old buildings, and all seemed clogged with the dank fish-rot filming the canals with a green, virulent residue.

"This is old cyber-crystal, not wine."

"You should be that lucky."

Macon laughed -- a hoarse echo redounding from his canyon dark throat. "Anyway ... If this 'Tomasi' dude comes back, I want you to let me know, all right? I'm serious, babe." He stared directly at her calves, studying musculature. "I promise you beaucoup bucks, and I'll square you with Tito if you're good on this."

"You're full of 'beaucoup bucks,' aren't you?"

"Honey, I'm Beaucoup Blues in the flesh, at your service."

She laughed at him. Macon hoped there was no double-crosser's glint in Jari's eye (that feral organ, opaquely cat-like), but couldn't be sure. He was at the mercy of forces conjured up out of Dutch pits of ignorance and timeless sufferings, and felt like he was becoming another slave of superstition, worshipping the female like he did, yet hating her too.

And Jari Vandeer knew this beaucoup bluesbaby was hurting. *He's crazy,* she knew, but realized all men were crazy. She felt that she could use him, quite easily, and forestall any of his power tactics. Macon was badly deluded, but that was how life went. She knew he wanted to dominate her, yet also press his acne-scarred face between her silicone-shot breasts and confess all to the whore-mater.

"Jari, what day is it --?"

"It's the day after the Beetles and the Creem reunited, or haven't you heard?"

He shut off the radio. "Big freakin' deal."

She knew this bloated male needed her, and would have to play her game like all the others. This excited her more than anything. She took a sip of wine, standing there provocatively before the bulb-fringed mirror, and eyed him in her practiced way. He had come full of bluster and threats, but now he sat there with a large hand to his forehead, looking desperate. She wanted to laugh at him, this displaced American, this browbeaten ex-G.I. who had gotten too big (in the wrong way) for his jock-strap.

"All right," she said slowly, finally. "I'll help you. But will you help me?"

She pulled the robe open, letting him see her wobbling breasts, and there was a feral intensity in her eyes. She pricked the tip of her nipples with a long red fingernail, simultaneously moving her tongue along glistening, freshly made-up lips. Holding the crystalline palm pilot behind her, Jari advanced slowly, kneeling before him, then pulling down Macon's trousers. He squirmed -- caught there -- a look of supernal wonder overtaking him.

Before he could rise from the chair, Macon's body was cybernetically amatorialized by Jari's palm pilot. He began to see the world's wonders coalesce for an eternal transitory instant in a mind's eye reaching into the farthest reaches of space, where only an ecstasy of reunion awaited him.

He was drowning, gulping for air --

Jari renewed the onslaught, and Macon knew the dimpled scales of her well-traveled skin in almost microscopic detail. He was one delicious megabyte now in a black hole in another galaxy, and he didn't want any star but the one collapsing within and without him ... Coming back, he tasted the unreconstructed saltiness of an amphibian-like skin his fingers serenaded, finding holes from which pungent smells and bright colors emerged. At the base of godlike buttocks wrinkled, red-furrowed flesh was discovered, distending the small blue butterfly tattoo which withstood such service through the years. For a second Macon was saddened, put back by the pragmatic application of some greater knowledge only the witch Eve possessed.

She performed on him in a way that Karin, his old lady, could never do. She was still a beautiful woman -- despite her occupation, her thirty-odd years of life, her sordid work on the street -- and all this thrilled a jaded and older Raul Macon, kindled a brief consummation to his pent-up fantasies; for money could never have bought him this. Not yet.

Now as he mounted her on the creaking floor, Macon felt he was entering some magical space of existence denied him too long. Tasting her rich digital blood, he was too spent to wonder about the crucible of things to come, forgetting all the wars on earth and in space that (like redundant newspaper headlines) had plagued Earth for a seeming millennium of failed "futuristic" achievements -- until the only true salvation was a regression into the sensual truisms of what machines could translate into a better reality.

When he was finished, Macon realized he failed to make ground zero.

2.

The boy seemed lost in the maze of people clogging the Dam square. He was always there, it seemed to Keller, feeding the pigeons or just walking them along the ageless and damp cobblestones.

It was a drizzly sea-gray morning, and Keller wished he was back in bed. He had no stomach for this endeavor, and was a mite confused. Slightly unhinged, he was too down for this anyway. The boy Mik -- standing there forlornly, waif-like in baggy pants, work boots, torn overcoat and soiled beret -- was an orphan of war in Sarajevo. A sad sight, he was the one familiar denizen (by virtue of lucklessness, no doubt) never failing to cheer up T.K. Keller.

Mik belonged to no one, it appeared, but this adopted city and Canal Street. Bastard son of a woman dead from cancer (was it rumor?), he was The Amstoy's unofficial mascot, a far cry from civil war or Euro-Disney. So it was that everybody on the street cared for him at ill-timed intervals, and he wore the orphan's eternal air of homelessness like another piece of tattered clothing.

"Where you been, T.K.?"

He spoke damn good English, this 10-year-old kid. Something T.K. Keller was beginning to appreciate more and more.

"Just hangin' out and around," T.K. finally replied, anxious not to mention his scheduled appointment at the Maradisa.

The boy put his white hands in his pockets and shrugged, "Oh yeah? Sounds like what I do."

"Absolutely, Mik-man." Keller glanced at the slow-running Timex on his wrist. Allowing for the ordinary slowness, he still had plenty of time. This gangster Tomasi could go diddle himself. He stood there feeling more at ease than anytime that hectic morning; it was almost like the boy in the square would always be around when necessary. "You need anything?"

"I'm good, T.K."

Keller nonetheless unwrapped a large guilder note, like a fancy handkerchief, and stuck it into the boy's vest pocket. "Don't lose that."

Mik kept tossing some stale bread crumbs to the strutting pigeons, humming as he did so. The two walked slowly along in silence for awhile, listening meditatively to city sounds. It was an early Friday morning and the square wasn't too crowded, except for the usual horde of Neo-huppies congregating around statues in the distance. Unaccountably this seemed the quietest place in a city bustling all around with swarming, noisy cars navigating through an ocean of people.

"How's Lelica?"

"She's okay," the boy replied. Lelica was the young digital escort babe who had virtually adopted Mik, though she was as suited for the task as Keller, perhaps.

T.K. uncomfortably felt the fall cold seeping into him, despite the long mauve muffler slung around him. "What do you say we get a cup of espresso?"

"Sounds, ja, good."

Coffee would hardly nestle soothingly in T.K.'s stomach like early morning dew on an empty lawn. Nothing would diminish T.K.'s reluctance about being a weak-kneed bloodhound on the scent of better kept secrets.

Later, out of the cafe's warm ambience T.K. would stumble, leaving his young charge satisfied among the busy patrons and their hunger. Feeling close to retching -- and laden with misgivings -- T.K. went back out into the drizzle-soaked morning. He headed for the Maradisa, that huge and picturesque old building where Amsterdam's drug-infested youth congregated.

Who would know about T-o-m-a-s-i? Raul Macon had ordered T.K. to get the dope on that mysterious individual, and T.K. felt as optimistic as he would trying to get an audience with the Pope. Moreover, continuing in an ironic vein, the czar of the Maradisa -- Lady Marva Claire -- was herself invested with a kind of Mother Superior majesty, and wouldn't be so sympathetic probably to T.K.'s plight either.

But T.K. plodded on, always the good troop. The airs of constricting secrecy bothered him most about the whole affair. He could see himself blowing matters before they got properly started.

Don't chicken out, T.K. told himself. His future well-being in Amsterdam might depend on what he could find out, and his bedeviling predicament might therefore be kept a viable secret. T.K. knew otherwise he'd be back in the stockade. If he was lucky, it would still be one on earth, not one in deep space where prisoners became equal to space junk ...

3.

Her face was something pristine beneath the blacklight: ebony crystal-like sculpture could only emulate the smooth richness, the glints of an inner light casting a nobility about the fine-chiseled features.

"You are so radiant," Marva Claire declared, subtly patting the regal young woman's hand with her freckled, heavily ringed own. By contrast the much older Maradisa owner was a bizarre concoction of womanly attributes, with a stark ugliness about her once mannish features. Red frizzled Afro hair, severely pancaked white face -- offset by horizontal punctuations of lipstick and eyeliner -- gave daring ambiguity to her strange visage. The jewelry she wore, like the gold crescent clasp clinging leaflike to her left nostril, was gaudy enough to belong on a bohemian fortune teller in the Uranus fold.

"I don't know why I love you so ..."

"You exaggerate, Marva," came the bland reply.

"No, no ..."

The stout woman paused to take another hit from her unfiltered cigarette, then marveled in her wondering fashion. "It's all so sensible, that I should feel this. Part of the great whole which is your beauty."

"Really?"

"Yes, yes. Absolutely magical Christina."

The young woman laughed, looking down at the ballroom-like floor from the uniquely styled fastness she found herself in. It was like a fairy-tale architecture dreamed up by Piranesi. Those erratic lintels and arches, those recesses in which people were grouped oddly (either hanging out, or sprawled around tables), informally watching the Bosch-like spectacle as they consumed a great variety of dope and soft drinks. The music seemed to emanate from the porous surroundings like an aerated tidal wave which threatened to engulf the Dionysian dancers parading in barefoot abandon. Indeed a sight to more than behold, though Christina had seen it (stoned or otherwise) more than enough times. The air of decadence never failed to enthrall and fascinate her.

"You are *not* beautiful, Marva."

"I know that, dear."

"But you are rather sweet."

The older woman closed her painted eyes in a broad display of threatrical passion. "Of that I am quite certain!"

Christina Alpreece felt that her high had stopped suddenly, leaving her with that sad clarity which followed. A poignancy would overtake her then, and she felt sobered by the after-effects of the inner journey she'd returned from. Once again conventional space and time were thrust aside, and this seemed to revive her interest in the mundane world one had to live again in.

"If you're tired we could adjourn to my offices."

"Oh no, not at all."

The older woman scoffed, but there was an implacable knowledge in her eyes. This was no ordinary otherworldly transsexual.

The great lady's attendant, Clendon, hovered nearby and kept a watchful protectiveness on their table. He was of an hirsute and muscular complexion, and kept his arms folded across his chest in the best manner of harem attendants. There was something uneasy in the air -- a cold, lingering fright in suspension -- and this disturbed and excited Christina like nothing else in the Maradisa had for a long while.

Clendon leaned over and whispered into the ear of his wrinkled proprietress. He acted privy to information of an astoundingly urgent matter. Christina sighed, wanting to go away, to sleep in beds of fine silk and perfumed pillows.

With a calculating shrewdness, Marva watched the large crowd of revelers now, her eyes alert to greater possibilities. Christina looked also, but the crowd proved an unbreakable barrier of costumed bodies bent on the thrust of a single rhythmic mission.

It ebbed in and out, this crowd, shuddering all the while. It was not properly fed on its ambrosia yet, and kicked about discontentedly while waiting for a super rush to descend. Christina watched more intently than ever, becoming afraid. On this top floor around her young people clung to the alcoved or recessed walls as if sculpted there, and bright primary colors everywhere vied to remain sovereign amid encroaching dark shadows.

"Piranesi," a knowing voice told her. "Piranesi's chambers of heaven."

A dancing male and female couple had quietly gained an ascendancy in the crowd. The couple moved in bewitching fashion across the floor, a long narrow swath which seemed to open for the dancers, until their bare and sinuously moving members could more freely perform upon it. All the on-lookers were fueling the moment of abandon, giving it new life. Amid turbulent smells of flesh and curling smoke, the couple executed a freestyle *pas de deux* of unrivaled emotional energy, celebrating the grand and communal sublimation of sex, pulling the ring of acolytes well into a flaying vortex. It was so deeply rich and alluring that Christina felt a voluptuousness declaring itself within her, crying to be unleashed in splendor.

But *who* was Marva Claire looking for? Her wraith-like lovely could only wonder, watching this spectacle gain in taboo-shattering momentum. Already a number of people leaned lewdly in an orgiastic direction.

"Don't stop them," Christina muttered, but only to herself.

Across the room T.K. Keller stood cradling young Mik from the jostling on-lookers, many of whom wondered how a boy had gotten into the place. Mik's presence was an oddity indeed within the gyrating event; but he was a fellow who got things done, according to Lelica, and what T.K. needed more than anything was someone to do the job he had no real gumption for. A child must lead the man, Keller had reasoned back in the cafe.

At least the available paregoric allowed T.K. to put a damper on the neurotic hypertension assaulting him. In the open drug-trafficking allowed the young here by the city fathers, T.K. managed to procure a quarter-key of Euro-hemp – which he clung to protectively, as if newly found balm, beneath an armpit. Amid euphoric celebration, he smoked and inhaled the stuff furiously from a silver pipe he never unglued from his lips, except in offering to the uninterested Mik.

An urchin to the core in his torn woolen cap and checkered muffler, both too heavy and large for him, Mik found small enjoyment in the whirling bacchanal before him. He had seen it all before, although under Lelica's wing. Mik even felt smirkingly above it all, in rather the charming manner some children have, feigned or otherwise. Wonderful hauteur was reflected on his oval-shaped, smoothly lustrous face, framed by a blonde bushel of hair mushrooming untidily in all directions. *A small lion,* Lelica called him, when she was usually not sober.

"Man, I don't want any, T.K.," the boy replied, pushing the pipe away while conscious of the faces observing him. There were some mellowly forbearing-looking ones, and a few of the opposite. Either way Mik was uncomfortable.

"Wow, these people are ripped," T.K. had to marvel.

Within his pleasurably time-suspended state, T.K. caught a glimpse of strange people viewing him from an upstairs vault. He couldn't make them out at first, except he sensed they were looking in rapt attention directly at him. He closed his red-veined eyes and attempted to wave the piquant-smelling smoke far from them, wiping his glasses all the while. *Wow.* Now T.K. believed he detected a couple of digital sluts standing up there, in that regal box, and surmised that one of them (the ugly one, naturally) was just the druid he wanted to see.

"But screw that dyke Queen anyway," T.K. muttered in tones of civilized contempt, angered that Raul Macon (who knew the druid well enough) sent others on such "covert" missions. This was something the beer-bloated Grit could better do himself. Besides, T.K. knew, the mission would prove an abortion anyway. He was woefully inept at junior espionage stuff, and wondered what would happen if he stood up to Raul, denied him, and refused to become part of this cockeyed scheme.

Reassessing the situation, T.K. knew Mik the wunder-urchin was the likeliest trump card yet to play. Somehow the boy -- with enough prodding – could worm warm secrets from deadwood.

T.K. kept looking up, pushing his way closer to the box, when he noticed -- in greater detail -- the statuesque younger woman standing next to Her Druidness. They composed a proverbially strange pair. On the one hand, there was that elder of freckled skin, pock marks, and red-frizzly hair: a testament to wholesale depravity of the heart (if such a diseased organ reposed beneath her flat-chested armor). By contrast there was that other visage of comely virtue, causing T.K. to nearly suffocate on too much hemp smoke.

The contrast was striking. T.K. felt like falling over from it, touching the sky as a sainted poet or madman might. Beauty & Ugliness became an icon of mystery in front of him, the sight deadly in implication.

"I'll never be able to pull this off," T.K. Keller told himself, "but maybe Mik can."

The commotion T.K. was aware of earlier hadn't subsided either. The dancing couple drew nearer, and what had been a wall of bodies around T.K. and Mik became an open path they stood in with dazed incredulity. Mimicking a slow-motion, the exotic dancers approached, and everyone around began flooding the thick air with gibes at T.K. and Mik, who resembled Salvation Army drop-outs.

"Get the hell away, Americans!" T.K. heard people yelling, and in his addled haste he tripped with slapstick clumsiness across the boy. Together they fell unceremoniously on the salty wooden floor. Momentarily frozen by fear and the sweet drug, the twin prostration of T.K. and Mik was an acute agony.

"Don't move!" T.K. heard himself trying to scream, but nothing intelligible emerged from his throat besides phlegm. The cold hard floor was now alive with foot-stampings and ricocheting voices, all imploring T.K. to hustle from the dancing procession's path.

A booted foot kicked into T.K.'s side. His facial spheres caught the mashing brunt of someone's heel. T.K. was choking from noxious odors and dust, yet could not rise. The power for motivating muscles had long left him.

He was now a beached jellyfish floundering without a vertebra.

The strong hands of Clendon, Marva's muscled cretin, caught T.K. by the hair, pulling him sled-like while on-lookers cheered. The pain was excruciating enough, the humiliation too real. His throat seared by hoarse intakes of breath, Keller caught an upside down glimpse of the ebony couple now dancing arabesques of design into space. He heard the crowd's growing excitement: the chanting exclamations, rhythmic clapping and foot-stamping now unified with the loud assault of the loudspeaker Rock music. It culminated with the Bluebottle Horsefly's "In-A-Dada-Da-Vi-da, Baby," and the assembled celebrants began entering a mystic realm long promised by pschodynamic prophecy.

"Get offa my damn face," Keller wanted to scream at the behemoth restraining him, but thought better of it. Things were off to a smashing start ...

Little Mik slumped like a discarded doll next to T.K., who realized with a nauseous start that the boy was hurt. Semi-conscious, his left arm held at an askew angle, the nearly emaciated lad bled slightly from the nose.

"How did that boy get here?" an excited woman's voice asked shrilly, but no one answered. The dancers leaped in the air like gracile acrobats. They reached a sweat-shivering crescendo, bringing a collective gasp from the throng in this mammoth barn. The young American, spreadeagled on the ground, felt his head was about to explode into glaucous fragments, spewing all with wondrous white, like the new milky way the news media claimed had just been discovered and where some form of life beyond the digital was certain to exist..

4.

In the baroque fastness of Marva Claire's offices, the boy Mik was taken and laid out on a sofa, his wounds attended to with careful meticulousness. Marva paced about distractedly, swearing, and said: "That boy could have been stampeded ... killed! My God, we have to keep greater security at the doors, Clendon. We have to keep minors at bay –"

"The clown who brought him works for Tito Van Meer. That's apparently how he was able to sneak the kid in. Apparently they came to see you anyway."

"Me? I should have been consulted first. You know that's the policy, anyway. Oh, damn it all –" She continued moving in her agitated fashion, sucking at a mentholated cigarette trapped between her garishly colored lips. "Well, Christina! Is the little bugger all right?"

"He appears to be, yes."

Kneeling at the sofa by the boy's side, Christina Alpreece made a strange Florence Nightingale indeed. There was a touch of nun-like devotion about her troubled features, so delicately beautiful, gossamer-like, beneath the soft effusion of overhead chandelier light. She still wore her long tan overcoat, buckled tightly, and – consumed by her nursing task – looked the ministerial angel, at variance with the aesthetic remoteness composing her persona of artist-dilettante. "I need more compresses for these bruises, Marva dear ... The poor darling should be all right. I don't think he's broken anything."

Thank Gods, muttered Marva. But suddenly she observed this touching tableau with greater criticality. "Why is the boy unconscious, then?"

"He's simply dazed. Listen to him moan."

"He's had a great shock," Clendon interjected, in his factual manner.

The proprietress of the Maradisa abruptly stopped moving, her angry frustration mounting. "Where is the other idiot? ... Have you let him get away?"

"Of course not. Nils is with him, in the other room."

"Is he in good enough shape to talk?"

"He's in bad shape, madame, but I'll get him to talk."

Clendon left the room. Murmuring endearments, Christina continued to sponge the sweat off the boy's face with a towel dipped in water. Marva sat sighingly behind an ebony desk, topped by a gilded ormulu which was (like Marva, perhaps) astoundingly out of place. As T.K. Keller was brought back in, the greatly fatigued Marva thought, *What a misbegotten wretch he is!*

"Here is the culprit, Msg. Claire."

A battered-looking T.K. Keller stared about him in an unfocused manner, finally spying Mik and that raving unorganic beauty on the couch. "Is Mik all right?"

"Of course, of course," Marva replied. "He only got the wind knocked out of him."

In quiet disbelief T.K. watched the sofa scene. The woman with the blonde, severely tied-back hair kept hugging the somewhat responding body of Mik, smothered with caresses.

Marva Claire snapped at T.K., "You, young man, certainly picked a bizarre method to meet with me."

"It was a pure accident," T.K. stuttered.

"Oh really. Since you know who I am, would you mind introducing yourself?"

Her irresolute captive seemed to think on this, then said: "I am T.K. Keller, and that's Mik. I work for Tito Van Meer at The Amstoy hotel." He smoothed back some rumpled hair. "I'm really sorry about this." For awhile T.K. stared at the formidable woman across from him. The sounds of incessant partying and Rock music from downstairs provided muffled accompaniment. "You're a friend of Tito's, aren't you?"

"We are acquaintances."

T.K. appeared to be improvising an explanation he knew sounded lame. All the while he was inordinately aware of the real raving beauty's presence nearby. It was her that T.K. really wanted to talk with and question, perhaps dispelling the extent of his fascination with her, which gnawed at him. Like a desire deeper than heterosexual attraction, T.K. realized this feeling frightened him also, along with everything else.

Holding a long-ashed cigarette, with a hand nonchalantly propped on her desk, Marva indulged an irritating habit of rubbing together two long red fingernails of her thumb and pinky. It sounded to Keller like the legs of a cricket grinding together. Suddenly yawning, Marva coughed harshly, as if the office were a gilded bathroom in which she was all alone.

"What is it that you wanted, Mr. T.K. Keller?"

T.K. allowed that it was a particular matter. He was looking for a businessman -- an Italian-American businessman -- rumored to be seeking a special brand of controlled substance T.K. possessed. It was a purely business matter, and of course T.K. was aware of the house rules about such a deal, etc.

Marva sighed, her eyes crying from the smoke. "I know of no such businessman, T.K. Keller. You have a bad lead."

"I thought as much." He believed she was lying. "Again, my apologies ..."

With a terrible grimace, Marva Claire said: "Enough of this. Obviously you weren't sent here by your employer." She looked over at the couch again, surveying with distaste Christina's benign ministrations. "Well, what of it, dear? Do I summon the doctor, or is the little bugger going to live?"

Christina stood up, eyeing her friend speculatively. "I think he'll still be fine." She carefully helped the boy -- who spoke for the first time, allowing he was thirsty -- into an upright, sitting position. "Mik? That is your name, isn't it. Do you feel good enough to stand?"

"I ache a little," Mik said, rubbing his creased features as if he'd been asleep. The other attendant to madame, called Nils, provided the boy with a glass of water, which was gulpingly consumed.

"Well," said Marva, expressing satisfaction. "He looks all right after all, the little man." She let forth an abrupt hoot and doused her cigarette into a small fish bowl (where a plastic goldfish floated amid the detritus of mentholated filters), and said, in her happier hoarse voice: "Clendon! Tell the chef to warm up some bami for the youngster. He must be starving."

"Are you hungry?" Christina asked, her voice gently maternal.

"Ja, I sure am," Mik replied. For the first time he noticed his sheepish co-hort T.K. standing a few feet away, cap in hand, looking half beat-up. A look of startled remembrance overtook Mik's features.

"You are an angel," Christina marveled, affably lighting a cigarette, then looking back to the doughty proprietress. "Marva? I simply must take the lad to the Quarters and see that he's looked after, at least for the night."

"That's a marvelous enough idea."

Christina gazed more coolly in this T.K. fellow's direction, sizing him up in her astute fashion, her face an impassive mask of beauty. "And you -- what was your name?"

"T.K. ..."

"Well, would you like to come along with your charge? We'll have someone qualified observe him."

T.K. made no immediate reply.

"You said the boy roams the Oudevoorburgwal, didn't you? I don't think he should be going back there tonight."

Marva arose (it was eventful), saying, "And on such a cold day." She was now beaming. Christina had bailed her out again. She wouldn't actually be unceremoniously turning these louts out, though she had a perfect right to.

Young Keller only knew that violence would be done to his person if he went "home" where Raul Macon waited ... T.K. sighed, resigned to the fact things were never in one's steadfast control, and that life (whatever it amounted to) remained a downer given to mystery. In a world given to pollution and intermittent, regressive global wars -- in a sense, where history endlessly and futilely repeated itself, if but in different guises -- how long would human existence remain intact, anyway?

The world governments had failed to colonize other planets in the solar systems, and there were only so many space stations built to contain a number of select humans, hybrids, and cyberclones. The result left Earth an endangered planet, T.K. knew, with only so many years of actual habitable life left beyond the current calendar one of 2037.

There seemed nowhere else to go -- but T.K. knew there had to be an alternative to what they were facing, even if it meant existing in a perfectly drugged one.

5.

What a messed-up day, T.K. Keller told himself as they drove along, *and it isn't even half-over.*

T.K.'s headache was the equivalent of a migraine, yet this moment's pain was subsumed by adventure. Headache be damned, he was riding in a sleek Citroen through downtown Amsterdam at dusk's rush hour traffic. Looking sedated, Mik was in the back seat cradling a soccer ball, oblivious to the event. Nearly slaying a row of bicyclists, the sublime young woman drove in haphazard fasion. In perfect calm she sat behind the wheel. Through the lingering effects of hashish daydreaming which totaled any chronological memory of the day's events -- beginning with an espresso somewhere which left his gut aching -- Keller suspected he'd soon faint and be unceremoniously shoved out the door into the street where he belonged.

"Do you really live on Canal Street?" the woman finally asked T.K.

Keller nodded listlessly, propping up his dark glasses and mentioning The Amstoy hotel again. In the rain-soaked kaleidoscope of lights (here red, there yellow or blue, everywhere rainbow-hued) creating patterns along the curb, T.K. resembled a pasty-faced specimen overindulged to the point of dropsy and beyond. A living testament to neo-decadence afoot in the Yappie-forbearing city he loved and hated -- so was Keller now a *Yappie?* No, he was a certain American-expatriate-outcast with a lousy secret threatening to land him in the stockade. He wondered if the girl-woman Christina read it in his mind. Along with everything else, she seemed a spooky parapsychic of sorts. This bugged T.K. along with the rest. Attracted yet repelled in alternating fashion, he wondered if he was going under.

Christina Alpreece was not Dutch, he knew that much. Was she American? A definite possibility, though something was affectedly British in her accents and manners. Now singing along to the radio, the young woman came off like a Scandinavian wunder-lass, purposefully more complex than the average movie queen crashing into your life.

There was something incantatory in all this, T.K. was wont to reason. Also there lurked something dangerous there too -- something hard to fathom -- giving Keller pause. He was nearly silent throughout the drive.

"This Tomasi," Christina said, as they cruised through a very old section of the city. *The Prinzengracht?* thought Keller. "Why is it so important you find him?"

"It's a great mystery to me, I'll tell you. At the moment he's about as real as Santa Claus in the flesh." Christina laughed, almost a sibillant sigh. "I think it can be arranged for you to find this Tomasi."

T.K. was frankly startled. "What? Do you know where he is?"

She turned her glowing eyes on him. "I said so, didn't I?"

T.K. felt that was hardly the point, entrapped by the surreal nexus gradually taking form. The sense of it overwhelmed him by degrees, almost vortically, and T.K. longed to succumb. It seemed foregone reality that he would, but tangible facts were difficult for him to keep a toehold on.

Then there really is a goddamned Tomasi, T.K. informed himself with chagrin. He leaned back, his neck jarring against the head-rest as their careening car nearly side-swiped a Mercedes.

"Mad bastard," Christina muttered, almost happily.

"Whoa," T.K. replied, finally getting a cigarette lit, but coughing fiercely before the first drag. There was a consumptive romanticism about him, which didn't say much about consumption *or* romanticism. Chemicals disintegrated within a brain he considered seedy, like the rest of him. T.K.'s dashing, unkempt "elegance" was stilted, but who in the city was sans pretension? Cautiously he gazed at himself reflected eerily in the roseate windshield, seeing the haunted form of a jazz musician, or a strung-out poet panning for gold in the river of human souls.

T.K. turned to question Mik in the back seat, but the youngster was too engrossed in uncomfortable sleep. No signal could pass between them. Mik the heretofore wise urchin was now -- in innocent slumbers -- bereft of his precocious skills, and more boyish than ever.

"He's a wonderful kid," Christina said, running a light. "Isn't he?"

"Damn straight," nodded Keller.

"But needy, man, needy ..."

Right -- we're all needy, baby, so take us to your promised land! T.K. Keller hissed, because who wasn't needy in a century where time had somehow wrapped itself around a backwards reel? Everything existed now, thanks to tortured international politics, only to be reinvented again in the past tense ...

Everywhere around town the upended state of things was evident to him. Even in the trendier bars there was always rows of video monitors showing a different war in progress around the world, whether in New China or the republic formerly known as Iraq ... As if that wasn't enough, there were also "interstellar conflicts" involving earth governments, on an off-and-on basis, taking place on distant, uncolonized planets as well.

Looking out the car window into the damp street, T.K. wondered if he himself weren't some entity dreamed of long ago by some deity who'd forgotten him.

6.

The seaport has its mysteries and dank secrets, archaic to the core, nurtured by a mythology known as popular history endemic to every culture. But modern traces within (and co-existing alongside) the ancient never failed to pleasurably astound young Keller of the opiate syndromes.

So with the same wonder, though aching with some physical and emotional fatigue about to drown him, T.K. looked upon the quarters of this young and talented woman he knew so little about. *The Quarter,* was it called? Joseph Beuys or some revivified *Sturm und Drang* Romanticist, whacked-out on Piranesi fantasies, might have had a go at it. How otherwise to explain the elegant outside niches, except as ingenious edifices created from that brainscape Dr. Caligari himself suffered within? The place was so impressive, so bizarrely beautiful, that T.K. wondered how, alongside a canal block with Dutch houses from earlier centuries still doggedly standing by, The Quarter was conceived in the post-Space Age.

"This is pretty wild," T.K. allowed. "How in the world --"

"My accomplices and I," the woman began, leading T.K. and the boy up the stairs into the inner foyer, "are the architects. A group of artists called Der Feuer erected The Quarter, I'm afraid, with a little financial aid from my fatherly uncle in New York."

"Fabulous," Keller said, still mildly suffering from the Maradisa experience. No doubt it colored his impressions of this studio-residence, where stark shadows and contrasts of black-and-white prevailed. "A tour de force ..."

"It does us."

T.K. was prone to exaggerate what he saw, on the wings of a fading drug dream, and this annoyed him enormously. He needed another pipe to validate his perceptions.

"Then you're American?"

"The veritable New Yorker, yes."

In the veritable flesh, T.K. mused. He stepped aside to usher Mik inside, and the youngster proceeded to ogle examples of sleek bric-a-brac art protruding from the wall -- or plastered thereon.

"How are you feeling?" Christina asked the boy.

"Better, thanks."

As they entered into what could be described a low-tech living room, T.K. asked: "Who all lives ... uh, here?"

"Myself and friends, T.K."

She produced some Geneva gin and poured two full glasses. T.K. grimaced inwardly, hating the stuff. "I'll get you some milk," she told Mik, departing no doubt for an unseen kitchen. "You may of course call me by my name, T.K., which is Christina ... I'm not royalty, you know."

T.K. would never have believed it. Christina had to be loaded with guilders, which explained her transcendental evasiveness. Why was she being kind to both of them anyway? Practically saving them from the wrath of Marva Claire's lackeys, who were ready to cast T.K. and Mik into cold turkey abominations.

T.K. still had an underexposed celebrity to track down, and something told him all motivating reasons eventually converged on the same ineluctable vector. *But let's not be seduced here by seductive magic,* he pontificated, not really sure of himself. His hostess knew of powers which a dark space cabbala kept secret, though T.K. was yet to learn of it.

Sloshing back gin, T.K. tasted nectar from a whore's netherparts. He gazed dispassionately at the tastefully baroque furnishings about him, wondering if one dared call them decadent. There were sumptuous wall tapestries of Oriental design; mysterious non-objective paintings of bleached hue and of a scale which dominated the on-looker; Bauhas-like furniture with a Constructivist icon here and there waiting for someone's obeisance. It made the tacky world T.K. inhabited offensive indeed, and he wondered if the woman was playing a joke on them. All the same, he would hate her for superior emotions she might betray. Allocating to herself the ministrations of a fey priestess, could she escape such self-canonization?

"Please relax yourselves now," she told them, "and pull up a divan. I was going to have a physician look at you, but it's later than I thought."

"No need," T.K. said, for he was certain that he and Mik had escaped serious injury, although his innards still felt queasy.

"Well, maybe tomorrow."

Christina sat carefully down, keeping her blue-gray eyes resolutely on her guests. She seemed to be framing some difficult pronouncement.

"You won't have to go back to the streets tonight, or be around that ... activity. You can stay here and recuperate."

"Thank you," Mik said, though his older overseer was preoccupied, moping about now in querulous and pent-up fashion. The liquor hit T.K. rock-hard, like everything else. He had acquiesced to his hostess' desire to hustle Mik off upstairs to a warm bed, and several minutes later T.K. wondered what was taking her so long. Damn the luck. Before probing Christina about her knowledge of the Tomasi character, T.K. was getting sick again and ready to puke on some priceless furry rug.

One suspicion nagged Keller. Tomasi couldn't be here, in The Quarter, could he? Waiting to somehow subvert T.K.'s quest ...

Later Keller would calculate that something went wrong at that moment. The ambrosial refreshments Christina provided included cocaine, and T.K. took a toot of that white line fever like any righteous jazzman. *Onwards & Upwards, T.K.!* So he was freaking out again, imagining the hostess had the power to create transmutations of reality inside his head, and drugs had little to do with it. Oh man, he was getting looser.

"Mr. Tomasi is your good burgher?" said T.K. when Christina returned.

"I would say he's a passing acquaintance to us all, always going in or out of port, but never staying very long."

"What's his line, then?"

"He does it all, love. It would fill a ledger."

"Shit. He's under your bed, I bet."

The vagabond bearer of dreams started laughing, reaching into the filmy layer obscuring his eyes. He was doubling over.

"The man's a freak in his own right, like you are."

"What *are* you trying to determine, baby?"

"I don't sweetly know at all." Falling over, T.K. went into soft shades of gray. "Hell if I know anything at all. It's Raul Macon, his baby. I'm cheap labor."

"The john is down the hall to your left. It has a bath going."

"Where we can genuflect before His presence?"

"I'll write down his number for you. Tell him nothing but dire truth sent you, from a distant star and another eon."

It was fact, all of it. Because T.K. could feel the weight of sacred hypocrisy, he fell silent. There had to be some better truth. Christina Alpreece? She was like the dancer who fucked to be in sin while also transcending it. She was a double-standard for what T.K. gagged on, chewing strange fruit. An unreachable apparition, gorging him sensually yet making him pay for it.

Not long after, T.K. passed out.

7.

Within the illusory T.K. struggled, borne through chasms of fear. Any concrete sight, such as a big toe with red polish adorning nail, was a vision of magnified evil, not just mammoth soft sculpture. Of course he realized this in a crystalline flash, as only a fine hallucinogen can provide. His insight had the weight of ages to a young fellow barely in his twenties, learning about life's complexities for the first time.

Prowling through the illusory and concrete, T.K. discovered a subterranean passageway within The Quarter. In her superior fashion, the art-sibyl Christina had misdirected Keller there, until he found himself quite alone.

"She has little sense of humor," T.K. remarked.

Intoxicating elixir still in hand, Keller lurched gamely along a narrow stone passageway, lit by overhead fluorescent tubing. Wondering where the Kid and Queen were, T.K. propelled himself further into the stark maze. Like his life, the whole fact of this underground matter was a vast clue whose significance he must unravel.

Yet somehow T.K.'d been disconnected, as his sense of chronological fixity was. He tried to remember what had happened, how he'd been moved chess-like from the marble-walled living room. Unfortunately the lacuna in his consciousness censored such recollections. T.K. began running – senselessly – until it seemed the corridor was part of some fabricated illusion it was his misfortune to be shuttled through. In sporadic flashes he recalled a windsong of warning, echoing endlessly, about finding the controversial Tomasi. The panting and searing pain nearly made T.K. collapse several times onto the pock-marked cement, glowing softly with dampness and decay.

Now he was outside again, wandering aimlessly along a canal of rust-hued water, its fungus growth creating a stark patina. Quietly he entered another dank building, as if he knew of its existence all the while, with his fate predestined by some controlling intelligence.

"I'm all right," T.K. said to no one in particular, but the individual waiting inside treated the remark as standard code.

"Identify your guide," the doorperson said.

T.K. mentioned her name, but wondered if it was the correct one. It hardly mattered. He was on the threshold of more than bargained for. Had he the courage to confront it? All this was suddenly too real, too urgent and important-seeming.

"And then I went inside," T.K. was saying to himself, the victim of his life. "It was like an old hotel, a brothel really. The contact took me on a tour, through the damn lot, and the place reeked of espionage and old sin ... The kind this city will never get out of its system."

There were strange characters standing around, bored and dissolute-looking, right out of a gallery opening and/or Rock concert. No one appeared to mind T.K. Keller's intrusion, perhaps because there was a ratty poetic elegance about him. The stuffy, fume-laden air was charged by a menacing quality, something T.K. recognized as the reason behind this facade: the homage to malice.

"You better watch what you hear," the doorperson said. In the flinty darkness, T.K. could see the hirsute man resembled someone singing nursery rhymes at a murder. "You may become hazy on what you see. On the entire situation here."

"What kind of club is this?" T.K. asked, as he maneuvered through a sordid ballroom trashed by low-lifers with their accouterments. (Were chains more than jewelry around the necks of white slave-looking eunuchs?)

"A place for radical chickens such as yourself," came the reply. "Your fantasyland ..."

Sick at heart, Keller realized he might be going nowhere. The city of canals had become his concentric prison, without a nucleus.

"Well?"

With a start T.K. recognized Nils Mupreen, that Maradisa employee who doubled as student revolutionary, staring out from a curtain-obscured corner. Politically active? Perhaps that would be judging Nils and his band too lightly, though appearances remain deceiving.

Feeling sick and powerless, T.K. was taken into a fetid storeroom where another youthful Dutch longhair presided, who announced:

"The message you have for your friend is this. His quarry is too big for him, and the financial angle has been co-opted by others. He would do best to end further involvement, is that understood? His accomplices are under scrutiny. If misfortune befalls them, then our advice is unheeded. Nothing beneficial will result."

Through astonishment T.K. stared at this studious informer. He resembled a New Provo, or student radical, highly averse to American imperialists such as Gaylen Tomasi. Anyone bent on furthering the "black-market-legality" of international business combines, the informer explained, was risking something serious indeed: banishment to a stellar Siberia in another galaxy.

"That's all we're going to tell you, my friend," the young Dutchman said, smiling indulgently while tamping a briar with his bony forefinger. "Tell Tito and his canal ladies. And don't come back please."

8.

Twisting and turning, T.K. awoke in his hotel room. On the bedstand his watch had stopped at 7:35. Groggily he sat up, still in the clothes he'd worn the night before, and realized he was suffering the after-effects of carousing.

In the small room it was cold thanks to the open window, which T.K. closed after getting his bearings and lighting a cigarette. It was gray outside, somewhere between late morning or early afternoon. T.K. wanted a shower but it meant going outside down the hall, and he had no immediate strength for that. Inside he sat on the scruffy bed, coughing and smoking while gazing disenchantedly at the multitude of drawings tacked onto the drab and colorless wall. He was hungry.

The hard growth on his chin reminded T.K. that his beard needed tending. He was debating what to do when he heard some scurrying outside his door.

"Are you up, T.K.?" came a woman's voice.

"Yeah."

It was Lissie, Hull-E.'s old lady and partner, who also ran the place. She probably thought T.K. was naked again and wanted to change his sheets (with him in them). Through the doorway she emerged: a short, middle-aged crone in a depressing apron and flowered shift. Too-thin, she wore gold-rim glasses and clattered about in honest-to-God wooden shoes. T.K. grimaced at the industrious sight of her barging in to attack his room with broom and wastebasket, etc. Under her perennial hairnet (hardly containing an oval mass of gray hairs) the vulgar hen was a hellion spawned from spoor-infested kitchens.

"Where were you?" she asked angrily.

T.K. was having a hard time remembering. Having entered the establishment while the night man tended shop meant T.K. had returned between midnight and dawn. Still, it was a cloudy remembrance at best, and he got no plaudits for it. With a start he realized he'd forgotten all about Mik, and couldn't recall whether they'd left the "white lady's" place together. It was all a mental blur, but snatches of his stay in the revolutionary's sanctuary kept aggravating T.K.

"Aren't you hungry, T.K.? You should go right down to the kitchen later."

"I will."

Unappreciatively Lissie fomented while performing her cleaning tasks. "I told Hull-E. you were sick, but he doesn't believe it. I'm not going to lie for you again --"

"I am sick."

T.K. nearly laughed at this admission. Looking fuzzily at this Dutch mother (and T.K. was habituated to calling many people mother), the discontented young profligate asked, "Is Raul or Tito looking for me?"

"Not that I know, honey."

"Damn."

T.K. had to nerve himself up for what was ahead, but the presence of this busybody was enough to make him forgetful. Didn't she realize there was deep trouble around the bend?

Keller shook himself awake. Luckily it was Saturday. He could afford to be lackadaisical. He believed himself in no immediate danger, but had been enough impressed by the previous night's lurid portent not to take anything for granted. All he had to do, T.K. told himself, was persuade Raul Macon to drop his infatuation with this Tomasi. But somehow it was as easy as stopping the 2037 war in Nu-Viet Nam(e), or ending American involvement there, just like in the re-emerging civil conflict in the former Nu-Bosnia-Herzegovina. Pig-headed Macon had reasons for his interest in the burgher-gangster (as someone called Tomasi once), and T.K. knew he'd have to decipher things before getting any further.

What worried him even more was the possibility of Tito and his courtesans somehow being implicated. If that were the case, then T.K. knew this business could become inextricably difficult, even downright unhealthful.

Perhaps T.K. would ingeniously sound out the hotel owner about the problem later that day, then gauge the next move. But how much time did he have? Unsavory circumstances were approaching, their political nature significant enough (in view of T.K.'s culpable past) to make him dwell on his own hegira from this salty paradise.

Lissie continued to annoy T.K. with her regimental cleaning, treating him like a delinquent soldier confined to sordid barracks. He managed to slip out into the hall and lock himself in the narrow, super-cramped bathroom, which reminded him -- a boyhood Catholic -- of a priest's confessional, only seedier. There he performed cursory ablutions with a wet cigarette in mouth.

"You've got work to do, idiot," T.K. told himself, trying to heighten his sense of urgency.

When he slipped back into his floor-creaking room, he found Lissie still inside, her manner towards T.K. considerably more devious. She was in her deplorable "sexy" mood, and Keller was in bad fettle to cope with it.

"I know you've been keeping a Love Diary, T.K.! What vixen are you in love with now?"

"I am in love with *no* vixen, Lissie. So you can spare me your prurient interest."

Lissie leaned provocatively against the nicked bureau. T.K. was shown a pair of veined and scrawny legs, which (for a 50-year-old) were unmemorable. "Ain't I good enough for you, baby?" she teasingly asked, a travesty of lust. T.K. wanted to gag (*Why me?*) but instead went about changing his shirt. "Take it off, baby!" the flinty woman implored, but T.K. kept his T-shirt on, gamy as it was.

"Get out of here, Lissie. You're not funny now."

"Ah ha --!"

Witch-like, Lissie cackled inordinately, tickled by her boy's discomfort. She loved him in her overbearing way, with years of experience catering to tourists from around the world, pampering her favorites until they left with tongues lolling -- irredeemably altered for the worst. It was her revenge for being the vassal-mate of Hull-E. and his alcoholic avoirdupois, which drove her into bitter moroseness over the years. A girl had to have some fun in life ...

"Give me a kiss."

"Get out of here, Lissie! Once again I must request you leave in peaceful resignation."

"Hahh!"

She was a noxious (ugh) knockout, all right. T.K. knew she was after his Euro-hemp stash. If she found it inside his room she'd have a fit, for Lissie frowned on drug-taking. The natural intoxicating agent in The Amstoy was Geneva, that patriotic gin Dutch customs are baptized by, and any other balm of joy was heresy, given to the outlawed realm of Hyperspace.

Quickly T.K. put on a presentable shirt and decided to make a run for it. Lissie harbored him during his military days of desertion, it was true, and probably saved him from being sent to a space station stockade to perform slave labor for whatever duration -- but to T.K. she was still a fang-woman in an almost drag disguise better suited for another reality.

9.

He'd slapped her hard ...

It was not reflexive, but a passion learned and shared between them. On the plush rug Christina writhed in a frenzy of cyber-masochistic lust, her male lover continuing his electronic assault on her legs and buttocks, until she nearly screamed from voluptuous agony.

Her middle-aged lover (with the prematurely gray hair) wasn't exactly thrilled by her performance, or his either. The tastefully furnished den was a shadowy arena where their ritual of interchangeable domination was played out repeatedly.

Now the man with the gray hair -- himself almost naked, with eletrical wires and leather accouterments adorning his body -- descended on his partner, flaying her sensitive areas with a large digital device resembling a polyethylene joystick. She arched her back, her buttocks indenting a mauve-silk pillow. Her staccato breathing made an odd counterpoint to the jazz music filtering in through stereo speakers.

"Now please shock me," said Christina Alpreece.

With a breast in each gloved hand, the man began to stimulate each nipple with the electrically charged digital device until Christina ejaculated harsh moans. Then she kicked him with simultaneous joy and revulsion, lost in a newly found galactic moment where she encountered distant space curving into infinity.

To a voyeuristic on-looker, it might be difficult to determine what was simulated, and what was "hyper-reality."

The man -- called Brice Rampoul (a pseudonymn), an American political performance artist whose greatest renown was achieved in Germany some years before -- finished his digital-shockings with mild exultation, pulling his device with a physician's adroitness from Christina's abdomen. With surprising strength, Christina pushed him back onto his side, usurping what was now vulnerable about the man's body and making it serve her own ends.

Each pleasure they shared was followed by more digital shocks to erogenous zones, so that ecstasy demanded its truly opposite to truly achieve the heightened experience their intercourse had become. In this act they yearned to become sophisticated aliens devoted to a unique gratification, as degrading as it was exultant, far from the simply human.

"I love this shocking," she finally told him.

"For a California girl, Christina, you're becoming more of a practiced liar."

"Oh, *shock* you!" she laughed, savoring the lingering sensations his joystick provided while Rampoul helped remove the wires and synaptic digital connections from her body. "How about some wine?"

"Yes."

While Rampoul poured their glasses full, Christina put on a fiber-robe and continued admiring herself.

"I think, Christina, you've actually become more Dutch than anything."

"Of course. I'm more cosmopolitan now. I was born in California, but my home is really New York."

Rampoul laughed silently. What attracted him to her was a quality of spurious innocence she managed to exude so coyly -- and skillfully -- that at times he believed Christina was a deranged virgin from the unknown planet she called Home.

They kneeled before the fireplace, drinking their wine and meditatively watching the flames. Rampoul lit his expensively ornate pipe. Christina's hair cast a sheen of radiant crystal that Rampoul savored. Tired, sated but not really content, they warmed themselves in the neo-art furnished den.

"Well. I suppose we have business to go over, Christina."

"What of it? I told you everything before, God damn it."

"Yes, but we can't afford to screw-up on this if we're to preserve any credibility with our German friends."

"The hell with your credibility. You sound more and more like a politician."

"You sound more like a Uber-whore."

They both laughed, somewhat in surprise. Everything was getting bizarre those days, but oddly believable too. One had no other course but to believe. Events in history seemed pre-destined to be repeated, if not manipulatively invented: from another "Viet Name" war, to German territorial division again into East and West, and even government controlled weather via digital satellites. Science was the tool of degenerate political rule, bent on terrorizing the masses into the acceptance of digital rule.

"We've got to find who's leaking what about the Tom." Rampoul smoked his pipe furiously. "Did you tell Nils?"

"Mupreen knows everything. He kept an eye on Keller at the meeting."

"This Keller. Can he *remember* anything? Addled like he is?"

"He'll remember what he's supposed to do. They impressed that on him, I'm sure."

"We're going to have to move on this Raul Macon. Find out what he knows. That's the logical next step." Christina raised her glass, a sly salutation. "The logical next step."

Brice Rampoul scratched himself, closing his eyes, the pipe still in his mouth. "When Tomasi gets here, there's got to be no outside interference, that's for sure. We can't pull this number otherwise." He opened his eyes. "Some meddlesome people might really get hurt."

Christina nodded, but there was a faraway wistfulness about her face now. (The face so many artists had drawn, or painted, and were accustomed to calling pristine.) Close to tears, she alluded to the fact she was keeping "the boy" for awhile, especially if Raul Macon proved uncooperative. He would serve as leverage, she told Rampoul.

"That little brat they almost trampled at the Maradisa?" Rampoul eyed her with a dull fascination. "I swear, Christina. You're a God damned mother on top of it."

They laughed again.

"I'm sure I know what I'm doing," Christina said.

From a nearby desk he handed her a folder. "Have you seen this material?"

She opened the brittle plastic dossier carefully. Inside was more speculation on their target, as authored by Rampoul:

ON THE RIGHT HONORABLE TOMASI, GAYLEN VINCENT. A PERFORMANCE PIECE INVOLVING HIS ASSASSINATION &/OR DETAINMENT ...
TO COINCIDE WITH THE CALIFORNIA BANKER'S JANUARY "GOODWILL VISIT" TO THE NETHERLANDS, 2037 ...

+++

-- involving diverse means & materials for the execution of an art form indivisible from the ultimate political Act ... into the futherance of Revolutionary Power & aims ... for the United People's union.

+++

(Terrible Tom-Imperialist, former entrepreneur for men's wear/ His wife of 32 years, frigid ... has 4 children, teenage/ Voted for Richard Milmouse Noxson, Fascistic Queen of Dementedness ... Plays golf, has large home, pool, pets, no mistress -- due to chronic non-digital impotence? Says The War Must Go On in Asia and Europe, until the gooks are soysauce, until the Nu-Commies overdose &

suck Sam's Dick

& Noxson becomes a God-fucker feared

/ is terrible tom a homosexual --? /

-- has 2 cars, 1 black maid

-- likes fine wine, cigars

-- is 6 feet 1, 185 pounds, balding (wears glasses, hearing aid)

-- in poor health, but won't retire

-- hot shit to the C.I.A.!

/ Tom is Christina's father's good friend --)

+++

MORE ON THE MODUS OPERANDI:

1. -- piano wire (his wrists red)
2. -- quarry by the sea to be taken yea ( )

3. -- *Put on brine & seasoned ... (for indefinite days)*
    -- *PERHAPS BURN*
        or baste in select Canal
4. -- *belated X-mass gift bequeathed to godless whore, mi lady /*
5. -- *Instruments of torture: music (atonal) ...*
    screwdrivers ... nails (Christian)
               days of hate judgement ...
acute dismemberment /
6. -- *Sodomy - involving animals (1 big pig)*
         &/or insects / excrement
7. -- *Epiphany For Satan:*

    "Off with his gender, into his mouth
        goes the pretender!"

    sticks

    rocks

    bolts

    weeds -- !

    EX NIHILO,
          INTO PASSION.

It was all drafted out, Christina Alpreece noted, this ultimate "performance piece" designed to merge Art with the Politics of Life and Death, becoming *revolutionary action*. And she was a part of it. In anonymous splendor the terrorist plan's execution would fulfill its ends via these artists of the human condition, who strove to give their madness constructive solidity. Who strove, and would strive, to put fear and trembling into the veins of the mainstream, "& craven creation ..." She couldn't wait to enter it into her laptop files.

"I think you're a little absurd, Brice darling."

But she read on, knowing an infinity of space awaited them. Christina also believed nothing could stop them -- certainly not the civilian police in Amsterdam, Germany, or any other European country. The police drove silver Porsches and attended chiefly to the unsolvable complaints of senior citizens. If anything, the current World Police -- a consolidated international body originally formed by the defunct United Nations -- was a more formidable, yet hardly visible foe, subsumed by yet serving the ruling technocratic-military complex of warring superpowers like America, China, and Russia.

The World Police existed in the way Santa Claus did, so Christina Alpreece and Brice Rampoul did not worry. They were ready to opportunistically use *the technocracy* by exposing its weaknesses -- by becoming, in fact, the greatest undercover "policing" body on the continent, and eventually in the Universe.

But to do so, the Feuer Bande had to first overcome the Forbrau Military Police, through which the C.I.A. flourished as the F.B.I. did in America's domestic heartland, where the civilian police were still viable and strong.

                   10.

She had a face too strikingly beautiful for her profession.

Such a face he'd looked at for so long, at first entranced, then gradually disillusioned by what alcohol and jaded effects achieved. Somehow she was a whore and a mother to young Mik too, and this combination caused T.K. endless moral difficulty. Morality was something he would have liked to do without.

To further compound matters, the thirty-year-old Lelica was a prostitute on strike. No wonder guilders were hard to come by, T.K. thought as he bicycled his way nearby Keizersgracht, on his way to Lelica's domicile. It was a rare sun-streaked afternoon, and a pack of Dutch children batted a soccer ball across the street. The noise of their feet padding over the cobblestones warmed T.K. Innocence so near had its poignancy, yet he was aware of never being able to share that ambrosia again. Not after all that had happened and was about to.

So T.K. bicycled along steadfastly, intent on reaching his destination. The usual souvenir and fish vendors were evident, proffering their unique wares to passers-by. The bustle of Amsterdam in perpetual motion never failed to gratify T.K. It made him feel authentically a part of something -- a rare and powerful emotion indeed, but among those few he ranked real.

Because he could become lost in this crowded port, yet knowing too where he was going, T.K. Keller was enamored of the picturesque trams and ancient architecture: the tobacco and tea shops, the winding side streets hardly wide enough for a car to travel through, the smoke smells against crisp air. Add the busy pedestrians, tourists and traders, all jumbled together to illustrate the freewheeling philosophy of a proud city where all societal strata (from low-life to wealthy patrician) mingled in equilibrium and forbearance. It was something to marvel at, and T.K. found a sense of freedom in it, something he could not find back in his Lost in Space, strife-ridden American homeland.

Yet none of the comforting scenery could entirely dispel the sense of foreboding he felt on his way to Lelica's. Near the Voorburgwal, climbing the steep stairs to her apartment made T.K. cough violently; and once or twice he paused to wonder what the hell he was doing. He was climbing too many stairs, seeing too many odd and potentially harmful people, getting deeper into trouble. T.K. was, however, inescapably *in* it -- this bad experience -- and there was no other course to follow.

The shapely woman in the baggy dress who greeted him was besides herself when he arrived. She'd been trying to reach him for some time. Peremptorily this Lelica wanted him to produce the boy Mik on the spot, like a stage musician pulling a rabbit from a silk hat. T.K.'s foreboding proved accurate. To his bedeviled chagrin, he learned from Lelica's pouting sternness that, truly, the boy was nowhere around. With a threatening ire, she had no idea of the boy's location, though expecting T.K. to provide some answers.

"I don't know," replied T.K., also besides himself. "The last place we were together ..." He proceeded to tell her all that had happened.

"My God," she said.

She wanted to pounce on him, drive her five purple dagger-nails into his throat's vulnerable shaft. Over espresso he momentarily convinced her to refrain from violence. (A digital-whore who had quit -- and rebelled against the oppressive digitalism indebting her to others, like Jari on Canal Street -- was an anomaly in this town, and had no business getting on his case.)

"You're in some kind of weird bullshit now, Keller, aren't you? I don't understand a shitting thing you've told me. You say Raul got you into this?"

"He made me his 'scout.' He ordered me to the Maradisa."

"Jesus ..."

Harried and distraught, Lelica sat down and lit her fourth cigarette. "I don't know what to do. Somebody help me. Call for help ... Get the police --? That's a laugh."

"It might not be a good idea exposing any of this, Lelica. I'll talk to Raul, don't worry, and we'll see about Mik. I know he's all right. I'm sure that Christina, the artist, has really treated him well, so don't worry. He's all right. Please --?"

She stared at him. On her taut face struggled emotions vying to express laughter or disdain.

"You had better do something. It's hard enough trying to keep track of that kid. They'll have good reason now to take him away from me."

"Don't fucking worry, okay?"

More slyly Lelica studied her guest, engulfing his features with exhalations of acrid smoke. "You're in some kind of other trouble --"

"No. Hell if I know -- but no."

"I want to talk to Raul. Immediately."

"I've been trying to find him all day. He doesn't even know about this yet."

"You're sure?"

She was utterly skeptical. T.K. didn't know much of anything at the moment.

"T.K. If Mik's hurt or something. I'll ..."

T.K. didn't wait to hear her finish. She was a difficult woman, all right. One undergoing some personal crisis he knew nothing about, and now this. All the way back to The Amstoy he felt like a royal heel, and realized for the first time how genuinely lost he was, in a world that appeared archaic compared to the Space Age one of his native superpower homeland -- with its equally bogus fabrications devoted to the hi-tech future nowhere -- which also was inescapable.

Looking up through the leaden air, T.K. thought he saw a mind-monitoring U.S. satellite flitting by. And looking down into the nearby canal water, a glow of crystalline eeriness floated by with the stealth of an otherworldly submarine.

11.

Blood was everywhere about her, like dried scabs shed by broken and brown larva. She'd been beaten up as severely as her Canal Street domicile (that cramped receptacle of pay-for-sin) was ransacked and defiled. Her nude body -- half-obscured by the tattered and spotted sheet -- was tattooed now by welts attesting to a professional cruelty, one whose perpetrator could be sickly proud of.

It occurred to Raul Macon that life was an unnatural proposition. If people were allowed to act naturally -- express their true emotions, thoughts and desires, without fear or persecution -- then maybe the world would be a healthier, less tragic, place to live in.

He had to laugh at himself for thinking all that. It was because Jari had bad secrets that she was beaten like this, left a now quite unattractive mess.

"Jari, Jari ..."

Macon tried to hold her, cursing himself, and realized he had to get her to a doctor. She was unconscious, apparently, but he could feel her heart beating underneath his hand. With some difficulty he managed to get her wrapped into a robe, over which he placed a heavy overcoat. She moaned as he sweatingly completed this endeavor, openly desperate.

So much had happened in the last few days, and now this. It made him murderously angry and befuddled at the same time. Macon felt guilty, morosely so. If he had simply stopped prying into this Tomasi business, none of this might have found its ugly climax. Someone of course had set Raul up, trying to use him to find out who in the Maradisa knew about Tomasi. The black suited C.I.D. nerds immediately came to Macon's thoughts.

Raul Macon was playing hard to get, weighing alternatives -- until this happened. Now he demanded of himself, "Did those Feds do this to her?" He suspected Jari had denied her attackers useful information, yet he wasn't sure anyone really knew anything anymore.

Keller, that little tit-wimp, had as much told Macon to cool down. But who could completely believe T.K.? Macon rarely believed the people he trusted to get him facts.

Only the night before, Macon had liaisoned with T.K. -- again at the bar of Tito's hotel near Central Station -- where they downed several beers and traded information. Perhaps Macon felt too serious following his interaction with the digital masseuse who'd taken his fancy, so that T.K.'s breathless admonishing failed to impact him beyond a comical exaggeration. In short, Macon believed T.K. was loaded, although this mention of an elegant and mysterious rich bitch was intriguing. The bit about underground "revolutionaries," however, stuck uneasily in Raul's beer-sodden craw. At the time he wanted to dismiss such possibilities, believing the C.I.D. agents were all one had to contend with. "They just want to know dirt about this Tomasi," Raul maintained, never suspecting they were after whatever and whomever Jari was connected with.

Now having cursorily dressed Jari, along with her wounds, Macon was afraid to speculate any more. He sat there, dumbly toweling her bruised face, and wondered whether or not to leave her. He'd bring hell raining down, though, on whoever was responsible, Feds or otherwise.

Peeking through the curtained picture window, Raul Macon (with the cunning of a soldier back in enemy territory) checked the street outside. He tried to wake Jari, but found it beyond his means. Hoping her brain wasn't a stew inside her head, Macon went out slowly, locking the door behind him, leaving the woman he now desired on the narrow bed where he'd found her.

"I'm shaking," he noticed irritably, trying to appear casual on the street. Ambling along somewhat, he didn't notice anyone watching him from the upper story windows of nearby buildings.

It was a frigid afternoon, the air heavy with imminent rain. A block away from Jari's window, Macon went into a digital pornography shop. He knew the owner casually, and asked to use the phone. (There was a current widespread interdiction concerning cellular phones due to the government's fear they contributed to people getting cancer, and Macon never owned one anyway.) Though outwardly calm, Macon's insides were in volcanic eruption, and he wanted to spit in the curt shopkeeper's eye. After a few rings Raul was speaking sotto voce to the booming voice of Hull-E., who was requested to send someone over in the Volvo.

"And hurry, Hull-E. ..."

Macon imparted some urgency into his voice, telling the bartender they would talk about it later in privacy.

Having thanked the shopkeeper, Macon went outside, moving to a point where he could still see Jari's closed window. He lit a cigarette he didn't really want. He would get a gun, he told himself. He would get an arsenal.

There weren't many people strolling about. The street was always half-dead during the day. Now each passing face Macon looked into was a potentially dangerous one whose shell he wanted to crack for a kernel of truth.

"Son of a bitch. Son of a damned bitch."

Macon checked his watch, pacing about, shoving gloved hands deep within his beige overcoat pockets, and wondered if the car would soon arrive. He couldn't wait forever. He was a seething mass of emotions out of sync, and he wanted to dismember something.

To Macon's relief the familiar brown Volvo drove its exhaust-popping way towards him. Driven by T.K., bless him. Quickly a door opened, and Macon hopped in.

"I was afraid you were gone," T.K. said.

"Back up," commanded Macon brusquely, his usually hoarse voice sounding worse than usual, when it was compared not unfavorably with a boozy English Rock singer's. "Jari's been hurt. That's her window over there -- whoa! -- pull up, God damn it."

"What's wrong --? Don't freak on me."

Before an answer was in order, Raul Macon was outside unlocking the beaten prostitute's door. Suddenly very nervous, T.K. saw his friend return carrying Jari's overcoated, unresponding body, which was placed carefully in the back seat.

"Get a real move on. I'll tell you where to drive."

Obediently T.K. had the car in gear and on its way.

"Is she all right, Raul?"

"I think so. She's been messed-up."

"Oh wow. Damn. Let's not get too serious here."

T.K. got a hurried glance at the woman's face in the vibrating rear-view mirror, and couldn't prevent a start from escaping him. It was one of those looks where the worst is verified. He was too intent on driving through the heavy traffic, across the tracks back into the heart of the city, to draw any immediate conclusions. All that would come later, after they got the woman to a hospital to be admitted for treatment.

"She's in shock," Macon would say later, bleary-eyed.

What followed (as recorded in their collective consciousness) was a helter-skelter montage of time-rushed events coming and going, entirely out of perspective. Frothing bear-like with a madness barely held in check, Raul Macon drove in bizarrely dangerous fashion after leaving the hospital. He headed for a necessary audience with Mr. Amsterdam himself, Tito. Hardly an announced visit, undoubtedly it would distress the hotel magnate.

As they drove, T.K. wanted to talk about the woman's beating in a way that wouldn't infuriate Macon, but it proved next to impossible.

"Her getting messed-up that way, Raul. After what I was told, man. The timing really sucks."

"So does your mother --"

Keller closed his eyes. With the flat of his hand he began massaging his aching temple. "Wow. I hate to say I told you so. I mean after last night."

Macon didn't want to think of the night before. All the hopeful possibilities he'd felt then was now bad acid in his mouth, and the trip had only begun.

"You think Tito knows anything?" T.K. said hopefully, remembering young Mik again, and believing grilling Tito wasn't a bad alternative at that point.

"Tito's got the key to the damn city. He better know something, right? You said your friends wanted him to be tipped about what's happening anyway, right?"

"Take it easy, Raul."

"I'm gonna kill somebody. I sure the hell am."

Keller felt his tension mounting. A bell in his nervous system was clanging bad news. He wanted out of the car, pronto. Raul Macon was combat-ready, and it precipitated a queasy dread within his co-rider, who had (up to then) dedicated his existence to the pursuit of aesthetic stasis. Now all his sonnets were nothing against the steaming animalism next to him, mercilessly ramming the car through the city, nearly flattening unwary pedestrians.

"You hear me, suck? Somebody better have heavy life insurance."

"All right, man. But let's not join the grim statistics."

T.K. sat up, propping his metallic shades higher on a sweat-streaming forehead. O for a spot of mitigating liqueur, or an understanding verse from Mallarme. They were really in shit's asshole if that girl died.

It had been so difficult finding Raul Macon anyway, until last night ...

After talking with Lelica and mercilessly concluding that episode, T.K. spent the day trying to re-locate his eminently confused partner. While searching a few bars and select places, Keller learned from a usually dependable source that Macon was conducting business at one of Tito's hotels. Yet after all the hassling, hours of travel and interrogation, by the time T.K. got there it was well into evening and buddy Macon was well into his Geneva cups. So T.K.'s dire revelation regarding missing Mik's plight, etc., didn't register in the cerebral nutshell of the Cro-Magnon man from Louisiana, who thought anybody from California -- such as T.K. -- was a stone faggot.

Why is this happening? T.K. wanted to know. *Why did it have to happen at this point in time and Void-consciousness?*

"Bravura Christina," he said with reverent sadness then, "the sibyl of unquenched desires in our brains. Yeah, right."

She knew so much T.K. feared to tamper with, like a painful secret entombed in nether-reaches of Id, or wicked-somethings. Sousing himself with nasty gin like his co-hort proved equally baffling.

Keller knew then he had to summon the will and courage to face that woman again if they were to get Mik back, only he knew facing her alone was impossible. It was a crippling certainty, and old Raul wasn't taking it in.

"Bravura Christina ... Bravura Christina!"

But Raul Macon wasn't listening.

12.

Nils Mupreen had to admire Her Grace with wonder, despite himself. She was among them, along with that sublime phony, the so-called "performance" artist. This fact would once have left Nils incredulous. But so much of the improbable happened over the last year, he'd become a jaded, head-shaking revolutionary.

Or so he'd thought.

In the crowded Think Room, a secreted den of a 19th Century building serving as underground headquarters, Christina Alpreece returned Nils' scrutinizing in her own manner. She expelled smart pluming smoke from endless Dutch cigarettes, and invitingly arched an eyebrow with sleek assurance. A ringed hand traveled across her colorful sweater front, then alighted beneath a braless breast which -- now and then -- jounced provocatively for Nils to appreciate.

All-American Bitch, Nils told himself, taking another sip of Geneva and looking away. *What use would she be -- besides the obvious -- if not for her hermaphroditic wiles on godless Marva, that transsexual creature mocking gender by her own defilement of it?* He burped from the unsettled bami maneuvering in his stomach. Christina's money (or her family's) was her saving grace, and it was the major irony for Nils to consider. It took bourgeois money to combat government repression. But what money wasn't bourgeois?

Christina believed Nils was a revolutionary whiz kid, and therein existed her respect for him. As far as New Provos went -- or even young Dutchmen -- Nils wasn't very good looking, but definitely a picaresque sort nonetheless. His russet-tinged long hair was kept in a fashionable ponytail, and his muttonchop sideburns were so large he nearly had a full beard. He wore granny glasses and smoked an evil-looking pipe which sometimes contained Euro-hemp. "I'm an ex-University student now majoring in 'freedom,'" he maintained. Poet and thinker, Nils had definite advisory power in The Conclave (as the Dutch group was known by its members), and Christina knew that being partner to his influence was essential.

"This is so much like a board meeting," Nils spoke finally. As much the leader as anyone, he never sported an official title. Sitting in a turned-around chair, his long legs straddling it askewly, Nils smiled at the reporting female member whose droning voice was now interrupted. "We are ostensibly such an unorthodox band of reformers, yet here we are at this underground meeting hall, a museum, a relic for civic pride's rule. So much for the 21st Century."

"Hear, hear," someone said with sardonic undertone, saluting repetitiously. A few of the informally sitting or prostrated members laughed, knowing that Nils' wit was an expected put-down of any group pompousness. He was the luminary in their midst, full of surprises that were displayed with skillful ease. "We should get right to the matter's heart, now that Mr. Brice Rampoul has consented to reward us with his contribution. We all know what happened in the past, and the repetitions of the past are what we're fighting now anyway."

Some scattered applause and mock-cheering were heard, and Christina Alpreece smiled extravagantly at the gentleman in question who, up to that point, sat unobstrusively before them.

"Go to it, man. Give us your recent findings --"

"Without delay," Rampoul said, smiling now at Nils Mupreen (who so resembled his brother, Kress, that it was rumored he was the other's clone, though Kress was schizophrenic). Brice stood up, finishing his drink and haphazardly searching through some papers in a folder. "Ah! Dear assembled Body, time as we know it is dwindling and becoming an outmoded thing. And the moment we've awaited, as they say, is at hand."

More applause and approving noises were heard, and Mupreen made an exaggerated benedictory gesture. There was an irreverent feel to the place all right, and Rampoul stood becoming more excited, priming himself for this inevitability. To become downright heretical, that's what he wanted all along. To perform his crowning achievement, some tour de force electrifying not just the art world but the World at Large. *Now* he had the opportunity.

Brice smiled again, now ready, observing the diversely intelligent faces of the surrounding men and women, many of them willing to sacrifice -- even die -- for the cause at hand.

"The X-Regent," Brice Rampoul resumed, "is due to arrive in Amsterdam two weeks from Thursday. Before you get your hopes up, realize that this is subject to change. Nonetheless we must proceed on schedule as if it's the real thing." Rampoul cleared his throat, and his strangely garbed audience murmured more loudly. "We should therefore have our people ready, with the procedural tasks rehearsed to a millisecond. And absolutely memorized, of course."

"We hear you, Mr. Rampoul," Nils Mupreen said. Next to him then appeared Kress (known as the Coffin Man for his violent tendencies, and soldierly role in this endeavor), who arrived seconds before through a cordon of men guarding the rear doors. Kress smiled broadly, having heard the latest revelations hours before, but overtaken now by communal exuberance. Slapping his brother's leg appreciatively, he looked about with excessive nervous movements, goofing on everybody in his fashion.

"Above all," Rampoul continued, "we have to agree on the procedures for attending to our Regent, once we get him."

"Julie and Lena are working on that," Kress said.

"And I with them," Christina added.

"Yes, but as resident underground artist-activist, I thought I'd go over the particulars. I've added some things along the way we might experiment with, if necessary. We are not simply terrorists, but fellow executors of a significant undertaking, are we not? Together with our German friends from the Feuer Bande, we shall abduct the X-Regent from his quarters at 2100 hours on Friday night, the 24th. It is that simple. Yet also this difficult: our teamwork must overlap in precise, synchronizing fashion, or the propaganda we can generate from this will be as smoke without a spark."

Reading from his notes, almost like a lecturing celebrity, Professor Rampoul inquired of the four teams (Red, Yellow, Green, and Black) regarding further questions. "You must be aware of your roles," he stressed, "and not overstep the specifics given you, or the procedure might get out of sync, for improvising even for a little while between the gaps could be disastrous. Understood? Red team abducts. Yellow team detains, at the 4th Quadrant. Green team commences Re-Orientation after the 8-hour interval. Black team commands, issuing alternatives ... That's the basic outline. Again let us go over the particulars."

Someone cried out, "Shouldn't his murder be our objective?"

Taken aback, Rampoul took a moment to collect his thoughts. "That's Black team's priority, if necessary. We don't have time to debate that at this point. Obviously he's more important if we keep him alive and our objectives are met."

Listening there, as in a dream, Christina could see it all in a clear vision. The X-Regent would arrive furtively at Central Station, surrounded by the cronies sent to greet him. After lunch and whatnot, he would be taken to a location where the C.I.A. would intercept their guest. He'd be informed of certain existing facts re the controversial marketplace for matériel of "a contraband nature." Involved as the C.I.A. agents are with everyone and everything, they'd banter about source material for their guest's edification, hoping to prompt consummation of that big-fascist-deal-in-the-making -- Space Hallelujah Blackmail! Tomasi, Mr. Industrial Black Market, would be the Feds' highwater mark for good. Neo-Commies lived!

But if The Conclave could wrest X-Regent away, then the C.I.A. -- and practically everyone -- would be suddenly hearing new directives from another source. And those directives had better be heeded, for Christina could hear them all explicitly, in splendid enunciation. Tomasi -- *X-Regent* -- would be theirs exclusively, in the coup of a decade. Only Christina's people would be the ones to capitalize.

She could see them seize him, smuggle this ambiguous magnate of many faces away to the 4th Quadrant, where the adventure of re-conditioning would begin. They would teach Tomasi new lessons of political objectivity, educate him exclusively on the overthrow of widespread corruption, etc., until Washington's favorite ambassador became direly missed by the pigs wielding such demented power.

Christina Alpreece could see it all, out of her crystalline and many-sided vision, and very beautiful indeed were these children of the new reich's Communistic coming freedom ...

More than once in his sonorously halting voice, Brice Rampoul continued going over "the procedure," minute by minute, hour by hour, day by day. Standing by him in rapt fascination, Christina Alpreece listened to what had been dreamed of for so long. She felt a queasy sense of rapture over the power they'd embrace in a dedicated union bold enough to rattle the imperial toads from their profiteering perches around the war-stricken, fearful globe, and once again re-unite a severed Germany.

It was all quite inevitable, this resurrection of world-wide Communism in history's repetetive scheme, a maze from which no one could escape.

PART II

TAKEN BY THE HAWK

13.

Reposing in the suds like a temporarily sated, still gargantuan creature, Tito's broad sweating face appeared nearly bronzed. Those features many of his underlings weren't privileged to behold displayed, in meditation, a gross sensuality only a jaded satyr could boast of. Called more than a Dutch gangster in his time, Tito was of Slavic origins. He arose destitute as a teenager from the ravages of world wars, fleeing Hungary later to make his fortune in the freer capital of Amsterdam.

Now Tito reclined in slothful obesity against a baroque, gilt-edged backboard depicting putti in various obscene actions. It was hardly less extravagant than the giant porcelain bubble bath he was submerged in up to his neck.

"What are you boys trying to tell me?" Tito asked, sotto voce, eyes closed and no doubt still focusing on some inner bliss.

"That Jari has been messed-up, Tito," Macon said again, wanting to splash some hot water into the turkey's face. "You remember Jari?"

The great man burped -- slowly.

"Jari ... doesn't ... work, for me ... any longer, Raul. She ... went ... independent ..."

In what could be construed comic book dumbfoundedness, Raul Macon stared down at his boss. Did it at all make any difference? Jari still worked her window on the Street, and Tito did huge business thereon. Tito practically owned the Street. Everything was interconnected.

"What happened to her. Raul?"

"That's what we're trying to find out. We'd like to know what the hell happened. Why she was tagged and who did it."

Both of Tito's bulbous, jaundiced-looking eyes slowly parted about one-quarter of an inch. His sonorously heavy breathing was all that could be heard for awhile in the large white, multi-mirrored bathroom, where many of his business dealings were conducted. To Raul Macon especially the place was creepy enough, and he half-expected to have his All-American ass pinched by the toweled eunuch who attended to Tito. But thankfully all the slimy gooks were outside, no doubt ready to intrude officiously with balmy substances to rub on Fatso, along with baby oil. Or fan him with that insipid plastic palm frond, whistling Yahweh all the while.

"How badly is she beaten, Raul?"

Macon's gorge kept rising. "Pretty damn good, Tito. She'll be unemployed for awhile."

The magisterial man's eyes were now fully open, blinking against the yellow fluorescent lighting radiating from the high ceiling above. "Get me one of those cigars over there, boy, won't you?" he said to a retiring T.K. Keller, who immediately obliged. "And take one for yourself, Raul. Potent blend if I do say so."

Macon declined, watching his boss laboriously priming the cigar's butt with his grossly lapping, cow-like tongue, before allowing T.K. to light it for him ceremoniously. Thoughtfully, for several seconds, Tito abandoned himself to sucking on the acrid smoke, which he exhaled indulgently in T.K.'s retreating direction.

"That's most unfortunate, Raul. All of that's most unfortunate. I'm sorry to hear of this. I want ... you ... to make sure it doesn't happen to any of the hotel girls, understand? This must not ... become ... *pandemic*." He paused, eyeing them sternly with a look indicating turgid gases were circulating uncomfortably in his stomach, and more foully sweet-smelling bubbles now joined the others composing his frilly bath of suds. "*Now* ... what's this ... else ... you've been babbling ... about?" he inquired, observing Keller with skeptical disdain.

Raul Macon approached with a deliberate slowness. He wanted to strike out at something -- the very embodiment of corrupt power, perhaps, dogging him all his life -- and this man submerged squeamily before him

was the closest thing to it.

"What's the latest word on Gaylen Tomasi?"

"What ... about him? He's .... wealthy, American ... old ..."

"He's wanted, Tito."

"Well ... I would never ... want to touch him anyway."

This comment struck Tito as highly risible, and he wheezed out an unattractive form of laughter, the oily follicles on his sweating, beef-caked face vibrating like aroused pin-heads. "Damn. I remain ... young by comparison! Do I ... not? Yes, I remain vibrant --"

"But old Tomasi?"

"A stooge ... A so-called Presidential close-friend." Tito's huge, crooking forefinger put this remark in quotes. "He goes on good will missions around the world, advising business interests ... on behalf of America ...

"Never met the slimy pus druid, I'm afraid."

Macon stared unblinkingly. Tito lied a lot. Macon was tired of hearing lies, old or otherwise. A sustained current of anger motivated him now, and he felt himself for the first time in years doing things he never would have believed himself doing. His anger was white hot, controlled by a fierce malice. Tito's fish nose was buried too often up the squirming rears of skinny-young boys.

"You've never met him, Tito?"

"Not that I recall, lad ... What's the problem?"

"Some Provos told Keller here that you should keep your nose out of Tomasi's business."

The gargantuan man gave forth a warble of hoarse laughter, stirring the bubbles into disarray. "Is that ... so?" He puffed deeply on his cigar, filling the air with lazy blue-gray smoke. "*Provos ...?* Where did you see these Provos, boy?"

"At the Maradisa, sir," Keller replied with lackluster spirit, feeling hardly up to it. "I went there with little Mik, Lelica's kid. We met this female friend of Marva Claire's. Well, thanks to her accidentally or otherwise, all this was passed on to me."

"Is that so?"

Tito became theatrically incredulous. He wanted to turn these impostors out. Disturbing his mid-afternoon bath. It was unheard of. This was business? He would turn the eunuchs on them.

"So I'm supposed to lay off this Tomasi ... Big deal."

"He's going to be arriving in Amsterdam sometime soon," T.K. continued, "on another 'fact-finding' tour. I leanred that much." He rubbed his nose self-consciously, clearing his throat, wondering how deeply he was getting into this and feeling like a first-class shithead. "Anyway, I lost Mik at this woman friend's of Marva Claire."

"You ... *lost* ... Mik?" (Tito was even more incredulous, and his ornate rings began to glisten like evil serpent eyes.)

"I think so. At any rate, he's missing. And Lelica's worried sick."

"That woman ... has a right ... to be worried sick. She deserves it."

"All this is getting more then coincidental, Tito," Macon said, chumily putting a foot up on the tub.

"So ... What do you want?" asked Tito, throwing a hand up.

"Help us," Macon said, leaning over the tub. "Help us when – and if – something happens. We hope this kid Mik doesn't stay missing, and I hope these protest freaks don't think they're gonna put a boot into us. But believe me, if they're responsible for beating Jari ..." He didn't finish. Tito was staring open-mouthed at him. Macon decided to test him, come clean just far enough. "Jari tipped me that Tomasi might be a good *user*. What a laugh. Who knew about this sucker? Just another faggy banker letting his hair down, right --?"

"So?"

"I went to where Tomasi supposedly was staying whenever in town. A pretty expensive apartment. I found some C.I.D. geeks there, U.S. prime, who want Tomasi too."

Keller was startled. He hadn't heard this much before, and wondered why Macon was telling it. Tito's face had become professionally sapient now, and with a new slyness he observed his accomplice. Tito was a big supporter of American politics, who would naturally be connected somehow with Tomasi more than anyone. Tito and Macon were facing off.

Macon pressed on: "I need to know who-do-you-trust, Tito?"

A pause. There was a buzzing of light fixtures, and an ormulu also flickered strangely in the background. *Tito's Heaven.* And now this, a challenge from a nobody who wanted *to know.* Tito's favorite saying was always a mocking, "What do you know?" *Answer:* That perhaps some expendable people were being white-washed at the service of corrupt political maneuvering, so that world powers could continue war mongering.

"Those C.I.D. -- or Federal men you saw, Raul," began Tito, sighing slowly as his cigar became enmeshed by filmy bubbles, "are probably interested in your Provos also. So you can thank them for this mess, since you've become their tracking device. They'll definitely keep a hammerlock on you. I know they will, because they're afraid like all hell their Russian counterparts are going to get to Ambassador Tomasi ..." Tito's eyes closed. "Raul? Wouldn't it be funny if those geeks were really Neo-Communists in disguise?"

"*Impostors.* All of them, my friend; and all history is a déjà vu carnival for freaks. Don't you believe that, Raul? That History is destined to disastrously repeat itself?"

Macon failed to reply. He was a terrestrial person, and like T.K. Keller didn't know what to make of a world trying to escape its own planetary atmosphere -- and failing miserably at that. There was nothing in interstellar space that would save the world from itself. Why hadn't Russia and the U.S. learned that searching desperately for intelligent life forms, other than human, beyond the Milky Way -- at the expense of letting earth life wallow in a warring recidivism no one understood as anything but inhuman -- was a resounding political failure?

One that never should be repeated, Raul Macon decided.

14.

The hurt invaded him with a searing fury: all that had happened before couldn't compare to the feeling of total degradation overtaking T.K. It was a slither through a drug dream, yet in this instance he was infrequently straight, and that lucid moment of insight made everything more difficult to accept.

Waiting in that domicile of sin for old buddy Macon to bail him out, T.K. Keller encountered an abyss of doubt. It wasn't the same anymore, being able to escape the specters threatening to disrupt his equilibrium of withdrawal. Now T.K. was forced to confront something like blunt-force trauma, and the closer he came to it the more agonizing was his fear and suffering.

It had come to this in typical pell-mell fashion, much too sudden for anyone to get any bearings. Only a few days ago, in fact, Macon and T.K. searched out the place where young Mik disappeared: the chic studio-cum-complex of the elusive lady Christina Alpreece, extraordinary dilettante. The Quarter looked impossible to home in on, so it was decided -- with some trepidation on T.K.'s part -- to visit Marva Claire's Maradisa once again and scrounge out the real panacea.

T.K. felt himself slipping, needing not a little dose of heavenly hits and escapist beers. He didn't like the look in Raul Macon's now devious and rage-furrowed face. Lordy no. The man was primed for the splitting of all the atoms in his brain (what little of that vaunted gray matter remained yet intact). The ex-ordnance sergeant driving so dangerously exuded murderous emotions. Never before had T.K. seen such a stark close-up, and he felt helplessly taken by that harmful vibration. He was getting very cold feet.

How to duck out of it? The enslaving signs were diabolically clear, with bodily fluids pumped-up. At least T.K. was glad they were heading for the Maradisa, that creaking emporiium of rank hemp-dealing, where perhaps he could fuel up. Anything to quell the cells of consciousness and such acute memory retention.

"I'm chickening," T.K. sadly allowed to himself, once again forced to reconsider the ramifications of that big secret in his life he'd been trying to hide and annihilate from resurrection: *I don't want to Know! I don't want to Know!* It was an admission that struck his core, promising no redress, portending only disaster.

"We've got to be cool, T.K. Man," Macon said as he ham-handedly wheeled the VW up to the Maradisa, still overcrowded at 4:35 p.m. with glaucous-eyed revelers converging outside in the street.

T.K. felt like laughing. *Be cool.* He hadn't noticed it before, but after the car was parked (nearly decapitating a curb-sitting flutist rhapsodically performing with nearby upturned Panama, ungraced by anything but coins), Macon pulled open the left side of his suede coat revealingly. The bulge T.K. thought to be new fat was actually a holstered pistol of considerable size and weight. T.K. nearly bit through the filter of his fifth straight cigarette, adding a broad double-take, thank you. *A gun!* Black, shiny, disgustingly real-looking. And now a knowledgeable Raul Macon was inspecting it swiftly, eyes down the barrel before snapping the baby in half, loading needle-pointed, copper-jacketed shells into the dark holes of that slowly turning cylinder.

"I'll get you one, kid."

"I don't need one, Raul."

Macon eyed him with severe disdain. T.K.'s weakness and fear were exposed like wee private parts displayed by old perverts at the train station. "You look sick, kid. But we gotta get going -- don't puke on me now." In step with this notion T.K. clumsily stumbled out, falling face first against the pavement, and garnered stares from startled on-lookers. In their colorful garb and sedated manners, usually oblivious to anything so disconcerting, they could not even abide this from Americans.

"Raul, this is all really ridiculous."

"Get the fuck up, T.K."

Now Macon was disgusted, ignominiously helping T.K. to his pigeon-toed feet. A whacked-out young lass wearing spangles in her long purple hair laughed at them. Some violent avengers they were. They elbowed their way through the crowd, T.K. nearly upchucking. Raul Macon waved the importantly embossed letter bearing Tito's imprint for the doorman, and demanded an immediate audience with her ambiguous highness, Marva Claire.

Macon had his other hand inside his coat, ready to unleash the Firebird, but the doorman allowed entrance after reading the potent missive. In they went, shoving, pushing, attacking that atmosphere of exploding light and decibel-climbing sound. Almost violating that Rock and Roll sanctum of countercultural revolt, the air was so rife with hemp strains that T.K. was buzzing immediately from proximity. Thank-the-gods, he might make it after all with the proper nourishment, and hoped to find Nils Mupreen perhaps busily smoking a bowl of dark hemp beneath the rococo entablature depicting two newly discovered planets.

They were met at the office stairs by a guide the doorman had notified. While waiting, T.K. made a quick transaction with a sinister Arab dealer cutting up a hemp key with a meat cleaver. Suddenly Keller was in business, albeit cleaned out of his guilders.

Nonetheless fortified, T.K. and the Arab began smoking after Macon only was invited inside. This oversight hardly rankled the smoke-clouded form of our young expatriate, who once aspired to write poems after Baudelaire, and was at least now doing his homework during this tense moment he yearned to disappear from.

So once again T.K. was reunited with the mystery of self-and-being, between which he'd experienced much exhilaration in the past. It would be all right again, he told himself. To hell with this character Tomasi, and forget Tito too. To hell with everything and everybody. No longer would he have to dwell on the worked-over features of Macon's favortie digital whore, or wonder over the fate of little Mik, or confront the fomenting revolutionaries reading him the writ. For a few moments of eternity T.K. could exist in subconscious bliss, his mind another chemical suspended in life's great elixir of Space.

And it was there that no problem seemed to matter, of course, since everything was answered without answer, if that made any sense. (It did if you were hemped.)

"I am ripped, my friend," T.K. told the Arab, who was slicing his loaf for other customers.

But what unfolded? The shadows of this dream of consciousness soon lengthened, and T.K. felt the onus of disturbing vibrations slowly possessing him. All the detritus from his conscious mind was returning, subverting his ecstatic communion with the netherworld. Inside/outside no longer, now T.K. was in Marva's office witnessing something having the overtone of an evil ritual. Marva, Macon, the bodyguards all appeared half-glowing, surrounded by lurid emanations T.K. shied from in wooden anger. He felt increasingly helpless, severed from any meaningful connection to this event.

"Where can we reach her?" Macon was saying, and T.K. saw a death's mask on his once pardoned friend's features -- but whose death did it belong to?

"Her whereabouts are none of your concern," the Maradisa proprietress replied.

Raul Macon took out his gun and stood next to the middle-aged woman looking much older under the lights with her make-up streaking. He pressed the long barrel flush against her powdered, flabby cheek and watched her two bodyguards go pale, their forms rigid with tension.

"One of Tito's ladies was worked-over on Canal Street. Tell them just to stand there and not move for anything! That's it. Did you hear me, dear? Things have to be accounted for."

Marva stood there by her desk, unbelieving, in a pose of contorted discomfort. Her made-up eyes blinked uncontrollably.

"Leave him alone," she told the bodyguards.

Macon took away the gun from Marva's face. "Also one of his lady friends has a boy missing who came here with young Mr. Keller that night. He says *your* friend took them out to her place. And that's been the last of that boy."

Marva looked searchingly at Keller, her blanched features still uncomposed. "Surely you know more about that than anybody?"

"He's been smoking," somebody said, very slowly, eyeing T.K.

Angered by this, Macon turned to his ripped co-hort and fixed him with an unforgiving gaze. *Of all the times.* He wanted to smash T.K.'s face in. Instead he turned back to the others.

"Tito does not like threats. This boy was threatened that night by people connected here."

"I've always had good relations with Tito," said Marva. "Things have been exaggerated, surely."

"Where is she?"

The proprietress turned a shade hemophiliac as Raul Macon pulled the gun's hammer back. The moment was beyond good taste. She regaled him with some lengthy information, avoiding certain finer points of rapprochement.

Perhaps she regretted it, for when this unusual pair left (unmolested, at her order, which upset her coterie no end), Marva learned only a few hours later of a terrorist incident that had one of her advisors remarking, "That's it. The Provos and the others might have you in danger, Marva. You've sent those Americans right into their craw. Isn't that wonderful --?"

"It's Christina's doing," Marva dismally remarked, attempting to sip a revivifying liqueur. "*God.* Of all the wrong timing." She cursed -- excessively, for baneful smells of violence contaminated her air. "Keep them in view. I'll notify Christina, if I can find her. Things are getting odd."

And out of hand, Marva reminded herself, hoping the innocent ones could be saved over the next crucial days. She knew some things in life never changed. But to kidnap a boy believed to be the bearer of some unearthly cosmic knowledge was beyond her understanding. Consulting her Zodiac charts, Marva Claire feared the coming disorder of planetary physics, then lit another gold-filtered cigarette.

15.

She did not really know why she did the things she did, she told herself. Was it an obsession on her part, another masochistic fantasy called Love Of Hate? She and Brice Rampoul took something from one another, but what it became continued to baffle this expatriate member of the Alpreece family.

Shivering on this morning of an impenetrable, gray-bleeding drizzle, Christina sat in the van's back. Still she was ecstatic because it was the morning they had anticipated for so long. And she was in on it. With Kress and Brice sitting up front, she was a privileged witness to this stake-out, and allowed to accompany the all-powerful Black team.

She and Brice Rampoul were in a state beyond anticipation, their nerves keyed to a hyper-sensitivity. It was hard to accept that it had all come at last. This moment superseded the intricate, dendrite-like complexity of their relationship, made all the past highs and lows inconsequential. Here was a spiritual foreplay of great excitement, with a feeling of unique dangers to come, never before known. Christina knew Brice was experiencing it also, for he'd never looked more adrenalin-pumped in his life. *Tomasi!* The X-Regent himself, somewhere right down the street at one of Amsterdam's more modern residences. He was probably the guest of a "prominent Dutch businessman" and partaking of a late lunch leavened by cognac and cigars, discussing the arms embargo of Venus.

"Tomasi ..."

That he was an obsession was the understatement of ages. What little Christina had so far seen of the man shocked her. He was more "adipose" than expected, though with a distinguished silver pompadour and mustache, adding to his officious air. Tomasi walked with a cane, occasionally wore thick-lensed glasses, and dressed like a Brooks Brothers ad for dour septuagenarian businessmen. Always beige-vested and dark-suited beneath an expensive overcoat, he sported a Homburg nestled almost defiantly on his head. He wore gray gloves constantly (except when smoking an infrequent cigar), carried a Samsonite briefcase tucked beneath his right arm, his other hand directing a large black umbrella. Tomasi was accompanied by a much younger aide endeavoring to manipulate the umbrella as they alighted from the limousine, but the task proved cumbersome.

"Idiots," Kress muttered, observing this spectacle in his emotionally tense manner.

"Old Tomasi is a badger who hates water," Brice Rampoul commented. To Christina in back he ordered, "Tell Oude Kerk they've arrived."

Christina obliged, crisply relaying the message into the radio microphone grasped by her svelte fingers. ("Oude Kerk" was the codename they'd given their chief museum-like headquarters; Christina's "studio"had a different designation.) They'd been discreetly following Tomasi's small entourage for hours, ever since he'd arrived around ten that morning at Central Station. Met by his host's aides who saw to the luggage, etc., the old man apparently desired some coffee and breakfast at the restaurant nearby Hotel Victoria. That visit eradicated another hour.

At a nearby café, Nils Mupreen and others were keeping their quarry under uncanny observation, and determining beforehand where-and-when the old man would go. Nils' contacts were planted everywhere, with every contingency plotted in advance.

"I want to know," Nils Mupreen had said, "when he pisses and what he shits ..."

"Spoken with the crassness of a true revolutionary," Christina remembered saying. But now there was more the ellipsis of their watchful silence than words. Following Tomasi necessitated a long, circuitous drive through the city and beyond. Several times they stopped to regain bearings via radio from Nils, who seemed better at tailing than anyone. But of course Nils Mupreen seemed to know everything, being an astute and perfectionist tactician clued to the digital world.

"Nils says the yellow Fiat following the entourage is C.I.A.," a Black team voice advised over the radio. It was that car they feared the most. Its four occupants had police stature and legal cell phones, were surely armed (though looking as stuffily innocuous as foreign bureaucrats on leave in Holland). Two of them, added Kress, met Tomasi at the train station and were undoubtedly bodyguards, heavily equipped with digital armaments. Thankfully there were no Dutch police around.

So the non-descript gang (termed *Revols* by insiders) wanted to strike before Tomasi made contact with any public officials, which he was scheduled for the following day.

"If we wait too long," Nils warned, "we'll never be able to get him."

Brice Rampoul continued inking notations into an omnipresent small notebook he kept on his lap throughout the wait. He slept very little the previous days &/or nights, and Christina was worrying about him. She kept refilling styrofoam cups of coffee for him and Kress, who both chainsmoked incessantly. They felt conspicuously parked on the large street for so long. Thankfully many cars used it for the same purpose. Quietly the van members assumed a good enough vantage point to carry on business.

"It'll be all right," Christina told herself. "It'll be superlative."

Now all through the wait into evening their chief worry became the Federal men inside the Dutch businessman's residence with Tomasi. It was another cloudy, gray-washed day, and evening came with a premature certainty. They had no idea how long Tomasi planned to remain in the residence, but if he stayed the night some vital plans would alter --perhaps disastrously.

The two cars of Tomasi's party continued to be watched. Both were parked close to one another on the right side of the street. The Revols' own van -- several cars up the block -- was parked on the left side. The uniformed chauffeur in the sleek black limousine never once left his car, so -- after lengthy consideration -- Rampoul decided they'd have to strike before nightfall, no matter how unfortunate this seemed.

"We'll go with the decoy plan," he advised Christina, who relayed the news with a hushed excitement into the unsquelched radio. *It is 3:46 p.m.,* she noted in her laptop computer. *Tomasi has been inside six hours.* She could have been more precise, but felt it didn't matter.

Christina was too hypertense now -- more expectant, she believed, than at any time in her life. This moment of incipient danger *was* her life, and cast everything she'd experienced before into a sad, pale intaglio. She almost had a mystical feeling of thanksgiving, waiting there, knowing things were now unstoppable forever, that some energy generated from the unseen reaches of a supernova perhaps guided her to the young boy who became her medium, her absolute contact, with those innerspace beings she'd waited for since time immemorial.

Sometime after 4 p.m., the station wagon containing two female members from the Red team drove onto Vijzel Straat and motored slowly past the closely watched residence. Knowing beforehand just what they'd encounter, the wagon occupants observed the limousine (with the half-slumbering form of the chauffeur inside) still parked out front.

As they pulled abreast of the limousine and its driver, one of the young women riding shotgun leaned out the window and asked some alluring questions in Dutch. Gruff-faced, the driver was a middle-aged, jowly sort who'd been slumping with his cap's bill at eye-level. His immediate comprehension was somewhat lacking. But the charm and naive flirtatiousness of his questioner brought him up straight.

Yes, he knew where such-and-such a place of sex-for-hire was, and he would also help the ladies with their car trouble. Almost too readily he replaced the young woman behind the wheel, ready to test the steering and brakes, etc. From the van Brice Rampoul strained to see the unusual happenings of the next few seconds. The straw-blonde woman riding shotgun leaned suddenly against the man in what appeared to be an amorous embrace. Briefly the fluttering wing of an upraised, white kerchief was slapped against the chuckling driver's face. The women also laughed throughout his struggling, until the standing female got behind the wheel, pushing the now slumped and unconscious driver from view.

The car drove off.

After some minutes the large station wagon stopped at a nearby side-street where another uniformed chauffeur waited. He received the incapacitated driver's keys and wallets, etc., and was driven back to the limousine, which he entered as if nothing was amiss.

The reaction was close to euphoria inside the nearby parked van. All through this little escapade -- which lasted just over ten minutes -- the area was dusky, with few passers-by about. And Kress behind the van wheel noted that nobody had seen anything from the residence, where living room lights now cast amber glints through huge, brocaded curtains aglow in the street's drizzle-thick aura.

"Red decoy successful," Christina heard the radio informing them. "Driver bound and taken from guest-site."

It all had to work this precisely, Christina thought. She fantasized about Tomasi, how the gray-bearded shit would react to what would befall him. She knew enough about him via media sources and clandestine reports, but seeing him in the proverbial flesh was another matter. Anticipating it gave her a brief sensation of excitement.

Meanwhile Kress had discreetly exited the van with a large backpack on his shoulders, giving him the look of a wanderer en route to some hostel. In the gradual twilight, he crossed the traffic-heavy street in the direction of the parked Fiat belonging to the American government men. He had to work quickly, Kress knew, yet he had to function with measured accuracy.

With alert nervousness, the van occupants peered out their windows. The crucial time was imminent.

"All Red units are in their sectors," the radio voice said. *Good,* thought Brice Rampoul, consulting his ever-present notebook under a faint penlight. *We'll soon know whether the abduction is a go.*

Sitting there, Rampoul had a prescient certainty that his actions would lead to the rebirth of Communism throughout the world. The Red rebuilding was at hand, and war -- guerrilla or otherwise -- was a means to that end. By the 21st Century's third decade wars raged throughout the Middle East, only to be extinguished by select nuclear missile exchanges putting countries like Iraq and Saudi Arabia under a cloud of radioactive uncertainty. Now Rampoul knew greater war in Europe was again historically inevitable, and his heart raced.

16.

For sometime -- in typical mysterious fashion, perhaps -- Gaylen Tomasi sat in an elegantly Old World study (replete with sea decor and oak paneling of great age), hashing out matters with his host and their mutual associates. Warmed by liquor, well fed, and sitting before a magnanimous fireplace ablaze, Tomasi had no idea of misfortune befalling him, despite being briefed by the C.I.A. about the existence of "radical fringes" in Amsterdam. They amounted to no more than the guerrilla theater protest antics so prevalent then, at which the resurrected Provos excelled so notoriously. But no one was sure.

It was hoped resultingly that Tomasi would realize the famous Dutch tolerance might prove unfounded on occasion.

"I'm only an American businessman," Tomasi replied, expecting it to explain everything. It was known he knew important people, had considerable sway in diplomatic circles, and his "connections" were legendary. And yes, this Medulla Raze business he was to safeguard could have immeasurable international consequences, and perhaps decide the outcome of the paramilitary actions in Asia and the Middle East.

Now Tomasi was being briefed on the possibility of a "mutual jurisdiction." Certain agreements were being discussed between the seated figures about the problems confronting them, and what influences they could share or borrow to consolidate their power. It was a business meeting, but the presence of the two C.I.A. men (who were privy to certain confidences and more) gave all a distinct political significance. This bothered Tomasi as the interminable hours passed. For the first time he felt the anomaly of his situation, which made it imperative he tolerate these officious boors to the cloak-and-dagger letter -- despite the fact he'd like to give them a rain-check for eternity. Upon lighting his fifth cigar Tomasi experienced the absolute intuition that things weren't right. He'd have to act as guarded around these types as if they planned to use him any second.

The host was a Dutch magnate named Van Groot, unabashedly more elderly and outgoing than Tomasi. Van Groot believed that their "cabal" should be anti-Communist and aid the American war efforts around the world. He argued that certain guaranteed emoluments should be provided him also. "In such a manner to insure a basic stance of disinterest for the NATO nations," Van Groot insisted, "so that more liberal and leftist factions in the Netherlands believe their leaders haven't capitulated to any imperialist reign."

Tomasi felt such a disclaimer was unnecessary, and not a trifle annoying, along with everything else bothering him that day. Just what financial outlay expected from him for Dutch willingness to support more clandestine activities of the American government, such as the continued dispersal of anti-war elements and other details of the accord, consumed more time than Tomasi believed possible. He was tired, yes, but at a point in his sixty-eight years where he wanted to show the world his continuing capability. His allegiance to U.S. President Richard M. Noxson made Tomasi doubly determined to see this all through, in order to secure every advantage.

Besides, should the Dutch agree to storing "the material" under consideration in Holland indefinitely, it would ease the tension in re-partitioned West Germany, where top-secret weaponry held an irresolute -- and possibly dangerous -- status. Tomasi had to convince himself the Medulla Project wasn't just business or another easy matter after all. It was *Politics & War*. It was possibly the answer in Asia and elsewhere, and the world conflicts waited in unrests of ignorance.

"You will notice," Van Groot whispered later, "that these other gentlemen have strong-armed me to a point where I must insist they carry out their activities without drawing attention to me, or making me take part. Do you understand? I can give them a certain impetus for going ahead, but I cannot unlock doors for them. And I must be privileged for not always explaining why."

Tomasi mused over brandy, and grew more discreetly angry dwelling on these revelations. He should have known better than to believe the President would send any ambassador on an ordinary trip, but learning of its ramifications in such an ungainly fashion was another matter. The President had to know what his C.I.A. men were up to, didn't he? After observing them for all these hours, Tomasi sure as hell didn't.

"Well, I can only guarantee my own end of things," Tomasi told his displeased host. "When I talk to them further, perhaps matters will be ..." Lamely he couldn't provide the right apologia, which would have been mere smoke anyway.

The two C.I.A. men present -- Brunasky and Larson -- would not disclose their own prospective doings, except in general fashion. "We're of course interested in finding out any connections between the Nu-Provos, or any Dutch radicals, with Americans in Europe. Particularly U.S. servicemen, etc.," Brunasky remarked later to the group. "Mr. Van Groot has been particularly helpful in that regard."

The C.I.A. men mentioned the acquisition of a great deal more names, but wouldn't go into any further specifics about any plans for such people. Tomasi wondered about the alleged American connection, but much information "disseminated" by these gentlemen apparently defied rational comprehension.

So continued the unusual discussions until about 5:30, when Tomasi begged off having dinner with his guest due to pressing hotel considerations and other activities.

"Then we'll have breakfast tomorrow," his host suggested, "and hopefully the contract will become formalized."

"Yes, of course."

Papers were withdrawn and carefully placed into dark-colored briefcases which were snapped shut. Tomasi's perennially tight-lipped aide stood at attention nearby, ready to open an umbrella. The rain shattering down unceasingly outside accompanied a wind-whipping sound tattooing the shutters. Everyone was finally standing, buttoning coats and finishing drinks. With a throaty command Van Groot admonished all to have a good night. Shaking his host's hand with his gloved own, Tomasi replied that of course they would.

Outside the progression continued more slowly, and Tomasi bent his head beneath the rain-speckled umbrella (already fringed by dripping water beads clinging like silver crystals), pulling his hat down snugly as they approached the street.

"I should have worn galoshes," he muttered to no one in particular. His aide Kreiger knew many of these asides were rhetorical anyway. The C.I.A. men followed not too closely behind.

What I should do tomorrow, Tomasi reminded himself, *is talk with the President, if possible. Something might be wrong here, or out-of-sync. I'm sure of it ...*

The chauffeur had the limousine doors open, awaiting Tomasi's arrival. The ambassador nearly stumbled trying to negotiate his way in, but was steadied by his aide. Fiercely rain punished the cobblestone street, and for a moment Tomasi's party was engulfed by the storm-like force, casting everything into a gray, permanent standstill.

"We will proceed to the Hotel Victoria now, driver," Tomasi's aide instructed with his official voice.

The driver nodded, checking his mirror, ready to pull out into the street. A sudden overcoated figure stuck its head into the car, waiting for everyone to make room. It was Brunasky, or so Tomasi surmised uneasily.

"I've been instructed to accompany you, sir," the C.I.A. man said. Tomasi looked peeved.

"Oh, I'm sure that's not necessary," he said, but the importunate official had already pushed his way in, slamming the door behind him. The driver nearly stalled the vehicle, attempting to put it in gear, upon the arrival of his additional passenger. In the rear-view mirror, had Tomasi been looking, he might have seen the figure of the other C.I.A. man getting into his Fiat, several parked cars behind. Just then the explosion which came unawares behind the limousine carried enough force to pitch its occupants forward in startled bewilderment.

"Good Christ," the C.I.A. man said. He tried to get out, but the limousine was already in the street and pulling away. "Driver -- stop this goddamn thing!"

Momentarily the driver looked perplexed, as if he hadn't heard. He turned to see Brunasky reaching inside his overcoat. The driver's hand quickly appeared holding a Firebird pistol fired point-blank at the C.I.A. man's crouching form.

Tomasi screamed. The C.I.A. man began to fragment into glistening, beautiful, iridescent parts that spun around him with cartoonish glee, each one emitting a uniquely musical sound. Meanwhile Tomasi's aide tried to shield his elderly charge.

The limousine careened to a braking halt, its passenger door opened by another device-toting figure who suctioned up the victim's essences -- whirling still like fireflies in the night -- into an elongated metallic canister. Then he took his seat inside the car in almost the same fluid and unbroken motion.

"Let's go," Kress Mupreen told the driver, and trained his menacing device on the two captives trying to fathom the lightning-like events. "Please sit up, gentlemen, and try to compose yourselves. Do you hear me?"

He slapped the stricken Tomasi hard across the face, jabbing his pistol at the aide also. "Do you hear me? You won't be harmed if you just sit there and quiet down, damn you --"

Tomasi was unaccountably singing an aria from a favorite opera, tears wetly flattening his mustache by the time the limousine penetrated the city outskirts, heading for God knew where. On the limo's small T.V.-computer screen a news program was boringly documenting the progress of a Russian spacecraft being attacked on the moon by renegade imperialist rebels planted by the U.S. government, and Kress Mupreen suddenly kicked the digital-tracker into a cracked and dysfunctional mechanism. It was incapable now of tracking the limo's whereabouts, though the C.I.A. man's dissolution no doubt was recorded on the Amsterdam police monitors. The broken spy-eye's sound remained operable, and the garbled voice of a portentous announcer declaiming the rashness of the moon attack was heard to say interplanetary war between the superpowers was becoming a grim inevitability ...

Still singing (as if at Carnegie Hall during his one man show), Vincent Tomasi briefly wondered why this now disastrous conference couldn't have taken place at the Hague, a place where peace was always a historic given.

17.

"You get yourself together, kid. You're coming apart like a Japanese radio, and nothin's happening yet."

Finally they found their quarry's unique residence again -- after scouring the Prinsengracht neighborhood for the proper location, eluding them even with directions in hand. By day, T.K. would never have recognized the place (except for the strange and ornately carved wooden door, which remained impressed like an iconic image in his mind, almost cauterized there), especially given his addled state at such legendary times. Right then he wasn't in much better shape, given the hectic events and helter-skelter search producing an undeniable strain, so that now his eyes were spent coals in some second-hand grate of implausible design.

They had staked the place out, to whatever end. Nobody appeared home, and waiting there for five hours in inclement weather for the renowned occupant to return proved fruitless.

Finally they left, figuring to return later that night, when darkness might aid their quest.

Raul Macon was distempered by the ultimately frustrating wait. More than ever bummed out, back in his girl Karin's apartment Raul consumed four straight shots of Geneva before deigning to utter any comment without curses. At that late afternoon hour Karin was still at work, of course, but T.K. wondered how she was taking her lover's hardly professional relations with a battered Canal Street courtesan. Did she perhaps know what was happening right that tension-heavy second?

Some intuition caused T.K. to answer this musing affirmatively, only increasing his wallowing self-pity and depression, not to forget old paranoia.

"That hole. That goddamn bitch," Macon was muttering.

In the dank, poorly heated apartment the phone abruptly rang with insistent jangling. Dangerously inappropriate, T.K. thought. Tensely Macon picked up the receiver and stood there almost wobbling, sweating out high-alcohol content from a face whose customary sullen mask was now gone with the winds of inner wars.

"Yeah?"

"*Raul*-ee?" the phone voice bellowed. "This is Hull-E. Are you all right?"

"Sure I'm all right, you solicitous bastard."

"Well, I've been trying to reach you," Hull-E.'s voice continued, quavering. "Somebody here wants to see you. It's about Jari, I think --"

Macon's face hardened. "What about Jari? Who the hell wants to see me --?"

"He says his name is Rolf, and that you've met before."

Rolf? *Sure we've met before, but probably in another lifetime,* Macon thought, his mind close to a barleycorn blank. *Don't sweat it.* He was told by Hull-E. not to worry; that everything was all right, and Lissie was still nursing the injured young lady. But if he wasn't busy, Raul had better come see this Rolf character.

"Thanks a bundle, Hull-E."

Was there no end to supreme tensions, T.K. wondered? He surmised correctly that his friend's emotions were on a trip-wire. His own weren't doing much better.

Macon threw down the receiver he saw as a dog's chewed bone. "Come on, T.K., we've got to make it over to The Amstoy," he slurred, wheezing words outs. Suddenly amused, his hoarse laughter was much more frightening. "*Rolf-stein* wants to see us."

Back at The Amstoy there was the tribulation of evil seediness inhabiting the weather-beaten walls, sodden with dampness from the sea's ancient presence. In malodorous splendor, Hull-E. stood in rumpled fashion behind the bar, his perennial maroon suspenders stretched dangerously across a huge, sweating girth. In rolled-up white shirt sleeves, his old-fashioned look was registered like a dossier profile in the gaze of one dark-suited man, beer in hand, sitting at a far corner table. In the wood-floor room the stillness was too pronounced for Hull-E. to bear without sweating.

The dark-suited man looked up finally upon the noisy arrival of his awaited party. Macon and Keller were convivially greeted by Hull-E., already pouring out beers, his one outsized glass eye glittering like a vitreous beacon. Macon lit a cigarette, coughing, pretending to ignore the man seated in the far corner. Replacing the matches inside his coat pocket, Macon felt the presence of the large digital pistol holstered across his chest.

Looking now at the patriarchal bartender, Macon asked, "Any change?"

"She's still the same," Hull-E. replied in whispered confidentiality. "The doctor will come again tomorrow."

Macon grimaced, thoughtfully sipping the beer and looking across the room at the man for the first time.

"There he is," Hull-E. said.

The man raised a hand in greeting, beckoning to Macon. *Count C.I.A. himself,* surmised Macon, who recognized the suit freak from that ugly morning at what supposedly was the mysterious Tomasi's apartment. Now another growing anger consumed Macon's overwrought self. *Too freaking fucked-up,* getting him there supposedly to sniff hemp, but instead telling Macon the shit was on him, that he better cool it and come into their corner. And why? They were using him like a sounding board, making him their decoy for whatever sweet scheme they were fixing to dope somebody up on. Maybe he could never escape that bust called his past.

But perhaps he'd see now what cards this joker was planning to play.

"Where's your partner, Mr. Rolf?"

The dark-suited man remained impassive, declining an immediate answer, watching in his intent manner.

"This is my sidekick T.K. Keller, who doesn't bite strange men or anything."

"Wonderful. Please sit down ..."

"Why? Is this so goddamn important or something?"

The C.I.A. man shuddered visibly. "I trust you're aware of what is happening."

"I ain't aware of jack squat. But let me tell you what I am aware of," Macon announced, leaning over the man significantly, his voice lowering to a whisper: "Somebody hit on a very dear friend of ours, Rolfstein. I trust you're aware of that."

"Who might that friend be?"

"Your dear Canal Street contact. The woman you silly bastards have tried to extort for reasons you will now divulge in all fucking honesty ... I expect you to contribute to Jari's welfare. If she gets any worse, your ass will be tied on backwards."

"This is hardly the time for threats. We had nothing to do with whatever has happened to Jari. She was paid to help us regarding Tomasi, and our interest in you was for the same purpose."

"You're a fucking liar."

"Let's not beat around it. I think I know who might have reached her. Have you heard the radio?"

Macon shook his head.

"Tomasi has been kidnapped by Dutch terrorists. Two of our own men are presumed dead ... It happened last night. You've got to tell me what you know up to this point."

Macon put his foot up on a chair. He uttered the name of Jesus Christ and couldn't suppress the short burst of laughter following it. "Two of your *men?*" It struck him as exceedingly hilarious. He mashed his cigarette out into a procelain coaster. "This is too much! I never found out jack shit about this Tomasi over at the Maradisa, which you clowns can't crack. I suppose now you're interested in those Dutch acid-brains, is that it?"

"Yes. Precisely."

"Precisely my dick. You're a devious fellow, Rolfstein."

"Our ends are all the same. We just take different routes." He shrugged and grimaced with exaggeration, watching some other customers arrive. "Perhaps we should talk elsewhere --"

"You're in a goddamn pickle, Rolfstein. Know that?"

"I don't believe that's actually the case. But at any rate, what you tell me you'll be well paid for, and it might eventually tell us who hurt Jari."

"You think it was these terrorists?"

"I'm sure of it."

Macon leaned closer. "It damn sure better be," he said, shoving the C.I.A. man backwards into the wall, where he collapsed into sudden disarray.

Now this, T.K. Keller thought, getting out of the way as Macon lunged for the government man, pulling him up by the collar and slamming him cop-style flat into the paint-peeling wall again, causing new customers to turn around in the bar.

"I'll tell you what, fucker," snarled Macon, his own face almost pressed against that of the reddened government man's. Shaken and crushed with a repeated slamming motion, the once manicured Rolf now resembled something for the dumpster. "I'll tell *you* what, and that's the sad fucking fact, okay? The sad fucking fact, man, is that your shit better be together or you're in the Canal without a paddle. So let's get the ground rules straight before we talk turkey."

"Let him go, Raul," T.K. Keller said.

"Well, shit --"

Macon finally complied, releasing the tall man and letting him dangle there in the moment's lull.

"Look at you, Rolfstein."

"This ... won't get us there ... Macon. Not at all."

"Shit."

Hull-E. stood next to them, towel in hand, watching with concern as the visitor composed himself, trying not to shake, and wiped his sweating face with a handkerchief. "I know how you feel," he told Macon. "I'm sorry about her ... We'll try and make it up to her, just give me a chance. Let's go over everything and see where it stands. We can't really talk here. Time is important now. They've got Tomasi, and if this gets too big, others are in danger."

But he didn't finish, for Macon was wiping the dust from him in a belittling fashion with Hull-E.'s raunchy towel, hoisting his beer in a mock toast with the other hand.

"Fuck time," Raul Macon said.

18.

She had seen it all, stung by its magnitude -- thrilled, even enthralled by the abduction. It was something exquisite, in the entire sense of that word, that had given Christina an unbelievably multi-faceted experience. At last it had happened. There was no turning back -- they were smacked hard by its actuality, and the jolt was a rush of ice water in a vein used to high octane.

And then this: a boar-like strange man waiting for her and Kress as they tried to enter the studio. He held a small-bore gun (Landmann-Preetz?) at them which resembled a submachine digital special.

"Is he here?" the man demanded, in the accentless tones of an American.

"Who?"

It was all *de trop*, as Nils would say. The man didn't have the look of some Fed agent; no, with his roughneck features he more resembled a bowlegged seaman. Then there was his sidekick. Though the kid was pale and looking away (with a Sherlock Holmes cap pulled so low its bill rested on the top of his silver-rimmed glasses), she recognized him as the one who brought the young Mik boy into the Maradisa that night. He was the screwed-up clown who called himself "a poet."

"The boy you took. *Mik*. The kid you took who belongs to a friend of Tito's. You understand?"

In hard-eyed malice Kress beheld the intruder. "You're crazy. Who the hell are you?"

"Let's just open the door and go inside. Don't argue with this mother," Raul Macon said, raising the digital firearm.

When Macon ordered him to search the pair once they got inside, T.K. experienced a seizure of unknown definition. No, you didn't refuse Macon at such a moment; so rather callowly T.K. feigned his best police manner and started work. He probed beneath the bulky overcoat of the large blonde man, now scowling, who resembled a young Viking warrior about to bite -- if possible -- T.K.'s chicken head off.

"Jesus," the poet *manqué* said.

"Well?"

"There's a gun in here, definitely, Raul," T.K. muttered.

The elegant young woman standing nearby had difficulty suppressing her feeling that this was sublime ridiculousness.

"Well, bring it out, shithead," Macon rasped, and with the Landmann-Preetz' barrel poked Keller in the butt.

Obediently T.K. complied, marveling at the small portable arsenal he was uncovering from various parts of the muscular man's body. Holding a shiny pistol which he'd removed (along with a stiletto and something resembling a grenade), T.K. went to the woman and searched her with the same hesitancy. Again he found a digital gun which he tossed over to an obviously pissed Macon, who skillfully snapped it open, checking it out with gun-handler's familiarity.

"Okay, people," said Macon, as if addressing a couple of recruits in his private army, "I trust we're alone here."

The captives didn't reply, but simply stared with an expectant quietness.

"Well, we'd better be. Hear me? The whole fuckin' C.I.A. has this place on its monitor, and they're hot to close in. You hear me? You people are suddenly item Numero Uno. You have blown away their goons, and they're gonna fry you a cheap asshole. I mean you people are in definite *big trouble*. That kidnapping of Tomasi is beaucoup big news."

The couple continued staring in resolute fashion. Finally the woman asked, "Then what do you want?"

"*The boy*. You got fuckin' wax in those other holes of yours?"

The young woman's face was more tense than ever as alternatives clicked in her ultra-chic brain. "If you mean Mik ... He's not here. He's at a place outside the city, and he's all right."

Stimulated by a flicker of fear he sensed in this Christina Alpreece, Macon approached her. "Why'd you take him, honey?" He nudged the ends of her long straying hair with the Landmann-Preetz. "Getting back at Tito? ... Trying to get back at hose loose-mouthed whores finking to Uncle Sambo?"

T.K. looked up. Sometimes Macon surprised you with some uncanny surmisings. But if he weren't right on, there might really be no way to get this asshole business straight. It was Just Too Deep, as the current popular phrase went.

When the woman didn't answer, Macon cleared his throat and emitted a gob of spit on the luxurious white pile rug. He looked then at the Dutchman.

"What's your name?"

"Kress."

"You're one of those Nu-Provo faggots, ain't you? One of those pussies who beat up a Canal Street working girl named Jari, 'cause she tricked for Sam? You don't like Tito's people down there, it's known." Macon stepped closer, pressing the barrel against the man's chest. "Unfortunately that woman was a friend of mine. That's the sad fucking fact."

Kress remained rigidly silent as the gun barrel continued its plodding course across his throat, ribs, abdomen, and finally scrotum, where it came to rest like a stick of living metal.

"What'd you come back here for, Dutchman?"

"To get some things," Kress replied.

"Oh yeah? Well listen. We are gonna make a deal here, people. You dig? Just a good old-fashioned deal. Or would you rather I turn you in right now and get my picture in the paper?"

"What's the deal?" Christina said, her voice composed, forceful.

"Ah-ha."

Macon pulled the gun out of the man's scrotum, though keeping it trained on his captives. He glanced at T.K. and said, "We gotta talk business. Find some booze in this freaking joint, dude." Then he regarded the woman with a leering grin, asking, "Honey, where do you keep the bar?"

"We don't have much time," Kress said.

"That's right! By God, that's a definite fuckin' fact. You goofers have captured a very important freak, and believe me, the radio says it's beaucoup important. What the hell will be happening? The whole world wants to know --"

"There's a bar in the den over there," T.K. said, having returned, now self-consciously wielding a pistol in each hand, as if part of a Wild West show.

"Let's move then, Bartender," Macon said, waving everyone along. "See if there's a radio in there we can get the news on."

"I'll check."

T.K. gratefully felt an inane rush of relief to be so helpful -- maybe this was becoming just like a house party now ...

Macon was a man of action after all. The bozos were so cowed, T.K. knew undoubtedly they'd acquiesce to bizarre party games if necessary, or anything Macon might manufacture. Whoever held the guns held the cards.

"Can I get you anything else?"

"Don't be a wise ass," Macon warned, lighting a cigarette. He wanted T.K. to remember the seriousness now of what happened; the fact they had to rescue the boy at least, not to overlook his lordship Tomasi, and then figure out everything later. He just worked in strange ways, was all.

"Enjoy yourselves," Macon told his guests once inside the den, and couldn't help admiring the ritzy furnishings and wall decor. "This stuff would go over big at the Flea Market. Eh, T.K.?"

"I suggest that we get down to whatever business you have in mind," Christina announced with an imperious air.

"Damn straight, honey."

Macon knocked back a tumbler of whiskey and gathered himself. "Suppose I tell you your game's in the outhouse now? You people have got to play ball with me, or I will reek vengeance. You understand that? I am *The Man* now."

"And what must we do?"

T.K. couldn't resist marveling at Christina's classical beauty. She was a staturesque Greek masterpiece all right, and a Pre-Raphaelite lovely in the flesh for good measure. Evil and divine, an unfathomable allure existed within her, and T.K. had to know about it. She was something to believe in, like some heroic saint from his Catholic upbringing, where the mystery of women possessed dark yet spiritual beauty.

"You must know, of course, that no matter what happens to us, the Mission will go as planned."

"That right?" Raul Macon asked. He snorted quietly, sitting clumsily on a divan, his dirty boots on an alabaster coffee table, and scratched his nose while letting the drink warm inside him. "Damn. Well listen, sister, that's too fuckin' bad. The way I see it, you'll definitely complete that mission any which way. You're gonna be right there in on it, and T.K.'s gonna take notes. How's that grab you? Provo Man stays right here." With his tumbler Macon saluted the Dutchman. "You are now officially our hostage, Provo Man. Which means if the boy Mik doesn't get delivered here all right, your ass is cracked plaster. Just plain *grassed*. You dig?" Macon debated the remainder of his confidences in a brooding manner before continuing, waving a forefinger at Christina again. "*Don't fuck up.* El C.I.A. would rather have you right now, but I"m holdin' the jokers, okay? It's your cross, letting me know where Tomasi is and what you're doing with him -- okay? He's your ace in your hole."

Macon couldn't resist a lunkhead smirk, for truly wit reigned.

For her part, Christina Alpreece was curious about what in hell Macon thought he'd be pulling off, but refrained from asking it. Things were too troublesome at the moment. Instead she'd let him feel confident playing out his gambit.

"Okay, it's an agreement. You get back Mik, we get our mission completed, and we go our separate ways, keeping the Feds at bay. Just tell me what you want me to do, what to expect."

"I expect, Lady," Macon began, "that you instruct your goofers that Provo Man here had an accident, but you managed to slip free. Etc. Or maybe we'll accompany you and work something out." Mimicking an idea man plotting a Madison Avenue ad campaign, Macon waved his gun like a blue pencil and enjoyed his role to the hilt, so much so he picked up a cell phone and smashed it -- then held the remnants to his mouth, continuing to dictate his message. "But now tell me. What are you goofballs going to do with Tomasi?"

Christina took a deep sigh, observing her partner before looking away. "The plan is to hold him as an example to the world and the U.S. government, as an attempt to disrupt the NATO war machine, and halt the worldwide conflicts." She looked evenly across at Macon, her eyes a pair of incendiary crystals. "Tomasi has been involved in negotiating the movement of a new war matériel through Western Europe, and some sources say it is a new weapon eventually to be used in the worldwide conflicts, especially in Asia. Something like the obsolete Agent Orange was, only more insidious, and to this extent: When detonated, it produces a fall-out vapor capable of reducing a human being's reasoning powers to mush. It makes a scab out of the brain, but the human relic remains neurophysiologically functional and alive, on the lowest level -- do you understand?"

"I hear you."

"So our group is intent on stopping the shipment of a weapon which Tomasi is spear-heading, fronting for, though of course we hope to find the matériel and use it to our advantage. Right now, we believe it to be in western Germany. Our sister band there, the Feuer, will also be involved in the eventual commandeering of this matériel ... That's as much as I can tell you. But as I've said --" At this point she asked Macon his name, which he facetiously gave as Ray King. "As I've said, Mr. King, this Mission can't be stopped at this point. I've told you this because I believe you're no friend of the C.I.A."

"I'm no friend of yours either, Honey," Macon said. He pointed significantly at her again. "If this new weapon is as hot as you say it is, maybe we can mutually make some guilders from it. Maybe other countries would like a little of it."

"Perhaps. But the Medulla Raze, as it's called, is to be used to *stop war*, don't you understand? We don't want this stuff to disrupt the earth's balance and affect our interspace colonies, especially those of another space species we're hoping to become allies with. We don't want it to proliferate where it can be dropped more frequently because it seems more safer than atomic weaponry, or be placed on a space missile's warhead. The world's full of enough decaying brains right now ... and if this weapon was let loose in Europe or the earth's atmosphere ..."

"You are one funny lady all right," Raul Macon scoffed, though chuckling admiringly. "Space species? And thinking about saving world brains! From what? *War?* That's a laugh. The best minds in the world make war. Some of our best geniuses got their gray matter knocked out in Nam II, but that don't matter, it jumpstarted the U.S. economy while others are poor ... You'd probably be happier to see that Medulla haze in the backyard instead of nuclear fall-out."

Christina stared intensely at him now for several seconds. "If you're willing to help us stave off the government executioners, Mr. King, I''m sure the members of our organization will accept you as an ally. And whatever profit you'd obtain from that union would probably be yours to dispose of."

"We *are* gonna work together, Honey. Or my name ain't Ray King Macon."

A calculated lust glimmered in Macon's eye as he surveyed the regal woman across from him. She was no digital factitiousness, no, but the real primeval Earth goddess. In time he knew his lust would be vengefully inflicted on her and others like her -- and on the black hole the material world had become for him.

19.

On the way back to The Amstoy, T.K. Keller felt bereft of his former self. The recent events apparently numbed his sensibility to the point where he had momentarily forgotten fear. But -- like everything else unpleasant -- it quickly returned to memory.

Riding along in the van of their Dutch "allies," Macon still pointed his murderous weapon behind driver Kress' ear, and kept swigging from a bottle of expensive bourbon taken along from the studio.

T.K. tried to make some logical deductions from all this, but was unable to, given his mentally exacerbated condition. Somehow he had to contact Lelica and tell her everything was all right; they knew where Mik was and were going after him. This fact gave T.K. enough strength at the moment to persevere.

"Are we still your prisoners, or what?" the woman Christina asked Macon.

"I'll tell you when we get to the hotel."

It was total daylight, just a few minutes after 3 p.m. on another cloud-ridden afternoon, and here was Macon acting like a freaked-out guerrilla fighter, T.K. decided. A gun in one hand, a bottle of booze in the other. And once at the hotel, things would no doubt take on a more ridiculously dangerous turn. Calling beforehand, they had alerted Hull-E. "to get some boys together," the kind of sadistic spoilsports who hung around Tito like syncophantic organisms. If Tito delegated them to the cause of The Counter-Revolution -- as T.K. now termed their great endeavor -- would they really stand up and be counted?

"Well, they'll be nursing this Nu-Provo homo over at Tito's for awhile," was how Macon put it after they'd arrived, "and lock him the fuck up in the attic."

They were all in the kitchen, Hull-E. and the irrepressibly busy Lissie (who fussed about the stove, moving pots, upset because something frightening was happening), Macon and T.K., with the beautiful Christina sitting out in the diner/bar area where one of Tito's men regarded her stolidly. With efficiently brawny malevolence, a short while later two of his clone brothers carted off Kress the Provo Man.

"Who was that young man?" Lissie wanted to know.

"A goddamn idealistic murderer," Raul Macon said, and waved away her ladle raised in shocked chagrin.

Macon finished his bottle and pitched it neatly into a corner wastebasket, burping sloppily as he did so. Hull-E. was trying to convince his dowdy wife it was all just "Tito's business," and there was no sense getting peeved about doing what the Boss obviously wanted done. "But not *here*, Hull-E. -- *not here!*" she maintained. Upon seeing the weapon Macon revealed from under his coat, Lissie nearly dissolved into a stewing meringue.

"Keep your woolly bra on, " Macon advised her.

"What the hell is going on? Who is that *woman* out there? You can't convince me Tito's behind all this!"

Hull-E. managed to put a bear hug on the diminutive woman, who continued to make remonstrating sounds of unique, gas-passing variety. Finally she was subdued somewhat, and Hull-E. approached the American pair, blotting acrid-smelling sweat from his forehead with a rumpled kerchief. (A task he habitually did following any physical exertion.)

"Raulie," he whispered to Macon, "is everything okay?"

Macon was methodically reloading his Firebird in a dour but determined fashion. "Everything's sweet-city, Hully. We're gonna cop some big guilders."

The hugely round bartender eyed T.K. with less than convinced assurance. "Well, we don't want you boys getting hurt. I don't care what the hell Tito expects. It's not worth the money, none of it is –"

"You're right there, Hull-E. None of it's worth a goddamn thing."

Leaning closer, his breath miasmic, the doughty Hull-E. attempted to extract still more specific confidences. But Raul Macon proved unwilling in that regard, claiming only that he was taking T.K. and "that beautiful bitch" on an excursion.

"You be careful then, Raulie."

Having finished his second cup of ultra-black and reviving coffee, T.K. announced blithely to his gorilla/guerrilla friend that Lelica should be informed of the situation. He ambled back to the bar area where only a few customers at small tables sat drinking, unaware of anything extraordinary.

"Mik's all right," T.K. told Lelica over a cracklingly poor phone connection. Unfortunately, he explained in slurred whispers, it might be awhile before Mik was returned, due to uncontrollable circumstances. T.K.'s eyes were trained on the elegantly stoic figure of Christina sitting patiently across the room. She emanated a tragic class T.K. found mystifying.

Upstairs the convalescing courtesan Jari supposedly reposed in a narrow bed, and T.K. was uncomfortably reminded of her while staring at this American beauty. The inevitable trek up there in Macon's wake provided T.K. a repulsive fascination, seeing the battered woman and her plight.

Like a recluse, Jari reclined on that bed in a surly remove from the reality about her, withdrawn to a point where Raul Macon was edgy regarding her for the umpteenth time. The same bruised and closed-off face. Smoking was her only compulsive activity, done with dour indifference. Macon touched her long hair through this difficult moment, telling her he was going to make some hard amends. He had just been dealt the right cards. In her bathrobe beneath the covers, Jari's only responses were bestial mewlings frightening T.K. Like coming into contact with an old acquaintance newly handicapped. She was some kind of still-born body he couldn't stomach looking at, and queasiness overcame him. (T.K. had seen her hanging around the hotel a few times before, because she was Raul Macon's significant other "partner," and remembered fantasizing over her body enough times to debunk any notion of sexual repressiveness. Jari had of course ignored his overtures, like many a snobby digitally-enhanced female before her.)

T.K. also thought of Lelica, who was going out of her mind with worry at the moment. She was sisterly to him in a quasi-maternal fashion, and he clung to the thread of their relationship almost desperately now when nothing could temper the starkness of cold reality.

And what would Macon's old girlfriend Karin think upon espying this maudlin scene?

In her fear or shock, the prostitute Jari wouldn't even reveal who had assaulted her. A dreadful amnesia imprisoned her without change. It was too appalling for T.K. to dwell on any further.

In this close proximity Macon stood surveying her, willing Jari into a deeper comprehension of him, imploring her to speak. There was a terrific intensity in the room. T.K. was riveted to this immemorial and timeless moment, grafted to its force until he wanted to scream, and unable to leave though ordered to by Macon. He was the voyeur impaled within the vise of the dark torsion Macon's obsession had become. As one deaf and dumb – though trying keenly to speak out against what he saw in all its sordid distaste – T.K. became both prisoner and witness to the event, sitting there at a small and chipped wooden table in the corner, wondering if he might pass out.

"Don't touch her, Macon," T.K. whispered. "Not here."

Because there wasn't time to dawdle in the face of their upcoming mission, Macon leaned over the prostrate woman and cupped her shoulders with both hands. He stood there regarding her, trying with his eyes to bore into some receptive faculty of her brain. "You are gonna make it, baby," he whispered into the vacuous distance between them. "Tell me who they were, Jari. Just tell me –"

Jari's unfocused gray eyes continued to stare out beyond him. All the while Macon kept fighting the notion (broached by T.K.) that she had betrayed for money. No, Raul couldn't handle that. She was extorted – used – and he knew she had no choice, and this happened because she tried to protect *him*.

"Damn it," Macon said, sobbing drunkenly, and lowered his patchily red-bearded face into the crook of Jari's neck, spreading out the woman's long and tangled hair rivulets across the pillow. T.K. feared that he might vomit. Macon exclaimed with difficulty that he was *going after them*. "And I'm gonna break out their brains, honey, and rip what's left of their balls off with a bayonet." His voice became incantatory, his muffled sobbing escaping into a rhythmic hiss. "Swear to God, Jari ... Swear to God."

A chill enveloped T.K., and in the ensuing silence, nearly intolerable, he heard a hoarse whisper come from the woman's lips:

"PRO-VO ... Pro-vo ... provo –"

Her eyes were still vacuumed marbles, and a glistening sweat broke out on her forehead. Macon slowly took his head from her shoulder. Chagrin and disbelief overwhelmed him. "Those rebel faggots? You hear that, T.K.?" A glaucous liquid inflamed his own eyes. "Provo. Nu-Provo ..." He wanted to curse, laugh, do anything but repeat the name.

T.K. was an unharnessed bundle of emotion. He couldn't believe how much the woman on the bed resembled Lelica, whom he wanted more than ever to be with then. In her maternal effigy he yearned to submerge his pain, assuage his torment, and perhaps succumb gently to a sweet madness more attractive than the diabolical one he now experienced at the barbarian's hands. He believed himself at the mercy of something inescapable, where self-immolation beckoned. *Yes'm,* he told himself. *Pull out or become a basket case.* Slowly he lifted his head from the buttress his arms created on the table.

Now Jari looked away, visibly exhausted and swallowing with difficulty until Macon offered some water and ordered T.K. to fetch Lissie. "That bitch should never let Jari out of her sight! *Hurry,* kid, we've gotta book up in a few minutes --"

O Buddha, help my ass, T.K. maundered, nearly breaking an ankle trying to navigate the vertical shaft of stairway he fell down. Like a musty contrivance of hazard from some animated movie, the stairway became an oubliette nearly skewering him. It was awful, ungainly, and ridiculous all at once, and surrealistically the stairs organically mutated-and-multiplied as T.K. plunged downward, finally coming to a ker-*plopping* rest on the fourth floor landing.

"Shit. I've broken something --"

Why did they put everybody in the top-story rooms? Luckily no one witnessed his pratfall, or he might have wept on the spot. Sitting on the creaking wood T.K. examined himself and determined, somewhat disappointedly, that he was reasonably intact. Add this to all the shocks yet to come...

After informing Lissie downstairs about Jari's revised condition, T.K. was stunned to find Lelica herself sitting at one of the tables and waiting for him. Expectantly her face was a wrathful visage. T.K. felt both relieved and horrified. Trance-like he wanted to reveal great secrets to her, make her regard him in a new light.

"Damn it, Lelica -- we're just about to pull out of here, I told you not to come!"

"I can't help it, T.K. I feel like going wherever it takes to find Mik."

With a grimace T.K. sat down in exasperation, and began tenderly kneading his right ankle, searching no doubt for broken areas.

"I fell down the freaking steps. Can you believe that?"

"Who is she?"

"Who?"

"The woman in there, with Hull-E."

"I told you, Lel, that I really couldn't go into detail. And now you're here." Keller began kneading the bridge of his nose for a change of pace. "Macon will kill us all. This is supposed to be Ultra-Secret. We might as well call the press in to make it official."

"My Mik. He's in no danger now, is he?"

"Of course not."

"Then why the guns? Why are you wearing a holster underneath your jacket?"

"It isn't loaded," T.K. swore, as if that proved anything. "Look, that woman can help us find Mik. She knows where he's at."

"I'm scared, T.K."

"Don't be. Just get out of here before Raul gets down and has a psychotic seizure. I don't believe his body can stand many more -- and neither can I."

"That woman. She's the one from the Maradisa you mentioned, isn't she? The friend of that T.V. tramp Marva Claire."

Keller nodded, lighting a cigarette with ungainly fingers, conscious of a bustling excitement becoming greater around him. This was supposed to be a commando-like party, but something told him it had the makings of a panty raid ... The enigmatic Christina in the kitchen was the key to everything, apparently. She could deliver the Nu-Provo den and the politically scalding Tomasi to the world. But at what price?

T.K. began to wonder who was using whom, or something. That neo-Marxist knockout babe was like a projected idea of his own anima he feared finding. That's why he yearned for the prosaic Lelica to aid and cover him with emotional blandisments only a sister could. So he'd become polarized in the right direction, and any horrific revelations would be cancelled, like another bad situation comedy.

"Are you all right, T.K.?"

"Hell, I don't know."

She sat watching, hunched over in a large coat of some imitation animal fur. Lelica, so demurely solicitous, so suddenly winsome that a pang shot through T.K. He wanted to really beseech this woman to give him a clue about life, and stave off the fearful reality of death.

Where are you going? was what she demanded of him.

Macon's eventual reappearance at the lobby bar wasn't exactly one of benign propriety. He was aflame with purpose, bolstered by Jari's resurgent spirit. Resembling an Indian war god, he was the keen embodiment of all political vengeance. The world had better bend over backwards, because Raul Macon was out to scorch somebody's territory.

Gravitating to the kitchen, beer in hand, he found a seated Christina being watched over by a portion of his entourage.

"Keep the street customers out, Hull-E."

"That's been seen to for the last hour."

"Bueno." Macon swallowed deeply from his green bottle, enjoying this moment of uncontested power. It almost made everything worthwhile. He eyed Christina, now sitting by the stove, a mellow distaste overtaking his features. "Lady, we're about ready to move. Suppose you tell us just where it is we're going?"

"Germany," Christina said with a disturbing evenness.

"Well, wouldn't you know," Macon said, indicating coyly it was quite a coincidence returning to an old stamping ground. *"Bitte schoen."*

Christina continued smiling her well-composed, Mona Lisa smile, basking in those interstellar radiations no one saw.

"Germany?" said Hull-E., wiping his neck with a towel. It was hardly warm in the kitchen.

"Damn straight, pard. Deutschland it is!"

The bartender shrugged. "Too much Army."

"Like the greatest of times."

Eventually black coffee with honey was being poured down Raul Macon's gullet. Java did not stem the tremens seizing him at times with visible nastiness. "We are getting there -- almost fuckin' *together*," Macon claimed, eyes beet-red cue balls. No one believed him.

"Give me another smoke, Hull-E., before I shoot everybody in the room."

"You talk too bad now, Raulie --"

"What time is it?"

"Almost five."

With a deep groan Macon massaged his forehead, and fought the bitch drunkenness although he probably functioned better in that state. He noticed T.K. with a strange silver-blonde woman talking heatedly among the empty tables. They resembled flattened mushrooms of burnt umber beneath the fuzzy light fixtures so aged, so old-fashioned, they might yet be gas fueled in a halogen-age. What the hell was that kid-bugger up to?

"We have to move, we have to move," a voice chanted with the insistence of a caucus vote inside Macon. Closing his eyes he could feel himself at some great outdoor political rally with banners streaming. That high-class bitch from La-la-land grilled him optically in her cold, imperial manner, like she was in charge and everything had been predestined to occur all along. She gave Macon beaucoup creeps up the buns, but he wondered how good her body was under the Bogart overcoat.

"She's a witch," he told himself, "a frigging space witch."

A bile of that old sickness began to abrade something inside Macon now, and the pain of it had him bossily back on his feet. What the hell was going on indeed? They were in on the biggest political kidnapping plot in a month of Sundays, and couldn't get the show on the road. He'd have to knock some sense into the slowboats.

Still there was that bitch from outside standing in the doorway with T.K., who apprehensively tried to pull her back. She looked tensely around at this heretofore secluded scene, taking in the militant ambience, finally focusing on the beautiful and strange other woman sitting with great presence in the far corner, a white rose gathering thorns.

"Where is my son? What did you do to him! Why did you take him --?"

"Who is this?" Macon wanted to know, trying to remember her. Grimacing anew because everything seemed to be going wrong, he felt like pitching his submachine gun through the wall.

T.K. was more than distraught himself. "*Lelica*. This is Lelica, Mik's guardian. The little kid, remember?"

In the corner Christina Alpreece sat in her same unblinking manner, staring back but not replying. Lelica came closer, still asking the same questions in her seething fashion, and Macon blocked her path with his beefcake body.

"Now I think you better get out of here, lady. I don't even know why T.K. let you in the first place. We've all got private business -- serious business -- to take care of, and you're interfering with that at this moment."

"Mik! What about Mik? I'm afraid she did something to him."

"Well, we're going after him."

Lunging forward, Lelica managed to upset the table and lash out at the seated woman -- crying in uncontrolled fury as she did so. With her long fingernails she tried to scratch the immaculately unmoving face of the American female (or she-male?). Glasses were overturned, drinks spilled, along with a clatter of broken ceramic dishes and butt-filled ashtrays.

"God damn it," Macon said, grabbing the irate woman from behind and swinging her around with frightening viciousness. Hull-E. began grappling with them too, trying to keep Lissie's kitchen from being torn up.

"Get this bitch outta here!" Macon demanded hoarsely. With one hand locked securely around her upper arm, he was still waving the Landmann-Preetz like a talisman. Macon's threatening admonition to shoot T.K. for this ruckus caused the young man to duck behind furniture.

A harried Christina, having been knocked to the floor, now looked up unsteadily. Eventually Hull-E., with the help of Tito's men, was able to get Lelica outside, where she was unceremoniously ushered onto the street.

"We're off to a roaring good start," Macon explained, rapping T.K.'s leg like a log. The sight of the quivering T.K. caused Macon's wrath to subside into laughter.

"You goddamn moron, T.K. I think they took the wrong kid ..."

But staring about the devastated hotel bar interior, Christina Alpreece knew otherwise. Violence was a good and bad omen. And little Mik (the one her stellar psychic powers advised her to kidnap) was the necessary innocent being, possessed of some indefinable beneficial charm, that her distant gods demanded be sacrificed for the cause.

The facts were indeed good omens, she mused again, and finished her drink.

20.

Now in deep foreboding T.K. regarded the jaunt to Germany. This time he had to endure the sight of Macon behind the wheel of Christina Alpreece's large white van, supposedly heading for a terrorist bastion somewhere within Teutonic boondocks.

Keller could have screamed. It was getting colder, snowier, with large banks of impacted ice adhering to the hills and scenery along the autobahn. Some low-lying white animals joined T.K.'s imaginary mental menagerie while Raul Macon drove in customary abandon.

Germany? T.K.'s time-tripping secret was in danger of being exposed. Back at The Amstoy, the moment he heard the country of their destination announced, T.K. couldn't believe how fated everything seemed. In cold clinical fact, it was the stuff of misery.

How could this secret be kept undercover, wondered T.K.? It gnawed at his reason's foundation, a wound he guarded for its extraordinary sensitivity. If it was ever exposed in public, Keller feared becoming uncontrollably divested of willpower -- and totally freaked-out.

T.K. had tried to skip out before their departure from Holland, but Macon had collared him, declaiming that none of them (due to the winds of politics and war) could escape any longer. It was inevitable. The risk had to be taken, before they were cornered in some canal alleyway and fed to roaming vermin, so loathsome were the poseurs infesting the polderland.

Now it was full-tilt road boogie and T.K., bouncing around in the van's rear, listened to Rock and Roll cassette strains. He teetered on the verge of vomiting up his mortal innards.

What followed more than justified his suspicions of the inevitable.

* * *

In her light tan overcoat Christina sat like an immobile icon through the long ride into New West Germany. Earlier she'd given Macon precise directions, and amazingly the chainsmoking driver followed them almost unerringly in hypertensive fashion: Mainz, Saarbrücken, Mannheim, Kaiserslautern ...

The winter-drenched hamlets were an unending roll call, poking holes in and out of T.K.'s shoddy memory, making the past real again. Farm land, hills, and forested terrain of the Saar region were all cloaked by the endless pall of winter cold and wind known as "The Hawk" by American G.I.s.

With a paranoid start T.K. recognized some of the terrain again. The fugitive's fear assaulted him, along with the knowledge of what could befall him.

But before he could express these misgivings effectively to the cigar-chomping Macon up front, a sound like rapid back-firing overcame the van.

"What in hell," Macon said, swerving the van suddenly so it fishtailed drastically on the ice-heavy road. "Get down, get down!"

They were somewhere on one of those winding rural roads leading through the hilly farm territory, due south for Saarbrücken. (Unpaved stretch; meeting little traffic; dense air leaking powdery drifts of snow ...) And now this, the unpleasant surprise.

"Who is it?"

The radio imitated styrofoam-cracking sounds, and Keller -- lying face-flat on the floor, center-aisle, in the van's back -- was getting his nose thumped by the careening vehicle. He smelled fresh vinyl and lubricants, and all those electronic panels in the van's interior (not to overlook the sophisticated recording devices) reeked of a pungent oil not even Macon's foul smell could neutralize. The nightmare was coming back.

"You all right?"

Her voice. Screaming.

"Never mind! I thought you said they knew --"

Earlier Christina had made the transmission in a code-like manner (in intermittent French too), informing her hidden colleagues of the situation: The fact that Kress had been "detained," that two new "accomplices" were accompanying her to aid the Mission, that she was in no way being "coerced," and instructions would follow. An enigmatic reply from Black Headquarters rogered the transmission. The van had then left the autobahn around five that evening, delving even further into the inhospitable forest regions where Christina's co-horts (along with German gang members) held the freshly abducted Vincent Gaylen Tomasi at bay, and doubtlessly planned their next move.

Yet here was this sudden road detour --

T.K. finally summoned enough fortitude to look up and estimate the damage. What he saw frightened him into looking away again. The windshield near the driver's side was significantly splintered. Macon had been struck across the back by exploding glass now deposited in crystal-bead abundance on the carpeted upholstery. Visible too were a few droplets of the rakehell driver's blood, which had been sprayed into T.K.'s downy-cheeked face.

Christina was balled-up like a beatific snail, trying to wedge her way further beneath the dashboard. All the while she commanded shrilly into the radio mike, trying to summon her allies.

"Cocksuckers," Macon muttered, accelerating as fast as possible given the conditions. Gears grinded as he employed all his racing savvy while scarlet lines formed arabesque patterns behind his neck. The bleeding infiltrated a map of weather wrinkles. "Got to zap this, my man."

T.K. puked (why not, adding to the mayhem?), making the floor-flotsam a sight indeed. For a second he believed he'd been shot too, and this caused his stomach to unload again.

It was the wrong road to be driving in such darkness, they discovered. Macon had long ago pulled off the main road, cutting a hardly navigable swath through icy underbrush, until miraculously encountering some little roads along which a few unlit houses were forlornly visible.

"This is the Old-fucking-World," Raul Macon said, pulling the van into a clump of trees where fallen pine cones lay in deep slow-slush. "I'm lost as hell. Can you reach them?"

"No," Christina said, near tears and shocked more visibly than she'd ever been.

"Shit --"

"Give me that towel," Christina demanded of the hunched-over T.K. A strange whimpering sound escaped from her throat with the same indiscretion of a fart. "Hurry, goddamnit."

"I'm all right." Macon was laughing. "It's like buckshot! I'm all right."

Yet Christina attended to him with devout ministrations, and with a thermos-dampened towel blotted away the blood. T.K. Keller groggily cleaned up the floor also.

"I can't believe this. Some homecoming."

"It can't be Der Feuer or the Puma. It just can't be."

"Lady, somebody did it."

Macon peered uneasily into the woodland darkness as he was attended to, breathing with difficulty, and sweated profusely despite the cold. In his hands now was one of his prized possessions, an obsolete American M-16 rifle.

He wanted to use it.

"The bleeding isn't so bad now. Does it hurt very much?" Christina asked.

"Stings like a bastard."

"I'll wash it with alcohol later."

"Might not have time for it."

But oh for a bath in good Scotch. Abruptly he began shining a baton-flashlight into the thick overhang of trees and nearby bushes, scanning for company.

"They'll see us," T.K. said.

"Shut up."

"We're sitting ducks."

"They could have hit us with more then that."

The radio now crackled up as a male voice speaking German entered their frequency. With nervous intensity Christina listened, then replied in an odd mixture of French and German.

"Ja, the Puma," she whispered to Macon.

"Your people?"

She nodded. Over the next minute or two she confirmed "the accident" -- for which no excuse or reason was forthcoming -- and assured the radio contact that her "American allies" weren't holding her at gunpoint. Christina tried to relay in detail what happened.

She looked up at Macon after a spotty transmission dissolved into unpleasant static. "They want us unarmed when we come into the vector-area --"

"No goddamn way."

"They believe you have abducted me."

"Bodies sure are cheap around here."

Macon began to cough violently, still holding the towel behind his neck. He lit another cigarette from Christina's burning one, and mulled over the cards they were holding.

"Guess they feel you're pretty expendable, Miss U.S.A."

"I wouldn't know about that. A job, as they say, has to be done. These people mean business."

"No shit."

Macon exhaled smoke with irritation.

"Three years in the Army and the only time I bled was after shaving. At last I've arrived at the war." He shook his head, laughing in a sardonic wheeze, his voice hoarse with pain. "Nice time to have arrived. You tell them I call my gun Lover Boy."

"They're not going to chance letting us into the detention point. They want to direct us to an uncompromising place, then check us out."

"Smart comrades."

"What should I say?"

"Just what I said. Don't sweat it."

"They're afraid you're C.I.A."

Macon laughed, savoring the irony. "Just tell them we're a couple of mercenary Americans defecting from two-faced Tito."

Christina knew she would have to sell her comrades, and that it would take some doing. They wouldn't buy the ambiguous "disappearance" of Kress, and Nils Mupreen would probably flay her dead or alive. (Believing she had little choice in the matter anyway, Christina hadn't planned on becoming a sacrificial goddess, praxis be damned.) If she told Nils this pair had once been stationed at the munitions site where the Medulla Raze was rumored to be, these disagreeable buffoons would yet be worthy of use.

And after that?

Praxis was praxis, she told herself, and the revolutionary war ethic was an unsentimental one.

A sudden galvanic spark enflamed Christina until she felt resurgent power like a greater will overcoming her. Muttering the word *Li-Us*, and becoming for one instant an all-encompassing electrode for forces unseen, she knew what to do.

21.

Night is eerie and cold in snow-shrouded Germany, and the woodland is potent with mythic beasts as well as real ones -- or even those from interstellar dimensions. What fugitive humans would inevitably confront, idling along in their now scratched and dented van, was something perhaps their repressed fears might conjure up. Some hubris from Germany's troubled past was evident, born from that degenerate conflict known as world war.

Up ahead in the road, such foreboding facts also were evident in those men who waited for the van. Stern-faced, ice-hard features made a garish frieze in the glare of headlights. Hunters of the Saarland, thought T.K., forming a makeshift roadblock. In turtlenecks, parkas, and every mountain climbing boot a roughneck dreamed of, men held automatic rifles aloft and presented stark angles as compelling as any nightwatch of figures a Dutch master might render. Behind them were other vehicles and standing forms alert with tension, and noisy engines sent steaming vapors into the dank-seeping air of darkness.

"This your reception party, Christina?" Macon asked her, his finger trigger-poised on the M-16 lying diagonally across his lap. (It was the first time Macon had used her name, or at least T.K. believed so. Perhaps there was a time and place for everything.) Globules of sweat fringed across Macon's still blood-scabbed skin.

Christina strained up front to get a better look through the fog-encrusted, partially shattered window. She still held the radio microphone in her tentacle-like fingers.

"It's them," she said simply.

"Your people?"

"Of course."

As they spoke T.K. noted their breath congealing quickly within the van, thanks to windshield damage and an ill-functioning heater. It was all suddenly a bitch. T.K. didn't know if it were the cold or the fright prompting his shakes.

"Please keep your rifle lowered, Macon. Don't raise it before them."

Macon vented his displeasure by spitting through one of the jagged openings in the windshield. "Hell. It stays where it is then." He killed the engine, leaving the headlights on.

"I'll go talk to them."

"We're gonna be partners -- better straighten them out."

T.K. could see the group moving forward in ominous fashion, stave-like weapons upraised. He felt they had reached their nadir, that they were all going to be blown away.

Unexpectedly, as Christina opened her door, Raul Macon also got out of the van, holding the M-16's butt against his hip so that the barrel pointed skyward.

"I told you!" she began, but Macon's jackboots were already cutting into the snow-slush. The approaching men stopped at this sight, their weapons still trained in the van's direction. Eye-stinging flashlight beams suddenly shone into the faces of Christina and Macon.

In the confluence of high-beams, T.K. thought he recognized Nils Mupreen, while the others remained surly strangers. T.K. heard someone announce Christina's name, and she in turn greeted the men formally, referring to them as "comrades."

"We're sorry. We damn near could have killed you," Brice Rampoul said, addressing Christina but staring measuredly at Macon's hulking form.

"Is anyone hurt?" asked the slenderest man, who was indeed (under a pile cap and muffler) the bespectacled Nils Mupreen, looking exceedingly out-of-place with a rifle in hand.

"My companion here has been superficially cut in several places. Please get some alcohol so we can attend to him."

Rampoul eyed this companion rather unsympathetically. "Is there a problem?"

"I took shrapnel in an Army accident," replied Macon, "but this has slightly pissed me off. You fire that buck shot?"

"Somebody did."

"I'd be more pissed dead."

"I'll say. But greetings are strange in these parts."

Their voices quavered through the damp air, and the woman stood there trembling. Mupreen put an arm around her for warmth, suggesting they get some hot milk into her, and asking repeatedly if she was fine.

"I'm certainly all right, Nils." She looked up with a somber expectancy. "Have you got *him*."

Mupreen nodded.

"Brief me immediately," she said, allowing a visible sigh to escape her. "This is Mr. Raul Macon King, who should be of service to you. There's another young man called T.K. in the van."

Mupreen and Rampoul kept their taciturn air around the armed stranger. The other member of their trio was a tall, well-muscled young man whose seediness overcame his handsome face. Dragging emphatically from an unfiltered cigarette, he brazenly studied Christina, all the while holding his gun like it was harmless balso wood. "You have certainly both shown admirable restraint. I am Gunther Hoffler, your liaison for the Feuer

Bande."

"Of course, of course!" Christina said, startled. "It is my great pleasure. I'm Christina Alpreece. I'm sure Brice has been telling you ..."

But the inclement weather and the presence of the ponderous "Mr. King" (hardly approved of by these bona fide terrorists) grounded conversation briefly. Hurried instructions were given by Mupreen to his aides for searching the van, and Christina was hastily escorted towards a well-heated green sedan.

"We will have to talk to this Mr. King," Rampoul said, coughing on some phlegm he was unable to expectorate. "But what's this about Kress? Why isn't he with you?"

Christina sighed, pushing strands of long hair from her eyes. "It's all been so confusing. I tried to tell you. Kress is ... still in Amsterdam. Once you take him fully into the operation, I'm sure we can get Macon King to release him."

Furious, Brice Rampoul demanded to know how this could have happened.

"We were waylaid, at the Quarter. That's how it could have happened! You can see the man is handy with guns."

"We should have killed him."

"Killed *him*? You nearly killed *me* --"

"Again, so sorry, Christina. There is mass confusion to say the least. We thought you had been abducted, and now we find that you are."

"They want the boy, Brice ... The one I brought in, before Tomasi was taken. He'll probably barter the boy for Kress."

"Barter? Who the hell is that clown, anyway? I doubt if all he wants is to barter, Christina. He probably wants more than that, and at a time like this! Things are quite sensitive, to say the least."

"That's exactly why you should be careful. Why endanger Kress at this point when the operation can continue on course smoothly? Why not use Macon King -- get what we can out of him -- and see how things go?"

"We can't trust anybody. And besides, what does he know?"

"Where the C.I.A. is ... and what it's up to, apparently. No, he's not an agent, believe me. He wants to derail the agency as badly as we do, for reasons I'll go into. But he's been a G.I. and knows about the Depot."

"Did he tell you that?"

"Yes. I asked him as much as he'd tell me, and I'm sure that's enough to prove his value right there. And his friend was *stationed* at the Depot more than a year ago."

"That's interesting, Christina."

"Of course it is. We must be opportunistic and make something positive out of what hardly seems so."

"Maybe. But at this point, our choices are limited. We have to proceed with re-orientation without delay. We have to seize the moment, because Tomasi is front page news, and our organization is about to make headlines."

Christina reflected. "Don't do anything rash with Macon King, then."

"But if he's an informant," Brice Rampoul said, "we must know when to neutralize him."

"He's not, he's not," the young and -- in the eyes reflecting herself-- hauntingly beautiful woman said. She knew what precious time they had would bear this out. Something in her features had mutated (if all but unnoticeably) into a feral amalgam at once human and extra-bestial, yet supernaturally so. Hearing all the forest creatures in an amplified instant was so excruciating it surpassed any feeling of pain or pleasure, and Christina smiled from being so loved. Soon she would see and know who bestowed this bliss on all of them.

There were stars radiating a light of power overhead no dark forest could obliterate.

PART III

"The 4th Quadrant"

22.

So this was Gunther Hoffler?

A person to be reckoned with, Christina decided, and perhaps the key to whatever success or failure they'd encounter. She found him handsome, charismatic, mysterious. Why hadn't Brice briefed her on his lupine swankness, which exuded a luxuriant evil. He would be perfect, just perfect, if only she could determine the right moment and place for using him.

Christina's speculation about Hoffler, intriguing as it was, would be overshadowed by immediate concerns. Taking stock of their forest emplacement would occupy the next few days, when they'd be burrowing into arboreal thicknesses like an animal gang the press would later nickname *Der Puma*.

They would virtually be living underground, Christina Alpreece saw that first night. After trailing her guides for several minutes through foot-snarling underbrush, the forced silence -- a wary precaution -- became excruciating. Moving with an Indian stealth she could but imitate, their wavering squad was stopped by a wall of

forest. Dwarfed by a hill slab, they were inside a cul-de-sac.

Christina sat down, grateful at least for this moment's rest. Her breathing became loud and labored in the surrounding cold. A stomach pain surprised her. Light, gauze-muffled like a white moth's wing flickering, turned into a flashlight beam. As it explored the unregenerate shadowland about them, Christina saw something always instinctually known. A colorless vacuum gained definition as bushes and branches were cleared away, unmasking the trompe l'oeil which had been there forever. The low voices and cautioning whispers continued more earnestly as she was ushered roughly inside. The gray outlines were dissipated by lantern beams illuminating an expanse of pitted, damp-smelling, and natural cave that at first frightened her.

"How extraordinary," Christina said, faintly sarcastic. Her now blistered feet throbbing within ill-fitting shoes, Christina nearly turned an ankle. There was acclimating to accomplish, she knew, if she didn't expire first. A good trooper, she shrugged off Brice Rampoul's inquiries about her welfare. She meant to study what so vied for her attention inside the strange and feral-seeming cave.

"This is just like a foyer, or corridor, my dear," Rampoul explained convivially, shedding some field gear and hoping to inspire her. "It leads to and is connected with several other passages. We're virtually within a mountain of caves."

"Extraordinary."

This time perhaps she meant it. In this hive were several other individuals unknown to Christina. Obviously they were from the brigade, and made preparations for arrival. All members from the Yellow and Green teams were infested within this underground network, furnished with camping equipment (military cots, canvas chairs, makeshift desks) and liberal food or ordnance supplies. Piled everywhere were canisters of some type, flanked by an undisguised cache of arms and munitions: everything from gas grenade launchers to obsolete and imported AK-47 rifles, which had antique connoisseurs openly gawking or grumbling. The irrepressible figure of Raul Macon -- with his thick-necked, linebacker's body -- lurked nearby, cavalierly inspecting the booty.

"Where'd you get this stuff, man? It's real black market and old stuff smuggling, some of it." Macon picked up a baseball-like grenade, olive-hued, and marveled. "This is vintage CS gas, U.S. Army, ain't it?"

Rampoul eyed him with cold restraint. "It is a formidable array, old man. Not for interstellar space soldiers, is it? Thanks in large part, if you must know, to the abilities of our German comrade, Herr Hoffler."

"Yeah, wow," said Macon appreciatively, almost looking around him for this remarkable individual. "This stuff could relocate this fuckin' mountain, Jack, if somebody tosses a match."

"By all means don't smoke."

Macon put the grenade back into its orange crate. "You people are at War, dude."

"That's the general impression."

"That's the general friggin' fact. Hey, honcho?"

Christina sat now on a crate. She whispered, "Where is our man?"

"Secreted within, naturally. And still in reasonable health," said Rampoul, "although his blood pressure's shot up and he's not coping with it. Not at all."

"Has Green begun re-orientation?"

"As far as I know. But there have been delays."

Christina sighed, relacing one of her uncomfortable boots. One of the female aides came by with coffee, announcing that a meal was being prepared. It was naturally quite cold within the snow-bitten cave, despite the gas stove churning on several yards away from the munitions. This warmth provided a hub the staff assembled around. Someone jokingly branded this contingent The Stove Staff.

But where was Hoffler? mused Christina. For the first time she surmised he was a presence even when not present. How these druidic caves of his homeland suited him. Indeed Hoffler was more than just guide in this neck of the woodland. He was, it seemed to Christina, already the leader.

She would have to consult immediately with Nils, if he wasn't already waylaid. They would have to talk, for unquestionably Christina was becoming afraid.

"When will I be briefed?" she asked Rampoul.

"Soon. Very soon," he replied. Checking his watch, he frowned at the crackling short-wave console living like a digital electronic creature in their midst -- almost watching them, determining their gene make-ups. "You must admit we weren't quite expecting you like this. We all feared the worst for you."

Christina stared back at him, gauging the glimmer in Rampoul's eyes. Sometimes the manner of his affectations bothered her, as sugar does when it is mistaken for salt. Rampoul, staring back, wondered at the way this Christina had changed in so short a time -- to the point where there were things about her he no longer recognized, or cared to admit were coming between them.

The Mission was all that mattered, after all.

23.

"Wie geht es Ihnen, Fraulein Christina?"

"Sehr gut, danke," replied Christina. She did not know German very well, but was an inveterate retainer of travel phrases from several languages.

"Gut. Very good," Gunther Hoffler replied, toasting her demurely with schnapps. Visions of Hitler dancing on pinheads glinted with myriad abandon in his green-flecked eyes. "Won't you drink with me?"

"If you have some Moselle."

"I have a variety," Hoffler said equably.

They were in a large tent apparently the camp headquarters, tantamount to a canvas conference room for bull sessions and decision making. In here Hoffler ate and slept as well. He was clearly a guerrilla officer in his own right, a Teutonic Che. His small army was probably, at that time, the most unique in the world and beyond.

The briefing held there earlier had gone well enough, except that Hoffler's flamboyance had created a strained atmosphere. He lectured and pontificated in condescending fashion, quite the firebrand given to the cause. After seeing him in such a state, Brice Rampoul dubbed Hoffler "The Black Patriot."

It was an illuminating experience throughout for Christina, who believed the German was the right transcendental shot in the arm. There they were, the original band members, ready to take the next step. Except for Nils, who Christina feared was growing disenchanted, even withdrawing somewhat from the proceedings. The first step was easy, but Christina knew the second wouldn't be.

How apparent that within a catastrophic maze of possibility the next dangerous gambit might soon occur. With terror and high emotion Gunther Hoffler was spreading a dictum of fear.

Christina was no longer an impressionable woman, yet she told herself caution was in order now when facing Hoffler. Digital music of strange melody wheezed from a thumb-sized box on the table, yet the volume was ear-racking, the surro-sound of absolute high-fidelity and more. Furtively they judged one another for possible use, but Christina knew this German was ahead of her. He was versed in terrorist and paramilitary activities on an everyday scale. So when Hoffler started making his will known, there was little arguing. The inevitable path could not be altered by anyone.

Hoffler desired to begin immediate infiltration -- "quick as lightning!" -- of the Forbrau Munitions Depot where the rumored Medulla Raze was stored. The American Raul Macon King would prove valuable to this aim, and Hoffler notified Christina of it. So despite the long day's activities, and the fact Christina direly needed rest, Hoffler wanted her to get "Mr. King" ready for his mission.

"I hope he's as capable as you say he is," Hoffler added through writhing cigarette smoke.

"He's tough. You saw that for yourself. And I think he's crazy, but just the proper amount crazy."

"Is he all right?"

"The last I saw, he was getting a compress bandaged on."

Raul Macon proved more ready for business than expected. He couldn't wait to see "the Rad," as Macon called any German. Hoffler actually pretended to like his guest, pouring him brandy after brandy, plying him with expensive hand-rolled cigarettes. It was a switch for Macon, who was sure he and T.K. Keller would have rough going convincing these tight-assed jokers about anything.

"I like a Rad like you," Macon said earnestly from across the small canvas table. "You're no chickenshit, are you, Comrade? Not like some of these college juicy-fruits hangin' out around here."

Hoffler laughed in his bellicose way. He liked entertainment as well, and this boor tickled him. Not all Americans were like this. Generally he hated the Fascist U.S. military on principle, and for occupying the Rhineland and Saar region for decades, despite withdrawing temporarily during the ill-fated reunification days before Hoffler was born. Now the U.S. military was back, and Hoffler's hatred had blossomed to extremes. It was an underground revolutionary wrath, vented also against the bourgeois Neo-Western "government of merchants" which Gunther Hoffler despised most of all, if reverently.

"I loathe my countrymen devoutly," Hoffler said. "I am a living oxymoron."

Though a university drop-out, Hoffler was an educated and even dogmatic pundit in his own right, calling himself a quasi-intellectual when necessity demanded. In ever growing rapture, Christina was discovering Hoffler's unusual intelligence, and marveling at it. Hoffler had a street waif's upbringing, and had lived a hard-edge life around cities like Saarbrücken and Hamburg. That's what Raul Macon was drawn to, along with the fact that when the Rad Man said *Ich will etwas*, it usually involved something violent, dangerous, perhaps irredeemably damnable.

Through a curtain of smoke, in dank and subterranean spaces, now Hoffler was briefing Macon with maps and photos of the bunker sites to concentrate on. It was a lesson in "classified geography."

"You know the place, ja?" Hoffler asked the squinting American.

"I know it. I've been through there. But that was before it became hot like it is now. My good pal T.K., though, was actually stationed there."

"Is that so?"

"Better believe it," Macon said, grimacing as he touched the brace-like bandage around his neck. "He got all fucked-up down there. You don't know what the goddamn army does to its guinea pigs! But shit, I don't know what he'll remember, or how good he'll be. We'll give it a good go or hock the gasthaus, Comrade. I can tell by your set-up and stash here that you are one serious dude."

The German's rough-hewn face broke into a smile. Beatifically he leaned back in his wooden chair, placing both hands atop his shaggy-tousled head, staring up now meditatively. He wore the old and badly frayed black leather jacket of a cyclist, and the turtleneck sweater underneath was another trademark which never left him, like the dirt beneath his fingernails. Under the flickering lantern light there was even an artificial aura of witchcraft about Hoffler.

"So let's understand one another," Hoffler spoke finally, quietly, in a more careful English. "We must somehow infiltrate that depot, Mr. King, and do it as quickly as possible while we have our captive Tomasi here to exploit in the media. Whatever sensationalism we achieve might better suit our purposes. You are to find a way into the bunkers where presumably materials, etc., for the Medulla Project are stored. You are to commandeer those materials for our own ends, if possible. And of course to re-con the entire area."

"So there will be a good old raid then," Macon-King said, almost in surprise, his cigarette ashes falling across the table.

The German blinked slowly, and asked Macon to provide any pertinent information about the Forbrau Depot. Macon cleared his throat, squeezing his eyes shut and grunting while picturing again the controversial site in his mind's blank eye.

"The bunkers, Comrade, are situated in the boondocks. It's a hell of a forest up there -- a real bitch in the winter -- and you can get lost easy as shit tooling through those crazy roads in a jeep. The area is huge -- it's called the Mag Zone -- and fenced all over with top-security gates, well-lit and barb-wire-rigged for electric shocks. The G.I.s hump that bastard 24 hours around the clock. A Military Police company's in charge of all that, which my friend T.K. Keller once was part of before he got cold feet."

Macon paused to light another cigarette, and cast a provocative look at the note-taking Christina Alpreece.

"What else? It's a huge Zone, like I said, but the Administration sector of the Depot's small. Very small. A few buildings, a P.X., and you got it. All the brass work up there during the day, of course. The peon Enlisted Men work out in the Zone loading bunkers and shit. Nice arrangement. There's a Main Gate with an M.P. shack next to the Provost Marshal's Office as you go in. NASA even has offices there.

"It's tight security, but we can get in. I don't think anybody knows just what the hell's going on out there -- it's a fucked place -- and I sure didn't until recently, thanks to the lady here. That Depot was for missile parts and munitions as far as I knew, but I guess times change, like they say."

"As far as everyone knew," Christina said, "until Mr. Tomasi informed us differently."

"How'd you get him to do that?" asked Macon with mock-leering innocence.

"You'd have to ask my associates, Brice Rampoul and Nils Mupreen. They devised this 4th Quadrant headquarters."

The German uttering all this betrayed nothing, but in his eyes there was a malice perhaps connected to his design, much of which was still private within him.

"How much time will you need to recuperate, Mr. King?"

"I'm ready now, Comrade," Raul Macon maintained. "But it may take a few days to get a good game plan ready, you know?"

24.

Out of a night of hangovers into this, a deliverance back into that country he once fled from, ice-bitten and starving. T.K. had reverted to his customary state of mind-ragged shock, as totally on edge as ever. *The reality was here again* -- despite how he'd fought it -- and the autobahn dash back to Forbrau Depot, that hamlet of greater nightmares which poisoned T.K. from the first, equaled a condemned man's journey.

Déjà vu of dooms, T.K. told himself with a cold-turkey shuddering. There was no way around it. He was a wanted fellow in these parts. His being captured by the Military Police he once served with would result in serious imprisonment. The penalty levied against any deserter was monstrous.

Macon knew of T.K.'s secret, had known since the beginning when he'd helped the young poetaster escape. Yet Macon was delivering T.K. back into the clutches of olive drab monstrosity again.

T.K. had small choice in the matter. Especially with the snout of a Firebird indenting his ribs. It was Raul Macon's comment on a ticklish matter. Nothing stayed contentedly in T.K.'s stomach either -- not even water, which he couldn't pass anyway. The point of no-return was beyond some vector never really intersected, except by wishful thinking perhaps.

T.K. was allowed to keep his name, or identity -- such had been pseudonymous for months anyway -- but Raul Macon was given another alias, *Warren C. May,* along with the properly forged papers. It was a name among many Macon had little use for. He was supposed to be one of those American civilians who worked in some administrative capacity for the N.C.O. Clubs on various Army posts in Europe. This suited Macon, who -- despite the fact he had almost drunkenly destroyed an N.C.O. Club in his time -- knew being around a bar was the best place for him. "These bad Rads ain't so stupid after all," he commented. "I told you I liked that Hoffler dude. I know he's seen a little combat in his time."

To simplify matters, Macon went by the initial "M." for accomplices such as young Keller, who couldn't even remember his own alias sometimes. T.K. pretended being a "student tourist" who was a cousin of one Forbrau Military Policeman, a Specialist Fourth Class T.K. knew during his tour of duty. That Spec 4 was as close to being a genuine inside contact for their purposes as anyone else in that unusual M.P. company, known for its eccentrics despite the tight security and classified nature of the post.

Possibly the fact that too much secrecy about the Medulla Project created an atmosphere where most everyone, knowing so little, became chagrined to a mutinous point at times. This enabled the infiltrating German terrorists to exploit what they could, since the Forbrau Depot was unpopular in the Western Germany rural community. Despite its being located in the forested, elevated area of the Saar region, there was a feeling among Forbrau residents, many of whom worked for the German civilian branches on the Depot, that there was too much corruption there.

T.K. knew it all at first hand, of course. He had arrived there as a young M.P. about 2 years before, nervously grateful that he wasn't on his way to the Middle East, which had become another recurring war. Life at this post grew insupportable for him, as it was for many of his fellow company members, who called themselves Haters dedicated to performing destructive acts against the Fucking Army which bedeviled them. The Depot command used these poor M.P.s, despite the fact more able ones might have done better, considering the importance of what was on base.

There were factions on Depot in conflict because of what went on, and this situation was allowed to fluctuate depending on however it could be manipulated by the Depot hierarchy. There would never be a "straighter" situation at Forbrau due to withheld reasons.

"It's still your basic crooked system," a member of the German liaison team said after arriving at Mam's gasthaus, near the Forbrau bahnhof. The members sat around an unadorned wooden table drinking beer from mugs, watching the dark winter's night through an open window. Weeks had elapsed since the beginning of the sordid business.

"Yeah," T.K. ventured to add, "and that's why I don't like it. How the hell can I get on that Depot without being recognized and hustled into the stockade? It's ridiculous. It just won't work. There are several unsympathetic individuals there who still haven't rotated. I'm a *deserter,* man. You know what that means in the U.S. Army? It means my ass is grassed. I could be sent to a space station stockade."

"Well, don't get uptight about it , Keller," Macon snuffled, pulling deep from another beer. "You're grassed anyway if you're not cool."

"We won't use you on Depot that much -- and especially not in the daytime," said the German, named Schiffer, who worked as an administrative aide at the Depot Headquarters Building. He was shrewd, thirtyish, and knew anyone -- and anything -- of importance involving the Forbrau Ammunition Depot. More of a black marketeer than terrorist, he'd made a deal with the Puma Gang (which could no longer be ignored) regarding the disposition of any matériel eventually commandeered during the planned activity to come. In exchange, of course, the Puma made it paramount that Hermann Schiffer render his go-between services as ably as possible.

There was no telling what Schiffer might be capable of. Even now his haughty, calculating air gave Keller uncomfortable pause. T.K. felt like a checkmated pawn in the man's well-structured game. For once, staring at this precisely manicured and dapper little Rad, rare sobriety gradually encroached on Keller. It made him take more than a passing slug from his Pils beer stein.

"I'm the one that's gonna be all over that Depot," Macon declared, "just like fuckin' Spiderman."

"Great," said T.K. " 'Cause I never want to see that sucker again. I hope they blow it away."

With a new hat on -- a wine-colored beret Schiffer had given him -- T.K. hoped that his yappie-long locks and beard would make it difficult for anyone to remember the crew-cut G.I. he'd once been. He'd been in this gasthaus several times before, but only as a transitory face unknown as a regular. With trepidation T.K. stared about in his alert paranoiac's manner, eerily taking in the patrons and scenery, knowing that he was fully thrust into that most diabolical of subconscious dreams he'd resisted all along, ever since he'd fled. Now here it all was again, and T.K. Keller was too fully conscious of it.

He sank more fully into the incipient, unconscious dream of trauma. Something within him was screaming from the attempt to awaken. It was not the beginning but the end, wasn't it? More than ever this hirsute young man felt a prisoner of war machines, and his absence from it had only been a temporary delusion, like all the other delusions his life had been.

"We're all gonna earn our marks on this one," he heard Macon say less than succinctly. All around the table faces became like those in a German Expressionist painting: ugly and brutal, gross and sensual. Mobile faces of men who talked boisterously as they flirted with the pair of homely barmaids circulating about haplessly with knife-like fingers; tongues splaying saliva around in clotted rain-drops; women whose painted mouths opened into sweating visions of genitalia.

"Wohin fahren Sie heute?"

To Forbrau. To *Forbrau* --

It was a strange place to talk business, and in some dull aural cavity T.K. heard Schiffer informing them about other people and places they must see. Keller through a dream-haze saw Hannah, the young and experienced Saarbrücken outcall masseuse who would shield and feed outcasts, acting like a sister of mercy (all men were degenerate wunderkind, though deserving salvation), her stricken and used beauty frozen in arrested development. Then T.K. wished to see no more, since this phantasmagoria of timelessness passed before his eyes like a writ of fait accompli, and he saw the final result as something hideous. That something was of dark hue from a spectrum rust distorted.

Of carrion weed, blank and dark, in the wrong-seeding mire, T.K. penciled on a napkin. Were they in a gasthaus, or a waiting room before hell?

The radio news hardly heard above the din wasn't encouraging either. It recounted the recently failed attempt of a Russian space probe which failed to locate a planet believed to be the earth's twin in another galaxy: a planet where the survivng lot of elitist humanity could yet migrate to, and attempt to subdue any threatening life form inhabiting it.

25.

It was too improbable -- what had happened -- what they were doing to him. He was too old moreover to believe he'd survive. The cave dampness had already worked against his badly flayed constitution, he ached with arthritic pains, and along with his inability to eat anything there was now a flu fever which cauterized every nerve in his head.

"I might be dying," a thought occurred to him, but that prospect became one enviably just. Yet something else inside him, a bitter and outraged resolve, fought back.

Although Gaylen V. Tomasi's recollection of horrific events was at best a mélange -- fever-blurred -- it was this outrage which kept him going, resulting from one of the deepest humiliations of his life. His man fragmented, rendered sputtering bits of cellular explosions, right before his eyes. It was an unforgettable sight whose impact -- and freeze-frame image -- played in Tomasi's mind with endless repetition. The elderly man had hallucinated from it, reduced to a groveling illness his captors would exploit and manipulate.

He could not remember much with any chronological certainty. There had been his aide's fragmentation, the sudden abduction in which Tomasi was whisked away through the rain's cold plummet. Profound shock possessed him from that moment, and part of him remained a soporific prisoner at best. The high-speed drive on the autobahn was endless, and it worsened as they disappeared into a forested, steep-hilled region. Tomasi had no idea where they were, or kept heading, except deep into some little-known woodland of Weir becoming more forbidding.

Fleetingly Tomasi recalled the unspeakable descent into these caves, where he'd been blindfolded and forced to wear the coarse clothing of a peasant or farmer. His head was shaved along with his mustache, leaving him little to be vain about, and certainly more susceptible to the underground chill his captors equated with that penetrating wind, know as The Hawk, which came and went at distressing intervals.

Tomasi could sense he was in some busy encampment. Even with his bad hearing the ongoing sounds of vehicles and a brigade of working people proved unmistakable. Only when he'd been sequestered within some plywood partitioned area was the blindfold removed. He'd been fed by a pair of young-looking German women who had a dissolute, unkempt air, and at times they handled him roughly. There were other shadowed faces, apparently male, appearing on Tomasi's visual periphery. Given a cot to rest and recuperate on, he'd been hopeful at first that this detention would not be a distressing one. The faces must see that Gaylen Tomasi was too fatigued to do anything, that he was actually a stricken and elderly man needing medical attentions, not the treatment of some radical interrogation.

This treatment, to Tomasi's dismay, was what he repeatedly got. His youngish captors evidently had some specially formulated and rehearsed program in mind. On awakening from his first hardly restful sleep, nightmare-plagued by an ineradicable image of cell erasure, Tomasi was gone over by a hirsute man with a student sensibility and Dutch mien. This young Dutchman immediately began questioning about Tomasi's recent business in Europe, and demanded to be told any classified information regarding unusual "military and scientific" projects the old man was aware of. A weasel-faced radical kept badgering the sly old fox, and the proceedings did not prove that beneficial at first to the interrogating party.

So Tomasi was bound, and made to stand for long minutes before a blank screen upon which brilliant light was focused, blinding him to a point where a blindfold would be welcomed. He was bombarded with high-pitched sounds better fit for a laboratory animal. Tomasi reacted in a disoriented, uncommunicative fashion that wasn't at all feigned. But his captors weren't so sure.

All through his treatment Tomasi heard voices: German, Dutch, English speaking tongues joining together in some corrupted melody he could not sort out or begin to understand. Tomasi was told only he was in the new United Nations, that he was on trial for American crimes of military imperialism (both terrestrial and interstellar), and that the penalty would be a unique and painful suffering. No one wanted him to die before experiencing it.

It wasn't long before Tomasi began to wilt. His captors drove him as far as possible, drawing back before reaching the point of ultimate harm. The Dutchman was joined by an older American of ostentatious dress, who appeared (at certain points when Tomasi approached collapse) to be meditating in some yogic posture before the old man.

"You must be more amenable, dear Mr. Tomasi," the American would say in a cajoling near-whisper, being careful not to further alarm his subject. "The Medulla Project, do you remember? You must tell us in more detail. Please. We would like to know more about the bunkers."

"You've learned all that I know," Tomasi said, having recovered from some dry retching. "This is a futile examination. I'm only a business liaison, as much in the dark as anyone. I've never been to the Forbrau Depot. That was not my assignment."

"Give him the liquid," Nils Mupreen said, checking some forms in Tomasi's folder, then making notations.

With a torn sponge, one of the women blotted Tomasi's sweating features, then coaxed him into sipping some clear liquid from a pear-shaped vial.

"Oh, my God ..." Tomasi groaned. Tears resurfaced in his usually rheumy eyes.

The American with the medallions around his throat stood up, every inch a regal-appearing sort, in comparison to the Dutchman's proletarian look.

"You're an invaluable accomplice, Mr. Tomasi. The world is interested in you. Your story has made front pages, and your countrymen are extremely interested in your welfare."

Tomasi reclined there in his wretchedness, breathing laboriously in a wheezing and sick-sounding fashion. Sweat bubbles still erupted like glaucous boils over his brow and wrinkled neck. There was a hangdog quality about his abject state, one of total and far-reaching defeat.

"I'm only an old man. This won't change anything. It doesn't matter if I'm alive or dead."

"Will you become our accomplice?"

"What choice ..."

"Will you let us inform the world that you've joined us in the denunciation of America's military ventures and imperial decadence, both terrestrial and in deepest space?"

Tomasi repeated his comment.

"We want more facts, Mr. Tomasi," Nils Mupreen said. "We want the complete and accurate names of everyone connected in your recent 'liaison' here. And just what the outcome of your meeting was before you were abducted. There is no immunity in this matter, Mr. Tomasi. All our lives are at stake."

The elderly businessman mulled this over. Dismayed, Tomasi noted he was being told to defect by a fellow American. Another young American would later enter Tomasi's blurred consciousness. A woman with pristine features, nonetheless chisel-edged, hovered there too, like an aesthetic wraith whose intelligence was cruel for its seeming innocence. The captured man saw in her gaze a child-like depravity.

A perfect complement to the other American, the woman now terrified Tomasi the most. All the collective eyes radiating a foul energy within the partition's moor-like grayness -- intercut now and then by the fierce light of lanterns -- made Tomasi feel like an incorrigible circus freak about to be unceremoniously dissected, bit by bit, for eternity.

To burn would be better, Tomasi thought. *To burn like the witch in morbid surrender would be much, much better, and the snow-ridden forest would be melted, wouldn't it?*

* * *

They came in like a shrouded procession, a few members carrying candles, into the darkness of Tomasi's partition. Paying homage to irrational deities lurking outside, the captors would subsume their hostage within some grand design.

They came to embalm his trembling body with poultice and herb, chanting in German as the taller gang member painted Tomasi's nakedness with swatches of thick paint, which became enmeshed with animal innards. They prayed for the elderly man, endeavoring to explain the cabalistic force behind the Medulla, how it would yet be used for a more constructive end.

The convocation of fear would give Tomasi new life, new blood, and made an Acolyte out of him. How he dreamed of release from moon-blanched rabble into the recognizable world again. Out there Tomasi would have no use for the sacrifice now offered him: that regal woman of sensuality now in nakedness, shimmering in sloat-eyed lust, pouncing on his destitute flesh and trying to work a miracle there, to bring something back from the Dead.

But Tomasi screamed with such anguish that the fabric of hope and possibility lost some momentum, thrust back into that nature of ancient woodland the snow buried with desolation.

PART IV

EVIL EDEN

26.

For Raul Macon, the interminable task began. Everything seemed burdened by the omnipresent long winter surrounding all with a pall of grayness. In this atmosphere of perennial damp, on his first morning in Forbrau, New West Germany, Raul Macon stood huddling by the Main Gate entrance to the U.S. Army's Forbrau Ammunition Depot.

It had been sometime since he'd last been inside, as a G.I. Now he was again, thanks to underground workings, ostensibly another mercenary American who fed off the troops -- even fleeced them -- via the N.C.O. Club circuit. Macon had the papers in his inner pocket to prove it, giving him access to enter the Administration sector, generally open to off-base individuals carrying valid passes. He would be known as "Warren C. May" officially, simply Mac to those who, like the slang-happy Desk Sergeant inside the Provost Marshal's Office, would get to know newcomers more familiarly.

It was just after 7 a.m. on a Monday morning. Macon had watched -- partially in awe -- the huge parade of military and civilian vehicles moving unendingly up the narrow entrance road, freshly snow-cleared. The bustling sounds of horns, gunned motors, and ice-spitting tires still resounded within Macon's ears. He tried to smoke a cigarette in the frigid air, but his numb lips tasted nothing. Slowly and inevitably, Macon gathered himself to make his grand entrance into the P.M.O. where the Desk Sergeant was, now visible through the large barred window facing the Main Gate cubicle where a lone M.P. stood forlornly on duty.

Macon waved to the white-gloved Military Policeman upon approaching, stopping momentarily to show his pass. The shivering M.P. nodded Macon toward where he'd been tending (in thought and action) for quite a while.

In this world of the American military the conventional block-like buildings were painted green as usual. Macon noticed this with displeasure as he stood inside the hallway, stamping his booted feet on the well-beaten mat by the door. Gratified, he also noticed it was warmer inside this building of depressing bureaucracy, where

uniformed clerks and orderlies circulated about inside their offices. The P.M.O. was attached to Headquarters Building, the Depot's center of administrative activity.

Behind the huge and elevated wooden desk (upon which, emblazoned on a gold heraldic shield, was the crossed-pistols insignia of the 76th M.P. Company), Sgt. Camrack sat typing out his log report. A strapping young man from the South, he usually appeared resplendent in his dress greens.

"Good morning," Camrack said politely to Macon's approaching presence, which the Desk Sergeant sensed but did not directly look at. "What can I do for you?"

Warren C. May introduced himself and handed up his papers, coughing extravagantly while peeling off his gloves. For warmth he stood nearby an olive drab radiator rail, and stared out the barred window.

"Okay for coffee?" Warren C. May asked, helping himself to a nearby pot without waiting for reply.

"Sure," said Desk Sergeant Camrack. "So you're on the P.X. and N.C.O. Club circuit, is that it? You probably want to see Del Mason, but I don't think the Club opens till 11."

"Where is it?" May asked, depressed by the sight through the speckled window, and grimacingly sipping the gruel-like "coffee". He was wondering how good an actor he was. He was wondering if he could pull this off without these Bums getting wise to him, before the inevitable happened. *You know the inevitable, Shithead,* he told himself.

"Ah." The Desk Sergeant stopped typing to think, clasping his large hands behind his head. "You're facing in the right direction. It's about a few hundred yards up ahead, just before the rail tracks and the brass yard, by Gate 16."

"Can't miss it, right?"

"Sure can't. It's new. It's on the end. It's one of the best places on Depot. My name's Sheldon Camrack, by the way."

They exchanged further salutations, Warren C. May lighting a cigarette which ended up in the same hand he held his dirty coffee cup with.

"You been in Germany long --?" asked the Desk Sergeant, making conversation.

"I've been in Europe quite a while. I get around."

"Oh really?"

Warren C. May believed the Desk Sergeant to be a nice, well-brought-up, somewhat credulous lad. Just a little older than buddy T.K., and built more like a decathalon aspirant. May could use the lad to run interference, to do a number of favors. He was another young sucker warming to the bullmoose impostor.

"Hey, *you've* got a great job. That's something I'd like to do when I get out. Stay in Europe, but still be close to the military," Camrack lamented. "I never get out of this office. I pull the same duty, week after week. Shoot, I wish they'd let me patrol or supervise or something."

"You're probably an invaluable man."

"That's what they tell me."

Camrack went back to his typewriter, sighing as he pecked away haltingly at the keys. Herr "M." still stood looking out, considerably pumped-up by his continuing sense of importance. At last he believed himself undeniably somebody *really* indispensable to the Forbrau mission. For the first time, too, he felt the thrill of being another James Bond in the throes of high espionage, certainly above the head of any average layman plowing snow all around, waiting for winter's end.

Macon & May came together at this point, creating the self-styled "M." -- dapper and dangerous -- who began affecting the pose of a cinematic lady-killer, used to eluding danger with great skill. Reflecting on this, Herr "M." knotted his tie more snugly, and silently paid egotistical homage to his many-faced self growing more stronger and unstoppable by the minute. Here was the stuff of real spy fiction: *"Super-M.!"*

And as for any dangers to come, he would certainly be ready for them, he told himself. But there were presences at Forbrau Warren C. May knew nothing about yet -- presences of an even other-planetary nature that regarded him unfavorably.

27.

As if things weren't bad enough -- as if the fount of his paranoia had not peaked -- T.K. Keller was unceremoniously dumped somewhere around Forbrau (by those seedy, Teutonic terrorists): straight into the callous hands of some Uber-Whore, and severed from his hell-raising guide, last known as Herr "M.".

It was maddening, that latter fact especially, since being in Macon's company was equivalent to non-stop masochistic tortures. At least those he knew about. But this? This introduction into the underworld had his dope-clean nervous system fermenting again, until T.K.'s heart felt like a time-bomb about to explode his body juices into the biggest geyser ever.

He was hustled via Volkswagen into this drab, overcrowded little city with its typically European streets of winding cobblestones, which reminded T.K. of some forgotten fairy tale. He had to walk -- or literally limp -- his Spanish booted way along slicker pavement. T.K. was physically thrust into the large, many-roomed building obviously used for activities of mercenary "sex." Enough appalled by proximity to the blunt-force surroundings, T.K. despaired. Gone was any past romanticizing about such an intriguing subject, which resembled a trip to the ill-equipped water closet for another desperate body function. Yep, the old wooden place (draped inside by a perpetual curtain of chiaroscuro) festered with the odors of such open practices, which hung about T.K. like badly kept secrets minus mystique.

The Uber-Whore was young, raven-haired, with what men called a "good" body. She was perfunctory in manner but severely conscientious about tasks at hand. T.K. felt she made a strange bedfellow for the terrorist gang, and wondered what her story was. In the depressing small room they occupied, she turned up the antiquated corner stove; let T.K. lay down to rest shakingly, on a wall-hugging divan no doubt used for digital business; and plied him with strong unfiltered cigarettes and some unappetizing bratwurst she later brought in, a servant unused to serving. Through it all Keller wondered if he could handle this, and cursed mad Macon for abandoning him.

Failure in this cloak-&-dagger mindlessness was a predetermined given, Keller told himself. Was it possible to flee from it also?

Of course speech was minimal with the Uber-Whore, since they couldn't speak one another's native tongue. Once again T.K. experienced the nightmare of being back in what he'd fled from, a long-buried fear again realized. And how long would the accursed "world wars" continue anyway? If they ever ended, maybe things would lighten-up in USAREUR-land. But that was unlikely, given the ongoing déjà vu lunacy of it all. A war ended in one place only to resume in another. Or maybe they'd fight it all over again here, as done before. The chronological year was inessential, even if the Yabba Dabba music superstar Duke had died. For T.K. these were dry realizations indeed, and World War III would seem like a rerun.

"Fraulein," said T.K. Keller. He indicated a desire to stretch his legs outside, around the old town.

Verboten, naturally, replied Uber-Whore in vividly graphic terms, displaying her unreserved alarm. An unshaved Keller fell back burpingly on his divan again, and was far from being the aesthete dandy of old. There was too much pregnant irony about what was happening, he decided. He would even pray for salvation if necessary, here in the *übermater's* nest.

If T.K. slipped-out — lost the handle on his brain, became a simpering mental-veggie — what would happen? What could they do — send him back, believing it? Or would they wreak some unspeakable punishment on him for the ruse. For T.K., just when to gamble was the ultimate concern.

"T.K., be cool," the disappearing "M." had told him.

Now T.K. truly wanted to disappear too. Perhaps even, Buddhas rest his soul, into some netherworld above or below. He couldn't believe all that had happened: Just several hours earlier he'd been at the bizarre subterranean encampment within the German forest, where something extraordinary was taking place. The woman there -- the space witch-like Christina, whom T.K. now regarded with greater trepidation -- was hardly diminished in memory by the living presence of the Uber-Whore. Yet he would like to forget them both. Keller felt corrupted, invaded by these females, and there weren't enough antibodies in his weakened system to overcome this creeping degeneration.

T.K. vowed to escape. The sooner the better, before the dark spirits inhabiting the ethereal airs coalesced into the celestial and alien *somas* that Christina Alpreece predicted would someday come.

28.

Herr "M." sensed mutiny. He sensed it everywhere he went around the Depot's Admin. Area. It wasn't a pronounced, obvious thing, of course. Rather it was a subtle emanation of psychic volatility Macon was easily receptive to, while initially exploring the Forbrau complex the next few days.

A curious place indeed, he decided. For a highly classified sector, it was almost identical to any other U.S. Army post in Germany. But "out-back" there was a whole different sector (totally fenced-off, constantly patrolled) where the hot stuff was, and Macon -- who never took anything for granted those days -- knew he'd have his work cut out for him.

There was something wrong on this post, Macon knew. Too many people from opposite ends of the military and political arena undoubtedly commingled here daily, unsure of anyone's status as traitor, spy, or informer. This lent unshakable paranoia to a festering olive drab circus, Macon knew.

He'd already made an important ally in M.P. Desk Sergeant Sheldon Camrack. Macon would make other allies, by virtue of his military experience and the fact that "Warren C. May, by God!" was the type Army sorts took to instinctively. He had come to entertain one and all. To insure that the N.C.O. Club (badly in need of renovation and new management for so long) would be better than ever, catering to any thirsts and desires to escape from this incomprehensible, forested fun-house, where everything appeared upside-down -- and perversion was the norm.

How far could Macon trust young Sgt. Camrack of Florida? This was a question he debated over for some time, from the moment he entered the N.C.O. Club that first morning and gravitated automatically to the large bar adjacent to the doorway. At that hour not many people were visible inside -- the place didn't officially open till past noon -- and Macon marveled at how easily showing his papers allowed his entry. There were times, after all, when as an old soldier he had to fight his way in and out of such a place.

Dressed in Neo-huppie fashion, an assistant (with beard and shoulder locks, all slickened) told Macon to go in and make himself at home until the interim boss, or somebody equally impressive, showed up. Grunting, lighting up a cheroot, Macon was allowed a 7&7 from a genial employee setting up bar. The newcomer had to admit that -- craning around, letting his eyes become adjusted to the low-lighting scheme -- the place didn't look half-bad, so the decor wasn't a problem. The people who ran the place were probably the problem, having misappropriated funds they couldn't get away with. Macon rued this sardonically, shaking his head and clucking tongue, because he'd always been able to misappropriate funds skillfully. But of course that wasn't his chief objective at the moment.

Macon knew this club could become the base of his operations. Looking into the mirror, he groomed himself slightly, hoping there were some good-looking women around. There always were in places like this. There were ugly ones too. And of course there were those who dated Blacks. He hated those women most of all. Savoring this hatred made him order another drink.

Already the young Desk Sergeant had told Macon more about Depot security than was bargained for. Already, thanks to that informing young man (who treated the newcomer like a more experienced older brother of impressive stature one must confide in), Macon would be doing some advance scouting of the hot Magazine Area that very night, when all the Forbrau employees left the Depot around 5 p.m. in another mass exodus, their workday completed. The gullible Camrack would even be the guide, and commandeer one of the Magazine Patrol vehicles on duty for the purpose.

Already Macon was thinking things were opening up smoothly, and he'd be becoming quite a familiar -- and important -- figure on base, having access to every nook & cranny. Would all the gates of this strange Eden open for him with similar ease?

"I trust they will," answered Raul Macon.

The M.P.s virtually controlled the Depot -- night and day -- so that was encouraging. There was a Polish Labor Army on base, but that "company" was more salvation army than otherwise, composed of beer-blasted World War refugees well into their advanced age. Some were even senile, and had done space duty. They formed a comic relief for the 76th M.P. Company of which Sheldon Camrack was proudly part of. Getting into this M.P. company was another large task for Macon, who feared the brass on Depot and wanted a way to neutralize, or keep in the dark, high-ranking American officers. There were a few other Ordnance companies on Depot, and that was it.

Outside, "M." knew the Admin. Area was a overused and congested site this time of day. The major buildings -- snack bar, P.X., bowling alley and theater, etc. -- were all packed closely together, and endless military and civilian patrons bee-busily filed in, out, and away. In their perpetual vehicles, military or privately owned, the traffic was also unceasingly congested and noisome. But it was quiet inside the Club now, although later Macon knew the teeming boozers would be in here too seeking discount thrills.

He had to curse, pulling at his cheroot and checking the sports watch on his wrist. It was all going good. Too good.

Then something inside the Club gave Macon a start. He noticed a suited man sitting in a far off corner nursing a drink and staring back, at oblique angles, intermittently. It wasn't somebody familiar, but a type Macon was unhappily acquainted with, and could detect even if blind in a snowstorm. *Them.* He said the word again to himself: *Them.* The buggers. The Brooks Brothers people with an electrode on each dick. The C.I.A. (or C.I.D.?) Perverts. That rat race hounding Macon everywhere till his nightmares had suits in them.

He turned back around until facing the mirror again. Could he be sure? Just once could he be gratefully wrong? Slowly in the mirror Macon watched the dark-suited man get up -- retrieve a folder from the table-top -- and move swiftly into and beyond the satin-curtained darkness, turning into a doorway near the stage.

Macon cursed more softly. He would find out about that joker. He would find out about everybody in the place.

It was a hell of a year. It was an absurdist era, in fact, in which the United States Government found itself (defying the great laws of historic lessons and cogent reasoning) back in another South East mini-war, similar to past ones; fighting another strange and strategic form of combat for terrestrial real estate in this inimitable year of 2037, decades since the American military had last occupied similar infamous terrain.

Raul Macon-May was much in love with the hooker who was implanted, forever amber style, in his 2020 psyche (around that unruly time when the Beetles broke up, and Rock heroes died at the hands of religious fundamentalists). Something of this hooker's heart was mired in that era, and Raul -- the burly, ill-suited man sitting at an N.C.O. Club bar in Forbrau, Germany, in another decade's torturous beginning when the world again played chicken with itself, on the brink of mass devastation, but always pulling out at the last second to vanish into space in fine cinematic style -- the *inimitable* Macon, had to retrieve the vital parts lost by his obsessed woman in a limbo of digital-dysfunction, shared by countless others.

If need be, to free this enslaved courtesan and allow her natural life again, Macon was willing to descend into the icy tunnel of time's standstill and set off an atomic firecracker that would turn the tide one way or another, by God.

He avoided his sweating face in the wall-long mirror, and managed to order another drink despite an ulcerous stomach acting up and telling him to do otherwise. For the time being, liquor cured his worrisome thought.

On the Club stage a band was setting up instruments for a rehearsal, and everything appeared as normal as could possibly be. Macon idly watched the row of overhead telegenic silver monitors depicting, on each screen, a different saga of broadcasted events (such as the space tracking of a renegade meteor striking with great force the surface of a distant blue planet), and sighed.

If only he could be like that meteor.

If only he had that devastating capability, life would be a piece of cake he could gobble with one nasty bite.

29.

It had to end, this Forbrau winter, along with that inclemently bitter wind called The Hawk by Depot veterans.

Yet for the grizzled man of a thousand aliases moving pell-mell into the inhospitable elements -- nearly falling out of the wind-buffeted jeep driven by Sgt. Camrack that gray evening of the first tour -- the privilege of entering such taboo fastness in search of secrets was more than one with a normally abnormal constitution could bear.

The roadays were treacherous. Glazed, slushy ice packed into cement-hard ruts threatened to overturn even a slow-moving jeep tire. Such was the natural state of the enigmatic Magazine Zone -- supposedly, in part, highly classified and verboten territory for sightseers.

Camrack's jeep passed through the entrance station at Gate 13 with hardly more than a squeal of rubber for the apathetic sentry on duty. Going farther into the vast arboreal maze, the jeep reached an area of double fencelines -- fences within fences -- concentric-circular fences and square or trapezoidal ones, all diverging at right and left angles into eccentric directions. *Maybe going no shit-assed where,* May-the-con marveled, hunched now in his parka, and unsportily wearing a stiff pile cap giving him a Cossack mien in the face-slapping wind. Camrack apparently knew *what was where,* and explained the sites to his guest as the jeep forged deeper into the woodland's expanse.

"Pretty huge, ain't it? It's like a separate country out here. Made up of a different community."

"So it's a different ball game out here," Macon sarcastically commented from a mouth corner.

"You better believe it. There's about 10 to 15 gate shacks and posts we man out here every night, and the men are so laid-back the duty officers never come out. They're afraid to. Too much weird stuff has happened out here, and the Bums think the place is haunted at night ..."

Macon brightened. "What kind of weird shit?"

"Ah, vandalism and shit like that. Shit getting stolen, generators breaking down. Dudes freaking-out, injuring themselves, claiming to see ghosts or space creatures."

"Oh yeah --?"

Macon was amused, yet pondering.

"It's pretty spooky and solitary duty for some of our personnel, May. And to top it off, we don't know what munitions are out here lots of the time. It's like the Bums are teasing us suckers, using us as guinea pigs 'cause we got sent here. There's a lot of irregularities for a supposedly 'classified' area."

"I'll bet. But what about those bunkers over there? Can you ever go inside them?"

They were coming abreast of a long row of C-Area bunkers, which loomed in the damp-heavy air like slumbering dinosaurs. Sheldon Camrack pointed out the fact these cement bunkers were all numbered and padlocked with aluminum seals bearing serial numbers. The seals were supposed to remain unbroken, their digits carefully recorded during each duty check. Inside these bunkers was allegedly the hot stuff: missile-heads, arms and explosives, munitions and related paraphernalia. *Maybe even the Medulla Raze,* thought Macon. Any unauthorized entry was a severe violation.

"Yeah, well, all promises are meant to be broken."

As they progressed along unsteadily, Macon wondered if things would become too unreal. He never liked to dwell on possibilities striking him as abstract. That's why he enjoyed having T.K. around: the kid's head was cloud-swimming, wrestling with intellectual vapors, fey shadows going nowhere, so that brainpower meant very little.

Strange and classified weapons of an indecipherable nature. Things could get out of control, and what then?

The Mag Zone bothered Macon with its stately wilderness of trees and bunkers, all rendered stark by the white ice clinging like animal skin remnants everywhere. It gradually took Macon into an avenue of emotional fear. Fear was something Macon had been unacquainted with for quite some time, and told himself (if his sanity remained intact) he must continue so.

The Mag Zone was like no other part of the forest. It was like a natural or supernatural invention, really, concocted by strange powers. Fabricated like a space community orbiting within the universe while appearing to stand still, it was too big a paradox to keep secret. Yet around it these intruders went as seemingly the Zone went around them.

The buildings were eerie, icon-like, cast into some futuristic architecture hardly resembling conventional cement bunkers -- barn-shaped -- the observing visitor expected. Whatever they were (and Camrack said they housed humming generators), they were metal-looking abutments geometrically devised beyond simple cylindrical shapes, and resembled stuff you saw at Disneyland, back in the U.S.A., when gamboling through Tomorrowland. Oh, what shapes *were* these? What function, what purpose? An exotic investigation might result from such eavesdropping. Yet Macon felt unsuited for it, as a bumpkin does when going to the big city.

"We're pretty close to Admin. II," Camrack said, continuing his tour guide litany with difficulty, trying to speak against the laboring jeep engine's whine. Inside the canvas-enclosed cab the hot air blower was malfunctioning, and the glass-scraping wipers failed to deflect snow particles steadily falling again. Numb from cold which seeped liquid-like into his shoes, Macon hunched deeper into his parka. Camrack's high-pitched voice came with staccato abruptness, fading in-and-out against the racket like a recalcitrant radio signal. He could get in trouble for what he was doing, escorting in Warren May like this. He could be hanged, and the Bums made that a speciality.

"You can see a lot of man-made lakes around here, May, when the weather's better. You can see a lot. That building to your right is the Polish canteen, sort of headquarters for our Polish Labor Army force out there. The Polacks are all old-timers with no other home ... There's another gate shack -- Gate 23 -- to your right ... And, of course, all kinds of bunkers and shit -- old and new -- some ruined ones even (like that half-buried one) from, believe it or not, WW II --"

"Surprises and ancient history everywhere," Macon said, squinting through poor visibility. He coughed rackingly -- feeling his ravaged stomach acting up -- but resolved he wouldn't let pain overtake him.

Along the way were tarp-covered trailers loaded with stacked munitions crates, and a deserted forklift and railyard items evident. Macon wondered where they were really going in this convoluted, snow-ridden maze. In the heart of the vortex, only Camrack -- who knew the area with mnemonic skill -- could tell. Macon wanted to inspect, take pictures, but it was getting dark and too cold for that. He would postpone such forbidden and detailed work.

Approaching the perimeter fenceline of Admin. II, the intruders saw an electric illumination of overhead lights (individually placed at 20-yard intervals) atop poles. It was a large fenced area within a larger whole, and the most extensively lit sector of the Mag Zone. Herein was the sector, according to Camrack, where some important weaponry was secreted. Before the imposing chain-link gates with signs and tumbleweed crests of barbwire, Macon could see the office complex with its huge generator room behind. It too was a sophisticated structure of cement and metal, with oblong picture glass windows, in which some fatigue-wearing sentries could be seen. One sat officiously at a desk where a phone was the only visible office equipment. "Now we're getting somewhere," Macon told himself, for this was where he'd wanted to come all along. And inside would surely be answers to all the questions this journey had raised.

The gates were unlocked and opened for Camrack and his rider. With a customary gear-gunning and tire squeal, their jeep proceeded into Admin. II's well-lit confines. The large and modern gate station the visitors entered was the most elaborate on Depot. Macon was suitably impressed standing inside thumping snow off his boots, and was engulfed by heat rays emanating from electric heater rails bracketed to the walls. The gate station was a paradisiacal sanctuary, with new and stainless desks, chairs, and benches occupying space throughout.

Who would have thought the forested Mag Zone was full of such exotic way-stations? Admin. II was the center and headquarters for security personnel in the Areas. Macon was informed of this while tugging off his gloves and pulling back his parka hood. Sighing, stretching, and shaking-out, he became immediately aware of the nearby generator humming incessantly, vibrating within the station itself (though it came from an adjacent building out back). He accepted a cigarette which Camrack lit with brown-nosing but equally friendly zeal, and noticed finally the seated figure huddled in a parka behind the desk, somewhat too large for its space. Emptily forlorn of any office equipment beyond phone and ashtray, the desk augmented the room's incongruous atmosphere. The only other figure noticed by Macon was the sorrowfully poised enlisted man standing before glistening and mist-heavy windows, in the corner opposite the desk and its mannikin-like occupant.

"Sgt. Lacer, this is the Mr. Warren May I was telling you about."

The desk occupant slowly raised his head, squinting, looking directly ahead and not at the cold visitors.

"How the hell did you get him in here, Camrack --?"

"Ah, shit," Camrack shrugged, revealing his best ivory smile. "No big thing. Tomley's working the Desk and said he'd call if the D.O. comes on Depot. No big thing."

"No big thing?"

The desk sitter roused his parka-bulky frame until his neck became visible, turtle-like. "Damn," he grumbled. "No big thing." He rubbed his fatigue-creased face with an unhurried, muscular hand. It continued up to smooth over the disarray of a blonde nest of hair. "No big thing? If the First Shirt saw this, we'd be stockaded for life on Venus and given strange pills for lunch -- not that I'd mind that." He turned to stare quizzically at his fellow N.C.O., perhaps underscoring the lengthy pause developing.

"Have a smoke, Wayman, and stop shaking. Old Shaky Rhinegold's somewhere in K-town tonight under the beer tent table."

The equally boyish-looking -- but harder-edged -- Wayman Lacer now stared at the formidable civilian in their midst.

"We don't get personnel like yourself in here every day --"

"So glad to be here," Herr M. replied with husky-voiced affability. "I heard you dudes were having a bad time out here and might be ripe for some adjustments."

Lacer leaned back in his chair, expelling a rapidly dissipating smoke haze to the accompaniment of an ugly-sounding wheeze. "Oh yeah? This just proves we get so many infiltrators in here that it doesn't really matter. Nobody knows a fucking real thing about nobody. How does that grab your scrotum, man?"

"Just where I can't feel it --"

"This place is adventureland, tomorrowland, nowhereland ... A junkyard for outer space parts. And supposedly a high-level of security exists in the Zone -- but all that's inevitably eroding, so that people like you aren't shot on sight."

The unusual civilian snuffled a sound out, somewhere between a laugh or expectorating noise.
"Just here to help."
"Oh, really."
Macon sat down heavily on one of the benches, slowly and more thoroughly observing his surroundings, almost theatrically marveling. "I'm all ears but close-mouthed, boys. I could get in trouble myself for being out here, starting a new job at the Club. Wouldn't do to endanger the job. That's what it's about."
Macon felt himself being regarded with suspicion. These days, he knew, everyone at Forbrau had ulterior selves at variance with their official ones. Yet he believed these younger men regarded him as another cut-above-the-ordinary black marketeer anxious to rip off Federal matériel, etc. -- just as they did. So the similar temperament was there. They were all Haters. It probably wouldn't matter, his terrorist connection: there were enough sympathizers for that cause on Depot anyway.
Something was *wrong* at Forbrau. Because his access to this privileged preserve had been so relatively easy, Macon wondered if the Medulla Project had been moved elsewhere. Yes, he wondered if Forbrau was only the decoy, a huge trap in which he was taking the bait for something he knew little of.
It began to irritate him, this something being wrong. Perhaps Macon's quasi-contacts were setting him up -- ready to nab him -- and he'd misjudged their Hate.
What's-Out-Here? was the only question he wanted to ask this hemp-headed Wayman Lacer, and answers of informative note were forthcoming.
"We, the guardians of the Mag Zone areas -- and all-hallowed Admin. II -- are the Moorlocks," Wayman Lacer began his monotonal monologue. "They, those out there in Admin. I, are the spineless Eli." Under the low-buzzing fluorescent tubes of light, Macon observed this Lacer to be bloodsucked of color, truly another forest ghoul who existed on chemicals not found in ordinary foodstuff. He was the kind of clown who hosted (from a coffin?) those cheap, late night horror movies on non-cable T.V., back home in The World. "The old Bums (or Eli) want to burn us out here, 'cause they can't keep tabs on things, or obtain complete control. That's it in a wild boar's nutshell, man. Everybody's faking each other out, or trying to, and the great rip-offs -- large and small -- are continuing, keeping the black market economy alive. I'm sure you're hip to this, Herr May, or you wouldn't have gotten so far in here in the first place. *This* is the microcosm of life! The grand culture dish of what it's all about, both home & abroad (as if they're such distinctions anymore). We are magnifying absolute corruption here as much as it can be magnified before your eye sockets explode. Do you dig?"
"Sure," Macon said, knowing Lacer was on something -- or something was on him. But who wasn't?
"Let me put it this way. There's something going on around here -- under our very boots, in the earth bowels -- that we don't know about. Perhaps no one aboveground really knows about it, but this *thing* -- this highly classified activity -- is continuing, and nobody knows just what the hell it will lead to, except possibly Hell. (But no greater hell exists then this claptrap called Forbrau anyway, ja?)."
Lacer sighed, stretching.
"So that's the deal. Something's here the Army Bums feel is so hot they can't even maintain under normal, strict security measures. They must feel the only way to protect it from being noted -- spied on, or whatever -- is to construct this bogus front we're all a part of."
"We're not just a front," Camrack interrupted, "this Depot has always handled military weaponry, hot or otherwise. There's a para-interplanetary nuclear capability here, and that's what everyone's worrying about."
"A 'para-interplanetary nuclear capability,'" Wayman Lacer mimicked, relishing the phrase. "That, Sgt. Camrack of hickland, is real military jargon. You truly have your ears open for whatever shit flies in there."
"Fuck you, fuck me."
Macon coughed, lighting a fresh Winston off Camrack's cigarette. "Keep going, man. I'm all big ears."
"Outstanding, my man ... Any-way, don't let me spoil your happy arrival here, but there's bad shit goin' down, and when it hits this snowy wonderland might be sizzling."
"Shit," Camrack said, laughing nervously.
"I'm serious. Leave it to governmental military mentality to botch this one. Teach the Germans good training, anyway."
"We need USAREUR, Lacer."
"Oh, sure we do. Affirmative. But hey, I think the Germans are working -- in spirit, tradition, what-have-you -- against this grand design, like it or not. How much is willful, how much *they* know, is another blind guess. But, man ..." Lacer leaned forward intensely, looked severely winter-blanched, his cheeks pinched. "This place is fucked, for black and white spooks only! I don't know if you're aware of the peculiar Depot lore here, Herr May. But it keeps causing day and nightmares for the troops here, right Cam? Oh, yeah -- does it ever. No end to the ghost stories and unexplained events around here, all contributing to the Story of Hate, brother. Another tradition! Yeah, just look outside, twenty yards away, nearby the fenceline. You see that half buried, large-ass, black shape out there, man? A German bunker from ancient WW II, with all its grisly secrets and goddamned bones preserved within. Get your heat goin'? *Fuckin'-A*, brother. And there's lots of stuff like that out here. This place is a regular natural war preserve, full of old horrors and forces seeking revenge."
"I love ghosts," smirked Herr M. "Especially space ghosts. We're all haunted, on earth as it is in heaven."
"Up the ass, we're sure haunted. So on the one hand you've got all *that* crap (not to forget the G.I.s with their stories & tribulations from humping the fencelines of this lonely fucking wasteland in arctic temperatures, some dudes freaking into madness and mayhem), plus this new munition mystique we're certain proves the existence of something so ugly, it can't be covered up! No way ... So here we sit, wondering just when and where this latest Army brainstorm will finally pop out for everybody's mutual disliking."
After a silent pause, Camrack cleared his throat and said to Macon: "Lacer here's been to college, back in

California ..."

No big whuppie, a gruff Herr Macon told himself. *That would explain it. Every funny asshole comes from California.*

"So what do you think of all this speculation, Mr. Herr May?"

Macon shrugged -- staring at the desk-seated, parka-clad figure -- and finally said: "What I think is, I'd like to find out more. I'm on your side, and I want to keep your asses covered like my own, if you're not against my 'investigating.' Being a civilian with connections at the Club, I can probably help you dudes in certain ways no one else could. So I'm optimistic on that score. *Let's Fuck the Army.* It's trying to fuck you, and you suckers already look like guinea pigs -- unwilling or not, it ain't a big difference. I know it's no picnic here, and you deserve some kind of leverage to pay the Bums back. In spades, man. In spades."

"All *right-t!*" Camrack sang out, though another unspoken part of him protested vehemently.

Lacer leaned back in his swivel chair, closing his eyes and smiling thinly. "Isn't all this unbelievable? We're almost talking sedition here. The ultimate disloyalty!"

"We're talking loyalty to the Godalmighty dollar. That's where it's at. That's the definition of politics."

"We are *Brothers of Hate* --"

"Damn straight, Sergeant. And we've got a job to do --"

Herr Macon requested an immediate tour of the Admin. II area, and he also wanted to inspect the controversial bunkers. There was no one else within the trapezoidally fenced-in area excepting the station anchorman, Wayman Lacer, and his taciturn companion of inferior rank. So Macon believed maximum opportunity presented itself. Sallying along the treacherously icy road in Camrack's jeep, Macon thought that if the Medulla was being stored in any of the large cement bunkers nearby, then pillaging these locked strongholds in one concerted swoop might be the necessary imperative for a terrorist takeover. Once achieved, Der Feuer bargaining power would improve tremendously, and the little world wars now playing throughout the globe would stop. If only to let the Last War begin ...

It was too miserably cold now to be out doing anything remotely resembling an inspection, but one positive factor was that the perimeter fenceline of Admin. II was well-lit. Macon stood shivering in the powder glare of the jeep headlights as he examined one of the bunker doors. He held the rusted padlock in a gloved hand, and noticed the aluminum strip seal, with its embossed numbers, attached for the prevention of opening any bunker door undetected. But could he devise a method whereby a bunker could be entered without breaking its seal?

This problem occupied Macon as he returned to the jeep and told Camrack to drive on. It might prove a difficult problem to solve, but things were going so well that Macon believed a functional solution could be discovered. Already he'd made significant progress in shorter time than he once believed possible.

A complete tour of Admin. II's winding, sometimes convoluted roads took about thirty minutes. It was a large, fenced-in area within an even larger one. Now and then along the fenceline an elevated, tree-housed guard outpost was forlornly visible. Unoccupied at the moment, in emergency periods Military Policemen would be posted there to "hump the area," and freeze indefinitely.

No wonder they go mad, Macon mused. Everywhere in this arboreal spread was the incessant electrical buzz of fence lighting, the only sound besides a jeep engine.

"That's enough for tonight, Camrack. It's too goddamn dark and cold to see anything. I'll come back during the day sometime to see the rest of this godawful Mag Zone."

They both laughed. If Lacer's hypothesis about an underground munitions facility was correct, could it possibly be somewhere in the near subterranean vicinity? The real Mission was just beginning.

30.

Once in the Forbrau *bahnhof* -- having arrived on another perfectly on-time train -- T.K. stopped at a nearby shop and stood idly for a few moments, window-gazing. There were souvenirs in the shop windows: toys, postcards, German steins, hand-carved briars, and assorted knick-knacks. In the white glare of late morning he stood appraising these items, as if hypnotized, transfixed, his breath panting out vapors that hung in the air like a VW's exhaust. These souvenirs struck a resonant chord of meaning within him, as iconic artifacts of a strange and special significance would. T.K. wanted something -- needed something right then to hang onto as a lucky charm.

In the far corner of this magical window T.K. spotted a small and furry stuffed animal, something like a panda bear. It excited him. Fortunately the shop was just opening, and young Keller went inside to further examine the novelty at close range. A wizened shopkeeper fished the panda out for inspection, and warily fluffed up the dark fur with an agitated and gnarled forefinger. Immediately T.K. swooned from the panda's cuteness and bright craftsmanship. He automatically produced several marks for the rather disapproving shopkeeper, who slowly and without comment added the amount to his till.

On a T.V. in the store a live broadcast from *Digital Control* featured the talking head of U.S. President Richard M. Noxson, his face sweating crook-like and darkened by a perennial five o'clock shadow, reading a prepared address from the White House declaiming the recent terrorist kidnapping of prominent Americans like Tomasi -- but T.K. was blissfully unconcerned, even when the President mentioned the ensuing grave actions to be instituted in bringing the terrorists to a swift and terrible justice.

T.K. proceeded back to the street, immeasurably lightened, in possession of more than just a furry stuffed doll with black button-eyes and sewn on zipper mouth. It was like a secret joy all the bustling and insensitive citizens around him knew nothing about, mired as they were in a black void of modern ignorance. The little bear

T.K. slipped inside his coat pocket was marvelous indeed. Casually his ungloved fingers stroked the fur as he walked the streets nearby the Depot, which was at the crest of the elevated town district resembling a forbidding, castle fortress.

T.K. knew the best time to enter the Depot was late afternoon, after all the workers from outside the base quit for the day and left. He had all the necessary papers needed for getting inside. He was even expected by his contact, though his appearance on this dismally gray day would undoubtedly surprise. So T.K. Keller preferred to enter from somewhere besides the Main Gate. In the interests of testing current security strength, he rather preferred to sneak in if possible, and wanted to try coming in from the Mag Zone.

T.K. dawdled outside Depot for awhile, defrosting in a *gasthaus* over a pitcher of beer, thinking over his modus operandi while the battered juke box spewed out the aural static of a new Rock band sounding like a long-ago favorite, Yabba Dabba. (*English!* The English bands were still best.) The Pils was strong and bitter. The more T.K. thought and drank, watching the cozy brown colors melt into sameness around him, the more he figured it might be less dangerous entering through the Main Gate. Either way the paranoia was growing upon him, despite the months he'd been away.

All things considered, with his current disguise of beard and lengthy hair, the man using the alias of T.K. Keller was still a deserter, and would be put on ice indefinitely if discovered.

The inevitable was at hand. Inescapably, for sure, and this risk was a dire something T.K. had always managed to avoid before.

Now he couldn't, could he?

It was a dream he was walking into: an oneiric mystery conceived long ago, perhaps, in the Pils-drenched mind of Old Smoky Joe, the ancient Polish Labor soldier who drifted in senile fashion around the Depot. Victims of other wars, leaning unsteadily on his wooden and gnarled black cane, Old Smoky Joe was a Forbrau prisoner who never left the Depot, and despite his advancing age refused to die. Joe would always be around, Keller knew as he passed the Main Gate and showed his papers to the surly guard. T.K. had decided to forego the P.M.O. for a Snack Bar visit first.

> *Old Smoky Joe,*
> *Don't you know?*
> *God's in Heaven*
> *& He's Not a Foe.*

T.K. felt his confidence returning, knowing he wouldn't be recognized by any of his old platoon members, because – thanks to his twenty-five month absence – all the Enlisted Men had probably rotated back to The World, and the Lifers who re-upped undoubtedly requested new duty sites. It was a comforting thought, this extensive turnover, and T.K. pondered it while eating a grilled cheese and slowly gulping Kaffee. His paranoia was timing out; he wasn't such a fool, having nimbly escaped the terrorist whore no doubt told to "work" on him. That something positvie from all this was developing became a welcome certainty.

The Snack Bar hadn't changed much. Nostalgically the well-dressed infiltrator began to graphically recall certain memories of his brief and curtailed tour as an M.P. Being a bona fide deserter was almost fun given the moment's circumstance, and all the glaring negativity of this place and its colossal, inhuman boorishness became temporarily overlooked. The old Snack Bar was always a cheerfully favorite haunt with its recreational juke box, pinball machines, and gaily decorated furnishings in a well-warmed building. Nursing his Kaffee, T.K. sighed as he lit a cigarette and felt more normally at ease than he'd been for several weeks.

Business, man, business. Now he was waking up and getting a hold on things again. Checking things out would soon be in order. The Snack Bar wasn't too crowded at this hour, and malingering G.I.s were scattered about conversing loudly above the omnipresent background of popular music. A crumpled *Stars and Stripes* left on the table had a cover story about Tomasi's kidnapping, and T.K. read it with more interest than he'd dreamed possible.

Sitting there, T.K. wondered if his euphoria wasn't a debasement, since he felt guilty about deserving it. Still he went through more rounds of coffee and cigarettes, envisioning his lifetime as becoming one long break.

This snack bar had a special significance for him. No, it hadn't changed much, and the fruity Rad women working the counter resembled maternal simulacra he remembered during his infamous, brief, better forgotten M.P. days. He felt superior to these women now, those fat potato-shaped sluts with unshaved legs, and yeasty aromas emanating from their armpits. The Dogs of Forbrau.

Time became garbled in this functional, aluminum-sided hall where T.K. came so many times before. Stoned out of his mind, he and the boys would assuage their smoke-thick throats with soft drinks during the inevitable, bittersweet coming-down period. Always they listened to Rock music on the corner digital juke and chainsmoked through controversial lulls punctuated by paranoiac laughter.

T.K. wished that time would be stilled; he became disappointed when it began moving in its temporal context once again. It was a profound loss for him, rife with that sorrow some called a religious understanding. Time, forever garbled those days, made it difficult for the deserter to recall whether it was the past or present he was in. But the eyes of a few leery G.I.s sizing up his unusual appearance, so theatrically sordid, could not deter the unique course of our time traveler, who catapulted through a distorted consciousness more unruly with each second. So the events of past, present, and future formed an interweaving network of ambivalent disorientation.

And weeks from that moment of hypersensitivity, T.K. Keller would yet again be sitting in this snack bar. He'd recall with greater vividness episodes of the recent past which had so marked current events and him. As if sentenced to absolve himself of the original curses afflicting him in this purgatory of tuna fish-on-rye-to-go, despite the human prejudices around him that made such absolution difficult.

He would remember meeting his contact, Sp/4 Heinsohn, in this misbegotten snack bar, and how breathlessly he'd been informed of prevailing urgent matters and company policies. And in turn, cautiously at first, T.K. would tell his contact, in rather general but titillating fashion, that things were now in some catalytic flux which would set the Depot -- and its fascist leaders -- on a new reamed rear. "Bust this ordnance farm into loose-flying ends, mister. Upset the fruit factory --"

"Yeah?"

"You'd better believe it, my man. Sure as I was once Sp/4 Gracinauto. Sure as I'm too deep into details, but we gotta get on with this A.S.A.P., okay?" Whispering hoarsely, T.K. leaned forward to address his listener more insistently. "The bunkers. We're going to get into them. My accomplice and I (and you too, man) will do this, hopefully before too many days and nights pass. Because my colleagues and I are part of something that's making front page news right now, Hein. It's gathering momentum now and will be exploited internationally to the hilt, if possible. If things work out right, we can put the scalding bits & pieces together before this puzzle gets too big for everybody concerned, and hits the old nuclear bull's eye for an old fashioned blow out."

Keller stopped to lubricate throat and gums with some tepid Coke, then resumed his head shaking.

"I don't know. Listen to me, man. The Bums are trying to develop something really hot on this Depot. Something for the latest war games. And some anti-fascist Germans want to steal it for posterity. If there is any --"

T.K. Keller stopped, looking pained and even frightened, unwilling to alienate his listener further.

"This place ain't cool, Grac, so watch it"

"Well?"

"There are plenty of nearly de facto defectors in the company I know you can count on, if you get the ball rolling. Look for Lacer. But you better hit all the pins, 'cause these dudes are in jail enough already. When you're ready, tell me who your boss man is. Or have him meet me at the bowling alley, which is cooler then here."

T.K. marveled at the ferret-eyed Heinsohn, with his taboo mustache and goatee. Things in the old M.P. company were probably in more disarray than ever. Keller toasted that fact with another sip of cola. Checking his watch (and imagining a reciprocal coordinate with Macon's activities down to the second), T.K. was astonished at how things were proceeding -- including his own now determined, scrupulously business-like behavior.

Keller had awoke in the snack bar, despite the fact he'd entered it less than positive. He was doing now what Raul Macon made clear must be done, sooner or later. Only now it was sooner, and screw the fact that he'd shucked the portentous direction of that whorish German counterpart, wherever her bodily sorrows were. He was doing this not for the kid within him attempting a breakout, but for Lelica's little gem of a dude, Mik, wherever he was then.

Thanks to Heinsohn covering for him, T.K. Keller was able to get around the Depot again nearly unmolested. He was able to rediscover old sites and encounter new ones. The location of each and every geographical detail was filed in his map-mind. He frankly didn't know where it came from, except why not attribute it to this enchanted hall-of-hallucinogens, The Snack Bar? That's what revisiting an old haunt could do for restoring one's willpower and direction.

For an instant he was back in the past, then again in the present: even in both simultaneously, thanks to the digital air-warp ongoing around him, so that T.K. became even more immobilized and locked into his predicament without consciously knowing it. He finished his coffee, a young M.P. in rumpled fatigues dreaming of going A.W.O.L., and ambled slowly out into the gray cold winter morning, when the very sky is blanched by its white blanket of space, a snow curtain no one can peer through to the other side.

He ambled down Waker Road, this Specialist Fourth Class Gracinauto, on his way to the company barracks where he would pull another day's company detail. It would prove a horrifying, numb experience of haphazard clean-up, where more of a mess would sometimes be made than cleaned away. Cursing, his fatigue cap pulled down, Gracinauto The Greasy One wondered how to extricate himself from this environment. With precise, photographic memorizing, he knew everything and everyone on Forbrau. The months in this stir-time only strengthened his detailed knowledge.

This was Gracinauto, who dreamed his alter-ego "T.K. Keller" into being on such walks into the future, or when meditating on guard duty in the Mag Zone, where he sat uncomfortably in some kerosene-heated wooden shack, graffiti-filled and gouged by abuse and decay ... Schizophrenic Gracinauto, stuck between extremes in a company of comical fuck-ups trying to escape time via alcohol, sex, and ever-present pharmaceuticals of every time, costing too many marks.

Gracinauto lived for his tomorrow the way some live in a season of yesterdays.

Now he must keep that surname a secret, one of many permeating the Forbrau environ amid the protoplasmic airs. A secret re-birth to guard. Hurriedly, possessed hopefully of redeeming purpose and new direction, Keller finished his cola and left the Snack Bar he judged hadn't changed during his dreaming absence. He was about to try the miraculously unthinkable, but must wait to after dusk to attempt it. When everyone of commanding significance left the Depot, then and only then would Keller venture a visit to his old barracks, home of the 76th M.P. Company.

He'd have to fuel his strength meanwhile, and not revert too far into the wraith of his former, ever-mocking self: that other reality.

31.

Around 5 p.m. each weekday -- once Retreat sounded futilely via a faulty digital tape, broadcast over the loudspeakers in the Admin. Area -- a majority of Forbrau's military personnel, having finished another day, would devolve quietly from official sorts to more personal ones. Over at the rickety 76th Military Police barracks (more fit for demolition than renovation), things would especially loosen up.

Perennial malcontent Bernie Beeschaum, for instance, would usually return to his upstairs Room 6 looking like an extra portraying some disaster movie victim. B.B.'s young but hoary appearance gave new but forgettable insight into the adjective usage of ugliness. Bernie's bestial likeness and behavior had a certain clownish cuteness, made palatable by his oversized black-rimmed glasses.

B.B. was extremely myopic to the point where he crushed out cigarettes on people's underwear. His putty face was highlighted by mini-craters of acne. In unregenerate bad humor, his crass witticisms and obscene remarks alternately baffled or entertained his low-life roommates, once regarded by the Army as the most elite M.P.s in the world and especially selected for their vital roles at the secretive Forbrau Depot.

Bernie Beez usually collapsed on the springs of his unmade bunk following a hard day's screwing off on company detail. He'd rack out for a fitful while until rudely awakened by some noisy interloper, usually a loud-mouthed soul brother laughing at a friend's jive. Then Bernie Beeschaum would painfully awaken from an unbelievably contorted posture, put his horn-rims on while distastefully licking dry lips, and check his watch. Mumbling some incoherent obscenity, he'd look around while slowly getting his bearings, irked to be roused yet also glad he hadn't slept the evening away past chow time and conversational hours of bullshit.

"Shoot, my fuckin' balls hurt," Bernie would say -- to no one in particular -- while lighting up a Winston and scratching himself, still idly in his reclining posture. Arm behind fatigue-capped head, one leg propped above the L-shaped other, he'd listen attentively to the soul brothers jiving invisibly behind the large row of wall-lockers dividing the room. A very popular young black -- Sugar Brown Bull -- bunked back there, and was perennially visited by other brothers from around Depot. They wanted to transact a hemp deal with the ever mellow Sugar, who couldn't send these visitors away without smoking a prime bowl of Euro-hemp, until it sounded strange behind those lockers.

Beez would keep listening, chuckling occasionally if some remark tickled him, and itched to contribute a "You know it" or "Ain't that the fuckin' truth, Bull?" He knew it was unseemly, because the brothers were best left alone while they sauntered in and out of Room 6, passing all night before Beez's slightly incredulous eyes.

Sometimes Sugar Bull (wearing a new suit and looking *b-a-ad*) would make a grand entrance, and sashay before Bernie while humming a recent soul rap ditty, looking quite The Man indeed. When he'd return from behind the locker an hour later, however, the slow exit took a more terpsichorean form, with great gyrations of arms, legs, and torso grinding to the electrified cadence. Any visitor accompanying Sugar Brown Bull would snap his fingers significantly upon passing Beeschaum's bunk, perhaps allowing a cutting remark as he did so.

In no way would a disinterested observer of these young men ever believe that the world was at a crisis state of immense proportions at the moment.

In fact, the Beez enjoyed more than ever the attention of any living creature -- human, animal, or vegetable. So ambling as he did past the second-story bay windows, in the hallway on his way to the latrine downstairs, Beez would sometimes pause to lean over the sill and trade insults with anyone lurking below.

On this particular early evening, Beeschaum spotted -- while yawning extravagantly -- the unusual form of a bearded civilian stranger coming up the Company walkway. Beez had to mutter "Jesus F. Chrise" despite himself. The strange civilian looked as if he'd went A.W.O.L. from a tent show of traveling gypsies, and appeared to be foreign yet American at the same time. A goddamn Provo-huppie was walking into the place, and Beeschaum wondered vaguely if the interloper were carrying a bomb.

Referring to his scourge of a Platoon Sergeant, Bernie said to himself, "If Big Dic Walden saw this he'd throw a fit. Holy Shit."

The interloper happened to look up at Beeschaum upon reaching the 1st Platoon entrance, his bespectacled mask-face unchanged by the sight of the scrawny figure staring back down through the encroaching twilight.

"You lookin' for somebody?" Beeschaum asked, shyly and hesitantly, sounding as deferential as a strong New Jersey accented voice could manage.

The civilian stranger stood there and appeared cold in the failing light. He stood as still as the Platoon's two wooden doors, which were formidably large with frosted windows. Slowly he turned, retracing his heavy steps back towards the Orderly Room. For a second, walking there, Keller became Specialist 4th Class Gracinauto again on his way to pull C.Q. duty for another long, misbegotten night. Spectrally fey humours revived themselves in the gathering mist, recharged from unseen atmospheric forces above. A myriad of snow-flecked butterfly wings fell endlessly in disconnected, scattered abandon. His fatigues were in need of laundering, his crease-cracked boots, beyond spit-shining, in need of extensive repair (or outright junking). The C.Q. of his dreams he was, immured in some private kingdom impossible to escape, where his not fine madness was tolerated – even nurtured.

Gracinauto's duty was considerably better than that of fresh Kruits like Beeschaum, who were forever condemned to menial clean-up tasks around the barracks or Platoon area; or, worst of all, dreaded Motor Pool duty where a testy Staff Sergeant Walden presided with no-nonsense exactitude. The jeeps, three-quarter ton trucks, and other assorted vehicles were the pride and mainstay of this Military Police Company. Pulling preventive maintenance became, under Walden's direction, more religion than ritual. This religious observance involved meticulous detail, requiring a conscientious application resulting in long hours of laborious attention, sometimes to the same nut or bolt. A part was constantly oiled – re-oiled – fidgeted with, taken apart, etc. S/Sgt. Walden, known as Big Dic to the men, wanted to see "assholes and elbows" even if no real work was needed except an endless repetition.

So pulling C.Q. was good duty because supervising Bums such as Walden weren't around. They fled the Depot for their wives and German apartments at Retreat's first sound. Yes, always Greaseball Gracinauto was in ethereal, hemp-induced splendor. The sights and sounds of all that mercilessly plagued him receded inevitably before this euphoric wave he struggled, at times paranoiacally, to control ... Yes, so many disagreeable sights and sounds were stamped into his impressionable consciousness. It took months of being abandoned in Forbrau's feudal conclave of barbed wire and concrete, until the last vestiges of soul – of worldly, civilian amenities – disappeared as leaves will with winter's onrush.

Gracinauto knew the Forbrau Depot with the same thoroughness he knew his gonads, more or less. He expanded on such knowledge daily. He patrolled roads on Magazine Patrol so frequently, and repetitiously, that he sometimes forged his own impromptu passageways, ripping through brush and tree limbs. Dirt and paved roads alike were raced over – sometimes dangerously, since their condition was poor due to erosive weather, or contained parked trailers with crates of exotic explosives and/or missile heads. Sp/4 Gracinauto became a skilled, veteran navigator of these roughways his lesser peers feared to explore. He committed each trail to the mind-map existing, sometimes to scale, inside his well-fed head ...

It would be hard to miss the Depot's sites even due to blindness, thought Gracinauto. Its chief macadam artery was mile-long Waker Road, an unbroken horizontal straightness extending from the Main Gate all the way to Gate 13, entrance to the Mag Zone. Traversing this uninterrupted roadway, one encountered the P.X., the Polish Labor Army barracks, the Ordnance and 76th M.P. barracks – along with Depot Headquarters building, the Motor Pool, and the Fire House, all roughly in sequential order.

Fabled Waker Road bisected the heart of the Admin. Area, but assumed a different perspective beyond Gate 13. Once into the Mag Zone, Waker began to peter out into lesser, more curvilinear and thinner roadways – paved and unpaved. These intersected crossroads led, to a neophyte eye, into confusing vastnesses of densely forbidding forest (made even stranger by the industrial lab dwellings, like forlorn outposts from other planets, encountered along the way).

At times, when Gracinauto whipped his exhaust-sputtering, engine-whining jeep back into the Company Area – having raced pell-mell and non-stop from the bewitching M.Z. – he would experience something like jet lag, or a feeling of having returned from the eternally unusual to the temporally mundane. It was inexplicable; sometime mildly frightening, baffling, and unknowable. What was it about such a passage that he would never really understand, or begin to.

To Gracinauto the Company barracks were *Home*. Once in their vicinity, despite any possible unpleasantness, one felt glad to be on safe and familiar terrain again. Around 5 p.m., after a long duty day of Company Detail (in which S/Sgt. Walden supervised an ongoing, if vain, G.I. Party of his Platoon Area: scrubbing floors, waxing and buffing latrine tile, painting walls greener, patching cracked plaster), the barracks would slowly deteriorate again into outright sloppiness and sloth. The occupants reverted to non-military ways impossible to eradicate, apparently, from the O.D. system.

Yes, all hell broke loose. Dirt was tracked in; floors were despoiled by ashes, liquor spills, various bottles, etc.; latrines were flooded by careless users, committing downright vandalism. Spoiled too: Orderly Rooms. They acquired vast amounts of junk dumped from lockers no longer inspected by the C.O., doubtless appalled by what contraband he'd found already. *Home Sweet Home ...*

Gracinauto thought, *The enemy within gnawing at its own innards.* A highly classified sector degenerating – thanks to the Army's ingenuity – into a military anomie, at least by night. And by day? The mask of Order, behind which lived hells of corruption. Amid all this Gracinauto had been buffeted, altered, turned around, maligned, abused, you name it. Behavior modification to the worst extreme. The man needed dope just to get straight. In a topsy-turvy world forever bent on destroying its own, there was nothing but a space lacking a common gravity to wade through, before finding bearings.

Yet the barracks were sanctuary, despite their unremitting drabness. Of course the men abused the place constantly with cigarette burns and general indulgences. "Better wear your boots down in the latrine," Bernie Beeschaum would advise, "the Wetback's down there jackin' off ..." Plus there was that manpower called *The*

Haters dedicated to the ongoing cause of destroying Government Property. Such property being sacrosanct in the fiery eyes of Big Dic Walden did little to change The Haters' attitude. Each week saw a new Hater being born via some ritual of destructiveness.

Every time a buffer was thrown out the second-story bay windows, a Hater was christened. When a jeep was deliberately or "accidentally" totaled, a Hater was behind it. Sabotage, vandalism, acts of indecent exposure and other unmentionable accidents could only be traced to fervent Haters.

Mysterious Sgt. Lacer was one. Gracinauto, a latent Hater who'd later surface full-blown. Bernie "the Beez" Beeschaum would become one, on and off, in born again fashion – soon enough.

The Forbrau woods were full of Haters, some undeclared or considering; others procrastinating, serving their time with prisoners' stolidness, awaiting that unbelievable day when they'd become Short-Timers about to leave what Beeschaum called the Whore's Ass of Europe. Hate existed, if fitfully, like another recurrent vapor in an atmosphere heavy with such spirit leavings ...

Ectoplasm. Propoplasm. All of it plasm *for Hate,* and it seeped into the very barracks walls with other rot. So Gracinauto might have been studying the pros and cons of such malignancy – like a college student might mull over some philosophical conundrum – and banish the vaporous doubts besetting him, to give definite purpose and direction to his actions.

Gracinauto had lost the faith of his Catholic upbringing while serving in the war-hungry Army, and needed something comparable in spiritual strength as replacement. Where and how to get it was the question nagging him perennially, as "Shakespeare's Dane" was haunted. It wasn't long before Gracinauto was dubbed *Stoner* in recognition of his long meditations, which some Platoon members believed stemmed from heavy hemp-taking.

There was animism in everything the paranoiac young Specialist saw in this unique environment. The woods in the Mag Zone were alive with woodland spirits – both good and evil – all struggling with the legacy of horror the terrain was heir to since World Wars II & III. Sprites, demons, doppelgangers of Neo-Nazi dead inhabited Gracinauto's vision of the execrable wasteland known as Forbrau, where bizarre scientific and military technological experiments were rumored taking place – constrantly – beyond Gate 13, in the almost Bauhaus-styled metal and/or plastic sophisticated bunkers the M.P.s weren't allowed inside of. Somewhere therein white-coated Army technocrats buggered Hitler's spirit, believed Gracinauto. How else explain the unnerving pall overhanging the place?

(Kress Mupreen of the terrorist Puma Gang would later attest to it, lost in a game of betrayal and counter-betrayal, becoming against his will a double agent after being discovered, with his Genome Reconstructive Cylinder at Christina Alpreece's The Quarter, by the same C.I.A. team tracking Raul Macon ... taken to a place he had no knowledge of, except it was in an underground array of hemetic labs and high-tech digital centers somewhere outside of Holland, in a classified scientific experimental center he knew had to be maintained by the U.S Government ... wherein he'd be questioned endlessly about his coming in possession of the Cylinder in the first place, meet the eyeball-bulging Project Director himself, Herr Freunderstein of the benign mannerisms, who invited him to watch how the genetic components housed in Kress' stolen Cylinder would re-construct the bodily form of the C.I.A. agent entrapped within it ...until Kress pleaded for his life, willing to divulge all he knew about the Dutch and German terrorists who once absolutely trusted him ...

"Behold the cloning of your immortal soul to an entirely different body!" Herr Freunderstein smiled back, laying his bestially clawed hands on Kress' naked back ...)

Gracinauto sensed all the strange things happening beneath and above him, stalling for a time he knew might exist in a disheveled warp only the government could control the way machines are driven forward or back. He knew every Platoon face and could see the truth in each, like some Italian gypsy who could morph his identities and personalities, being the ultimate psychic reader of faces and souls. Fates good and bad converged upon his sense with a rain of atomic-ray-like vibrations, and at times the intensity was too much for him like the new drugs given to him. Each day he lost more weight, becoming ultra-thin like the other Company Heads. He knew what constituted his health was in bad shape and getting worse. Yet he smoked and drank all the more, like the others did, because the self-destructive price of existing in Forbrau demanded it.

Naturally Gracinauto fantasized escaping it all, and at times worked on perfecting the details of that civilian personality he'd become: *Mr. T.K. Keller,* poet-pretender, who would also walk into this Company Area – with its parking lot, Supply and Arms Rooms, trim hedges hiding ghouls, and partitioned grounds which became lawns in spring – one more time.

Everything now was déjà vu – even the memory of it ...

So shambling along the sidewalk towards the Orderly Room, T.K. Keller got the shock of his life.

In the doorway near the stairs leading to the Day Room was the little New York Puerto Rican, Juan Ortiz, standing by the grated Arms Room window. Ortiz! The greatest hemp-eater in Platoon history – still in Forbrau. Ortiz the O.D. Kid, the same unique individual Keller talked and dealt with so many times before. In mincing fashion Ortiz danced there, trying with heavy accents and high-pitched singsong to jive the disbelieving clerk behind the window. When Ortiz glanced dully at him, Keller's stomach went upside-down for an instant.

I'm dreaming things past & future, Keller knew, *but which is which?*

Keller thanked God as the fraily diminutive Puerto Rican looked away, too fucked-up perhaps to recognize anyone or anything. And finding it difficult to sign-out a .45, undoubtedly.

Ortiz had once – in a drunken rage, having been fleeced at the N.C.O. Club one night by a waitress professing love for him – checked out a weapon by claiming he was on the midnight shift, but instead used it to terrorize and nearly shoot the woman who wronged him. He was busted to P.F.C. and on S/Sgt. Walden's shitlist indefinitely. Like his comrades who shared a similar lifestyle, somehow Ortiz was up to his old tricks again, despite all the disciplinary tactics imaginable. Despite how all the commanding Bums had tried to burn and hang the little guy, Ortiz survived within the system ambivalently tolerating him, as a ship does barnacles clinging to it.

Anxiously T.K. scurried on, wondering how many other misfit holdovers from his Gracinauto-days existed. It was possible he could be detected that very night, his mission dismally thwarted before it began. The thought terrified him. He had Lelica and Little Mik to think about. He was their last hope, and couldn't afford to fail.

Only one man in the Company should know who Keller was, and that one man T.K. expected to confront shortly -- or at least before the night was out.

Doubts nonetheless overtook Keller as he entered the Orderly Room. By "escaping" the German liaison-prostitute when he had, T.K. failed to wait for proper notification from "Herr M." Macon. He was in effect jumping the gun and acting on his own, simply because his fear and distrust of the German terrorists were so great. Still, T.K. was doing what Macon said must be done inevitably -- when the word was given, via the whore's mouth. Might not T.K.'s overweening initiative be just what was needed? For all anyone knew, Macon was incommunicado due to some error which would only eat up irretrievable time they couldn't afford to lose from the menu. Trumpets blaring heroic strains implored T.K. to *Seize the Hour!* as he mounted the steps to his long-awaited destination.

"Well ...?"

Bernie Beeschaum was there, talking on the phone and smoking sloppily as he sat on the First Sergeant's large desk. "No shit ...?" Some of his ashes fell on the desk's surface, coating randomly stacked but official-looking papers. "Well, then where the hell is he, for Christ's sweet sakes? We got somebody off Depot in here, a goddamned civilian named *Mr.* Tees Keller. I ain't shittin', you goddamn Bum ..."

It was probably Desk Sergeant Camrack that the Beez was talking so candidly to, Keller decided. It had been a long day's wait for T.K., most of it spent wandering about the Admin. Area as inconspicuously as a Rasputin-looking clone could. He spent time in the bowling alley, explaining he was a tourist visiting a relative on Depot. He augmented this story somewhat in the N.C.O. Club, where he killed enough time drinking mixed drinks and half-expecting to find Herr Macon, who was reputed now to work there -- but no such luck. The rest of the afternoon was divided between the P.X. and the nearby "Polack Zoo," a small fenced-in menagerie of common, unattractive fowl maintained with a rather zealous pride by the Polish Labor Army.

Fortified by the liquor awhirl within him, T.K. was mesmerized by the Zoo scene before him. Ducks, geese, an occasional agitated chicken were located in this small penned sector nearby the railroad tracks with Gate 16 and its Brass Yard. The fowl paraded before T.K.'s straining eyes, evoking a poignant feeling in the lone, hunched-over viewer. There was a fairy-tale atmosphere about it all, something Keller had never noticed when stationed at the Depot. As he watched, a solitary peacock suddenly came into view from behind a crate. The bird looked radiantly beautiful with its variegated feathers at attention, and T.K. felt -- despite his surprise -- quite delivered. A frigging Peacock! Queen of the mundane lot, diamond in the rough, it was something T.K. felt was a beneficial talisman regarding his mission.

He watched -- for how long? -- eyes agleam, and almost watery.

The reverie was rudely dissipated by the mad onrush of vehicles exiting in a torrent behind Keller. The workday was ending, and the workers were beginning their habitual exodus through the Main Gate and off Depot. An awesome sight to witness indeed, T.K. thought he'd seen it many times before as the Main Gate guard. Though nearly run-over, Keller made his way towards the P.M.O., waving at the guard standing dead-center at the crossroads. Ineffectively the M.P. kept trying to direct the traffic steadfastly ignoring his signals.

It took some gumption on T.K.'s part to actually enter the "hallowed" P.M.O. again, but he knew most of the Headquarters officers and non-coms were already gone and on their way off Depot, vanishing in minutes like the other civilian and military personnel had. He'd entered this building so many times before as a working M.P. it seemed only fitting, once inside, that nothing had been significantly altered or tampered with beyond a much needed paint job.

Alone with Desk Sergeant Camrack in the P.M.O. thereafter, T.K. tried to conceal sweltering emotions as he stood gazing at the old place again. Chairs, tables, and bulletin boards had been relocated, but other than that -- sameness. The same old P.M.O., drab and bureaucratic as ever. The same giant platform desk so many Desk Sergeants had occupied before this current one, now staring benignly down at T.K. from all that abutment of brown, walnut-stained wood with its familiar heraldic M.P. shield. The visitor knew it only too well.

T.K. summarily explained his business, showing papers, and found Camrack only too amenable about the matter. The Desk Sergeant insisted on calling the 76th M.P. Company and notifying T.K.'s "cousin" about the situation, as soon as he could be reached.

"Beeschaum's the C.Q. runner tonight," Camrack said. "You can't miss him. Just proceed to the Orderly Room. Do you know the way? Halfway down Waker Road. On your left. I'd get the Patrol Super to give you a lift, but he's at Landstuhl right now ..."

So T.K. was allowed to pass readily enough, despite the qualms he felt activating guilty signals across his face. What luck! The exquisite papers did their deed. The Desk Sergeant was an upstanding American young man, o sons and daughters of ancient revolutions, and that's how Keller found himself back in the dreaming past-present state, as well as the Company Orderly Room, a perennial station in hell, with Bernie Beeschaum ...

T.K. listened to that disheveled Specialist still arguing on the phone before hanging it up with slamming abruptness.

"Don't know where the hell your cousin is, Mister, but he's supposed to show up. Sit down, he'll be along. I gotta go check on my laundry. If you need me, I'm in Room 6, 1st Platoon, upstairs." He extended his hand.

"Bernie Beeschaum ..."

"Thanks, Bernie," T.K. said.

Someone else entered the room then, saying: "In this Army they kill you if you're a hero and they kill you if you're a coward. You have to be a little of both to survive." It was the finally arriving C.Q., a young buck sergeant whose name tag read "Lacer."

"The ring of prophecy in those words," T.K. replied. "A 'big' thought too, man. I love that, speaking as a civilian who dreamed thoughts here, and big ones too, like polymorphous perversities."

"Yeah? A flaming intellectual, then. Not to be confused with one of our resident geniuses -- Bernie Beeschaum -- who you probably ran into."

"One guru of the flesh and senses. I've never seen anyone so ..."

"Unabashedly something-or-other?"

"Sure. Never such unabashed grossness, without a shade of self-consciousness. The young man even blew his nose like a farmer not long ago, using his thumb."

Lacer was sitting with his feet up on the First Shirt's desk, lighting a cigarette. "That goddamn pig. *Hicks*. I mean we're talking some back-hills boys in this Platoon, no shit ... Is it any wonder Forbrau's biting The Big One?"

"I'm talking to a live intellect here."

"Goddamn right. A lively mind, at any rate. The Army's got your body -- nothing can change that fact. But getting your mind is another story. Know what I mean?"

T.K. Keller shrugged, lighting his cigar off the Sarge's Marlboro. "Be cool, *everybody* be cool. That was the line when I was here, mind and body both practically grossed out. But then nothing's ever been the same since those Iraqui terrorists blew up Hawaii with their homemade nuke, back way back when, right?"

"No shit? Hey, whom I talkin' to here besides a dude who looks like a session player from a Rock and Roll band. Not who the hell I think it is."

T.K. nearly winked. "In the flesh, man. Code name fuckin'" -- here Keller whispered -- "*Greaseball!* I sat right in that chair, months before you got transferred here. Shaky First Shirt of a bastard letter-of-reprimanded my ass to Death here."

"You're the Real McCoy," Lacer said, consulting a pocket notebook amid swirls of thickening smoke. "About goddamn time! I'm your cuz tonight, instead of Heinsohn."

"Wow, and I thought I was obsolete."

"No way. Talked to your honcho Herr M. just the other night. Mag Zone ..."

"Where-the-hell is he?"

"Wouldn't everybody on both sides of his Depot like to know. He's a disappearing act, off and on. I know I didn't hallucinate him. I've been straight for three days now. There's no Ecstasy on Depot ... You got any? They're cracking down here. No Librium lollipops."

"I'm clean, though my head's a buzz. I've had too much on my mind lately." Keller paused, allowing himself to reveal -- at the buck sergeant's prompting -- a tiredness he would ordinarily have suppressed. "I'm dead on my feet."

"Tonight I don't sleep, but I don't even when I can. I've waited for this! There's a lot of plastic karma to settle here. We're gonna screw a few Bums for a change. We're gonna screw the Army, and to hell with thinking twice."

"Spoken like a fire-eating radical."

"Damn straight. And I read the Gita. That radical enough? ... This Depot loses even if we fail, man. Then it's total Teutonic conflagration, with blasted bunkers. The Bums started all this, Uncle Sambo screwed up the earth's ecological equilibrium with his missiles, satellites, and ozone incineration. Why not exact the next logical step and make this planet an abyss? The only hope is to relocate the species to other hospitable planets, my friend, and leave this one to devolution. That's the grand plan. Whether the U.S. capitalists or the neo-commies get the benefit of the nod from those unseen powers in space calling the shots ... You know there's more than intelligent alien life when it's controlling the fate of the universe."

"Jesus," T.K. said. "Let's not get carried away, man. Let's not crucify ourselves."

"No religious terms please," the buck sergeant said.

Keller absently began massaging his face. "This is getting surreal, Sarge. I don't think it's just the Euro-drugs causing it. You know the Puma Holland headquarters has gone down following what's been front page headlines. You know Der Feuer has a fat-cat American businessman who's 'condition red' now, named Tomasi, supposedly privy to Noxon's every move. They'll grass him if the bunkers aren't full of Christmas goodies, namely the Medulla Raze. And they're holding a friend of mine's little boy they might get serious with."

"You don't trust these Germans?"

"The Puma is fucked-up. Everybody's fucked-up."

"Don't tell me about it, I only work here."

"And here we are on an early winter's evening talking *classified* business, right? I mean it's surreal. It's like this winter's going to be one long one, care of I wonder who."

"Don't get paranoid. The walls aren't bugged yet. Or at least they better not be. Anyway ... nobody's around at this dead hour. So keep whispering so nobody'll notice. And you sure dressed inconspicuously, didn't you? Beeschaum told me he nearly gagged seeing you."

Keller figuratively embraced the Orderly Room with outstretched hands. "You certainly picked a great spot for a family reunion, long-lost relative."

"Yeah, right." Lacer produced a large key and flipped it to Keller, who watched it fall to the green-tiled floor. "That's the key to my room -- upstairs, number 3, 1st Platoon -- where later we'll rendezvous at a specified time to iron all this out more intimately."

"The excitement is killing me. Just when does Operation Plunder get under way -- ?"

"In two nights, if the honcho has his way. That soon enough for you?"

"Two nights?"

"Don't crap out on us, 'civilian.' "

Keller was startled despite himself. Two nights! Things were rolling for sure, but -- like somebody facing the reality of going to the dentist's for root canal work -- he wondered if they shouldn't think on it awhile. He stood there in his wavering dream remembering this varnished, oak-paneled Orderly Room he'd seen in another lifetime, which was untidy now, but would undergo waxing and buffing before morning. (If Ortiz could be convinced to work again, of course, incoherent as he was at the moment, his squealing and hurt voice still sounding like a trumpet outside.)

"Jesus Christ. Two nights, man? That's *murder.*"

32.

"Beeschaum --!" ... Big Dic Sergeant Walden was speaking: "Do you see that gate shack there? ... Do you see how terrible it, uh, *looks* because grown babies in this Platoon got nothin' better to do then write on the walls?"

"Yeah, Sarge," Beeschaum said haltingly, mop in hand. He pushed back the bridge of his glasses with a forefinger. The Sarge was pissed. Definitely pissed off. The Sarge's voice got higher and scarier the angrier he got. At that moment it resembled an operatic diva's about to either kill or commit suicide over some wrongdoing.

"*Why,* Bees-chaum? Will you tell me that? Will you tell me why some members of this fuckin' Platoon treat Government Property like jack-fuckin'-shit? Will you tell me that?"

"I don't know, Sarge," Beeschaum replied, uneasily fidgeting still with his glasses. He cleared his throat during the ensuing strained silence. Why, indeed, him in this Beetle Bailey routine? Jesus.

Big Dic continued: "I brought you and this work detail all the way out here to this gate because I wanted to show you men what you do to Government Property! This is my goddamn Home, and I do not appreciate people screwin' up my *Home.* I been in this man's Army too long for that. Would you men act this way in your homes back in The World? Like fuckin' hell you would. So why can't you act like that *here?* This Government Property is your Home too, why not treat it like that instead of a goddamn shithole?"

His tirade over, Platoon Sgt. Walden stood like an ebony tree trunk scarred by life's difficulties, still unbowed though some branches were missing. Six foot five inches of angry Southern Black, age thirty years, you'd swear he'd been a Lifer for most of them. Literally born in a king-sized footlocker, Wayman Lacer would say sarcastically about his boss, who he respected and hated equally.

Most members in the 1st Platoon felt this way about the venerable Big Dic: they both feared and loathed him, but were big enough to forgive him for being Olive Drab flotsam. The Army was indeed his home -- his *only* Home -- while they at least had better homes and better careers to resume. Nonetheless they respected him for being a capable and good soldier they would follow into combat, wherever the current wars moved to.

"Beeschaum! I want you to come with me and have a look at the inside of this gate shack."

"Okay, Sarge."

Beeschaum looked at his three helpers, who were also holding cleaning tools, ready an hour ago to begin scouring. Dutifully all four of the E.M. trooped behind S/Sgt. Walden as he slowly, deliberately, made his significant way into ramshackle Gate 26, which was located (or lost) in a forlorn section of the Mag Zone's least-traveled boondocks.

"This gate shack looks like fuckin' shit, people."

Disgust overtook the stolid, heavy-moving features of S/Sgt. Walden as he stood surveying the interior devastation of Gate 26. The wooden insides looked gutted by a fire bomb: pock-marked and gouged walls overwritten with extra-obscene graffiti, composed by the M.P.s during their long and unbearable guard shifts; cracked window panes ineffectively mended by masking tape; a roof about to cave in; a wrecked kerosene heater which lay crumpled in the corner like a disassembled tin man; and a fire hazardous slat floor, soaked by oil and gasoline, which creaked like the topside of an ancient frigate when walked upon.

"Jesus H. Christ."

Big Dic looked as if he might spit.

"You men get busy now. I want this place cleaned up before lunch. And I don't want you fuckin' around on my time, is that understood? If the First Sergeant saw this he'd have everybody's ass before the Old Man."

Mumbling sullenly, his lips still moving, Walden leaned forward almost grimacing to inspect some of the grease marker graffiti pertaining to himself. SGT. WALDEN SUCKS BIG DICK, one of the scrawled lines said. Others were equally uncomplimentary, to the point where the authors' mental states could definitely be accused of profound instability.

Walden turned away, saying nothing, his face unchanged. He might well have been looking at some rune on an ancient wall; something difficult for mortal man to understand.

"I want this fuckin' shithole cleaned up," the Platoon Sergeant said before leaving.

Of course Beeschaum reacted ambivalently to the Platoon Sergeant's invective, and knew one thing: the shithole had better be cleaned with asses and elbows, and no bullshitting, he told the three-man detail of raw recruits he supervised. The brash young trio of Neumann, Ladd, and Halston -- all P.F.C.s barely a week in

Forbrau -- were a violently unmanageable lot prone to foul-mouthed horseplay. *These Kruits will fit in nicely,* Beeschaum thought, *as soon as they learn who's boss, and which hole the shit flies from.*

Hard Dude Bernie was the designated Company Bad Ass. Weaned on tough New Jersey blocks, it was his job -- "though it sucked" -- to break in difficult personnel to the hard facts of Army life. If they wised-up, as most of them did, then everything was okay, and they'd get a break from any shit details to come. If they didn't wise-up, then they'd literally get their necks broken, and spend the rest of their live-long days visiting Landstuhl Hospital -- where the nurses weren't attentive, and the doctors only badly so. Nice choice, thought Bernie, but Forbrau was no winter resort, and it only distempered G.I.s the longer their duty tour was.

"Better get in there and G.I. that fuckin' shack like the Sarge says," Beeschaum said, lighting his habitual cigarette while coughing and rolling up his sleeves by way of example. "We ain't got all day, and Big Dic'll be back before Retreat."

"Fuck this shit," said disgruntled P.F.C. Timothy Ladd, the oldest and wisest of the Kruits (who were Mid-Western farm boys used to silent obedience), and the only married one ... Nonetheless he picked up his pail and scrub brush, getting down to the nitty gritty facts below knee-level and perhaps dreaming of his lonely wife. As soon as she arrived from Missouri, he'd be living off base with her. A school teacher in civilian life, believe it or not, Ladd joked that "this shack's beyond cleaning, Beeschaum. They ought to tear it down with the rest of this rotten Government Property --"

"Sarge Walden hear you say that and he'd have your fuckin' balls, boy. No shit."

"Oh, sure," Ladd laughed. "Well, then at least he'd have a pair."

There was more work besides the shack to clean up, and Beeschaum had a three-quarter ton truck for the purposes of carrying the men and their equipment to the other sites in the Mag Zone indicated by S/Sgt. Walden. (It would prove a long day, Beeschaum knew, but the shit had come down, and they better get it straight before it hit the fan big time.) So Bernie made sure the three beleaguered men did a good job, one that Big Dic couldn't bitch about. Before long, the three P.F.C.s were grime-laden from tackling the initial shack with their mops and brushes. "We're soppin' wet," said Ladd disgustedly, comparing his dirt-defiled uniform with those of the other workers. "Sweet Chrise, I feel sick already."

"You better believe it," said Halston, whose comment equaled a speech for him.

Bernie even pitched in and did some work, though he didn't have to. It took his mind off things he didn't want to think about. Lately there were many things he didn't want to think about: the rumors about Forbrau and the controversial goings-on in the Mag Zone (were there predominantly nuclear war-heads in the area again?), which Bernie knew was haunted by space spirits, gory-goblins, and what-have-you from other war years. Here men died or suffered on the same ground he relentlessly drove the three-quarter over.

Bernie had yet to see any ghosts, but he knew they existed, yet the place was too spooky for them not to be around. He'd heard strange noises and seen unusual flashes at night, when the woods were densely clay-like amidst skeletal tree limbs. The heart struck a hard tattoo, and any form within eyeshot portended something paranormally interstellar.

Bernie's comrades fueled such legends of fear and hate with their own accounts of disturbing hallowed realms in the damnable Mag Zone, discovering some spirit-plasm which scared them into never humping the area alone again. Some were scared enough to quit the bottle for awhile. *But what the hell,* Bernie told himself, *why get excited about it?* It was all above his head anyway, and as long as it stayed there it wasn't his problem. So he really didn't have to deal with it, unless he was cornered and had no choice.

As Bernie Beeschaum drove the men around from site to site on the shit detail, the gray and cold-darkened day seemed to suck itself and the woods into a holistic rag-blur -- like a charcoal smear might absorb details within a drawing -- and Bernie feared his vision would desert or play tricks on him, a not uncommon occurrence for men in the Area.

Considering what optical hijinks were to come, perhaps Beez was right to weigh his fear. Over him in the high trees a gigantic, lunar-like face with hornrims floated like a Macy's Thanksgiving Day Parade balloon, beneath which the neon words "FREUNDERSTEIN, INC." blinked.

PART V

The Depot Raid

33.

Who was that idiot speeding around in that truck? wondered Gunther Hoffler, cursing to himself while straining his eyes through high-powered binoculars.

Across the paved road outside Gate 25, about 100 yards away, Hoffler and his comrades had been ready since dusk. Secreted behind a tree-infested vantage point, they were dressed like laborers who might well be working for the Forestmeister -- perhaps out to perform some tree surgery, or about to knock off work any minute.

"It will be getting darker soon," Brice Rampoul said, brandishing a truncheon-sized flashlight. Wearing an Air Force jump suit, his eyes were hidden behind opaque, lead-like glasses. "If there are any military personnel around our bunkers, it might ruin everything."

"Then we'll take out any intruders, the same way we de-activated their computerized security alert functions," Hoffler said, lowering his binoculars. The resolve on his face was straightened as one might straighten a slack bedspread. "It's that simple -- but of course we want no firing heard. Discharged rounds might alert other M.P. sentries stationed in the Zone."

Nils Mupreen looked nervously around, because things were getting too serious for him. Yes, he was wondering if they could really get away with it, this commando-like raid they were about to pull in hopefully secret fashion. He'd been impressed by the way Hoffler -- thanks to insider info provided by his new contacts on the munitions base -- had found in Headquarters Building the computer room monitoring security and surveillance cams for the Mag Zone, and how Der Feuer members had de-activated the security functions with remarkable success. Never had Mupreen been a part of anything so daring, which for a moment rendered all his student philosophizing about political violence almost insignificance, even laughable. For now they were about to do something only legitimate guerrilla terrorists did -- things Nils had read mostly about in newspapers, from a distance of great safety and uninvolvement.

Am I scared? Nils asked himself. *Yes, I am scared.* He really despised violence, and to taste -- if gradually -- its full measure was like running into an iron curtain of depravity. One buzzed futilely against it like a brainless insect.

This, after all, was deep into the New West Germany -- where the real terrorists without conscience were. They were distant offspring of Hitler, according to the media. And Hitler's spirit lingered still and could never be exterminated, Hoffler jokingly told all ... Hard-bitten Hoffler was unafraid, almost glamorous to members of his tactical band. They gathered about him, waiting in crouched or prone positions within a thick copse, their weapons aimed and ready. They too were young and hard-bitten, like their dogma-spieling leader, who had a library of Marx and Lenin in head -- and symbolically the guns of revolutionaries in hand.

And T.K. Keller? He was wondering more than ever what the hell he was doing there, dressed like an Israeli commando. (And where the hell was his ever-unbelievable cohort "Herr M." at the moment?) T.K. was mired in this debacle, for the Feuer Bande had picked him up again one night, as he left the Depot after a drinking spree. Yes, he was needed, never mind how Der Feuer knew what he was up to. It was time to receive vital information, and Keller would be worked over if he didn't give. "We'll turn you back over to that nanny of a whore in Saarbrücken if you don't," T.K. was told menacingly.

"Anything but that," Keller said while being plied with coffee in a nearby *gasthaus*. Now, at least, he had accomplished something "on his own" (or had he been really on his own?) that no one could deny would prove useful. He'd once been an actual M.P. on Depot, and now was friendly with a 76th non-com who had access to keys, privileged information, etc., not even the metamorphosizing Raul Macon could come up with. How did lowly T.K. come up with the precise location of a bunker with munitions the Feuer Bande needed to freeze Europe with paranoia, and hold the world at bay ...?

This fact was no less valuable than all the expert Teutonic torturers could get from the kidnapped old man Tomasi, rumored now dead anyway. M.P. Sgt. Wayman Lacer trusted Keller more than anyone, and wasn't going to betray that trust despite knowing T.K.'s ass was in a sling of trouble. The Germans threatened to use T.K. as dog meat, so he had to come up with something quickly.

Eventually Lacer's trust would pan out, though that very moment he was probably wondering where T.K. was, now that they were underground partners. If telepathic, Keller would report they had little choice right then, and had to cooperate with the Bande -- in whose company he was presently in -- *A.S.A.P.*

"Ready, T.K.?" an ebullient Christina Alpreece asked him, posing like a fashion model he might be accompanying to the beach.

"Sure, I guess so," Keller mumbled, without much heart.

She blithely hoisted her M-16 like a cheerleader's baton, treating it like Napoleon's jeweled scepter. "Don't look so down, will you!? We're going to make history this day."

"I've made enough History lately to last a lifetime."

"This is *War*, T.K.," the guerrilla model said in curt dead seriousness; and he saw in no uncertain terms a cold ferocity on her face which hadn't surfaced often, but couldn't have sprung up overnight. He almost fumbled the trusty U.S. Army .45 he had in hand. "And you must be prepared for War. You -- an old soldier! -- should know that better than anyone."

"Yeah, but I went A.W.O.L.," T.K. said with a low voice and measured slowness. Any end to this wunderkind's talents, now that she was playing Annie Oakley?

"Well, you're back in the Army now, my friend."

They said little after that, preparing more in isolated privacy as each soldier went over assigned details for the specific task at hand. Inevitably darkness suffused dusk with an opacity of cold shadows. In tense concentration Hoffler was still observing the site across the road behind that chainlink fence where the three-quarter had dawdled unmovingly for so long. It was still there, of course, and now parked besides a dilapidated gate shack which a few men were still repairing, all glimpsed in shadowy intervals. The perimeter fence lights had been turned on, along with the interior gate shack illumination, so observing the work crew in detail continued for a disapproving Hoffler, who hoped the sad sacks wouldn't be at it all night.

"The Zone is pretty well-lit at night," Rampoul commented nervously as he stood near the German. "Maybe it's too well-lit, don't you think?"

"Inside further by the bunkers it is not so well-lit," Hoffler said.

"Well, I don't like it," Rampoul said, and felt like the German terrorist was idly watching a peep show only he could see.

"Use your night vision, Brice," Christina said in a coy whispering, idly touching his arm as she did so. "Or don't you remember how to work in darkness?"

"That damned truck. That gott-damned truck," Gunther Hoffler said slowly.

Miraculously and finally -- sometime after 7 p.m. -- the truck left. Much to the Feuer Bande's disbelief, the remaining men and equipment found their way back into the three-quarter ton vehicle; the moth-ridden yellow illumination inside the shack was extinguished; and with an abrasive roar of engine and peeling of rubber tires, the truck departed (leaving behind a plume of fumes almost purplishly visible, T.K. noted to the inappropriately scholastic-looking Nils Mupreen).

"Gott *damn* that truck," Hoffler said again. After another thirty minutes' wait in virtual stone-faced silence, becoming nearly unbearable to T.K. Keller, the German gave the word they were ready to carry out RED PLAN "A."

In the dark nocturnal background outlined shapes took greater definition as other bodies and matériel began to move readying for the event. It was not that difficult an exercise, Hoffler maintained, if everything was done correctly.

"That's it," he had said. "We must simply minimize the possibility of error -- and not panic if we do, but keep such within the entire perspective of controlling our mission."

So it was not that difficult for two of Hoffler's spider-like point men to move silently across the paved highway. It curved outside the entire perimeter fenceline of the Mag Zone's northern side, although the speeding traffic of civilian vehicles remained constant, and the men had to wait until no onrushing headlights were visible around the bend. Dressed in workers' outfits resembling military fatigue uniforms, anyone sawing off the Gate 25 lock and chain wouldn't seem that unusual to passing motorists. But the Bande wanted to resist being seen anyway. The chief worry of being spotted from inside the immediate Zone would be from the gate shack which had just been worked on, but Hoffler was sure no personnel remained inside it.

Once inside the gate (which was closed again, but left unlocked) the twin point men crept with that quiet stealth suited for a mine field. They passed the forlorn gate shack and found the lighting inside the Zone to be a low, fuzzy-edged radiance wavering between oil-black areas of darkness. Nimbly, aided by long flashlights with screened lenses, the men navigated these interstices with tense cursory movements, until finally arriving at the bunker marked B-12.

Heretofore the bunker had been a dark shape marked on the maps of Bande members. Now they were before its iron-rusted huge doors, professionally examining the heavy padlock they would attempt to cut off -- then later replace, along with another undamaged and duplicate aluminum seal bearing the bunker's code numbers.

In a few minutes the deed was done. The ominous silence which reigned usually in the Mag Zone was interrupted by the sound of iron doors sliding open stubbornly, at times stridently abrading their cement foundations. Outside across the highway, a grumbling Gunther Hoffler -- still secreted behind the large copse -- had his glasses trained on the area, although the men had been out of view for several minutes. Eventually Hoffler saw the waving flashlight signal appear, which meant the bunker was infiltrated and all right for the rest of the plan to proceed.

Across the road they went -- silently, in pairs -- dark-shrouded figures all, some crouching like hunters creeping up on prey. To T.K. it was all a blur, and each sound was an amplified agony terrible with its insistency. A dim moment of Creation was being revealed to him, something supplanting his human understanding, and unfathomable pathfinder Gunther Hoffler was leading them now into the nexus of it all, into the interstices of dark and light; into the shades with striated branches intersecting this surrealistic pattern so-called reality became; into the very desert of a failing winter's land, where no bounty of salvation was actually awaiting them. *Nein:* nothing but a forever lost kingdom of wilderness awaited them. This was their means to an end, by no means ending; this was their maze, and they were forever the circling, imprisoned rats.

For an instant T.K. felt genuine hate for their starry-eyed leader, hating him the way Hitler was once reviled by a world needing an anti-christ to vanquish. Yet pseudo-Nazi Hoffler was an extraordinary terrorist, perhaps even a gallant guerrilla fighter, the way Che Guevara must have been.

Now the Bande members were near that gigantic-seeming bunker with its opened doors. Somehow all of

it was eerie in the gauzy light of shielded flashlights, which penetrated the darkness with uncongealing radiances equal to a stellar glow. They were invading some temple to a technological god, and T.K. knew such desecration was always attended by some unshakable stigma.

He watched as Hoffler and his officers, oblivious to the possibilities of contamination, entered the bunker. It might only be a Medulla bunker for storage, but what transmitting disease lurked inside? What digital surprise? To T.K.'s disappointment, the interior was a trifle primitive for an undertaking of such classified complexity. There were indeed some troubling loose ends regarding this matter, he reflected. What they were stumbling into -- a tomb-like, ultra-frigid interior of stacked crates and assorted boxes -- couldn't hold that important a matériel. Not the real meat and bones of the controversial operation, but more like its superficial nuts and bolts.

T.K. watched as some of the crates were opened and inspected peremptorily, with a clumsy reverberating noisiness, for what seemed a never-ending period. He shivered, feeling totally useless like some kid watching adults perform the important part of a task he'd forever be excluded from.

"It's not Medulla," Hoffler's voice sounded with sudden harshness. Somebody began a wracked coughing adding to the general unease. "It's not Medulla ..."

"Goddamnit," Brice Rampoul said.

"It's not *Medulla*. So much for the accuracy of sources." A panicked mumbling was brewing, which Hoffler quickly cut short. "But we can use these munitions anyway."

"What are they?" asked Christina Alpreece, who now hovered nearby with a pale nimbus about her.

"Small arms. Ammunition, American military weaponry ..."

"Crates of old CS gas grenades back here," Rampoul's voice said hurriedly. "A cache of M-16s which should be useful ... grenade launchers, M-79 ... Hell, this bunker's an armory."

"Tell them to bring the first truck up," Hoffler whispered urgently. "Let's move all this quickly."

Silently the shadow-like figures began to carry out the task of divesting the large B-bunker of its goods. Voices became insisten, more hurriedly audible as the event proceeded. More powerful but gauze-sheathed lighting was deployed, causing an unreal -- even interstellar-like -- atmosphere to develop. The ungainly, canvas-shrouded three-quarter truck (secreted in the copse beyond the curving highway) slowly trundled through the gate toward the bunker. Another vehicle would soon follow.

For the next several minutes the shadow figures carefully carried and loaded the crated matériel, with an ensuing confusion Rampoul and his people were just able to control, despite distempered expressions. For the most part these anomalous soldiers worked as one largely motivated unit, and even doubt-ridden T.K. Keller suspended his misgivings in the adrenalin-filled task unfolding. It was like robbing some sacred temple in a way, and this fact had an undeniable appeal whose spell transfixed T.K.

But there was little time for any of the individuals to savor the excitement of plundering the Mag Zone. A warning whistle came from one of the Feuer Bande sentries posted several hundred yards up Waker Road. Cell phone messages and radio transmissions were equally alarming. Rampoul and Hoffler lowered the crate they were hauling, their grease-camouflaged faces (awash with the delicate glints of palest moonlight) poised like frozen masks on stooping, almost posing bodies. With the feral eyes of something unleashed from an unknown aviary, Gunther Hoffler saw the twin orbs of some vehicle approaching with a steady, if fog-veiled, glow. Standing next to the German, T.K. felt his anxiety mount to a near nerve-synaptic dysfunction. His mouth open, some cry would have sallied forth had his lungs been capable. Instead there was simply the sheer horror of waiting to be discovered -- caught in the act with the precious evidence scattered all over the rock hard ground.

For one interminably long instant, Bernie Beeschaum -- the driver of the approaching three-quarter ton truck -- did not immediately comprehend the strange scene ahead. It registered within him like no scene from any movie he was used to viewing at the Depot theater every other night. His shaking headlight beams revealed a blurred mass of shapes in a chaotic state. Like ions resisting a galvanized resolution of some physical law, or just plain pinballs hurtling into his unclear line of vision, suddenly vicious shells exploded against the windshield and truckside metal. In another frantic instant Bernie swerved the vehicle off paved road, just before the gate shack, and managed to execute something resembling a fishtailing figure-8 around the open, treeless yard adjacent to the shack. Usually trailers loaded with ammunition were parked there, although there wasn't one then in sight.

The pandemonium ensuing among the Feuer Bande was formidable, something in keeping with the forested wilds about. As the retaliatory rifle fire of fleeing members broke out around him -- pock-marking the frost-heavy air with flashing, yellow and orange patterns -- T.K. stumbled and dropped to his knees, the fear he'd always dreaded totally upon him. The once known terrain had quickly become a foreign one of battle. Within the din confused shouts and imprecations resounded in his ear drums.

From the cold and inhospitable earth T.K. pantingly looked up to see the wildly careening vehicle which disturbed tonight's clandestine endeavor. The bouncing headlights of that vehicle -- impersonal as any ghostly metal behemoth -- bore down inevitably on the rutted ground T.K. sprawled over. No onslaught of rifle fire slowed down the invading craft, rising tank-like in the foreground of this embattled landscape.

"Fuck," T.K. thought, though his thought processes were suspended in the immobilizing instant. Then automatically -- reflexively -- he raised his weapon when the approaching vehicle was some fifty yards away. The old M-16 surprised him by jetting out a minute's length of semi-automatic crackling, spark-like fire. One of the chaotic headlights zeroing in on him -- revealing his prone plight momentarily in a relief of icy and silver-tinged shadows -- abruptly expired like a dead flashlight. The vehicle-beast seemed to viciously execute a 90° turn, nearly overturning in gear-grinding labor as it tried to right itself, swerving away from that curtain of fire becoming a wall of resistance.

"Fuck!"

Someone lifted T.K. by the seat of his pants and pushed him roughly towards the gate where another truck was about to exit. Endlessly T.K. felt the ravaging assault to his lungs as he tried to run all-out through the gate and across the road to the truck which waited with engine revving. The field equipment he struggled with bore him down like punishing weight. His eyes squished through sweat, his throat dried out and became an empty culvert, yet Keller drove himself toward that truck the others ran to in the confused flight from battle.

At last T.K. was reduced to a pure animal fear which later strained his ability to see himself as human ever again.

34.

Just beneath First Sgt. Rhinegold's usually florid complexion, the rage wadded in slow fission gave his skin a strawberry-mottled quality. It exceeded the red-devil skins of his alcoholic, non-com underlings. The news throttling him so was enough to automatically entitle him to 10 extra check-ups at sick bay. Such floridness wouldn't dispel the cold treachery of winters.

"G-goddamn t-this f-fucking D-depot," the First Shirt stuttered early that fateful morning, simmering in the Orderly Room at his overcrowded desk. He waited in dread for the Commanding Officer of the 76th M.P. Company, good Lt. Bivvy, to call him in.

In his spacious office located down the hall, Commanding Officer Bivvy -- seated with regal composure at his desk, as if advertising correct military decorum -- listened impassively to E.M. Bernie Beeschaum drone feebly about "what happened." The C.O. found the roundabout tale unfolding to be extraordinary at best -- or worst -- and very doubtful. It was the most preposterous tale he had ever heard. So much did he doubt it, in fact, that he was waiting any moment for then P.F.C. Beeschaum to commit a fatal error of such obvious prevarication, it would forthwith be debunked entirely, putting an end to the "scare" while sternly reprimanding everybody involved. Yes, Letters of Reprimand and Article 15s would be in order for these men, and the C.O. wondered how Beeschaum had avoided such for so long.

"... just drivin' down Waker Road, Lt. ..."

"For what purpose, Beeschaum?"

"Like I said. To see if we got all the cleanin' equipment outta Gate 24, 'cause Sgt. Walden" -- almost meekly Bernie acknowledged the Platoon Sergeant's disapproving presence, as if seeking corroboration -- "always wants Government Property taken care of, 'cause it's *Company Policy,* and I was in charge of Company Detail out there that day, so I was makin' sure we got everything." Beeschaum paused for a throat-clearing, and with a substantially nail-bitten forefinger pushed back his large glasses.

"Is that right, P.F.C. Beeschaum."

"Yes, sir," Bernie replied, looking uncertainly again at Sgt. Walden, who glowered like some transplanted sic King Leer.

"Go on. Run through your 'story' one more time, Beeschaum," Lt. Bivvy said wearily, rubbing his immaculately pale hands together. Bernie was half-transfixed by Lt. Bivvy's gleaming wedding band and the expensive gold wrist watch the good-and-conscientious Quaker wore with noblesse oblige, for all his men to see. A court-martial might be in order. An Article 15? the C.O.'s look continued to say.

"It's like I said," Beeschaum sighed again, disheartened still by the prospect of telling his story aloud for the third (and no less difficult) time. "It's like I said, sir. The visibility was bad, but I could tell somethin' wasn't right when I got out there. I don't know how to put it. I just felt it. And sure enough, I was comin' up to the gate when I noticed somethin' off near the bunkers ... A *glowin',* that's what I seen, and a dark shape I thought was a boar or somethin'."

"Were you armed, Beeschaum?"

"No sir."

"None of the men are armed on Company Detail, Lt.," Sgt. Walden interjected dutifully.

"Hm," said Lt. Bivvy. He pondered this fact a moment. Everyone would be armed from now on if what occurred truly occurred.

"Then," Bernie said again, continuing, "it's like I been sayin'. All hell kinda broke loose, and I see all those shadows runnin' about -- lights goin' every which way -- and some rounds were fired. One hit the windshield of my three-quarter, and I turned off the road real quick not knowin' what the hell to do, surprised as hell. I did about four wheelies -- still hearin' that shootin' -- and I could see they had what looked like military vehicles back there ... but they looked like ours, so I didn't know what the fuck -- excuse me, sir -- I was kinda confused then, and a little surprised, so I kept doin' wheelies ..."

"Wheelies," Lt. Bivvy said, pronouncing the word as loathsomely as he could.

Sgt. Walden allowed a brief scoff. "You had the milk scared out of you, Beeschaum ... Isn't that right?"

"Yeah, Sarge. But still it was all crazy, all hell broke loose! And don't tell me I shot up my own three-quarter."

"No one's implying that," Lt. Bivvy said, wondering if it could have been accomplished nonetheless.

"Tell the C.O. what you did," Sgt. Walden commanded in his loud voice, which always sounded to Bernie like a saw grating across his nervous system.

"When the truck they had headed for the gate," Bernie continued, somewhat dismally, "it dawned on me they were tryin' to get out, and had no business bein' there ... right? And I could see a few of these jokers runnin' around in my high beams, all dressed like they were on ski slopes -- and all armed with rifles they definitely were firin' my way -- so I kept dodgin', but came as close as I could, hopin' to stop them from gettin' out the gate. And, well, they musta been shook up too, 'cause they just wanted to get out the gate, but when I rushed 'em like I did they jumped off the road for cover."

"You hit the gate shack. Isn't that right, P.F.C. Beeschaum?"

Beeschaum looked down sheepishly. "Yes, sir. Actually, I hit the porch posts. There wasn't much choice. I had to swerve from their firin'."

Lt. Bivvy closed his eyes, listening perhaps to privately heard music during the charged interval of silence which followed. "That gate shack is *leveled* -- isn't it, Sgt. Walden?" the C.O. asked in his level-toned manner.

"I'm afraid so -- yes, sir."

The C.O. opened his eyes.

"They got away, sir," Bernie continued. "One of my tires was shot out! ... I started skidding, couldn't control the truck much after that -- and didn't want to stay in range where they could nail me."

"You saw them get away, then?"

"Yes, sir. I saw them go through the gate. The truck took off down the road. Then this other vehicle came out from the other side of the road -- from near the fenceline -- and picked up the people on foot.

"That was it. It happened pretty fast ... I couldn't pursue -- though I wanted to try. The truck gave out on me," Beeschaum added, again sheepishly.

Sgt. Walden, with his perpetual clipboard in hand -- and wearing a dully-shining, green helmet liner (due to the Depot Alert status) which gave him a more ferocious appearance -- acted as if he wanted Beeschaum to start crying. The elegantly seated C.O., whose men had been standing at near-attention throughout, closed his eyes and rubbed his upraised hands again in meditative silence. The *unexpected* had happened -- no doubt about that fact. None of the platoon members could have accomplished the remarkable feat of riddling Beeschaum's truck (into a sieved metal hulk) with antiquated AK-47 rifle fire -- without murdering P.F.C. Beeschaum in the process. It definitely had to be the work of unlawful interlopers.

"Sgt. Walden? Please tell the First Sergeant to come in here."

In an instant the fomenting First Sergeant appeared, saluting the C.O. with the usual exemplary formality, though his red-splintered eye-bulbs seemed about to short-circuit with a snap, crackle, and pop. With a more difficult formality, the seated C.O. ordered his First Sergeant to be at ease, and then filled him in on what P.F.C. Beeschaum had been reporting (although the First Shirt, of course, had heard the story from the P.F.C. just as many times before).

"That'll be all we'll require of you right now, P.F.C. Beeschaum," the C.O. said. "You can wait in the Orderly Room."

Awkwardly, P.F.C. Beeschaum saluted his Company Commander, then had another significant exchange of eye contact with the platoon sergeant before leaving. On the way out Bernie accidentally kicked the door jamb, which everyone elected to ignore.

"Give me the word and that man is up for outer space stockade duty," a trembling First Sergeant Rhinegold declared.

The C.O. reflected, then said: "I don't think P.F.C. Beeschaum could have done more under the circumstances. By all accounts, he tried his best to stop the robbery -- endangering his life -- and to apprehend the suspects."

"Well," the First Shirt said, "to my way of thinking he's partially culpable for the destruction of thousands of dollars of *Government Property,* and probably for allowing those bunkers to be broken into and robbed of vital matériel."

"We'll discuss that later, First Sergeant," Lt. Bivvy said with a sigh. "Right now, I want to know the situation in the Mag Zone."

"The entire Depot is on Alert!" the First Sergeant uttered apocalyptically, somehow controlling his stuttering and rising to the occasion. "Every man we can spare is posted strategically throughout the area, in full field gear and rifle-armed. We've got to keep a contingent out there from now on, sir. Of course the Gate 25 bunkers are the heaviest stocked with troops and vehicles, as you ordered earlier. I've revoked all passes indefinitely, and all men living off-Depot must now remain at the barracks indefinitely ... Every man is being utilized in the Administration Area as well. The Polizei has been briefed and I'll be in direct contact with them now, until we apprehend the suspects. Main Gate security has been doubled. I've got men foot patrolling anywhere there's earth. We're covered tight, sir. *And waiting.*"

"Good, First Sergeant." The C.O. paused, looking at his two top sergeants in turn. "So the Polizei feel it's the work of ... 'Terrorists'?"

"Absolutely, sir. Judging by Beeschaum's description of their uniform and modus operandi, that appears to be the case. I don't have to tell you what's been going on in Germany and Europe lately -- you need only read the papers. Kidnapping ... sabotage ... violent intimidation of civilians. Now this." The First Sergeant's wracked voice sounded on the brink of self-destructing. "I told you something like this was inevitable, Lieutenant. The men here are not worth one shit. I've told Sgt. Walden this a thousand times. They think they're vacationing. They think this is an asylum for their bed-wetting. Now they're in for it ... Now we're all in for it. *We've been hit, sir.* We've been robbed ...! Caught with our rear exposed ... You'd think we were surrounded by an unseeable but colossal-numbered army of ruthless zealots. And that's what they are, these 'new terrorists' -- ruthless, immoral, godless zealots bent on turning U.S. military installations into their private playgrounds, stealing everything they need, leaving us looking like fools. When will it stop, sir? When will the shoe be put on the right foot -- the truly righteous one -- where it belongs? No act of treachery is beyond those animals. No act of perversity is unknown to them. They're *killers* -- another pack of wolves in these hinterlands -- and they'll spill American blood like so much hops if we're not careful."

The C.O. stopped rubbing his delicate fingers and palms together. Mildly surprised by Rhinegold's outburst, he stared in some astonishment at the still wrinkle-ravaged and hoary face before him, with its crown of a perfectly starched green fatigue cap sporting the insignia of the Army's more unique rank. Rhinegold was a vengeful rarity, the C.O. thought; and here he was stoked to the hilt for this unfortunate occasion. This life of evil was a waking nightmare, the C.O. thought, with no room for sleepers.

"I'm glad to hear you're doing what you can, First Sergeant. Keep the Depot on indefinite Alert. No one gets through the Main Gate without official business, Sgt. Walden. Please post that on your platoon bulletin board. No one but workers with passes get on this base indefinitely. It's a matter of grave importance, First Sergeant, and I'm to meet with Mag Zone technical supervisors connected with top-secret projects this afternoon. Thank God for one thing: only matériel of an unclassified nature was stolen. The classified installations underground in the Zone remain impregnable *and* untouched -- their sectors preserved by electronic and computerized perimeter surveillance -- and they'd better remain that way. If *those* sectors are ever broken into, Gentlemen, then *we'll* be on the way to the stockades, and I'll be the first to lead."

"Then maybe we've got something to be thankful for, sir," a gruff-sounding Sgt. Walden concurred.

"For now, anyway," the C.O. said, reaching across his desk for some bound papers he was about to review with his non-coms, before addressing the men in a company formation. "But how long is *now*?"

One touchy thing was certain: Lt. Bivvy knew he'd be busy "indefinitely" reviewing data and policy on this matter with his key personnel, in rote-repetitious fashion, until they had it all down pat -- and then some. It was his severest test as a Commanding Officer, one he wanted to measure up to with flying colors. So following this session there'd be an even lengthier one with his junior officers, all of whom would be properly impressed by himself and the First Sergeant. He would personally inspect the Mag Zone several times during the week. He would do everything in his power to preserve the Depot's security, and prevent in the future what had lately happened to mar his once spotless military escutcheon.

He would even pray. Lt. Bivvy was a devout military Quaker, and praying for guidance -- and ultimate deliverance -- was part of his official procedure, though he knew his subordinates felt uneasy about it and rarely joined him. (If they did, they were self-conscious to the point of mutual blood-letting.) Yes, he would pray, much in the manner his commander-in-chief, President Noxson, would. And in knee-bending prayer he would find a way to vanquish the godless ...

Bivvy would need to pray, for one key member of his company was -- at that moment -- difficult to locate, and that individual would be instrumental to his preparations, the C.O. felt. Namely Second Lieutenant Morris Penscay (Sgt. Walden's Second Platoon Officer -- young and impressionable to the point where his effectiveness diminished -- was supposedly an "expert" on international terrorists, on earth and beyond, and his talents were sorely needed at the moment.

So the C.O. began to pray. There was one angel of hope in his invocation, the fact that in his ramblings Beeschaum had revealed clue-wise a potential suspect: a tall, red-bearded yahoo-civilian-type whose mysterious (but heretofore unremarked on) presence apparently alluded to dire happenings they had failed to keep an eye on.

35.

"By Gawd, Lacer, get me to the Church on time!" a recently despondent Lt. Penscay had cried from that inebriated sloth he'd fallen into, along with an unattractive prostitute at some Saarbrücken sex store. "The Depot is under attack and I lay like Ripped Van Wrinkle in the lap of *ig-nom-i-ny*. O, sordid wastes, befouled virgins!"

The proverbial shit had hit the fan, as it was once said, and Sgt. Wayman Lacer had the gas pedal of his jeep floored as he sped along the autobahn, hell-bent for Forbrau. Errands like finding and driving home a controversial 2nd Looie like Penscay (known to be the worst officer in Forbrau) nobody needed. To have had to locate and then drag this miserable sucker out of a gott-damn whorehouse was about the worst duty Lacer had ever performed, and he hoped the C.O. and Sgt. Walden appreciated it. Probably no one else could have done it this successfully, Lacer mused despite the cold, wind-whipping, Hawkish airs assaulting the jeep's canvas cab cover, which threatened to blow away at any second. (Small screws, etc., already had.) No one else could have extricated the besotted Penscay from his indecent obsessions so expertly, and Lacer rued the fact he'd prevented a pimp from slicing up Morris.

Duty, Honor, Country, smirked Lacer.

Though things were heating up in Germany -- in Europe particularly -- nothing could staunch or melt the unnaturally overlong winter which ebbed, then prematurely (and unaccountably) returned to vanquish a fallow spring. Nature had gone haywire, along with everybody else, and scientists claimed it was but an aberrant, out-of-sync "ice age" of sorts caused -- unbelievably -- by the world's abuse of neo-nuclear devices and botched effort to reverse global warming, which had upset nature's balance and the the earth's once natural equilibrium, alarming the world's population along with everything else.

Nice timing, Lacer thought, considering the terrorist attacks which had burgeoned to this point of incipient, all-out, guerrilla warfare or worse. Ja -- yow indeed, sirs -- the merde had hit the fan, the old globe was on the front burner, and maybe the long averted Armageddon was around the corner after all (as the C.O. maintained during his dreary, soul-less lecturing). It had all started with the kidnapping of some international big wig Lacer knew wasn't worth a fuck, but the powers-that-be weren't noted for their dependence of reason. On the proverbial contrary, they needed to encourage and glory in just the opposite.

"This is war, Lacer! *War!!!*" the lieutenant was howling risibly above the wind, and Lacer wanted to punch him out. Any other time perhaps he would have, but the buck sergeant knew duty required his delivering a conscious body rather than an unconscious one. Though in Penscay's case, those states were hardly dissimilar.

"This is 6 mega-inches up your keister," Lacer muttered, "and I got your war hangin' between my legs." But Morris Penscay could hear only comments that were usually screamed at him, or else broadcasted in a manner saluting his insuperable skills; all that mere mortal men had no inkling of.

In the rather unbusy confines of the N.C.O. Club at mid-day, Raul Macon sat nursing his fifth rum and coke, saturninely awaiting the man he was to receive crucial information from.

When that man finally did arrive -- apparently on duty, wearing starched fatigues -- Herr "M." Macon raised his glass slightly in a mocking toast of disapproval.

"You were supposed to show up around lunch. Here you are closer to dinner, Lacer."

Wayman Lacer sighed, removed gloves and fatigue cap, and sat down with little apology.

"Just happened to be re-orienting the man in question, after unexpectedly taking him to Landstuhl to get his dyspeptic stomach fixed up. Lt. Penscay -- besides having Moselle on the brain -- has something of an aggravated ulcer."

Macon grunted, not enthusiastically. He was not into his role at the moment. Anyone studying him more closely (and with greater impartiality) might detect he was dropping his assumed mask with an alarming clatter. Herr "M." was fed up. Events were getting out of hand, now that the Mag Zone raid had been so ingloriously botched. Macon half-expected to be found out any moment. Surely that dodo Keller -- that *crawling* bad luck charm -- had contributed enormously to the astounding failure. If it was a ball game, they'd be deep into their bullpen. Having some prescience, he should have benched Keller -- permanently.

"So what's the dope on that fathead?" the M.-man asked, keeping his voice conversationally low.

Wayman paused to drink from a water glass of stagnant liquid. "The dope is, the lieutenant is supposed to be some kind of expert on terrorism, according to the C.O., whose heart is bleeding pure bull at the moment."

"With his head up his pray-for-me buns," Macon added.

"Everybody is ape-shit in that orderly room at the moment. You'd better start praying for your cover. Everybody on this Depot is going to be watched more closely -- civilians included. The old man wants to pull file on everybody. He's smelling inside connections on this, and there's no doubt his sniffer's getting keener by the minute. I don't know what to tell you. What can I say? I tried to throw him off a bit, but he's not going for it. T.K. had better stay off post for awhile. It the C.O. heard a dude resembling a walking flea circus was on Depot, he'd bring smoke down on us for sure."

Lacer went on to recount, in some telling detail, just what had happened during the lengthy meeting between the officers and the N.C.O. staff of the 76th M.P. Company. "Probably the most suspect M.P. company in the new USAREUR at the moment," Lacer declared. It sounded almost like a boast. "And I'll tell you one thing. I never want to go through another uptight meeting like the one I went through this morning. It was chickenshit to say the least. You're lucky you're on this side of it. 'Shaky' Rhinegold was something else -- a man with a terminal brain -- and he's got the C.O. listening and swallowing his bullshit. They're gonna comb the Mag Zone inside out, so that means no more spying. No way I can get you back in the area. Perimeter fences are being patrolled on the outside now, too, as well as the inside ... Is that what they wanted?"

"They don't know what the shit they want. But the more classified, the better."

The young buck sergeant shook his head, looking around the unlively, sparsely peopled N.C.O. Club dining area with its satin curtained stage to the right. Behind them was the long bar with its slot machines and drinkers' tables. "And how you been makin' out in here?" Lacer asked almost furtively, his voice lowered. "I can't believe you're working in this place."

"I *drink* in this place, Lacer," a surly M.-man said, finishing a lengthy rum swallow. "Keep one low profile, stay in the back here with my ears and eyes open. I'm technically 'the assistant manager,' okay?"

"How the hell did you get a job like that?" Lacer asked, his voice California flat. He clearly felt that fat ass Macon had lucked out.

"Because the Germans actually run this club. You didn't know that -- did you, dungkopf? They're into most everything on this Depot's administrative side of things. That's what G.I.s get for sleeping with so many German girls."

"I don't believe it."

"Okay, maybe they don't run everything, and there's only one good or bad German at Headquarters who helped arrange this sinecure for me, in conjunction with Hoffler."

"What German was that?"

"His identity I can't give you now. You're the one who's supposed to be laying facts on me."

Lacer lit a cigarette, shaking his head again. "It's gonna get bad."

"Good. Then I can quit this job and go back to that bitch in Amsterdam, who says the Rads shoulda let Jews alone." Macon finished his drink. "I don't like Germans or Jews. I don't like this N.C.O. Club. I don't like the asshole manager either, who's getting wise to the fact somebody made a mistake putting me here. But lucky for me he ain't around much, shackin' up with some white dogmeat off post. He's a yammer, naturally."

"Naturally."

"So now you know it's best things happened this fast anyway, 'cause they sure can't go on much longer,

Lacer. At least not around here, where I get stuck taking inventory for the food service, and all I know is how to eat the stuff."

"The Army sure frags up," Lacer laughed.

"Oh yeah. And so did that Bo Jangles I'm gonna get."

"Save it for Rhinegold, the old fuck. He's the one looking for people like you." Lacer beckoned to a not-so-pretty waitress and ordered a drink. "I hope somebody knows whatever the hell it is we should be doing. Why did the Germans get militarily ambitious again and cause a goddamn civil war which gave the U.S. and Russia an excuse to wage political ones again? Why is history a cyclical repetition, more or less, with unanswerable questions?"

"Does your Penscay know anything?"

"I don't think he knows his ass from Rhinegold's or his dog's. 'Expert on Terrorism' my sweet peter. I had to sober him up, get him under a shower, then practically dress him. It was sad. Somewhere along the way he read a magazine article about 'terrorism,' and the C.O. thinks he's an expert. Penscay is an expert on jack shit. He's a clone-decoy -- but question is, whose decoy? But he and Rhinegold are teaming up to prepare a 'counteroffensive guerrilla maneuver,' and we're gonna be out in the cold running through it all for the next two weeks, *in addition* to regular duties. I feel like jumpin' ship now. If there was a Martian side to this business I'd join it. I'm putting my money on the final space solution."

"Hang tough, Lacer. I've got to see Hoffler very soon to see his side of things, and what they're planning now. And if T.K. Keller's still alive, I'm gonna roast his sorry ass. He sure ain't been no good luck mascot."

There was more mulling over these sad facts in dour, prolonged silence, until Lacer's eye caught a familiar figure entering the Club's dim confines. Morris Penscay in the civilian flesh (or garbed, rather, in one of his most ostentatious and appalling "new" gabardine blue suits) was standing at the bar, drinking some fizzy concoction. Something nobody else would drink, thought Lacer. That fact, coupled with the general irony of Penscay's appearance, distressed Wayman Lacer. That jerk-looie of a faux man was standing there joshing in his *shee-it* horsey demeanor, loudly asking the bartender whether "the world had ended yet?" The question (followed by a snuffling guffaw) approximated Penscay's version of wit, and he stood there visibly pleased by it. With one of his hands in pants pocket, he looked to be standing and drinking in the midst of some bustling party which was in full swing.

Lacer uttered "Oh no" to himself, and noticed that Herr Madman Macon was still too deeply mired in dull-eyed moroseness to see anything. Inevitably Lacer knew that shit-kickin', grit-faced Penscay would turn his hirsute head from side to side in search of some lucky fellow drinker to share levity with. Unfortunately no one was around but a puffy-eyed E.M. performing a humdrum custodial task. Just as inevitably -- his mustached face cracking into a hot-damn-it grin of recognition -- Penscay would spot Lacer and friend sitting isolated in corner splendor.

"How you boys doin'?" said the lieutenant, bringing with him a full glass of Singapore sauce, still fingering an unlit cigar the size of a hot dog. "Jeezus F. Christ, Lacer. Who's yer friend there? Whom have I the honor here of joining."

"This is the new assistant manager of the Club, sir," Lacer said, pulling himself together. "Mr. Warren C. May ..."

"And I'm Lt. Morrie Penscay," gushed the second lieutenant, affably sitting with great flair at the table, before extending a glad hand which Macon gripped gingerly, as if it were a wet eel, unscaled. Not flustered, Penscay put the cigar between his large, too perfectly white teeth and allowed his great chuckle to unfold itself over the men. Raul Macon believed an indiscretion equal to some noisome burp occurred, and stared back with marble-eyed impassiveness at the interloper. *This* was the very yokel they'd been talking about, acting like a lobotomized barker standing outside the peepshow he starred in? Expert-on-Terrorism my flamin' ass *in* that peepshow, Macon further thought, not even noticing the arrival of a fresh round of drinks.

"Say! This is one heckuva N.C.O. Club," Penscay marveled, letting his wide eyes pan around the patterned ceiling and walls. "Now I know where you spend so much of your time, Lacer. And I commend you for it."

"It's about the only place to go on Depot, sir. There isn't anywhere else to go really."

"No shit?! Well, that's a g-darn shame, boy. That's a sin of magnitude." Penscay reflected on this, licking the cigar which he rolled almost elegantly between his ringed and manicured fingers. Then he emitted a hoarse coughing laugh of some duration. This too was regarded by Macon with an unflinching lack of expression. Penscay made pooh-poohing gestures while hurriedly irrigating his throat with huge gulps from his beverage. Effusively he wiped his mouth, mustache and nose with a bunched-up linen napkin that seemed to be attacking him more than anything.

"Ah!" the lieutenant said, finishing.

"You okay, sir?" Wayman Lacer asked.

"Just fine, Sergeant," Penscay replied, though condescending. Clearing his throat with regained composure, the lieutenant sipped more elegantly once more at his drink. His face was still adorned by the extravagant smile he had greeted all with. Finally Raul Macon picked up his fresh drink, consuming it with one swallow. Lacer watched all this out of a paranoid eye-corner, squeezing his own drink like a rubber ball.

Do not blow up, Raul Macon. Don't blow it, my man! He watched Penscay reach into an inner breast pocket and extract a pair of tinted glasses some of the hemp smokers on Depot wore when communing with spirits, and Lacer felt that askewed presence on the lieutenant's face was an abomination of sorts. Acting unsuccessfully cool in a hopeless way, these props couldn't save the lieutenant's lack of *savoir faire*. Lacer knew now why the other officers of the 76th wished Penscay an early funeral.

"Some weather we're having," the lieutenant said.

Macon couldn't restrain a wheezing sound of either amusement or disparagement. Lacer could tell M. was about to speak, that he'd gathered himself up and was the old cunning man again ready to exploit this surprise occurrence for whatever worth. Damned if there still wasn't a war to get on with, and the Holy Holocaust just around the corner.

"Excuse me, Lieutenant. Wayman and me were just talking about how bad things are gettin' around here -- especially after that fucked-up commando raid and all -- and he told me you were going to play an important part in catching those bastards, right? So it's kind of a surprise to see you in here decked out for a wedding, considering the whole Depot's in a state of alert."

Penscay coughed, again clearing his throat and letting his lips work over the cigar, then eyebrow-shrugging as if at a loss for words. "I'll tell you boys one thing. The C.O. would have a fit if he caught me in here. But thank Gott he's a Quaker tee-totaler. And thank God everybody's too busy to be in here, except you boys." He winked. "I know indeed that the shit has hit the fan, and I've got some powerful thinkin' to do if we're ever going to right the ship now that it's been hit ... You know all that, and I know the world's smack dab in some kind of whacko Ice Age -- and I know things could get worse, and that our days might be numbered."

The lieutenant lifted his drink, poised for a gallant salute.

"But by *God* I am not about to shit in my diapers over it. I am not about to get so wrought-up that I can't come into a place like this and loosen up a bit with you troops, am I? Hell, I've been stationed in this hell-hole for months, and never got to really see it until now, when there's a crisis on, when everybody's runnin' around with their dick cut off. Why can't they relax, and realize they brought it on themselves because they got their heads up their assholes.."

"Because sanity's beyond the common man," Lacer put in.

The lieutenant smirked, and began gesticulating with his cigar in a politician's manner. "It just don't make sense! *If they'd of listened to me beforehand, we'd have rounded up all these fuckin' terrorists long ago and hung every one up by his balls* ... There'd be no problem at the moment if we'd of done that. No big-time diplomat woulda been kidnapped. No goddamn break-in would of occurred in the Mag Zone, no illegal unleashin' of weirdo weapons (and God knows who did that) would have whacked the weather outta shape, and we could all be sittin' at this moment in some fancy whorehouse with a sweet little lady in our saddle! But shit, that ain't what we're lookin' at now, is it, boys? Oh shit no. We're lookin' at the goddamn hours of reckoning. We're lookin' at things we got very little control over. I'm tellin' you there's bullshit out in that Mag Zone we don't know jack shit about. There's another world out there -- underground or whatever -- and for all we know, it might be bigger then this one. Oh yeah ... a sight bigger for sure. *So whatta we do?* Do we just sit around boozin' our brains out, or do we finally override these chickenshit leaders we got *and go blast those commie bastards outta the woodwork and roast 'em in fuckin' hell!?!*"

The lieutenant's voice had risen dramatically throughout this tirade, and Wayman Lacer was even more paranoid and appalled when a few heads turned inside the Club. Macon, meanwhile, had resumed his deadpan stare which -- at bottom -- was the essence of disbelief. Slowly the M.-man finished his drink, eyes still on the lieutenant, and allowed his features some ambivalent marveling. It was a marveling of some depth, however coarse, and it told Sgt. Lacer that the inimitable Macon had good use for this Army's irregular officer; if-and-when.

"Okay, sir," the hot gravel-voiced assistant manager said, "how do we go about gettin' those commie bastards and roastin' their tasty butts?"

Perplexed, in dismay Morris Penscay shook his head and wiped the crumpled linen napkin over his sweat-pocked face, stopping to windshield-wipe the anomalous glasses he still wore.

"I wish I sure as hell knew, gent. Your guess is as good as mine." Penscay checked his watch. "I mean here we all are with not much time left, and we gotta get on the ball. I mean those Feuer Bande bastards are probably planning one knock-out attack again, somewhere, you better believe it -- and we have to beat them to the punch. We have to spoil their party."

"I thought you were a goddamn expert and all on this matter?" Macon snorted.

"Well, I know a sight more then the average nincompoop around here, Warren C. May, I'll tell you that." The lieutenant put his hands together prayer-like and reflected, burping at one point. "I know *this*. I know mine enemy, and he is a godless, wanton animal *of the Damned*. A cunning, ruthless guerrilla who's out there under one big rock plotting the next move now. And I know another thing! Mine enemy is no fool by any stretch of the imagination. Mine enemy is as wise as Satan, and a worthy adversary."

"Cut that claptrap," hissed Macon-May, "and get down to specifics. How you gonna get to this Feuer Bande?"

"By going out there and confronting them," Morris Penscay said. "By socking it to the bastards, as they said long ago. By attacking where it hurts most -- in the field, in their backyard ... Believe me, I know these degenerates, May, like I know the feel of my dick. I know them inside out. I know who their leader is."

"Who's their leader ...?"

"One Gunnar Hoffler. A hell-bent for leather neo-Maoist who's wanted for bank robbery, arson, and other anarchistic anti-christ acts in half a dozen European cities. An absolute *criminal* who's been allowed to run around for too long, and that's one name -- and one piece of vital information -- that the Commanding Officer didn't know until about 12 hours ago when I straightened his ass out."

"Gunther Hoffler," corrected Warren C. May.

"Whatever. And I'm also sure some Americans are involved in this mess -- and I intend to rout their asses out as well," Penscay declared, taking a swig from a glass he was too wrought-up to notice was empty. "There's a whole lot of shit connected with this you wouldn't *believe*. And I believe I'm the perfect candidate to bring it to the world's attention. Don't you?"

"I wouldn't doubt that," Macon said, studying the lieutenant. "You know a whole lot about this Hoffler?"

"*Enough*. Enough about how he runs his gang of murderers, and what his next move might be." Penscay again consulted his watch. "Enough."

"I'd like to hear more, Lieutenant Penscay," Macon said, standing up. "I've got a bottle in the office, and if you've got a few minutes, maybe we could get into it ..."

Morris Penscay returned a look of sudden sobriety. "Oh, I don't know about that, my friend. I don't know about that at all. I find it wonderful that you and Sgt. Lacer have the opportunity to afford these sessions yourselves, due to the circumstances. I find a lot of things around this Depot difficult to believe, but don't get me wrong. I'm willing to take a lot of things at face value."

Macon's own look grew harder again, and his face was no comforting picture to dwell upon as he watched Penscay, with an effete wave of his hanky-holding hand, depart the premises. There was just the faintest emission of green ectoplasmic vapors left in the officer's wake, Macon noted.

36.

The dream had reached a new significance: it seemed to be going on forever and ever. Repeating and expanding on the same imagery, it gained a resounding power within an absorbing consciousness leaving no choice but acceptance. Its content was like a schizoid picture of an inverted reality, showing two halves which bumped exteriors but never met, though remaining uneasily contiguous. Of course the halves were the yin and yang of the human condition, all the opposites of existence vying with one another for supremacy.

In the dream he saw the golden apple balanced precariously on his head, and waited (in a horrified suspension) for the bolt arriving to pair the fruit. He saw again the dark figure some yards before him raise the crossbow, or arbalest, aiming it with unwavering fixation at a point just above the target's head.

But the bolt never arrived ...

Instead he was perambulating again, roaming the German countryside in an out-of-step formation with nature. Dressed in fatigues, a cigarette in mouth, he was heading for the company area ... This is the eternal Soldier's March through time and all time. Does it lead to Anywhere or simply to Nowhere and beyond? Gracinauto doesn't know -- or care -- though at times he has, and labored mightily to preserve such regard. But fate and circumstance have taken that away from him. Once, as a young man in military training, he'd been force-marched by head-high superiors inflicting facts of the modern soldier's lot on him: He must stand tall, look good (carrying his sleek, neo-automatic rifle slung over right shoulder), and be prepared to fight and vanquish the Unknown Enemy in mortal combat. Though his tired feet in their gumboots dragged through this indoctrination, a part of Gracinauto told himself believe, accept it, or there'd be little hope. Because this is all there is left, and it is your immunity from total damnation, though you're damned irreparably enough already like a pinball target.

So keep marching, young Gracinauto, through the war zoned and occupied forests of the world -- the modern Netherworld, now -- and remember how it all fell apart on you. Remember marching into that 76th Company Area long ago, right into the barracks and the bay area (where Kazu, the Darvon-wired and wiry little Puerto Rican, buffed the bay area throughout his elevated or decelerated state, finger-popping to some music you didn't hear then), up those drab, cold, green-painted stairs where you passed P.F.C. Leare -- perennial scumbag from East Coast 'hood America, reeking of no-shower and stale hashish breath, his eyes a dull & disconnected come-on for a share of those insensate glories -- who said something profound like, "Hey, Gracinauto, I got your mojo hangin' ...!" -- until you reached the second story landing and entered Room 6, your room, with all its stagnant air of hopelessness disturbed only by the heavy, suspended sounds coming from some demonic composer's always spaced-out sound tracks. Those sounds were/are familiar to you, though a mishmashed echo of a tape played at the wrong speed at times. Yeah -- oh yea -- there's Beeschaum on the corner bunk by the radiator in some contorted swami's pose -- completely nude -- jackin' off to the great Void and chanting some commercial jingle he picked up from Armed Forces Super Radio: "Does yer chewin' gum lose her flaver on de sex-aide over-nite -- ?!" ... You stare a shade unbelievingly, almost laugh despite yourself, realizing in a satori-filled hangover the complete appropriateness of it all; the almost sacredness of The Act here in a neo-decadent Forbrau, where Gott has given you a Sign to pursue through all the dusty, crenellated epochs of Thyme. "O Beez-man! You got it, Babe -- !" ... And who the hell's this out beneath your own bunk, you wonder, removing your cunt cap almost respectfully as you squat down cowboy-like and prod the unmoving form of some dummy-like, faceless body wearing old fatigues and unshined boots? You just can't make that face out, man, and small wonder since most of it's decomposed, maggot-warted, and stinking with a gagging odor that's become such standard whiff you aren't really offended by it. Any more than you are by the dried patches of excrement lying here or there, or the forever sweet-but-acrid smell of urine which has soaked into the cracked woodwork.

It's all perfect, perfect by its just presence and (il)logical rationale here in Forbrau. You search through the stiff-body's pockets, looking for anything of value, and come out with a cat's eye marble and a dried stick of chewing gum which you pocket greedily. You rip the E-5 patches off the poor fucker's sleeves, 'cause he don't need those sergeant stripes any longer; and you pocket those also, whistling along with Beez as you do so, hearing the panting litany of his voice in sync with yours. Great. You stand up, prepared to navigate your way further about the Room, but the tile floor's pretty ripped up. It's as if an explosion or gun-fire ravaged it. Turning to go around the lockers, you damn near fall into an ugly-looking crater the size of some fat-fanny's foxhole, and notice -- looking down-deep into the obfuscated interior -- that some of your relatives might be down there, man ...

No shit! *There's Mom, fer Chrissake, all soot-cheeked and scary-eyed, huddling sick-like in a corner; a body there looks like Pop's, or maybe Brother Will's ... can't tell for sure, and the longer you look, the worse it gets. So you sidle around the Hole, ignoring the pleas for help, thinking perhaps it's a bit too much. You expect this room to be your Asylum. That's what it was and always will be, your safe haven, your pseudo-salvation from the unknown pitfalls outside. Now it's all inside, and you shake your head, despite the fitting logic. You could be down there. Mom wants you. Her naked, flabby boobs bouncin', she's callin' you to join her, and you don't like that. You shake your head.*

You move on to the next scene, the next bunk, and see an overweight, half-naked German female prostitute lolling there, smiling back at you. You laugh. If the First Shirt could see her, his high blood pressure would come undone, come out every which way. The most elite band of M.P.s the Army has ever devised via long years of "experimentation" has come to this, gang-fuckin' a downright ugly bitch on the steel-springed, creaking bunk with its nearly flattened mattress soaked brown from old blood-lettings. The Rap Soul Brothers are to blame, of course. Two of them, Sugar Brown Bull and so-tall Toper (from Harlem), are gathered around this flabby, pink-white old hammerfrau. They're wearing knock-out suits they scored on the black market; both look fit-to-kill, there's a silk cravat in Sugar Brown's vest pocket, a stolen Homburg on his Afro-haircut head, a whiskey bottle in one white-gloved hand, a mean-looking cane in the other. Toper is equally made-out. They be badd, Jacks. They be fit to do business, and the hammerfrau there enjoys it all, her purse well-fed with marks, her gorging "sex" large enough (as Toper learns when, guffawingly, pulling down her panties) to fit both their whiskey bottles inside it.

Gracinauto has seen enough, doesn't want to see what the Brothers are about to do, have done before. This ain't the Home he had hoped for, no doubt about it. Some colossal clerk's error was made in sending an idealistic type like him to Forbrau, where all things are out of kilter, where polymorphic perversity was/is the natural norm -- and pity be upon any misguided, ignorant Innocent raised in the idealistic traditions requiring service & dedication to God, King and Country.

Of course that very motto -- God, King and Country -- was graphically tattooed in a prominent position on the whore's anatomy ...

So for Gracinauto this is the decadent Apotheosis which America-in Deutschland has become, and he steps as a blind man round the fatted calf being defiled in low-life celebrations. Out-of-time, out of synchronization with any idea of past or future, his present has become an ultimate unreal fragmentation of schizoid dimensions -- and this, he never really realizes, is the penultimate temper of the times which he so feebly embodies.

Walk back through the rubble, Gracinauto. Leave this minor holocaust of flesh & sin -- give birth to the other self foaming in your visualization of being-becoming -- and give that good citizen-to-be to the peaceful workings of yet authentic civilization, proclaiming yourself the Right Honorable Clown of Slaves, "T.K. Keller." Forget that animal band of subversive renegades about to cut your throat, and the abyss of a black eden which your land's become ...

It was in the miasma of another Time now, or so T.K. Keller thought. It was a primeval period whose ooze he was borne along precariously by, into the first Cave of caves where Cro-Magnon aped Plato in everlasting futility. And it was death-in-life warmed over a hot potato not even the beasts could eat.

The World had stopped. Immobilized, it bordered the brink of its (un)naturally scientific Cataclysm, a satellite-pinball careening volatilely, out of orbit around the flickering sun: The Nu-Apocalypse, in short, awaited one & all, existing outside T.K.'s (un)consciousness as surely as it did within. But his fire-wounded eyes remained shielded by amber lids closed to the shadows moving about.

Firefight-stricken, T.K. remained prostrated upon the cold earthen cave bed, realizing there was no escape. Though perhaps he'd escaped body/spirit, still this had to be ground zero, for only months earlier he'd deserted to escape the marital specters alive in World War (wherever it was) again, and now here he was embroiled in combat, the quasi-hostage/soldier of anti-American guerrillas of Teutonic stripe.

He'd reached ultimate nadir. He'd become an actual *traitor* -- by default or otherwise -- and wondered how in hell he'd accomplished such a feat. All T.K. ever wanted was to be far from the maddening crowd and toking on his hemp pipe.

There was Gunther Hoffler's voice, however, inflicting aural assault with unrivaled grandiloquent declamations. T.K. was awakened by vitriolic, pagan tempers: " ... Now there is no turning back, and this is the turning point, the point of no-return, ladies! ... Does the radio lie when it says the American military is sending its finest marines into Germany at this very moment, poised for a lethal exchange with so many fine citizens of Deutschland like us ...? Though of course, goddamn it, ladies, *the U.S. can't tell the difference between us and the great bourgeoisie of Germany at the moment* -- and that's the bloody fact." Hoffler shouted with an encompassing Wagnerian air, stentorian lungs exploding, both his arms upstretched in an Ike parody (his fine ivory teeth unveiled, in this rare instance, and proving less than Hollywood caliber). He leaped about still dressed in fatigues and Castro-like field jacket, body blood-and-sweat lacquered, his facial grimace a Protean god's mask unable to disguise a lost humanity.

O Lordy, thought T.K., rising like a shot, and straining from his miserable state to view Hoffler's rallying histrionics, hardly enthralling the tired and captive audience of Feuer Banders. Only the enraptured figure of Christina Alpreece believed, squatting nearby in her undiminished bravura, acting open-mouthed as if a young Olivier or John Wilkes Booth now leaped upon the stage of a loaded ammunition crate nearby. Hoffler threatened to explode it with one point-blank shot from the .45 submachine gun gripped -- scepter-like -- in his hair-mottled, pale hands.

Deliver us, thought T.K., *but not that way, my man. Send in the medics, not this "ballet clown" from East Berlin -- and be quick about it!*

"So what now, *people*? Now that our country has been divided again by the Superpowers, and it suffers from the inevitability of civil war?" Hoffler was asking, more than rhetorically, after a moment's charged beat. The submachine gun's barrel still pointed downward, casually, with a poised finger on the trigger. "Will one of you great moron-minds please tell me that, now that the lines are drawn ...? We who have awaited this colossal moment are overshadowed by its scope and implications. We're just a supporting cast now, people. Events have proceeded beyond our influence, and our kidnapped Tomasi is hardly the trump card we figured on at the moment ...

"Is there any *body* here who can contribute some worthwhile suggestions regarding a plan of action? *Ein Krieg ist schön, ja ...?*"

"Let us lay low," came the measured voice of Nils Mupreen from nearby. His simple statement was uttered with great disgust. Exhausted and beaten-looking, his spectacles still covered by grime, he sat sipping from a water canteen one of the veterans was unable to commandeer.

"I quite agree," said Brice Rampoul, who looked the least shaken of the lot, and with a lupine air settled next to the alert Christina. "No sense hurrying our own immolation, is there, Comrade? The world's gone a bit topsy-turvy at the moment, if we swallow that earth's axis tilt-trauma the papers are full of ... Not to overlook the latest invasion by good old Uncle Sam. We're simply out of the turkey shoot, old man. Our raid didn't do a damn thing but give Washington leverage for finally instituting the brunt of inevitable propaganda threats ... coupled with unnaturally perverse weathers. I hope you're following all this. I just hope that much."

"Whatever happened to good old nukes?" Christina asked blithely, in an inept attempt at off-handedness, or perhaps naiveté. "Once upon a time they were the earth's scourge, threatening one and all, until Australia was accidentally hit ... and then Hawaii ... and the ocean seemed to cave into some kind of aquatic dark hole, terrorizing scientists who claimed the earth's stability was upset, as has apparently been borne out."

"You've answered your own question, dear, per usual," said Rampoul, almost hugging her. He'd been drinking.

"That was certainly the true beginning of the end," said Christina with a shiver, almost excited by history's most controversial fact, which made soothsaying a moot science practiced now by genuine fishwives in the alps. "The nuclear arsenal became neutralized -- even 'obsolete' -- replaced by exotic space-stuff like the Medulla Project I'm wondering if really exists. What's so *hot* about that Forbrau Mag Zone we just got shot up over?"

"It's all underground, Baby," said Rampoul, winking. Lighting a cigarette, he cogitated bemusedly on this remarkable fact. "There's a technological underground lab complex at that Depot. It's the equivalent of a massive bomb shelter. Only trouble is, they'd better hurry if they're going to evacuate what they have on a *safe super* satellite into emergency space," Rampoul chuckled. "For some reason they had to work on, or *under,* good old *terra firma,* and it might cost them at the moment if Mother Earth suddenly bites the big one. Or does it matter?"

"How do you know of this," Hoffler asked, releasing the tension hold on his weapon. A crystalline nimbus silhouetted his thick bushel of hair garishly from behind. "How the hell do you know --?"

"Double agents abound in this business," Rampoul allowed, but the guerrilla captain was unamused. He pointed his weapon towards Rampoul's body mass, and said:

"This is what the double agent gets if he's not with us. *Verstehen?*"

"Ja, ich verstehen, old man. Sprechen Sie langsam unter *all Death,* ja --? Reserve your judgement for the right Man."

"Be wise, mein Freund. Be wise."

"Mein Deutsch ist sehr schlect," lamented Brice Rampoul, raising a thermos cup by way of salute, if not homage, to the overhead standing figure. *"Entschuldigung ..."*

"Regarding the alleged preposterous facts of your underground complex," announced Nils Mupreen to the group, "I've never heard more insensate, fucked-up bullshit."

"That's it, Nils," one of his male followers seconded from the shadows. "That's certainly it."

Rampoul swung his thermos cup towards Nils. "Each to his own factual opinion, dear fellow."

"Dear fellow my scrotum," Nils replied, causing some raucous, and for the first time merry, verbal exchanges within the Bande. For a moment cold, weariness, and defeat were forgotten.

Keller propped his head back on mother earth. Trying to relax in this hallucinating realm -- at the moment equally comic and surreally scary -- was, he believed (or imagined?), burying him in a phantasmagoria from which some intervening grace had to relieve him. In his privately spellbound eternity, after a passage of what amounted to hours, apparently no one bothered to inform him much of anything. By then the sports-jacketed Raul "Herr-M." Macon was back on the scene, adjudging it like an inspecting officer in danger of losing rank and life. T.K. wondered if there were much of either left. So much for a Purple Heart following his first taste of battle. Per usual, he was spitting dregs from cold-cracked lips, yet gamely nursing his enervated body. Macon's undisguised voice moved T.K. to that extent, in the guise of a digital bolt reconnecting to synaptic dysfunction, so with some difficulty he managed to sit up again, going, "Yow, baby," imagining himself a good slave about to be freed. *Yow, be a good nigger* he told himself, battling brow sweat as inarticulate cheering and toothy smiling possessed him, child of a distant puppet meister.

"You managed," he heard Macon's smoke abraded voice saying, "not to zap a goddamn soul, Hoffler, not even a boar. Nice raid. But you sure as hell stirred Forbrau up. I don't believe what's happenin' out there, man. It's like the crown jewels been tampered with."

Hoffler had his submachine gun testily pointed again at this beefy intruder, regarded by the German leader as being too stupid to know fear. "You were a big help, 'Herr Dumbkopf.' One big help indeed."

Almost nattily -- too coolly -- Macon lit an unfiltered Camel, pretending he were in some well-furnished living room, perhaps, or on the set of some Hollywood location between takes. Puffing out hazy pulmonary emissions, he squinted his customary squint, coughed almost smilingly, tensing the vertical elbow of one arm (atop which his cigarette hand casually rested) on the other buttressing arm held horizontal, chest high. "Jesus F. Chrise," he muttered, unenthusiastically surveying the scene.

T.K. was mesmerized by glints of diamond-pointed light reflecting off the gold ring and bracelet on M.'s amply fleshed wrist. One could easily overlook the smudges of muddy wet weather marring M.'s debonair appearance, for in the bitter cave of primordial cold he was cool like fire was in the grate and a brandy on the table.

"Just a fuckin' minute, Hoffler, before you pull that trigger and get your ass kicked six ways from sundown for it. *Verstehen, cocksucker?* I mean your shit's in the wind."

A pall descended over this terrorist brood, whose assorted performers and motley extras never heard or saw their leader confronted so. Collectively they awaited an inevitable burst from Hoffler's submachine gun to indent the fat heretic before them. Such a discharge never came. Keeping an impassive face (and that wicked-looking weapon) trained on his questionable associate, Hoffler let the challenge pass into the staid suspension of things. Finally he descended with measured portentousness from his crate-vantage, a wafer thin smile compressing whitened lips, the gun's snout still upraised. An unfazed Macon -- one hand now in a jacket pocket, J.F.K. style -- seemed to enjoy the moment's limelight.

When he was just inches from the fatso, Hoffler emitted a hissing but subdued invocation in German, which a now rapt T.K. figured had to be obscene. Good enough reason to have studied the Deutsch at that point, instead of imbibing uppers and downers. Then the Der Feuer Bande leader said -- in English, in the same sibilant undertone -- that he promised right then to cut Macon to gooey red shreds if the bloated Herr-Man did not do more than show up for a house party. It was, in essence, time to deliver something besides kibbitzing, to put some hold cards on the table and purge that gleam in the eye of any "enemy."

"I hear ya!" Macon said with relish. Convivially he held his restraining hand like a stop sign. Between its fingers his cigarette's monumental ash swelled, dropping. "I do hear you, brudder, and that's why the Herr-Man's here. To get you out of this Polizei-crawlin' mess, ja ...? To take the heat off this iceland." Macon now thoughtfully reflected, pacing and taking a final drag from his Camel butt before flicking it into mid-air -- a few yards south of a loaded ammo crate. "To put the heat back in our kitchen where it belongs. Right, *Comrade* --?"

"Ja," said Hoffler, though his eyes indicated otherwise.

"I know what you're thinkin', bro," Macon went on, addressing everyone. "All of you. You're thinkin', Jesus Chrise, this Macon clown ain't worth a shit, right?" Raul M. paused -- snuffling, gauging the effect -- before clearing his throat and continuing. "Sure, he ain't worth a turd in a Turkish toilet ... I hear ya." Macon shook his head now imperatively, underlining his own declaration, delighting in the moment's immediacy. They were really listening to him, if you could believe it, like their lives depended on it. War was no taste of honey if your Boot Camp was at *Fuck U.,* and the sissies had to accord him that much. Sure. Macon knew from first-hand which way the winds of war blew, even Hoffler had to admit that much, by Gott. Even if they were humoring the M.-man just to use him, it was to save their precious asses from the big hurt. (And look at the la-dee-da blonde bitch staring at him now, like he was really Jack Shit with a cross come to save them: she was about to cream there, sitting cross-legged as if at a Rock concert ... O Lovely Bitch, Macon thought, sweet lady with a mental orgasm, *Your time will come.*)

"Yeah, you're all proabably feelin' a bit let down by this Confederate cracker here, ain't ya?" Raul continued. "Betrayed by another Judas from candyland! Well, listen up, cocksuckers. You're up shit creek at the moment. I mean it's hit the fan, clowns. You might as well make reservations right here for your own mass cremating."

"That's not what I think we're entitled to hear," said a disgruntled Brice Rampoul, interrupting the deep silence always following Macon's pronouncements. "We are, in short, in need of some seriously beneficial advice at the moment. We're more than willing to be all ears for any."

"Oh, is that fuckin' so?" said Macon, for a moment mildly irritated. He punctuated his own remark with a trademark braying cackle. "I'm glad to hear that, Comrade Asshole. I mean that just pleases the piss outta me. Jesus F. Chrise, you should take a bow for somethin' that profound, man ..."

Suddenly enlivened, Christina playfully poked her sidekick Rampoul once in the ribs, to his chagrin. Rampoul was in the midst of taking another thermos sip from a liquid now lukewarm, and his distaste was dramatically evident. He looked older than his years.

"Anywho," Macon resumed, having indulged in enough chortling inspired by his wit and wisdom, "I got your advice hangin' ... Hoffler? I think you and these animals should lie low for awhile until we can stick our heads out again and see what the board's like. But I did come here with some tactical ideas I wanta go over with you, sorta in private."

"I think we should be present," Rampoul announced, indicating the slouching Mupreen nearby as well.

"We'll have to decide on that," snickered Macon.

"Just what the hell's the story here," Nils Mupreen asked, sitting up. "I personally am hard put to follow you at times, Macon, or whatever the hell your name is at present. You don't seem to have much to report or inform to us, and I'm frankly wondering if the American military at Forbrau isn't shielding you in a way ... letting you proceed unhindered in an attempt to betray us. (I say this because no one seems to be listening to anything but war plans at the moment.) You're a man in the middle, comrade. That's how I see your place here, and frankly I think it's the worst position anyone can be in. So what do you think of that? You're a fall guy, Herr Macon, whether you know it or not -- and maybe you'd be better off to yourself and everybody concerned by just, as they say, disappearing ..."

"We must be prepared to fight," Hoffler said, as if answering for Macon.

"Perhaps. But not with Herr Macon, in my estimation, who will only expeditie our predicament into a Waterloo of sorts."

"We must be prepared to fight," Hoffler reiterated.

"Let us try to use our advantage with the old man Tomasi," Mupreen said earnestly. "Let's test his political usefulness to us in the near future, and see if he's still not the answer. We can use him as a bluff, can't we? ... Maybe the world will believe the old man's Mr. Medulla Raze himself -- the cloned Einstein of it. We can fabricate media information about this around him, descrediting the Americans. We can 'expose' the Medulla Project to the masses, inventing our version of its reality to the people ... and perhaps create a counter-paranoia for the Americans to deal with. Perhaps it will weaken them, this secret being exposed. Don't you see that ... Gunther? Let us proceed tactfully, rather than shooting it out Western style. If the world believes the Medulla is another time bomb directly accountable for the bad weather's greenhouse gases in the ocean of ozone -- and imminently perhaps much more, until we all die of carbon dioxide overdosing -- then perhaps mass panic and even rioting will break out, all across Europe. What can the Americans do at that point if the snowball's rolling, ja? Ach so. The Russians will gain sway ...

"We must exploit this moment, Gunther. That's all I'm going to say. We must exploit it -- and hope for the best, perhaps a turning point in our favor, which will allow us to proceed ... perhaps get more of a beach head, a *real* hold against the U.S. military, ja? ... We must at least try. The other way is suicide, simply that."

Lowering his weapon, the young German leader was definitely considering Mupreen's plan as an option.

"All right, Nils, that's a good alternative ... since we have a few days before moving, at any rate. I want you to work on that in detail then, and get it back to me ... Christina and Rampoul can work with you, and maybe -- God knows how -- you can get some real information of value from the man as well, yes?

"In the meantime ... Herr Macon and I have much to discuss regarding the facts of *Krieg,* which will be prepared for our political body as well. We'll see just which one of these alternatives we will need the most. Ach so, I have a feeling both will prove useful -- and perhaps together."

Rampoul saluted this with an upraised mug, though his heart wasn't in it. He smirkingly began to hum his version of The Battle Hymn of the Republic, but no one was listening.

37.

Her face appeared to phosphorize, within a limpid moment of eternity, into a living mask from myths of Mara: and with such powerful but potentially spiritual destructiveness she wielded a will over the men, driving them against the wall of whatever capability for resistance they possessed.

Out of the ice haze she gamboled about, taunting and cajoling, inspiring and denouncing them for becoming cravenly hesitant when "the battle," she maintained, "has not begun."

How could any bitch talk and act like this? Macon wondered in a moment of pure dumbfoundedness. He could understand her being able to confound the American and Dutch wimps so easily (they, after all, belonged in a university museum studying one another's castrated members); but that she could have such sway apparently over Hoffler was another thing entirely. *Was Hoffler getting soft?* Had a measly firefight unnerved the bugger into some chickenshit cowardice, he wondered.

The Witch Bitch. Macon had heard stories while impersonating the fictitious "Herr M." How she had overpowered the kidnapped old man (who now was on the verge of croaking, perhaps), systematically torturing him for key revelations -- which never came -- regarding the Medulla Project. At first Macon had refused to swallow it. That sophisticated looker just didn't seem capable of doing anything worse than stroking a professor's beard as Dietrich had done in *Blue Angel*. Now in the secluded and subterranean terrorist fortress, what he witnessed made him believe otherwise.

Christina Alpreece looked to be playing both ends against whatever middle there was, doing a compromising act regarding Der Feuer Bande's next -- perhaps crucial -- tactical maneuver. She backed the bespectacled Dutchman Nils' pleas for attempted media exploitation to the hilt; yet she cast knowing looks of agreement at Macon, hoping to establish bona-fide allegiance with his kick-out-the-jams, Rockin' out dogs of war mentality.

The night following their mega-meeting on strategy, Macon didn't know Gunther Hoffler had presented Christina with certain "artifacts" found in the bunker from their ill-fated raid. In their headquarters' tent they'd been arguing over recent events and sorting through another chest from the bunker raid when -- almost in a pre-destined manner -- Christina extracted a stainless steel box she wondered about. Unlocked, it opened creakily to reveal old photo albums and personal articles that clearly enough were non-military -- so totally out of place in a cache of arms and munitions, Hoffler knew.

"My God," Christina said, after opening the album. There were old black and white photos of obviously German civilians in formal group poses. "That's my great grandmother, see her? I'm sure that's her, Gunther .. I can't believe this."

Studying the photo with others, Hoffler acted startled to see Christina's likeness portrayed, right down to her present age, though the World War II photos were ancient and near mildewing. The date "1942" was clearly written on the back of some, yet Christina's first impulse was to regard them as fakes -- a hoax of some kind. Then Hoffler told her what he knew, using the items to help her recall things she had somehow forgotten -- as if once she'd been hypnotized and now it was time to bring her back.

"These things were planted in the bunker -- by Nils' brother, Kress. Purposefully put there by him. He left a letter there, as you can see ... So he's been working with the U.S. government all along, though I've no idea how voluntarily. We only know he's somewhere probably on the Depot, or wherever the Medulla Project's being carried out."

"This scares me," Christina said. Hoffler studied her facial features in the wavering lantern light, watching how shadows flitted across them as she turned to afford him a stolid profile. "My great grandmother ..."

"So she was German. Sort of a coincidence you didn't seem fit to tell me about."

"No. Because I don't know much about her -- hardly anything, really ..."

"Perhaps Kress Mupreen does, if we can ever find him -- and alive."

"We'll have to speak with Nils. He has to be a part of this. How else would anyone have known which bunker to have placed these in, unless he was part of us?"

"Don't worry about that now. I think the best thing is to play along for awhile, and keep quiet. There's something about you they know about, Lady. Things that may have to do with what we're all doing at Forbrau. Here, look at this ..."

Hoffler extracted more photos from another album showing a curious-looking statue of a temple god from some undisclosed jungle location. The large stone deity reposed Buddha-like, only it resembled a cross between Egyptian and Indian gods with animal characteristics conjoined with human ones. There was also an obviously once classified and official-looking typewritten report, again dating from the World War II era, describing how -- for certain unknown reasons -- it was imperative this particular piece of temple sculpture remain unknown to the world at large, "no matter what steps are necessary to insure it." All the while Christina incredulously examined the material, Gunther Hoffler kept studying her intently, hoping to determine just how much she was acting or not. He remained undecided.

Christina Alpreece was shaking her head. The word or name *Li-us* was printed beneath the temple deity's depiction, and she tried with difficulty to pronounce it. "I'm just wondering how any of this could relate to my great grandmother."

Hoffler had no answer. He knew only that the artifacts had a timeless reality about them and would somehow be a key to finding out more about the Medulla Raze, when and if that time ever came. And time would prove Christina Alpreece was definitely a part of it all as well -- though for now he believed she was telling the truth, that her ignorance on such matters were greater than his own.

Did anyone else in the Feuer Bande have any further links with what was going on, such as Raul Macon, who later gave no such impression when Christina herself approached him to further discuss his plan for the Bande's next -- and most crucial -- martial tactic. *Just Blow Them Away*, Macon told her, and eradicate the Depot fanatics guarding the supposed underground Medulla Compound from intruders like himself.

Katzenjammer those Klowns, growled Macon further, displaying Janus-like dissembling powers. "Time don't matter, Comrade Lady. The time be *now*."

Coughing over the smoke from the Euro-hemp pipe passed his way, the Alpreece woman had her elegant white hand over M.'s tempid forehead, stroking it as if to deter fevers. Somehow Macon had his own hand on a private anatomical part, squeezing down under until his man o' war reached the *Present Arms* position. Christina hardly noticed, and Macon fantasized his own hand thrusting him into the dry ice zones of indulgence belonged to old flame Jari even. Yet this jarred his enjoyment. Old Jari was only another pin-headed, cum-fading centerfold in memory, while the fetching Comrade Lady here was one of those *radical intellectual femmes* (so the sometimes reliable T.K. Keller said) with a PH.D. in something besides cocksucking. The fact eventually expunged Macon's self-excitement. And he wondered why he no longer thought the same way about the unavenged Jari he once did.

Gunther Hoffler wasn't noticing any of it either.

Hoffler the spartan, the ascetic, was subsisting on his own will -- sans stimulants or depressants, or even food at times. Now through the maze of hemp and cigarette smoke he stared. Squint-eyed, imperturbable, he perspired greasily beneath the incandescent battery lighting which painted his figure an icy yellow. The German shimmered in an aura of ecclesiastical spuriousness, and affectedly tried studying the enlarged map of numbered-and-colored Forbrau Depot gates and fence perimeters. Despite facts at his fingertips, a flashing speck within his enlarged pupils spelled The Unknown. Something of Hoffler's own medulla matter softly unraveled the more he studied, or squinted. Even the Alpreece woman who insisted they engage in some kind of group prayer to invoke the spirits of Li-Us could not bother him.

I can't believe this, Macon said, growling dissatisfaction, pushing the woman's faith-healing hand away, wanting to drag her down on him but instead putting the pipe between her Princess-like lips and going to work with probing fingers at her still unresponsive crotch.

Sure, I can tell you beaucoup things yet about Uncle Sam's game plan, Comrade Lady! He didn't know where that Dutch wimp or that gray-haired New York Sugar Daddy of hers were at the moment, but he wouldn't take his hand from that one true center of warmth in the cave -- even should they arrive to find the little lady and him bare-butt naked. Such were the ways of undercover operations. This lithe beauty came to Macon off the cover of some swank erotic tabloid, yet she verified for him more than indisputably that she existed in the flesh like a risen martyr from a ghostly Gestapo tea party censored from history's record.

"Don't stop. Your grunting is eloquent. Your scar tissues are ample for this ... oh god ... I'm your *Angel of Life*, aren't I ...? I'm the one transplanting life into your veins, stirring your blood with its protease inhibitors."

"Shit," Macon said, fondling the elegant flesh warmth, hirsute as his own. (Was it his own?) He was succumbing, inadvertently or not, to a fatal taste for beauty, and the stars were lit in his mind despite its inner space of darkness.

"Brice," she moaned, "Brice."

"Honey, call me *Raulie*," Macon said. His straight days of playing Brooks Brothers suited intelligence dupes were over, he thought exuberantly.

So he would later tell T.K. Keller, when confronting the damaged young wastrel in an attempt to procure a long overdue "intelligence report."

Understandably at first the lad wanted to voyeuristically hear Macon's detailed and downright obscene rendition of just what happened (in more than titillating close-up) inside the 4th Quadrant's headquarters those long hours before midnight. Macon decided wearily to oblige, though the hour was past 2:30 a.m. and he was dead on his feet, having somehow survived the paranormal lady's investigating advances.

"That bitch! That Betsy Ross and Mata Hari all in one -- and don't ask me to explain who the hell she is, was, or comes from, Keller. She's a raving insane spook with revolution on her mind, that's all I know. She's from another dimension, man. She's transsexual Jesus Christ with a hard-on from the Planet X in an all new body -- *and what a bod, T.K.!* ... I have tasted that sweet flesh and feel Born Again."

Raul Macon was shaking his head but smiling, reflecting on it all. Some poor drooling miserable bastard T.K. was, just like in the old days, a captive audience with the fear of God & Satan having bowed him into childishness. The boy had tasted bad things, and their effect on him at this hour clearly amused a rank Macon, whose suit now looked sadly soiled and wrinkle-lined.

"All I can say, son, is that she's a mouthful and a half ... *I can't believe* I did that in there, but facts are freakin' facts. I fornicated the goddess upside down, rolled her over on Der Fuhrer Hoffler's desk, and now her spoor's all over that poor bastard's military maps!" Macon couldn't restrain an outburst of sibillant then guffawing trademark laughter, counterpointed by T.K.'s sick-sounding own.

Pausing to wet his whistle with another pull from a Moselle wine bottle -- and thoughtfully flicking a long ash from his cigarette T.K.'s prostrate way -- Macon continued like they were just having another bullshit session in the old N.C.O. Room, instead of deep in some godforsaken cave with icy stalactites overhead adding to the general phantasmagoria, what life in a hit-and-run war had become from here to Bosnia and back again. "I *shit* you not. Too bad she's the best lay I ever had, and too bad Hoffler, Mupreen and that Rampoul creep are a bunch of sick puppies."

"You did it right on Der Hoffler's desk?" asked still laugh-quaking T.K., trying to stop long enough for some miscegenated oxygen.

"Goddamn right," yawned Macon, eyelids heavy in an almost amorous fashion.

"Then -- Hoffler saw...?"

"Hell yes. They all saw, the sick shits."

"Oh, Jesus *Christ*," a no longer laughing T.K. said.

"That's what I mean, laddie. I told you they were all crazy, didn't I? That they're a bunch of cocksuckers on the half shell? I mean The Bitch has more of a pecker then they'll ever have," Macon chortled, enjoying the reaction he was getting. "We're talkin' *Clit.*"

"Better keep it down, Macon. You're not bullshitting me, are you? I mean everybody's had a long day and night ..."

"I ain't bullshitting," Macon explained in a louder, angrier voice. "What the hell's wrong with you, besides your cheap-ass 'shrapnel wound' scratches -- and the fact you pissed all over yourself and can't stand the fact. The Shit Has Hit The Fan, Son. *Dig it?* The world's gone haywire -- bananas -- and every Doomsday fucker from here to New Delhi is out *protesting* and raising cane because the brilliant 'scientists' have screwed this ball of planet earth so -- okay? This green ball of wax, T.K., practically don't even spin on its axis any fuckin' more, or so the papers are sayin'..."

"Jesus Christ."

"I told you, didn't I?" Burping extravagantly, Macon tossed the empty bottle away, and began thoughtfully chewing a fingernail. "Nobody's together in this place. Face that fact."

"We gotta do something. We're like rats down here, Macon. Our chances aren't lookin' good --"

"You're tellin' me? I just convinced Hoffler we're gonna have to find that Medulla Zone somehow, while there's still room to move. So that means another commando mission, son."

"Oh ... great. Just great ..."

"That's right. As for whatever they're planning with that Tomasi character, I doubt if any of it'll come off. I damn near knocked out that fuckin' Mupreen's banana brains anyway for smartin' off when I dicked bitch-face, so I doubt if he's capable of doin' much thinkin' hereafter, the scumbag. Serves him right, cryin' at The Bitch for *'treason'* or some shit, until I had to slap the fucker." Macon laughed again, though now it sounded unpleasant. "And that old joker Rampoul she hangs out with got the shit scared out of him likewise ... though he didn't open his mouth, the smart ass. Just stared like a dumb fucker while I peckered his old lady."

"I don't believe this, Macon."

"You better, son. It's the sad fuckin' facts. I hate to spoil the party, but this is fuckin' war, where fair is unfair. You *know* that, Keller. And you're right in sayin' we're gonna get out of here. And if it means slapping these silly mothers around, then by God ..."

"I hear you."

"Damn straight," Macon said, squinting heavily as he field stripped his cigarette butt. His lies had to be believed, his truth had to be disbelieved. "Don't worry about a goddamn thing. I told them I was gonna come out here and get the low-down from you about Forbrau. I told them you were holdin' back out of fear for your sorry life. I told them you're more valuable then you proved so far."

This news did little to improve T.K. Keller's febrile state of mind. With a moan he leaned back down, trying to digest body & soul all that was told him. Suddenly the alluring woman Christina Alpreece, with the beautifully enigmatic Hellenistic face, was reduced to ashes and not just mortal whoredom in his stereopticonic recall of her. Only recently she had attended to and bathed his inflamed, pinpoint-speckled wounds with the devout, soul-uplifting ministrations of a Florence Nightingale. He had wanted to believe -- as he always had -- that she was a miraculous creature of rare device: a madonna-like figure from antiquity's gilded pedestal ... He had wanted to believe, perhaps, because he had never really known his own Italian-American mother, any more than he'd ever known the true faces of women who were bent, he believed, on somehow betraying him. And now this: an intimation she was an addled hedonist trying to rebound from the hard row of battle?

"I don't believe it," T.K. Keller said.

"Well -- fuck you, then. I ain't got all night."

Macon slumped back against rock-abutting crates and undid his tie, for the party was over. His suit coat's once brilliant blue color was now smudged by grime and traces of slushy mud; his face, red-mottled by fatigue, cigarettes and drink, resembled an excavation in progress. Sighing with eyes shut, rubbing snot from his nose and belching, the show nonetheless had to go on. *What kind of Shit have you for me?* was the question. T.K. at first regarded it with hesitancy, still wanting to vomit, his body assaulted by cold cave vapors. Macon slapped his different dude's thigh with a weather-chapped hand displaying an expensive ring. Evidently being the pseudo-manager of an N.C.O. Club had its rewards.

"I know what you're thinking," Macon said. "Any fool can tell, right? You're wondering if I got a little strange at the Club -- whether I've gone over to good ole Uncle Sam -- which maybe you'd like at the moment. I tell you this, I ain't suited for that job, but Hoffler's contacts impressed hell outta me. All I've been doin' is tellin' the coolies where to stack the beers, and no questions asked. The real fuckin' manager, Berston, comes in twice a day too crocked to give a damn. Without doubt the Germans are into that guy -- or have somethin' on him to keep him scared shitless, and mum as your dead mother. *Anyway*, son, I don't believe that scene, but Hoffler's got some pull, I wanta tell you. The First Shirt's been the only one tryin' to give me shit (you know the old fucker, his ass is into everything), but Berston cooled him off for me, and I'd of never gotten off the bar stool until this latest ruckus, thank god.

"Now *tell me*, Keller. Have you gone over to Sam with cold feet?"

T.K. Keller shook his head, reflecting on life's absurdity which this moment -- and this "dialogue" --

crystallized for him. "No way," he said.

"I'm sure glad to hear that," Macon said laughing, reaching into his coat to reveal a U.S. Army .45 pistol (with a loaded clip inserted) which he pointed, after bolting the slide back with angry suddenness, at T.K.'s unflinching presence. "I oughta blow your ass away, you damn quisling wop."

Keller knew the play was serious. "What more can I tell you, Macon?"

"You can start with what you and Lacer been up to on the Depot."

"Lacer? Wayman Lacer? ... I thought he was your boy! Doesn't he tell you anything?"

"I'm beginning to wonder, man. Just beginning to."

Keller tried to laugh disdainfully, but was too tired. Keeping his end up in this laborious exchange required some great effort.

"I saw what you saw, Macon. I got the same tour as you did. Of course I hung around the Depot, hiding out in Lacer's N.C.O. Room, waiting for you to show up and the Shit to hit the fan. Now it has. We've seen changes in the very format of our existence, man. We've traversed into transcendental territory -- the future of humanity is mutational."

Macon spat. "This is big bizness, son, and you and that loony buck sergeant have whiled away the hours smoking hemplines and adulterated Medulla shards in that Room -- and all around Depot -- nearly getting your half-assed cover blown in the process. The First Sergeant's on to you, son-son. You can't go back to Forbrau again in that drag disguise, or you'll get us all busted. And a greasy mouth like yours would spill secrets just bein' tickled ..."

Keller closed his eyes. *Raul Macon. Man of great subtlety. Right now holding a .45 on me, threatening to give me the bullet my pain-wracked, bruised body just narrowly missed several hours ago. Raul Macon-May-King-Alias-Yahweh ...?*

"Okay, Raul, we checked the Mag Zone out as best we could. That's what you wanted, wasn't it? And everything we could note I later told Herr Hoffler in the recon report. Don't you believe it?"

"Everything?"

While Macon took his .45 safety latch off, T.K. Keller went into greater detail, rehashing once again what was already common knowledge. How he had covertly photographed vital points of strategic interest in the Mag Zone, as Hoffler had requested. How they had run into members of the suspicious Polish Labor Army also out on patrol, and how Lacer had reassured the old Polacks (who nonetheless knew their business in the Zone -- to a point where Keller believed *they* really knew what was happening -- and drove new green, well-heated, nuke-powered Broncos making U.S. jeeps look shabby) that everything was all right, that Keller was a classified visitor with a valid permit, etc. Of course T.K.'s forged documents were in order; he might as well have been sent by the Army to perform this mission, like some declassified wonderboy well-versed in the arcane high-tech arts of Medulla alchemy, and nobody had more say so than Lacer's Floridian pal, the quarterbacking Desk Sergeant. Yes, everything had gone smoothly enough -- didn't Macon believe that? -- and the coming snafu certainly couldn't be attributed to any faulty information from T.K.'s end. "No way that could be possible, Raul. You know that."

In T.K. a mass of intangibles made him doubt everything he'd seen and did: as if fate, that skittering ball on ye old roulette wheel, had stopped on the wrong number. So the odds for the right one remained slim. Perhaps, T.K. had to admit, Lacer and he had too much fun on their clandestine recon mission, where they glimpsed the faerie goddess of Christina Alpreece's alter ego, ready to spring forth and save the woodland universe. Perhaps that vision fouled their luck up. Could there be a better intangible reason?

It had all been like a reunion in a way: a trip down a once loathed memory lane made exciting because -- at last -- the coming plunder of *The Zone* made them feel they now had the final power over it. That was a remarkable feeling indeed, one undoubtedly intoxicating T.K. and his accomplice.

"We need something better right now to go on, T.K.," Macon coaxed, not lowering the gun. "We need it bad! Think, you bastard, think. We gotta find a way down under to that Medulla motherlode in a hurry."

You damn illiterate, T.K. thought. *A way to the Womb-pussy is what you're after. A way to that Medulla cave in a hurry, where the ghost of great terrorists like Usama Bin Saden stand sentinel therein, before the plug is finally pulled on surface land-mass Earth. I kid you not -- & ol' Tito our founding father will cash in on all this at last, Macon, mark me...*

In those reflective moments of bottled eternity, T.K. sought to purge his memory for something overlooked: some clue for them to go on during this fateful wait between things. But the more he tried, the less his bankrupt mnemonic software yielded. He almost prompted Macon to pull that trigger and induce merciful murder-suicide. Instead he moaned, sweated, did his damn best to concentrate meditatively on the remote pictures of Forbrau being dredged to the crepuscular mental topside from his unconscious. Details emerged -- but in diffracted, random abandon they came, forced up from an implosion equal to his head being split around nuclear gray matter.

The events from that recent time had been traumatic enough: emerging again as a quasi-spy into that dread Forbrau bastion of now rumored and complex techno-experiments. Once there was a blessed ignorance, T.K rued, but no longer. Now there was fear and tremblings, and the divining rod he had figuratively wielded began shivering in every direction but the one where the real hotspot was.

...And it certainly wasn't just in Lady Alpreece's Z-spot, where a penis was said to be burgeoning like a neo-biblical miracle, courtesy of some undefined and mysterious science.

38.

Once there had been an idyll as he and Lacer had jeeped around the Mag Zone, immured within the now endless winter which, at times, changed to an unaccountable Indian Summer. The manifestation of this aberrational season in all its uncontrolled wavering (or was it really a predetermined, controlled wavering?) amounted to the startling sight, here and there, of cone-bearing, green-needled fir trees -- heavy with spring blossoming -- hovering above an ice floe bank of cold, encrusted mud.

Once (as in *Camelot*) there had been a brief idyll of digitalized hemp smoking in Lacer's N.C.O. Room, then the dangerous but exultant journeying forth at any hour into the wilderness where the mission of espionage beckoned. They were cheating probably, T.K. thought. They were consciously or otherwise making it more difficult for themselves by increasing the risk factors in their flirting with dangerous consequence. In a way, too, the Fire Band's future could well depend on these two young men who -- like Egyptian tomb explorers -- were threatening to uncover some ambiguously contained scientific taboos in a region where they didn't really belong.

Of course, T.K. reflected in his subterranean desperation, there was something to be remembered from those fateful jeep exporations with a drug-dazed Lacer. Despite their attempts to make it a game, a marvelous escape from predicaments depressing, the brush-clogged ruins they circumnavigated were pregnant with a riddle of ineradicable import. Not even the voluptuous peace pipes of Medulla-tinged hemp (smuggled by T.K. from the break-in of that bunker cache of munitions, etc., exhumed one ill-fated guerrilla night), smoked in the seclusion of Lacer's N.C.O. Room, could ease the ongoing pain of ambiguous truth. "There's no easy out," Lacer had confided, knowing it didn't pay to be philosophical at times.

Yes, the day T.K. remembered most vividly now -- thanks to Macon's brutish prodding -- was taboo-tainted, and therefore the most difficult for his mind to recall in detail. A block, maybe, always has significant meaning wedged behind.

There was something else T.K. didn't want to go into, even a greater reason for the block. It was something he would never dare confess to a Cro-Magnon like Macon, though to T.K.'s disbelief perhaps he wanted to.

Ridiculously enough, it was a prolonged staring into Lacer's inveigling eyes that brought the problem on, and generated the mistake to come. Maybe it was the hemp *and* the staring, but whatever the reason for T.K.'s coming under that non-com's sway, it was enough infatuation for the gorilla Macon to eternally train a gun on. Lacer had the eyes of an alchemical magician, the all-knowing illusionist of dark love T.K. believed he'd become prey to. Yet how significantly? How much time for Keller to set things straight, to clear himself before the executioner exacted payment, before -- thanks to his now bitter self-awareness and damning knowledge of it all -- he'd be rejected, jettisoned in one hairy bullet-gouged splat into hells where it was too late to say you're sorry?

These were qualms that went by the wayside as Lacer, the great illusionist, hypnotically offered up the host of some exotic chemical, "D.M.T.," while jeeping down Waker Road on this reconnaissance tour of the Mag Zone at nature's most august dusk. T.K. had wanted to refuse. There was a job to do, after all. But you-don't-talk-to-a-man-with-a-shotgun-in-his-hand as the song goes. Wayman Lacer was overriding T.K.'s non-violent leaning of late, only to cop, control, and subvert it into the future expression of a grander violence T.K. would be, yes, the mindless cog of. Oh that D.M.T. was the ultimate mental fender bender in a totaled era where even prescription drugs were hard to get, with water having been replaced by alcohol. That D.M.T. made going through Gate 13 a moment equal to the penetrating of some heavenly portal. Once again T.K. was delivered, saved, brought into the penultimate gilded paradise of fir and exotic plastics shimmering with crystalline essences.

A moment of pure Ascension: of the truest and most devout meeting with Nature ever conceived of or promised by the febrile prophecies of mad saints and outlawed poets! It was wanton yet divine, the perfect conjunction of diametric forces brought into powerful alignment, until a greater energy arose within-and-without, scalding their mind screens with satori, intimations, visions and the kitchen sink, as the ride became roller coaster wend into taboo territories there was no turning back from.

There in the forest they saw the vision of Christina Alpreece as Joan of Arc, glittering like an ascending space projectile into the distant waiting tree brances a fading sunset graced with a brush stroke of crimson on the horizon. There T.K. saw the face of Ulrike Meinhoff smiling from the outlawed reaches of the dead 20th Century ...

How could T.K. describe these things to anyone, when he couldn't even begin to tell himself about them? Christina's Vision brought T.K. into the mega-source of things, where spiritual nanotechnology engineered every drop of moisture coating arboreal bark, and the celestrial visage of her mentor Li-Us appeared to be either a bad likeness of Hitler's, or that of Mona Lisa with Dali's mustache affixed. To quote Frederik L. Polak, the Dutch sociologist and utopian thinker: "If Western man now stops thinking and dreaming the materials of new images of the future and attempts to shut himself up in the present, out of longing for security and for fear of the future, his civilization will come to an end." There existed Ylem, as perhaps Aristotle postulated, and this was the nucleus of all great visionary energy culminating in the Medulla compound. Ylem was taking them over, believed T.K. now, and D.M.T. was the means to this infinity of awareness, where nature's runes became the most marvelous artwork, and it was hard to tell a sculpted tree from a figerglass totem: both were from the same artist's hand, now inseparably equal and linked to one another for all the general ages, including The Eternal One.

There were so many signs, so many trail markers inside the glittering Mag Zone's artificial paradise, that T.K. was at a loss to catalogue them. Somehow they were seeing this all with privileged eyes, Wayman Lacer euphorically exclaimed, because D.M.T. was officially the most classified new U.S. Government drug, or uncontrolled substance, type rara avis. "We're the first," Lacer maintained, speed-shifting along and cuffing T.K.'s cheek, "to ever See this place. We're pioneers, Keller! We're Marco Polo and Daniel Boone. We're Yin and Yang ..."

Burning with the vision, T.K. did not know he would yet be persecuted for it. He only knew Lacer's version of the sight picture before them was possibly a profanely sensual one, fraught with the slow playback of a one-track mind. A mind bent on an unholy armageddon equivalent to mass Friday night fights in the Pleiades star cluster. This supernatural creativity was a geometry of tangled equations, all making sense in a perversely nonsensical manner of seemingly haphazard fact and fancy. There was no need to move or uproot this universal landscape of mind and matter. T.K. had glimpsed his apotheosis, accidentally or otherwise, and saw a beauty unparalleled for the first time in Forbrau's kaleidoscopic panoply of earth, space, and fragmented laboratory dreams. And instantly he understood:

WE ARE THE EXPERIMENT.

That much was broadcast in any electric rock or edible grain of space sand falling from the heavens above. He and Lacer were traipsing across Uncle Sam's metaphysical playground, a golf course Bob Hope or Ike would have loved to play.

"Try to imagine what I'm telling you, Macon. Try to see some detailed pictures in all this great landscape, which is on the same conceptual plane with a landscape painting out of Hieronymus Bosch, and stop looking into the darkness which is only your whore-mother's womb. You can't handle that darkness anyway. That's why you and the others are verging on apeshit murder and trying to pap that nothingness with blood. 'What is my nothingness to the stupor that awaits you?' asked Rimbaud."

The cave was a perpetual space hollow that could never be escaped from. The D.M.T. journeying over an idyllically transformed landscape was now a passing dream whose reverberation still assaulted T.K.'s consciousness, leaving a presentiment of the Medulla's ultimate location.

"Stop your bullshit, Keller, or these bullets will eat your fucking mind ..."

What could he say? A good lie would be preferable to a bad truth, but perhaps he was no longer able to distinguish one from the other. That made him unfit to stand trial, didn't it, or testify on his own behalf? That made him mentally unfit, and deserving of other prisons.

T.K. continued: "It was a beautiful evening, Macon. Suddenly we weren't afraid, we might as well have been driving into a park. Time was halted, the weather enjoyable despite the piles of unmelting snow all around, like styrofoam or wet cotton. Suddenly everything was okay, and we didn't care about any goddamn reconnaisance mission, or if we acted out of your jurisdiction or our own. Nope, we didn't care then if we were in danger, or if we'd run into some hidden cave in the Zone we'd be hung for entering, and end up being tortured as spies. Spilling all the beans and finking on you and beloved Führer and his crossbow ... We didn't care one bit about any of that, and I guess that's what rankles. What can I say? Call Lacer what you want, he's just a space cowboy looking for greener grass in that jeep. *That's* his mission in life, I tried to tell him, not overthrowing perennially corrupt governments. But he listens about as much as you do."

"You both were wasted," Macon said, wishing the wine bottles weren't empty.

"For the first time in long-assed months we were *free,* and that temporary freedom was a high like I've never known. It was something *religious,* Macon, and I know how that must turn your guts profanely. It made us feel like giving thanks, like we were entering the kingdom of life rather than the Mag Zone of technological hells ..."

"You're just wasted, Keller," Raul Macon laughed. "Admit that fact. You muffed the job, and deserve to get yourself iced all the way."

"This was like the Promised Land suddenly, and we knew it all as such, sensed it as such! Something beyond our ken was ovulating all right. The most significant ovulation in history was taking place thereabouts, and we were part of it. Millions of brainwashed proletariats around the world would cheer *en masse* if they knew of it, beneath this media-propaganda fostering of a reign of fear and terror, my man.

"Believe that or nothing. That the World is trying to be reborn through the technological marvel under government auspices, with a little help from our galaxy friends. What more could you ask for? At last all the wars will be vindicated. At last slavery will have its extenuating circumstance, because healing the public weal would sanction and forgive it, see?... Sure, once the world is brought under control, then we're all contented slaves for good, instead of unhappy ones. Isn't that what you want? To be part of the greatest enslaving power ever known, First Sergeant R. Macon?"

Macon's finger was still trigger-poised. "And what did you see that might be of real use to us, Greasy? Begin from the beginning."

He would have to continue, Keller decided. Even if he wasn't believed — even if it meant taking the bullet — he would still have to tell it now, for what it was worth.

"It's Disneyland," Keller began, realizing his friendly foe's tenseness following this remark meant a trigger-tightening forefinger in close-up. "By that I mean it's Fantasyland. It's Hyperspace! It's the garden of Hieronymus Bosch in a terrestrial space station. O, man — it's everything and nothing, heaven & hell, a place nobody should be forced to go to, because even your mother would go insane there.

"Lacer *really* knows, I don't. He knows the place inside-out like a tour guide, like he's part of it all. I was scared shitless finding that out, the way he cruised through there, fearing no evil, showing me the super-tech industrial highlights you'd have to see to believe. Can you dig that much?

"We went *down under,* I guess you'd say. There's an intricate array of incredible, tungsten-tough *tunnels* beneath Mag Zone terra firma. Are you hearing this? It's like an industrial subway city down there — super-secured by computerized vault doors -- with a thousand different sectors leading to departments you wouldn't believe... to the Medulla Complex itself, for all we know. *An actual subterranean city of military & scientific complexes at work there,* just like Nils Mupreen of the Puma once speculated, with white-and-blue smocked zombies in plastic skullcaps zealously investigating secrets of the Universe's fate, man, and taking off where Einstein and Dr. Mengele began. In fact, Mengele's probably down there in fine fiddle. He or someone like him even shook my hand. I think he wants my body for further research, though technically I'm still a virgin," Keller laughed. "Anyway, that's *it,* Macon, in one big thundering nutshell. What more can I say? That's the box score. That's the biggest underground laboratory in creation, apparently devoted to bringing-to-life whatever in hell is The Medulla Project, of which I haven't the faintest idea in a snowstorm might really be."

O fear has no zenith such as this, T.K. told himself. This was *the ultimate.* Why had Lacer done such a thing, putting him on a spot like this? Did he so believe T.K. was made irredeemably dumb -- by virtue of a fearful complicity in something that reduced human proportion to a nil, and forever would keep secret some garish, unbelievable fact?

T.K. wondered. He wondered why Lacer would preserve these discoveries from Macon's and the Feuer Bande's immediate knowledge, for such a course was suicidal. That course was hastened now that T.K. had "informed," to temporarily stave off execution.

There are no two ways about it. We homo sapiens are in bondage now to a Project which leaves us on a par with dust motes within this Cosmos dimension.

Morever, T.K. had to suspect Lacer's being affiliated more than ever with the mad powers that be, and was nothing more than a deceiving agent there to root out and entrap the mercenary devils of violent terrorism -- such as Macon, Hofler, and the rest. Whatever happened to the good ol' United States of America, which (once in bondage to terrorist attacks itself) long ago was a republic in dire opposition to all threatening the tenets of its Constitutional freedoms, yet by the 21st Century slowly became imprisoned to forces it became powerless to hall: forces from within its own government as well as those harbored in distant space regions. This certainly caused Keller an even more impossibly growing dismay.

T.K. remembered how the forest captivated in its dark enchantment that fateful dusk they excursioned into the Mag Zone -- and how they were never conscious of it until the spell took effect. In the beginning there was never consciousness of anything, except the density of frost-heavy foliage in a technologically aberrant winter, plus that clinging opaque air through which detail never resolved beyond a few feet. Still Lacer jeep-chugged through it knowing the Mag Zone like a lover's genitalia in darkness, and the putt-putting sounds of his cranky engine approximated a defilement within this woodland sanctuary.

Was this the madness of "War," T.K. believed, or the true fruits of that earthly paradise one envisioned in the same spectrum as a Divine Kingdom? War was Hell, yet here secluded within its premier fortress was a bastion hinting at the haunting pleasures of sense and sensuality, at all that sustained the warrior during respites from battlefield rigors. Here indeed, remembered T.K., was an architectonic Valhalla from the future-past, poised somehow incongruously in their ever mundane present. Hadn't a greater race or an advanced civilization built this magical cyber-ruled kingdom for a battalion of military expendables to continually recrudesce within.

That's why now Christina's face darted up as Joan of Arc's (or a death mask's facsimile) to startle him... The Sciences of WAR were achieving greater scope and identity, for here was truly a once uncivilized activity reconstructed, digitally and otherwise, in the service of the soul. A new definition of Human Being was being clandestinely formulated. Here were edifices emanating the same vibes as any tabernacles in a supposed holy land, yet here the bunkers bore the living fossils of humanity and its accouterments, such as a once technologically advanced military firepower (including strange chemical components of archaic "bio-terror" capability). a force undying in spirit or fact.

That purveyor of Ylem, Wayman Lacer, was going to show T.K. where the entrance to the subterranean Medulla Complex was. Keller became incrementally astounded by this realization, recalling it in the past now and in its present-future context, and knew thereafter things and alliances were changed forever. The more he discovered, the more he discovered what he did not know. The scope of such knowledge was dangerous, and how necessary? Somehow he would have to desert yet again from another Krieg. But weren't all the wars the same One?

They followed a dirt road behind a ridge of foliage where the entrance was. They dismounted from the jeep after Lacer radioed an "out-of-service" from a false location to the P.M.O. Then the buck sergeant unlocked and upraised a cellar-like, iron door enabling their passage into a fluorescent-lit antechamber with something astronomical about it. They were in another capsule-like earth stratum, wherein a humanly made, underground supercomplex existed Lacer referred to as The Lab.

Down through the curvilinear, hospital-like corridor the pair cautiously went, silently, though their boot steps on the concrete stairway reverberated in echoing accusations. "I know all the alarm codes to punch in, don't worry," Lacer cautioned. The lighting, too, was scarily blinding to one nerve-jangled T.K. Keller, who felt this passage to be as surreally unreal as any he'd taken via the auspices of drugs.

How much of a knowing dupe was Lacer about all this? a dubious Keller asked himself as they continued into verbotten territory. The same question could now be applied to everyone, T.K. knew, and suddenly all his inner apparatus of trust became compromised, suddenly he could believe only in White Rabbits, not human beings.

"What chance does a poetic soul have in a world of Medualla Raze and super-technology?" T.K. would ask the void later ...

Macon breathed out, releasing the trigger finger, apparently pleased. "You're a life-saver, Greaseball. I mean that ..." He bit his flaccid lower lip in thoughtful concentration. "I gotta believe you better know the entrance to that earthly or unearthly chamber of heavenly delights, all right. Don't go tellin' me only Lacer can navigate us there. I got other plans for him for holdin' out, him bein' a two-faced agent of a Grand Conspiracy."

"I was afraid you'd ask me that," Keller said, a bit disheartened. "Again, what can I say? The place is an incredible maze of roads and cul-de-sacs going everywhere and nowhere. Give me a break. You seen one tree you seen them all, Macon. Even during the day it looks like night out there. I will defecate a brick, damn you, just imagining being ambushed at every point. You *know* that now —"

"All right, all right, shut up," Macon said testily, putting the lethal-looking pistol back into the shoulder holster inside his suit jacket. "Don't piss-out now, but you better get your beauty rest and your act back together, 'cause you and I and the Fireball Band got some hard rockin' to do out in that Mag Zone fantasyland, okay? I mean shit, shave, and let's get rollin'..."

Macon chortled. He finally had some classified information to withhold or dangle tantalizingly before the Feuer Banders — and that would give him time to calculate his final critical moves for the Super Battle to come.

39.

She held a face within her hands. It was not a face of stone — nor putty — but one she had never felt before, one she had never molded. The male head was distinguished, with a fine and noble forehead above a thick mass of dark hair flinging itself back in scraggly disarray. The head belonged to a living warrior, savant, and philosopher of wars. For a moment she was Judith holding the head of her Holofernes, except the power she derived from such tactile possession was one of love, not loving hate, and it derived from not severing this head from the man's beauteous body in sanguinary, ritual sacrifice.

Not yet, anyway.

Instead she was engaged in succoring it sexually — the head *and* all of the body — as befitted the ongoing talents of Christina Alpreece, who sought to generate heat within a mountain of cold. *Time was of the essence* now, as her colder Dutch confidants reminded her just hours before, and not every woman could have pulled off such a cool seduction given the circumstances, nor with the individual enjoying such favors. While she worked on strengthening his distended digital member within her hands, the elegantly denuded young woman reminded Gunther Hoffler of his shortcomings between his hoarse inhalation and exhalation of panting breath.

"We-must-make-use-of-Tomasi-now!" she insisted, uttering these remarks concurrently with the buzzing measurement of scrotal-seismic activity displayed on their palm-held cybernet device, linked to so many others enjoying the same digital linkage. "The world media must be notified in a cogently effective way, Commander Hoffler, or else Tomasi will be absolutely useless to us, and we'll have lost any advantage we might have had."

Hoffler was trying to ease into a relaxed state following the triumphant mass measurement, but the *femme* would never let him forget the real business at hand. Not for a nano-second. Perhaps he'd made a mistake, succumbing to her digital linkage, but he was a very tired man given to the same weaknesses of others, despite his extraordinary talents and character. He needed a cyber-jolt of something — things being what they were at the moment — and this supersiren was a marvelous narcotic to the group she invigorated in her relentlessly succubus-like fashion.

Alpreece had the mask of a cold virgin with a cyber-whore's warm body, a combination that men did cartwheels for throughout the European continent, so strongly did they wish to connect with her exquisite Somatic circuitry, which had a muscular leanness almost like a man's.

"You are a mean goddess," whispered Hoffler, for she allowed little savoring of enjoying beyond the machinery's obvious beeping. *"Bis demnachst."*

Within the subterranean aery vaults, she covered his trembling mega-mouse with a U.S. Army blanket, though remaining herself there almost dauntlessly unclothed, as a show of strength perhaps. She knew Hoffler was seriously thinking over her demands, and during that thoughtful interval she lazily smoked one of his cigars. She knew he would say, Ja, now we must use Tomasi... *Aber sicher! In Ordnung —*

"Ja, this might be the right time for the Old Man — if he's still alive. This might be the only time, in fact."

"Precisely," said a nearly purring Christina. "And Nils is ready to coordinate Tomasi's media appearances, etc. I'll tell him forthwith to carry through on it, A.S.A.P. Every minute is crucial now, Hoffler, and hell could break loose if we're not careful. Our main intelligence source, Herr Macon-May, has told us the American Army is planning a search & destroy mission against terrorists in the Saarland. We're living like rats now under a sinking iceberg anyway... Normally it should be a pleasant late spring weather to cope with. Only nothing is normal any longer. The goddamn world scientists have screwed things up, intentionally or accidentally. But what difference does that make? Our people are sick, tired, hungry and disillusioned. Our life here in the Cave is one of luxury by comparison.

"The War has begun, Gunther. The enemy army is advancing, and soon you'll be spilling blood instead of seismic emissions. Our trump card Tomasi had better work miracles — to cool some heels — or we're in a world of hurt, as Macon likes to say. But if we can forestall things, turn the brunt of world opinion in our favor, who knows what an advantageous turnaround might not be achieved? The Medulla Project is the key. If we can make it seem, to the world, as if we're preventing the U.S. from using it like they would an old-fashioned nuclear missile warhead ... then maybe 'the people,' as they were once known, will grow wary and mutinous to a point where we can muster enough strength to continue our efforts, and even commandeer the Medulla itself. Even *use* it on those who would like to rid the planet of those like ourselves -- the true renaissance activists."

Hoffler arose like a cheek-sunken Lazarus, head-shaking. "The effects of their Medulla experimenting are already manifest by this endless winter. We must try and strike the Forbrau Depot again and find the Medulla. Somehow we've got to get into it. Then we'll really have the Army at bay, especially if we can threaten the world with whatever it is, freeze them to death if need be in an ice age of final judgement that could perhaps last years."

"Macon agrees with you in that regard," declared Christina Alpreece, almost crowing. "He can't wait to initiate the strike force for that sortie. You've heard his proposals. Some of them, even one, might work. That's all we need. He's the demolition expert. At last you'll see how valuable and instrumental his contribution will be. Shall I give him the go-ahead?"

"Tell him to meet with me again ... tomorrow. When he's more sober, that is. Perhaps then we can more effectively plan the counterthrust."

Christina's countenance lost its ebullience. "He says the Americans are really beefing up security in the Mag Zone. He hopes to somehow subvert one of their lieutenants from within, and give us the access we need for attacking the right sector."

"Let's hope so," said Gunther Hoffler, still trembling. He put his hands between the young woman's offerings, yet discovering solace within her heat-radiant shockbox, the truly proportioned digitalized cave a deluded neo-Platonic philosopher might begin marveling at, if times ever changed.

PART VI

THE MEDULLA RAZE

40.

Night: it sinks into the bones, draws a border around the soul. Impenetrable. That is the way of all leaden flesh, the underground guard thought, lighting another cigarette and coughing out smoke like a fire-eater's horribly histrionic belching.

Inside the small abandoned church, the guard knew his prisoner (half-awake, half-asleep) was having a tough go of it. Especially considering his advanced age. Tomasi's being still alive loathsomely struck the guard as a blasphemous miracle; and religion, as all knew, was in danger of becoming extinct, despite the world's precarious position at that moment just begging for some salvation.

The guard was peremptorily dismissed by a regally arriving Christina Alpreece. Her attire resembled a cross between a forester and Peter Pan. An unsettling necklace of large animal teeth dangled from her neck. In her sleek right hand was a large, glinting broadsword that may have been lifted from a nearby Teutonic knights' castle. The sentry noticed a feral intimidation in her eyes as he left, nearly bumping into a small boy with long blonde hair he'd never seen before.

"The time demands an ultimate action," she muttered into the surrounding darkness.

She would confront him, Tomasi, the subjugated one now half-nakedly prostrated on the abandoned church's makeshift altar, where he lay like a sweating marine creature in the crepuscular air of another world. Young Mik, the perfect offering of a boyish innocence, was groggily pushed forward in a dazed condition by the sword-carrying dominatrix, who had dubbed herself Saint Joan for the occasion.

"We shall sway the right honorable Tomasi with something he can't apprehend," she intoned solemnly.

Spreadeagled inertly on the stone altar slab all the while, Vincent Gaylen Tomasi resembled Mantegna's painted image of a moribund, once divine messenger.

Emanating an aura of evil Christina Alpreece entered the altar area. Within the dark, sepulchral chamber she would finally make Tomasi do her bidding. She knew he would not choose death, though now she ominously held the sword's blade over the elderly man's head, just inches from his neck's wrinkled flesh.

"You will know the coming of your true savior," she whispered to her hostage. Tomasi blinked once, his unfocused eyes staring up beyond the talismanic sword towards a blackened ceiling once displaying a fresco of flying cherubs. He dreamed he was in hell, and knew he wasn't dreaming. Despite the cold he was sweating as Christina ordered the boy to fully undress and stand like an enfant terrible before the desecrated altar.

"I know your sordid personal secrets, Vincent Tomasi. If you wish to live you must accept my offering, then reveal those classified government data I need to know. It's strange to think our world's well-being may hang in the proverbial balance," she calmly proclaimed, slowly circling the altar while keeping the sword angled uncomfortably over the prone man's body. "But indeed it may be so. These are strange times, aren't they?" She removed the blanket from her sallow hostage and prodded him with her sword tip, muttering a brief litany of imprecations, her eyes tilting towards the darkness above. "You degenerate capitalist, I've brought you your salvation. The fruit to succor you. The balm of your recovery, without the onus of shame and all your despicable fey secrets. Can you still find the faith to renew yourself, in flesh and spirit, and help us save this misbegotten world?"

In the umber space surrounding him Tomasi was softly crying, his eyes as unseeing as ever. This deluded female presence saw herself as a saint, he knew, along with the rest of the avenging Feuer Bande. He wanted to scream, but his voice was also hostage to the apparitional woman's presence. Her very essence was mendacity, yet he knew she was serious. And she *knew*. She knew about him, and that was the hard and almost unacceptable thing.

How had she found out, and who could have betrayed him? She was more terrifying because of her ability to lie always along with her skill in exposing the mendacious shields of others. She'd pierced him and his defenses, now they amounted to very little, and Tomasi knew she'd pierce his brain in the same manner she had his honor.

She ordered little Mik to lay his digital toy on top of the old man, which was easily done. Tomasi recoiled from digital shocks. The boy added a weigh which seemed the collective guilt of ages.

"Vincent Tomasi, will you tell us what we need to know? Will you tell us where the Medulla Complex is, and how we may access its labs?"

She raised the sword higher over both of them, then uttered a Latin pronouncement, her face almost radiant with a perverse spirituality Tomasi was glad tears blinded him to. (His eyesight was failing naturally enough anyway during this confinement, along with the rest of his health.) He realized with a flickering madness the boy was attaching feathery wires to him as commanded, and knew -- along with everything else -- he was a greater prisoner of his own weaknesses than his dying strengths. A dance of stuffed teddy bears now commenced their ballet directly overhead, serenaded by a background music of unseen violins. The young woman laughed when she saw Tomasi press the animal circuits against his face, where they swished like a horse's tail against aggravating flies. He felt himself now becoming a giant orifice engorged with all the sweet liquid passions of a sweeter galactic hell than any he'd known before.

In a far corner of the abandoned church, the unseen figure of Raul Macon watched all this in candlelight shadows. Around him a chorus of neo-tech toy demons sang a lustful accompaniment through the endless night. For a moment Raul feared this feral priestess who materialized Fuseli-like nightmares (with astonishing ease) from the world of aesthetic illusion into that of endangered reality: feared her in a way the dreamer does his long-awaited succubus, or the mother of some unholy god.

For her part, meanwhile, Christina Alpreece achieved a fleeting communion with something that irradiated the core of her most starved being -- and she saw a way out at last.

*   *   *

Brace yourself, T.K. a voice told him.

Wars forever revived themselves, Gracinauto-Keller knew, from neo-Communistic Europe to the Orient. Sometimes the names changed, sometimes not. Peking to Beijing -- Sarajevo to Bosnialand -- Viet Nam to Viet Name -- Kabul to Kabullam, it was only the jingoistic mutationism reflecting the trapped human condition, despite whatever age. And T.K. knew the Age of Medulla war was all but upon them. As surely as he found himself reverting to the mad poet ways of his alter ego (which, though apparently aesthetic, were just more manisfestations of a personal and universal schizoid dysfunction), so too would the uncured world of mass humans revert to the cave.

As he waited to meet with Macon-May in the Forbrau snack bar, Gracinauto-Keller knew they were having trouble keeping their acts together. Nobody, least of all the C.I.D. or the C.I.A., was fooled.

Of course Time was of overwhelming essence, now that much of Western Europe was suddenly entering the throes of a faux-modern Ice Age. T.K. sat uneasily worrying about his erstwhile Amsterdam love Lelica and her boy Mik; the latter's unknown whereabouts and current condition gnawed like leeches at him. T.K. was afraid again, and pal Raulie had to help out. No longer could they continue being a half-assed espionage team more befitting a bad American T.V. show than -- well, whatever. Whatever they learned immediately was lost again.

Even recent memory escaped T.K. like evanescent dove wings.

So the reality of terrorist warfare was something he needed again to escape from. He even feared an unaccountable desire to escape into the Medulla Raze mystique itself.

"And why is that?" he incredulously demanded of Macon-May.

"Sounds like a personal problem, T.K.," Raul responded, inhaling strong cigarette smoke the way unsuspecting victims once did anthrax spores. "Once again you're freaking out before the play's over and the curtain falls."

"Don't go Shakespeare on me, scumbag. This is beyond seriousness."

All Macon-May knew was that he now saw things more clearly than before. He recalled in detail what T.K. had revealed about his sortie with Sgt. Wayman Lacer into the privileged sanctuary of the mysterious Medulla Complex. In Raul's mind it proved conclusively that dubious Lacer had to be a C.I.D. informant, perhaps even agent, well aware of what he and T.K. (though long out of the picture, and almost obfuscated by time and current disguises) were up to. All that despite the fact Sgt. Lacer had never really met Macon or Gracinauto until their second coming to Forbrau.

T.K. had a general idea of where The Complex was -- but gaining access would be virtually impossible without Lacer, and it was the buck sergeant that Macon-May had to lose. Their sortie into that enclave had been a mini-adventure, if T.K. were telling enough of the always questionable truth. According to him the Complex was an incredibly computerized operation -- huge, encompassing many high-tech underground bunkers affording them a brief glimpse into the U.S. Government's controversial new world. Yet Macon-May wondered how much of the Complex was really Uncle Sam's. He was hunch-wise sure that it was an extensive international cooperative involving many countries, excepting of course the neo-Soviet Union and its revived 21st Century brand of communisms.

THE RAZE OF MEDULLA

"I don't want to blow your mind, T.K., but the Feuer Bande's about to move on the Complex. Tomasi spilled his beans to Christina on the whole operation – including its vital coordinates and access codes. We're going in, thanks to him. Almost walking in, in fact. At least so in the beginning... So get your shit together because we're about to take a long pass and quit these freakin' Forbrau barracks again, something I know you'll enjoy –"

A disbelieving T.K. was almost cheering.

"Any word of little Mik's whereabouts? I know Lelica's worried sick back at The Amstoy."

"I'll tell you that later, when you're mission-focused. Right now you've got to prepare for a quick exit."

Other things preyed on Macon-May's mind as he downed his coffee. *Mission Seizure* was their biggest, best, and perhaps only chance to turn the tide and gain the controlling momentum they'd need against the U.S. Government and its accursed army. He would have to accompany Christina Alpreece and the rest into the Complex. And then? That was the delicate part. The part everything resembling his successful takeover depended on.

Indeed Raul Macon-May was planning a takeover. As meticulously as his fervid thoughts would allow. Standing in his way, he knew, was the damnable Feuer Bande leader Gunther Hoffler. If only he could banish the spell of having seen Christina in the old church with Tomasi and the boy. Something about it equaled a curse hammering him down, minute by minute. Glancing at his watch, Macon wondered if the time on it was still real.

"Everything depends on how well you get Lacer to help us when we hit the Compound," he instructed Keller. "We have to make certain he's not a C.I.A. plant. We have to make sure he'll be there with us – and that's your job now, T.K. To make sure we can count on him, and that there'll be no surprises once we try to take the Medulla."

41.

The Hawk is Blowing. So T.K. knew, preparing for the coming armageddon with as much focused concentration possible. The once natural winter reappeared with lightning abruptness, and an Icelandic wind blew fiercely through the abandoned city warehouse they occupied. T.K. pulled his parka more tightly about him and sipped his scalding coffee.

A few minutes earlier he'd shared a simple breakfast in the disturbing presence of Christina Alpreece. (No more fancy Depot food now, he knew; no more snack bar tuna salad on rye, or specialty soups. Only stale crackers, cement-hard bratwurst, and an odorous cheese extremely distasteful.) Her transformation from glamorous *femme* into something resembling an androgynous Che Guevara – sans beard, of course – startled T.K. He knew the hour of *The Usurpation,* as she called it, was at hand.

"I want to thank you and Macon for doing a superlative job for us – without being detected," Christina had complimented, pacing about in her fatigues while stroking the fur-flaps of a pile cap held, kitten-like, in her arms. "It was a dangerous deception. We didn't think it would go this well. But tell me, T.K., would you expect more than this in the way of a last supper?"

T.K. wondered for an uneasy moment what she really meant. Then he continued methodically chewing his slab or burnt toast. The Hawk whistled like a teapot through the building's poorly insulated walls into the huge void above them, where dimly visible ceiling rafters lurked in ominous configurations.

Her face has a savage streak marring it now, mused T.K. *No longer the Vogue cover girl* ...

Once again he thought of little Mik and questioned Alpreece extensively about his possible whereabouts. She tried to reassure T.K. everything was all right, that Mik was staying in her Amsterdam home and would soon be reunited with his mother. But of course Gracinauto-Keller did not believe her, and knew cunning remained a better taciturn play than outright angry desperation.

"I need some proof that Mik's all right. I can't proceed otherwise."

"You'll get your 'proof,' but you know you're in for the duration of this. You're committed to us, and young Mik's well-being might well depend on your performance."

"Don't threaten me."

"I'm not. I'm stating unavoidable facts. The real world as we once knew it is like this, T.K. Keller. You've grown some with suffering, as I knew you and the others would. Myself? I'm simply a protean-being in my own right, refashioning the masks of a female deity's thousand faces – *Mater Mara,* perhaps? What we can never truly behold ... You're in with us. Don't try and look away from this. We know where – exactly where – the Medulla Complex is, and Herr Hoffler's preparing our strike force. Everybody goes."

Something in T.K., despite himself, relished Alpreece's inspired irrational moments. They were more insidious than his could ever dream of being. The world itself was in a *dream-state,* he realized: one where the collective unconsciousness of humanity was at stake, one way or another.

If they awoke, what creatures would behold them?

The edges between sleep and wakefulness gave way to clearer perception, and T.K. saw a vast assemblage of soldiers, vehicles, and equipment gradually fill the warehouse. Christina was gone, leaving only an ectoplasmic trace of her sensual perfume. Everywhere growing noises abraded his consciousness, and Raul Macon stood winking, the legendary giant from native folklore, at Gracinauto-Keller's woebegone form.

"I need a light, T.K.... Fire, bitte!"

"How much time's left?"

"Not much. I hope you know how to use an obsolete M-79 grenade launcher."

"Of course not, Macon. Like I'm your munitions expert?"

"If you can pull the trigger, you're my man."

They were eventually in a blue van with windows tinted so dark it appeared, T.K. thought, like a *nouveau riche* hearse. He was just glad to be clear of the depressing warehouse headquarters. His stomach churned with an almost welcome fear because they were going beyond the no return point.

The stripe patterned ski mask Macon-May now wore afforded him a classical terrorist's look. Even an old-fashioned one, believed his shivering protégé. Raul the elder chuckled watching T.K. struggle with his own mask, then his attitude grew somber. A tenebrous air existed between them as he loaded a clip into his assault rifle. The van was moving bumpily along now into the woodland's unpaved territory. T.K. couldn't bear the look in his companion's eyes.

"I hoped it wouldn't come down to this," Macon-May said, "but you want the facts. Always the frigging *facts*. It's better to remain an ignorant fool in this life, but people life you don't believe it. They can't stand secrets. That's why governments are so hated by their citizens." He paused, breathing with panting labor. "They've still got the boy Mik out here as you probably suspected. The bitch Christina has practically turned him into a child porn star in order to break down Tomasi. It worked on the old pederast finally, I guess. *C'est la vie.* I'm sorry to tell you what that kid's been through, T.K. I really am."

T.K. stared back unbelievingly, anger and dismay clouding his still visible eyes.

"We got to do somethin' for sure, that's a frigging fact, and not just to keep the boy's health intact."

"I don't believe this ..."

"I told you she was a fuckin' crazy bitch, didn't I? They all are." Macon's gloved hand reached out to steady T.K. "This is gonna be touch and go, but we're getting out of this mess, hear me? I've got some surprises in store for those turkeys. And by the way, amigo, this *ain't* as good as it gets – it gets worse. Your hash head friend back at the Depot -- namely, one P.F.C. Heinsohn? -- is without question a C.I.D. plant working for good old Uncle Tito. You can bet your ass he knows about us -- especially *you* – having strung us along with his bull hoping to find out more about Hoffler and the Feuer Bande."

"He didn't get nothin' out of me," a trembling T.K. replied.

The van ride became bumpier.

"I know that, kid. That's why you're still here." A protoplasmic menace emanated from Macon-May's bulky form. "You did good, T.K. You told everyone what I wanted you to: pure horseshit. Even ol' Tito thinks we've split to England! And you're technically A.W.O.L. again, on your way to Limeyville."

T.K. gingerly removed the large gloved hand from his shoulder. It felt like a large spider had left him.

"I sure as hell hope so, man."

"The only way he can know is if the Medulla people inform Tito that Tomasi is leading us into that top-secret compound for a technically very classified visit. Which of curse they will." Raul almost spat. "I don't trust Hoffler and the Bitch -- their plan won't work. And I'm counting on them to screw up."

"So? They've told the world media about everything!"

"So you better be ready for some high-level ballistics, dude. We're going to commandeer the mission and whatever the fuck that Medulla Raze supposedly is. And frankly I think it's a load of crap that *shouldn't* make the evening news."

T.K. was too inquisitive and intrigued now to lapse into his usual silence, especially now that he knew of young Mik's actual condition. He recognized a hatred then transcending old despair, and desperately wanted to turn on Christina Alpreece. But more than anything he wanted Mik back alive.

"We better not be walking into something we can't get out of, Raul."

"We're not, believe me. We've still got Tomasi as a chess piece, and President Noxson wants him back intact, according to Alpreece. I believe that much. So their plan is that we're the escort team. We get in the Compound along with Tomasi, the troops remain a mile or so outside. The Bitch thinks the plan's a winner: a simple trade-off with the Feds. We leave with the Medulla Raze, they get Tomasi, and Tito loses a bundle."

"That's a sure-fire way to get ambushed after exiting, ain't it? Can Lacer really back us up?"

Macon winked back. "That's necessary, since Hoffler's guerrillas have a battle strategy planned out. They know we have inside access to certain Forbrau bunkers, that we can enter almost at will -- thanks to our own Depot contacts and all that we know. And *they* know the Forbrau Depot could be turned into a fiery shithouse if we're taken too lightly."

It was true, T.K. knew. The Forbrau Depot at that moment was still, despite their recent sortie, as ill-conceived a "military" misadventure as ever. That might change in time -- possibly a great deal of time. That was on the Bande's side, Raul maintained, by their going for *the grand slam* so soon.

Still worry and doubt seized T.K.'s facial features beneath his ski mask. Could they really pull it off? Wrest something from a high-tech cyberspace nexus that seemed, in a way, a real world government of its own at the moment, with the fate of Western Europe in its cold grip.

"And you're seriously telling me you can take it all away from Hoffler and the Bitch -- just like that?" T.K. demanded in his mocking voice.

"If we don't we're as good as dead anyway. They have no use for us after this, don't you see?" Macon's voice became a rushing whisper. "They took us in because of Forbrau and what we knew -- I don't trust them beyond that, kid. We'll offer a no-win deal for the Feds, all right. But that fuckin' Hoffler will be out of the picture then." Raul Macon raised his weapon. "You follow what I'm sayin', or do I gotta learn sign language? There's gonna be a change of command."

T.K. could almost see it, if the projected picture held sway. But it wasn't Hoffler that worried him so much as Christina Alpreece. She loomed larger than any great wall of cyberspace. She was still a burning vision in the underside of his mind waiting to explode.

42.

There's a Wheel of Time we're caught up on -- swinging back and forth, from past perfect to future imperfect -- an illusory ride that distorts our version of conventional History. All thanks to some mysterious & corporate underworld of collusive governments, overseen by the spuriously mammoth democratic one of America's ...

So scribbled Nils Mupreen, riding shotgun in the blue van, into his notebook as an uptight Brice Rampoul drove them along through rut after frozen rut. Nils had almost forgotten their two heavily armed passengers sequestered in the back. *A ride taking us to what quasi-historical juncture at this moment in so-called space and being?* Having suffered so and witnessed so much, Nils now wanted -- if ultimately nothing else -- to make sure he understood completely this terrorist "liberating venture," whether it succeeded or failed. If only for a more accuate and historical record, he told himself. *We are not suicidal holy terrorists, such as the Islamic al Qaeda group was at the beginning of this benighted century. We are scientific, with a faith based in empirical rationality, far from the recidivism of fanatical religions ...*

"If we don't get stalled out here it'll be a miracle," the driver Rampoul uttered in a loud New Yorker's accent, laden with his patrician affectation.

We've so distorted the nature of our world into a shifting morass of deception... We've been betrayed by our own technological tools to a virtual point of gridlock -- even a kind of enslavement. No governing body can free us from it ... only, perhaps, our experimental anarchic-liberation movement, which our enemies brand a terrorism ... Beauty in the service of Death. Death in the service of Freedom.

We are destined to come closer to the truth than anyone else, because our lives have achieved the full measure of dedication in pursuing this goal. We are the new human saviors because we choose not to believe the inveigling deceivers ... but as the ultimate truth of an actual and perfect idea we shall yet prove to be its truest expression.

The peoples of the world shall someday make the rules and explore the solar systems' ultraspace -- and not their ineffectual, lying governments' ...

"Fooey," Rampoul said. He could hardly keep pace with the exhaust-spewing white van leading him, which Hoffler and Christina were in. But then lately he felt far behind them in just about everything, and for the first time realized he was jealous. Decidedly so. They were becoming a "couple," Hoffler and Christina, and that fact rankled Rampoul. He'd begun to fear the German as well for his obvious military talents which made Brice Rampoul resemble a pretentiously aesthetic wimp at times. He knew things were getting away from him as he speed-shifted the van precariously over an unending rocky surface of crater-like gullies only a four-wheel drive could handle. Was it all too late? The reason for his being was vanishing hour by hour when just the opposite should be the case.

He nearly hated Christina then, but told himself it was all Hoffler's doing. If the German with his arrogant militarism fouled-up the next crucial stage of *The Usurpation* -- then what? Christina must side with him then, out of bitter necessity, the way Rampoul hoped. It had been days since she'd even allowed him to touch her.

The van leading Rampoul's also contained Vincent Gaylen Tomasi, still a key passenger despite his fast-fading health. For days the diplomat-businessman had resembled, thanks to Christina's doing, a pale mannikin compared to his former self. Rampoul believed the old man's disintegration was an alarming one -- that soon they would need a doctor -- but Christina Alpreece kept vetoing the idea. "He'll live as long as I want him to," she confided. "I'm like a wonderful daughter to him. He needs me now." She paused, thoughtfully scrunching her brow. "When all this is over, though ..."

It mystified Rampoul that any individual could be as valuable to the U.S. Government as dear old Tomasi, but that certainly seemed the case.

"He could still tell us so much," Christina believed. "These are classified things he's holding back. I wish we could hold onto him forever."

They were nearing a barbed-wire fenceline that Rampoul knew was an anterior part of the Forbrau Depot. Elsewhere, key components of the Feuer Bande were that very moment discreetly congregated at various strategic points surrounding the Depot. Some of the guerrillas were posing as German forest workers and wore corresponding garb. In their trucks, however, were a variety of munitions, but hardly any forestmeister tools. All had walkie-talkie radios and were making site checks that very minute with Christina, who was designated "Control One." It was 4:40 on the afternoon of a very somberly gray day, and Rampoul was surpised things were going as planned, without the slightest glitch. He knew if they pulled this off -- somehow utilized for themselves the so-called Medulla Raze agent, or hindered the Feds from manufacturing it -- they would be home free. And the world's suicidal clockwork would be stopped like any shattered timepiece -- perhaps forever.

It will be history's greatest work of art, demolishing the world governments' genocidal political warfare, Rampoul's co-rider finished penning into his creased notebook as the wind whistled its mournful wail outside, deep into the arboreal fastness of crosshatching limbs and branches.

In the lead white van Christina Alpreece was hardly pondering any similar historic destiny. Instead she was finishing her radio check with her armed unit groups strategically positioned, as unobstrusively as possible, around the wooded Depot perimeter. She glanced rearward at the stately figure of Tomasi (bundled up in his parka like a proverbial Eskimo), still sitting motionless. The small boy Mik sat equally still besides him, also bundled up, but wearing a grungy-looking baseball soft cap more wrinkled than their esteemed hostage's face.

"Gunther, before we reach the complex gate ... pull over for a second so that Brice catches up with us."

Grudgingly Hoffler complied with her request, and Alpreece confided that none of the units were being unduly noted or questioned really by any Forbrau military personnel in the area. It was like they were being invited in, or going to a dinner party they were expected guests at, somehow cowboys in Indian territory.

"If things go exactly what we've planned," said Hoffler, sighing heavily; but he didn't finish the thought. Instead he parked the vehicle and waited for Rampoul's blue van to catch up. "And if your two idiot U.S. stooges don't screw things up ..."

"They won't," Christina assured him. "And if they do -- by then it won't matter."

Hoffler's magnificent silver arbalest lay like a talisman between them in the van, its scope dully reflecting the white winter glare. She marveled at Hoffler's prowess with what amounted to an ancient (if re-tooled) crossbow, and rued her own so-so ability as a "swordsperson." She had purposefully left her own knightly sword back in the abandoned church, knowing that a reliable pistol (such as the old Ruger P944 .40 S&W she now carried) would serve her better than indulging any ego-pretentious wand. Hoffler also had a Colt AR-15 tactical model rifle stolen during the earlier Depot raids; it sported a 16" heavy barrel with removeable handle and a lug for Hoffler's gleaming bayonet, still bloodied.

The Gods had been good to them. They were prepared now for ultimate battle.

To Christina, seeing the ready weapons equaled a mild religious experience. She told Hoffler she was going to talk with Brice a moment, just as the blue van finally drove up. In her vest pocket (sequestered next to other ammunition) was a single 62-gr. plastic bullet from the revived German Democratic Republic she carried for good luck. A souvenir from her hard months of guerrilla training.

"Mission Seizure's about to begin," she told a sweating Rampoul once he lowered his driver's window. "How are your two riders doing?"

From the van's interior she could see Raul Macon-May giving a thumb's up signal. She told everyone to step out and stretch their legs awhile, "before we actually reach the Complex gate."

"Then everything will get really serious, won't it?" Macon-May said, walking up to her and displaying a huge smile. He held up his wicked-looking Kimel AP-9 blowback pistol and kept smiling.

"You got it," Christina said, "just don't get too excited yet."

"You're what excites me, baby."

"Tell your friend T.K. I want to show him something over by our van, Herr Macon-May, and save your excitement for the wild boars."

Raul smirked over his cigarette smoke, wondering what she was up to now. When he saw her pull the bedraggled and trembling boy Mik from the van, his mind-hackles arose. Nearby T.K. also was visibly altered for a moment, and cried out the youngster's name.

"He's all right," Christina answered for the small boy, literally dragging him along. "Just tired like you and I, T.K. ... But perfectly fine otherwise."

Staring dully back at T.K., the boy's eyes were the equivalent of stony secrets. He did not seem to care about what was happening around him, and resembled a portable puppet. He hardly noticed the red apple placed carefully on his head by Christina Alpreece, with the aplomb of a kindergarten teacher. She had backed her small charge up against a magnificently stout pine tree trunk with a large enough girth to accomodate her own version of a William Tell overture -- or encore?

"You'll be okay, little darling," Christina confided. "This is just to show everyone how brave you are, how you always do what Christina tells you to." She looked around at T.K.'s palely disbelieving face. "If only everyone else had your absolute faith, Mik, what a miraculous world it would be -- instead of the unnatural mess it really is." She laughed, gently patting Mik's behind. Then she retreated several steps from the coniferously-heavy tree to consult with Gunther Hoffler, who stood holding his silvery arbalest like something magical in his hands.

Watching all this Raul Macon-May shook his head as a guttural laugh snuffled out from between his blistered lips. Oh well, he told himself, remembering back to the night in the abandoned church when little Mik was ceremoniously offered to the lust of unknown primitive gods -- and how Christina's form shone with a chilling radiance through the sepulchral gloom, surprising Raul. Making him wonder at the occult connection she possessed, like an otherworldly priestess praying to the aberrational spirits Raul had glimpsed momentarily as, sword upraised, she called them forth while "consecrating" the boy. It was something Raul knew he'd never be able to fully explain to T.K., so unreally repugnant was it to its blasphemous core. At that instant something turned noticeably within him, thanks to a revelation of true blasphemy and damnation seen for what was, to Macon, hopefully the first and last time. It was something worth fighting to stop -- along with everything else.

Now as he watched from a guarded distance as Hoffler readied his arbalest, aiming it carefully for what was a pulse-stopping eternity, Macon knew a lot would end that day. The arbalest's wickedly gleaming arrow tip was a harbinger of Ebel that remained for Raul to witness, and finish on behalf of his struggle and its ultimate triumph. He hated the ancient missile like he hated the obsolescent weapons they were forced to war with, vowing something almost prayer-like as Hoffler's arrow was abruptly released, and all of them watched hypnotized its speeding flight through leaden air until the apple on Mik's head parted like a miniature red sea. The arrow wedged deeply in the tree's stout trunk, still vibrating from its impact, and Christina was applaudingly whooping loudly.

T.K. had watched in silent agony all along before finally rushing towards Mik to discover him standing immovably frozen before the tree, a harbinger of his perpetual fate.

43.

To escape the onus of creation & the milky way of retribution ... Before T.K. jotted that into his mental files, an irreversible series of events took place. He had witnessed the unthinkable, and now realized he was thinking "it" – and its possibly boom-boom bad conclusion.

They traveled rather easily into the Medulla Compound. Astonishingly the large twin metallic gates – despite what seemed warning lights and unusual alarms triggered by their approach – opened fluidly, the way impressive ultra-tech machinery should. The gates of another Eden were now parted, remarked Keller, D.M.T. soggy to his core, and standing like a conscious dreamer in the midst of this greater dream whose air weighed against him like an ocean current.

"Something is wrong with this, along with everything else," T.K. said in his B-movie announcer's voice. "As it has been from the beginning. *O salvia divinorum.*"

"And so it was written in texts we'll never translate," ventured Christina Alpreece. "Into a reality we can't understand. But that's metaphysical show biz."

She, more than anyone, might yet steal a page of that great book. But their time for collective speculation was like a clock winding down. One whose hands were functionally illiterate. Now before the Feuer Bande leaders a brigade of formidable military and technical personnel appeared. Though uniformed, the lot rivaled poorly costumed extras in some unremarkable play. It was strange to believe that military pride had been so reduced, but this was – after all – still Forbrau.

Raul Macon had thought he'd seen it all, but knew this would be the transcendental mishmash of events, perhaps. Before him was a small phalanx of semi-important looking governmental officials – some uniformed, some not; some wearing suits, others casual, or even ragged khaki attire , and surpisingly unarmed, for the most part. Raul held his rifle at an intimidating port arms, but knew there was no need for it. The Compound reeked of peaceful, even tranquilized airs that reminded him of an olive drab monastery. Stepping gingerly forward was a skeletal greeting party of four (two bespectacled and civilian-like sorts flanked by a pair of army colonels), the lead individual extending a frail hand towards the expectant Puma warriors. "I'm Herr Freunderstein," the lanky man said. "And you're the terrorists, I presume?"

Before Gunther Hoffler or Christina Alpreece could mumble assent, the limping form of Vincent Gaylen Tomasi ambled forward. "Hello, Richard," he announced, struggling to steady himself on the tree-limb crutch now supporting his awkwardly bundled body. "We are here. We are intact."

"Vincent," the khaki-clad technician replied, recognizing him. The two men embraced one another before the startled guerrillas. "I'm so glad to see you. You must receive some medical attention, my friend, you've been through an ordeal."

"I'm all right," Tomasi lied through his coughing. "I'm just sorry for all of this."

"No matter," scoffed the Medulla Project's Director, a spry man in his 50s. "It's been inevitable, in a way. Everyone's to blame for it. The day of reckoning was inevitable ..."

"Yes, wasn't it," Tomasi agreed, stepping towards the intimidating Compound's main doors.

Macon-May pushed T.K. along with the others walking heavily towards the doors. This would be a piece of tasty cake. So touching was the scene he almost laughed. Herr Freunderstein's English was only mildly accented by his native tongue. He was probably just another German scientist the U.S. Government was historically prone to recruiting for its special causes.

Inside the Compound, Raul and the others had to marvel despite themselves. They were in the presence of a computerized technology awesome in its breadth and scope: The true cybernetic *Zeitgeist,* in all its mechanized variations and formats, was present in the huge bunker they had all but trespassed into. T.K.'s own mouth dropped open like an Edvard Munch silently screaming portrait subject. The strange humming sounds had a contrapuntally impressive accompaniment.

"What you see is basically our control room," Herr Freunderstein announced, without looking back, to the group trailing him into the massively computerized chamber. Already his voice assumed the patient, even impersonal airs of a tour guide. "All of what you're seeing has been extremely classified and very secret for quite some time. This, the command central for the Medulla Project, sposored by the U.S. Government in conjunction with the New West German Republic – and other partners I'll get to shortly." In his drab smock and lowbrow shoes and attire, Freunderstein indeed resembled the true low-profile technician. "I've been Director of this project for quite some time – an endeavor scheduled for completion in the calendar year 2100."

"That's a long time away," remarked Gunther Hoffler, obviously relishing every optical inch of what they were now seeing. His eagle-like baby blues looked briefly into the adoring gaze of Christina Alpreece, making the moment extra special (even, Gunther thought, highly mystical). The rest of the trooping-in Feuer Bande members were no less impressed, including the wan Nils Mupreen, who continued scribbling away into his metallic gleaming notebook.

"This entire facility, or mega-bunker," continued Freunderstein as he watched the technicians busily at work around him, "is officially dubbed The Alpha Sphere. We have virtually been sequestered hermetically in it for several months, which explains my complexion's pallor." The Director grimaced out a smile of sorts. "Today is the first time I've been out, in greeting you, for over a year, and we've been keeping the outside weather very cold (as you all know) for virtually that entire period, while inside here – as you have noticed, by your apparent relieved looks – them temperature inside this part of the sphere is a constant balmy 70 degrees." Freunderstein nearly chuckled while adjusting his large spectacles, which in fact more resembled wrap-around, amber tinted goggles.

Hoffler turned smilingly to observe Christina in her joyful radiance. They were twin conquerors who felt, still possessed of weaponry and power, like Hitler upon his unimpeded conquest of Paris in another century. Though warning Freunderstein and his aides (who were equally and now impressively armed) not to encroach on their personal spaces, the occupying group felt more comfortably at home by the second. It was a foreordained moment decreed by their destiny, Christina whispered excitedly to Nils. Possessed of their righteous spirit, they were the enlightened beings overcoming these computerized barbarians. She rued the fact she left her magnificent sword with its baroque handle behind, for Christina would smash all her digital aids with it, so liberated did she now feel. *We are the embodiment of the true powers of Li-Us, all that has guided us to this predestined moment of transcendence!*

Freunderstein saluted them with his continuing *noblesse oblige*. While Christina and Hoffler remained basking in it, Raul Macon-May and T.K. Gracinauto-Keller observed all this in much different fashions. Their looks were guardedly incredulous. Raul's hand turned white gripping his pistol, and – looking away into the more distant and dim reaches of the control room, he noted the military presences of certain individuals of the 76th Military Police Company watching one and all. There was old Big Dic Walden himself sucking up to Commander Bivvy and his trembling First Sergeant Rhinegold; there was Lt. Morris Penscay with his gleaming teeth poised in a hick smile beneath the ragged fluff of his russet mustaches; and there was Sgt. Wayman Lacer and a host of subordinate soldiers like Bernie Beeschaum and Co. holding their rifles at port arms while lining the entire wall of the amphitheater-like chamber, all of them drab sentries who – at last – were poised to discover their real identities and perhaps violent last reasons for being, or having been. All around them electronic putti flew in terpsichorean heavenly abandon, like beatific flies hovering protectively over some festering feast. They composed an impressive background, Raul Macon-May decided, and tactically his thoughts devised ways to obliterate such traitorous presences if the time came.

Still by the Director's side, Vincent Tomasi gamely raised his cane to punctuate his host's remarks. Then, coughingly, the frail dignitary whispered some urgent comments into one of the Director's oversized ears.

"Yes, Vincent," the Director replied patiently, "I am prepared to tell them virtually all. In fact, I've orders from Washington to do just that. In spite of everything, the world must remain poised for its union with a greater one."

Hearing the Director's remarks, Tomasi visibly blanched as if he could turn even whiter, yet managed to control his coughing. The Sphere's temperate climate apparently was having a gradual beneficial effect on him, and he refused the immediate medical attention offered by an Alpha Sphere paramedic.

The Director – still accompanied by that phalanx of gray-smocked aides and bodyguards – motioned for the group to follow him through an adjoining chamber of the Alpha Sphere, saying: "There is indeed an exigent shortage of normal temporal time, for reasons I will attempt to clarify for you."

The pallid Director began reciting some debatable factoids that T.K., for one, was already acquainted with. The Project had to do with the scientific formulation and production of what Freunderstein called The Medulla Agent (or "Raze of Medulla," as it was nicknamed), an "entheogenic chemical" derived from psychedelic plants, mushrooms, etc. "What amounts to a unique amalgam of *P. harmala* and *P. cubensis* extracts, along with the sacramental *psilocybe* mushroom, and various other compounds into an undisclosable formula, ladies and gentlemen. This," the Director allowed, "has involved years of research to produce what is, in my opinion, a still very unrefined yet in other ways very rarefied product, which – when induced into the human bloodstream and nervous system – has the distinct aim and power to create reactions restricting certain undesirable activity in the human brain – primarily the medulla oblongata ... In order to eradicate primitive violent urges in the human species permanently."

As they approached another imposing corridor leading to what was called the Morph-1-A Chamber, Freunderstein continued: "Much of our research into these areas were once connected with what were considered 'psychedelic experiences' involving the exploration of realms of Consciousness – dubbed *Ultraspace*, a term still used, dealing with the dissolution of barriers between the many discrete realities of Infinite Space, in order to perceive a greater power or 'alien soma' being paramount in that psychic Ultraspace... But in our own time that aim has changed, for the Medulla Agent (or M.A.) is considered a dangerous weapon whose design was, at first, to immobilize the human nervous system. Unfortunately its effect and chemical properties have changed since then, so that 'the Raze' is capable of having many diverse and uncontrollable effects on its subjects. Effects that are unusually good or bad, depending on your viewpoint."

Christina Alpreece suddenly said, "Whatever the Raze is, we want it, Herr Freunderstein ... We're here to either extract enough of it for our own ends, or to stop the U..S. imperialists from further fabricating and threatening this world (or those beyond) with it. Do you understand, Mein Herr?" There was undisguised menace radiating from Christina's eyes, for now – with her blowback pistol halfway raised – it was clear the Director to her was on a par with the nearby trembling Vincent Gaylen Tomasi.

"I, of course, understand," the Director drily replied, his dull eyes looking off towards the omnipresent ranks of guardian M.P.s standing like centurions in the computerized machinery's flickering light, buzzing like a great electric bodily organ around them. "But it's not just myself or Washington that you must make understand, Ms. Alpreece." He blithely gestured to the huge double entrance doors of the Morph-1-A Chamber behind him. "You must make the manifest alien somas of the *Cranachs* understand as well, and please do not bring your weapons any further. Should you misuse one, the entire Project could be jeopardized. You know how incredibly rare this network is."

"We are not, dear Director, surrendering the use of our weapons," Gunther Hoffler announced through the ensuing tension. "They go where we go. As Christina said, you must cooperate fully – or accept the consequences."

"And you must refrain from any harshness," the Director quietly warned, still the objective spectator.

Brice Rampoul -- who was now directly standing behind Christina, and the only unarmed Feuer Bande member -- indicated he, for one, would prove that rashness was not their primary objective.

"Shut up," Christina told him. Then turning to the Director, she said: "So far you've been spouting what sounds to me a load of rarefied bullshit, Herr Director. Don't forget that exigent time factor."

To T.K. entering the Morph-1-A Chamber was similar to trespassing into an ancient Egyptian or Etruscan tomb -- in this case, one extremely ultra-tech enough to resemble something NASA would devise for a space project. Maybe it went beyond that, T.K. decided. None of them were prepared for the gigantic totem-like structure which occupied the Chamber's center (gave it, in fact, reason for being) and emitted a light so volatilely coruscant it resembled a comet's tail of diamond-like brilliance -- at times freezing into a cold blue flame of glacial emulsion similar to what a rocket lifting-off exhausts on the pad.

In short, the sight stunned, and Christina was immediately affected. Dancing isotopes of radioactive stripe bounced off her eyes, stimulating a connection to that celestial energy she knew had guided her this far, as nylon strings do puppets for a children's show. But that wasn't all ...

There was a huge figure trapped within this cylindrical column of nuclear light -- or "crystalline sheath," as Director Freunderstein put it above the Chamber's noisome drone.

"What you see is the projected figure of the Cranach god-child," said the Director calmly, quietly, as if they were in a nursery. "Its name is Li-Us, for the record."

So totally was T.K.'s mind boggled (as was the collective guerrilla group's) that he was sure the chemicals coursing through his own bloodstream were locally manufactured, if not from the Beta-C-2 planet, or that giant space station the Cranach alien somas called home, Freunderstein reminded them. To T.K. the Brobdingnagian deity entrapped amber-like before them revealed (as any space baby god would?) a cross between Egyptian stele portraits of Osiris and some choice Art Deco exotic female figure depicted by Gustave Klimt, perhaps, except this was clearly an hermaphroditic being. In plain view, Li-Us' super genitalia was a mixed bag, surrounded by ceremonial accouterments like some of those the Puma gang had taken from the plundered Mag Zone bunkers.

It was incredible, Christina Alpreece muttered, seeing this living imago from god-knew-where. The others were equally impressed -- to an even frightened point, since Raul Macon was openly gripping his blowback pistol and assuming an offensive stance.

"Is this real?" Gunther Hoffler asked, his neck craning back the way a tourist's might when viewing a mechanical dinosaur. "It's the size of a construction crane!"

"It's real enough," the Director assured them, his voice raised. For him that was the equivalent of a shout.

A fascinated Brice Rampoul moved closer (despite the all but blinding light) to the column's base, noting a smaller horizontal cylinder -- resembling a crystal coffin -- with diverse hoses connected to its greater Host. Moving back, Rampoul shook his head.

"Would you mind, Herr Director, telling us what's in that torpedo-shaped capsule?"

The Director cleared his throat with an unpleasant sound. "Of course. That's the cryonically preserved alien Cranach body of PQ-31, ladies and gentlemen. In its crystalline cylinder, the Cranach's like a sleeping shaman 'dreaming' -- or projecting -- the hologram-like revelation of what you see. With our computerized assistance, you can see how the manifest Soma and its celestrial offspring are inextricably bound to one another -- and in a very real sense, neither can exist here, in this environment, without the other ..."

Nils Mupreen now moved closer to the cryogenic cylinder, trying to make out PQ-31's indistinct form. An unattractive and amorphous lump with unseeing, jewel-like vernal eyes, PQ-31 rivaled an underwater entity in its fluid sac of computer-linked crystals. It was, more specifically, parasitically sustained within its very ultra-techno cocoon, and -- most upsetting of all to the wary observer -- it had a babyish face unquestionably the spitting image of Christina Alpreece's.

"This is incredible," Mupreen gasped, backing away contortedly and shaking his long-tressed head. "That can't be, it looks almost like ... and the stink, it smells like afterbirth." Mupreen struggled to retrieve his camera from the lumpy burden of his backpack.

"Don't let your imaginative fears get the better of you, my friends," the Director cautioned. "Fact is fact. Truth is truth, no matter how inalienable. And that's why you all came here. To complete a destiny prognosticated long ago by the keepers of this great flame, from the very dawns of our reputed recorded history. To see the very source and reasons for this Medulla Raze -- and now you're beginning to see that, without question, and you've been under our auspices a very long time, though it may seem simply an earthly hour that we've been together... So, are any of you growing afraid?" the Director laughed, slapping his compatriot Tomasi on the shoulder. His mood was jovial, despite an unaccountable reticulation of blue wrinkles now clotting his forehead unawares with the visible clarity of a brain scan. "I should think not. Here we survive the strange permutations of our unsure human flesh. The Medulla Agent is the answer to our terrestrial humankind's ills, or so the Cranachs of Beta-C-2 have decreed -- and the U.S. Government has little choice but to cooperate in the matter, not wanting to see our planet decompose fatally before the grand aim of all this is achieved, of course ..."

Herr Freunderstein briefly gave instructions to one of his aides, and in a matter of seconds the impenetrable Morph Chamber walls started to part and roll back in sections, the way the roof of a domed stadium might. Where there was darkness there was now light, T.K. Keller realized, and he could see what the Director referred to as the artificial bucolic spaces of the Medulla Compound where the Neo-Cranachs were treated, tested, and observed like prized specimens of some wayward evolution within their huge crystallized bell jar.

"Those are the chosen people," Tomasi suddenly avowed when the milling crowd of Neo-Cranachs came into full view, staring back through the glass partition the way sea creatures will at a marine exhibit. "They are the hybridic salvation of this entire planet. Part human, part Cranach -- fully evolutionary for transplanting to another sphere where only they can adapt, live, and carry on. They are a minute example of what the Cranachs hope to make of the remainder of our human species, or whatever specimens are able to make the great evolutionary leap to ..."

"They're freaks," Nils Mupreen said.

Herr Freunderstein endeavored to calm his associate, but Tomasi was having none of it. Insistently the old man banged his walking stick against the overwhelming wall of curved glass, trying to rouse the numb and sightless Neo-Cranach figures milling unenergetically about. Among them Mupreen thought he recognized the shamefully altered figure of his brother, Kress, who returned a gaze of utter abjectness -- almost an accusingly hateful one akin to a prehistoric beast-man's. Nils cried out, dropping his camera to the tiled floor. He was jostled by the mewling Tomasi, who would have smashed on through a boundary of synthetic crystal and plastics had he the divine power to do so, but instead crumpled to his knees before the insuperable barrier and wept.

"No Christ, or anit-Christ, will save us from our sins," Tomasi said, as T.K. Keller felt an unmistakable chill course through him with the same rush a heroin injection might.

"The old man needs help," Brice Rampoul said, watching T.K. and Macon-May help an unsteady Tomasi to his feet. "Those are stroke symptoms ..."

"I'm only dying," Tomasi quietly agreed, "and that's more than helpful enough... But the rest of you might well need some chemical 'purification,' so that you too will achieve peace with those you now see."

The Director nodded, all the while motioning to some of his uniformed aides busily speaking into radios to keep their distance.

"Yes, they were once Human. Now they are in-between being that and also aliens. That of course is one of this Medulla Agent's indisputable side effects." The Director openly marveled at the pitiful sight of several hundred Neo-Cranachs so nakedly revealed. "In a sense they are very beautiful somas, because of being in their transmutational state. In what direction will they evolve into? They've been reborn to populate a new artificial space continent soon. You must agree they are placid, their Ids removed or negated by the Raze, more or less. With no more primitive instincts to kill one another, or give destructive expression to their once uncontrollable subconscious passions. They are scientifically holy. Don't you see? In a sense they've been purged, recreated into what you *see* they're becoming. That is a very miraculous state, what they're becoming. What the entire lot of us will become if the Cranachs get their way.

"And now the rhetorical Q & A session ... How did all this come about, you might ask? Because several decades ago a greed United States government made the unsuccessful attempt to create 'space colonies' out of other susceptible planets or asteroids, never expecting to encounter alien life on another space station deep within distant star clusters. The Cranach somas can't live in our earth environment -- not until the Raze changes us and them, not until our own earth's atmosphere is 'purified' -- though now it's too late for that. Centuries ago they gave it a try, but died out in remote African jungles, or South American ones, leaving behind strange artifacts of an unidentified cultural hybrid that remains unexplained by our archaeologists and anthropologists, and some items still classified by Uncle Sam, though some has leaked through into scientific circles for rogue uses and study. PQ-31 there before you is their important emissary at the moment. Its mission is to keep the Li-Us deity 'projected' from the reaches of intinite space, until we can someday fully realize it in somatic form on earth, or elsewhere, for the Neo-Cranachs to worship. To do that we need the DNA transfer of a very sought-after individual who's the direct descendant, and currently the only living one, of a coupling between a human being and a Cranach which inexplicably occurred many decades ago. One which holds a key bit of information for successfully completing our Project's mission in both the 'natural' and 'supernatural' senses, or the new human and the new divine. (So that we can successfully transfer this 'Li-Us Genome' into the necessary clones to come, and impart those crystalline components borne by our redeemer into all those chosen as well.) That is what the Medulla Raze must really become, my friends: the stuff of genetic experiments dealing with this classified attempt to breed hybridic-clone humans into the proposed saving race. Our lab has built a nanotech device that's part biological and part mechanical, with molecular-size rotors -- what we call a 'nanometer' -- for injecting microscopic chemical implants into human bodies until we create the desired clone transformation, manipulating individual atoms to create both mechanical and information machines within these new creatures to come." Herr Freunderstein paused, letting his words sink in for whatever worth, and stared tellingly at Christina Alpreece's obviously agitated form standing nearby. "We've awaited that person's coming for a long time, have monitored her whereabouts from afar for as long -- until losing track of her during this present Ice Age, which caused no small consternation here..." Freunderstein now slowly approached Christina, gathering up her well-muscled hand to lavish it with a kiss similar to those which osculate the rings of Popes. "Now we give thanks, in the name of so much, that the individual descended from the bloodline of Hitler is here before us, so that hope will remain for our species ... And for those behind the large glass, those who have the very Cranach god-child before them, but have as yet been unable to worship and grow into all-consuming faith before it. They wait and always have for the moment of connecting with such a promised savior ..."

That might be true enough, T.K. decided, because the Neo-Cranachs now pressed up against the glass and gyrated with expressions similar to old-fashioned holy rollers. Many tongues licked the crystal barrier, many grotesque faces of unparalleled ugliness nonetheless radiated a poignant bliss in sensing the presence of an awaited one, and thus transforming their fleshly features crushed so implacably against the glass -- so that blood began freely staining it, and those closest to the wall were swiftly squished to death on it, their mouths open yet in silent screams. Many of the Feuer Bande members turned away, disgusted by the sight -- but T.K. watched mesmerized, feeling a second-hand alien energy tugging at something within him as Christina no doubt did, knowing these grim multitudes of fallen humanity were supplicating an *Ubermater* that mysteriously had obsessed his own subconscious mind for an infinity of years.

"They are damned," Gunther Hoffler cried, spitting at the glass. "The corrupt world governments would give us all to such 'entheogenic soma' abductions as this? No wonder events have been what they've been. These wretches, the new lot of humanity? Supposedly to be treated till they're converted into pseudo-aliens, thanks to this gott-awful Medulla Raze we've come to plunder, if not destroy, surely as rampaging Christians once seized the Holy Grail ...?"

Freunderstein couldn't refrain from laughing at these remarks, until Hoffler's face reddened. The Holy Grail as Medulla Raze ... It was all too rich for him. Didn't these intruding reprobates see – thanks to the C.I.A. and C.I.D. government agents now lurking within the Sphere – that the Feuer Bande had been *encouraged* by Washington to commit all their renegade terrorist acts? Perhaps the sudden glints in T.K.'s eyes (like miniature halogen lamps switched on) gave proof that somebody saw what was happening. All along the C.I.A. clowns had shadowed them, Raul and T.K. knew, turning them on to their Forbrau connections like Sgt. Wayman Lacer, who all but swam in contraband chemicals and turned everyone on in his nark-like way, monitoring their actions through Holland and Germany with the Pumas. Though no one knew then Washington and President Noxson actually wanted T.K. and the terrorists to actually disrupt the Medulla Project and confiscate the Raze, which was "unrefined" anyway and probably incapable of achieving entheogenic alien conversion, and thus throw the ultimate monkey wrench into the distant Cranachs' plans.

Deep down humans did not want to become spaceniks, T.K. reasoned. It was all too perfidious and wildly evil somehow. *His ol' Dutch mammy Lissie was right. Beware of alien dealers with strange candy.*

"There is only one government: the supreme Space Government," Herr Freunderstein said to himself.

All about them now there was a foreign buzzing from the surrounding cyber-machinery, and the super Li-Us deity began to writhe like an exotic snake within its restrictive cylinder. No longer able to restrain herself, Christina Alpreece rushed towards the coffin-like capsule Freunderstein had designated "the PQ-31 appendage" earlier, prostrating herself before it in benedictional fashion, then reverentially kissing its plastic casing. Looks were exchanged between the Director and members of his scurrying staff. Christina next stood, mouth agape, and stared up at the archaic deity's writhing dance, seemingly like an Indian god's many-limbed lament for the sad mysteries of creation only it knew, and could perhaps alter within its now swirling red cylinder.

"Stay back," Hoffler commanded, but Christina wasn't listening. A beatific expression unfolded over her facial features. She passed space trilobites that were being incubated as timeless pets along the base of the Alpha Sphere's circular wall, and felt that the exigent power within her was the predestined one somehow guiding her all along to this moment.

"Stay back, Christina!"

Herr Freunderstein knew a key to breaking the psychic telepathic control of the Cranachs over the Compound would be destroying the link between PQ-31 and its hologramic projection of Li-Us, a super realistic "illusion" more real-seeming than life itself. Li-Us was the alien soma of Ultraspace (& actual space) that some earth researchers, in more primal eras, thought they'd discover a variation of via exploration with D.M.T., psilocybin, or Kelamine, etc., while taking computer-linked journeys into their own consciousnesses being scientifically monitored. But now that such consciousness had become alien reality, Freunderstein hastened to expand it – knowing that only someone chosen, in a sense, by the deity itself (much as a virginal victim was sacrificed to more obsolete earth gods) could temporarily sway the distant aliens into modifying their control within the Compound.

It was a gamble, finding that long lost sacrificial descendant – but Christina Alpreece was the one. *She* would be the greatest explorer of any spatial consciousness, alien or human. (*Where Ultraspace and actual Space converge there exists the Aleph Point,* Freunderstein conjectured: a nuclear juncture of consciousness providing access to transcendental powers of Supreme Being, explaining and governing all reality throughout the Solar System and galaxies. It was at that Point the Li-Us deity sought a rendezvous via the services of its earthly cousins, many of which proved difficult to recast in the image of cosmic creation. Except for Christina, whom the Cranach deity was now remaking in its own image.)

So when Hoffler tried to stop Christina's ascent toward the cylinder, the Director lurched forward to block the guerrilla warrior's path. It proved a fateful physical intersection of another kind, and the Director fell with his head bleeding to the ground. A blue pus oozed from beneath his scalp.

Watching all this in a flash, the hulking figure of Raul Macon knew the moment had come. With his antiquated Kimel AP-9 blowback pistol, Raul fired several shots into Hoffler's back and head until the German approximated an aerated bloody mannikin on the floor. Unfazed and unhearing, Christina continued her climb to the cylinder's base as Brice Rampoul and Nils Mupreen dove for cover during the shoot-out.

Lying on what he knew were storage vaults containing components of the Medulla Agent, Rampoul managed to retrieve Hoffler's fallen rifle and pantingly hold it chest-close as sparks and red tracer-like bullets whizzed about him. He realized then that Christina was walking towards something she wasn't coming back from: the light of another nuclear power few have ever seen, where destructive and creative forces become One. He wanted to cry out. The bullet-struck bodies of Tomasi and the Director now splayed before him, leaving curious flesh-marks splattered against the great crystal glass wall hundreds of worshipping half-aliens still peered through.

At the cylinder's bottom, oblivious to the raging fire-fight going on all around her, Christina Alpreece raised her arms to the dark heaven not even the spiral cylinder's blinding light could blacken out – then leaped through the burning crystal encasing Li-Us. Miraculously or shockingly enough, the projected image accepted her small form against itself, a vision both male and female in awesome hermaphroditic splendor, and a fire-spurting orgasm of special-effects smoke exploded over a concourse of lava. Christina disappeared into the smoldering formidable elements apparently good enough for Li-Us to dance with even more excited and uncontained frenzy.

Still the fire-fight continued unabated, and T.K. (for some reason never clear to himself) began firing his M-79 grenade launcher indiscriminately, hitting a nearby computerized station and assorted other targets, including the glass wall itself. All proverbial hell was breaking loose, and Macon mowed down many of the Forbrau M.P. guards that T.K. once served with in another lifetime, including Big Dic Walden and First Sgt. Rhinegold, whose decapitated heads rolled about like sanguine soccer balls. Only Lt. Morris Penscay remained smiling throughout the fight, yelling compliments to the very man shooting up his guards -- until he too caught a Kimel round that fatally ruptured his cranial anatomy.

"God damn!" Brice Rampoul was shouting.

T.K. realized he'd no idea where little Mik had disappeared to during the initial bursts, and began desperately searching for the boy through a welter of debris, bodies, and burning metal. At one critical moment he peered through the smoke and saw Raul Macon-May hovering above the cryogenic coffin of the alien PQ-31 itself. With a gleaming bayonet Raul severed all the hoses and disrupted those eletrical circuits connecting the Li-Us deity to its somnambulistic little parasite. PQ-31's capsule exploded like silly putty from its plastic egg shell, rendering the space emissary into gluey nothingness, while Li-Us emitted a roaring jet-engine sound somehow dwarfing the surrounding gunfire. Then the deity began its agonized dance into vaporization, with all the incredible force of a tornado snuffing itself out in a vacuum chamber.

Soon the cylinder contained only the sacred smoke of the deity's acrid remains, a residue lingering like a cloud of doom above everything in the now gutted Alpha Sphere.

And with the deity's disappearance, so too did the Neo-Cranachs watching from behind the glass wall fall like dead puppets to the unfeeling ground ...

Sgt. Wayman Lacer abruptly stopped, the way a remote-controlled toy does when the power's turned off. Trembling in his suddenly static and indecisive state, he was oblivious of the slaughter going on all around him, and stolidly held his automatic rifle like a broom staff, fighting something greater than himself.

Inside the buck sergeant's mind, distant telepathic laser commands evaporated, powerless against the dysfunction seizing him. A chunk of his memory evaporated also, so that Lacer stood dumbly, his eyes unseeing, as any instant amnesiac might. When his sight did return, it fragmented so that he saw triple-images of everything on a plane of vision becoming a mirrored infinity.

He murmured: "Li-Us, Li-Us ..."

Everything had gone wrong. Lacer had been programmed telepathically to apprehend, then exterminate every member of the Feuer Bande -- swiftly and irrevocably, without posing hazard to the Alpha Sphere and its inhabitants. Through a force resembling something like individual free will, clearly that hadn't happened, and Sgt. Lacer felt the way a child does when abandoned by a parent. What was he doing now in a world he had only a vague inkling of?

Turning slightly, Lacer somehow electromagnetically registered, then computer-recognized, the triadic presence of T.K. Keller still wearing ski-mask and camouflaged fatigues as he stumbled about, wildly firing his pistol at the green shapes of U.S. soldiers in disarray everywhere.. Human blood, along with alien soma fluid of a faint yellow color, was also evident everywhere.

"Lacer!" T.K. screamed out. "We're bottled up in here ..."

The buck sergeant no longer remembered his programing. He no longer remembered he was supposed to kill Lacer, Macon, and many others with the elite guard of M.P.s forming this special detail. Now several of the guards sprawled like bloodied sacks at Lacer's feet. Everything had gone haywire, but Sgt. Lacer only fuzzily recognized this wonderful fact.

"Goddamnit, Lacer, get us out of here! Get the doors open --"

All within the smoke-filled Sphere sirens and alarms rang in emergency fashion, but Wayman Lacer's face had the composure of a meditating saint's. Who was this strange young man now yelling in front of him, if not a good friend he had spoken with only a few days before, when together they'd mapped out a strategy for attacking and escaping from the Medulla Compound? It was *T.K.*, he knew, without benefit of his internal cyber-verification. There was also *Raul Macon* kneeling next to him, shooting ferociously from a blowback pistol in both hands, so that the ground rocked and rolled with earthquake shock waves.

"Take out the door, Lacer! The *doors!*"

These two guerrilla fighters were his friends and allies, Lacer remembered (if foggily), and were being threatened by the government leaders they wanted to betray. Like a series of subliminal snapshots, Lacer in his mind's crippled eye saw again these leaders -- such as the Amsterdam double agent and Dutch black market Burgher Tito, along with Vincent Tomasi -- who had gained his confidence and given him his orders.

Now all Lacer could fathom was that these leaders had failed him and were indeed about to kill his friends, thus preventing him and Keller from commandeering the sought-after Medulla Raze, which all the world wanted to know about, like a bad soap operatic secret no longer concealable.

Whoever has sullied me will see a threefold death. His rifle swung about to begin firing back at the true enemy, for Wayman Lacer was able to see eternity no longer equaled an eternity. Working his way to a computer console protected by a wall of bullet-proof transparent material, he quickly punched in the numbers of a classified code while still firing his weapon. An act of bravado, it brought whoops from T.K. and Raul Macon, still scurrying through the smoke and devastation. They could see authentic daylight filtering into the Chamber and its mammoth twin portals slowly beginning to part.

"Mik! Mik!" T.K. yelled towards the opening. He knew the boy was somewhere there still waiting hopefully with the remaining Puma contingent, told earlier by Gunther Hoffler to standby: all waiting in a large vertical rectangle of light that shimmered with the true hyperion air of some lost heaven.

"Mik!"

Leaping from the vibrating ground, T.K. and Macon hurtled through the opening provided by the now stalled doors. Unfortunately their leap was from one battle zone to an even hotter one. With concussive explosions rattling the air around them, they saw a cadre of Feuer Banders shooting it out with Forbrau civilian and military personnel. In this diffracted spectacle of battle, T.K. and Macon recognized some individuals they wished they hadn't. There were several C.I.A. agents (including, Macon noted, the infamous "Rolfstein" character from the Amsterdam days) side-by-side with such Forbrau M.P.s as Sgt. Sheldon Camrack, P.F.C. Bernie Beeschaum, and a host of other heavily armed paramilitary sorts. All of them firing back at a bevy of Puma vehicles, some gutted or lying smoldering behind the electric barbwire fence where the heroic figure of Nils Mupreen strove to direct his small army against an unbowed enemy still fighting fiercely. Forbrau Germans shot back at their apostate Puma Deutschlanders, and Macon subliminally saw an international cadre of English, French, and even Dutch soldiers engaged in the fray. Fortunately Raul was approaching from their behind, knowing most hadn't noticed the Medulla Chamber's now opened south doors.

All around them the air scalded from discharged weaponry, and T.K. nearly passed out. In his backpack he was still carrying canisters of the Medulla Agent taken during the melee in the Alpha Sphere, and the dorsal weight almost bowled him over backwards as he tried -- shadow-like -- to keep pace with Macon. There was no trace of the boy Mik, and T.K. strained to see him somewhere against the forest's impenetrable backdrop.

Immediately Raul Macon began firing at the fence-moored Feuer Banders, and young Sgt. Sheldon Camrack -- along with the other Forbrau M.P.s -- expressed shock seeing Macon emerge like some griffin-beast from an unknown hades...

44.

It was the fire-fight long ago prophesied in dreams. There in the midst of several vehicles of every make and description (from paramilitary assault vans to plain old, yet how obsolete, army jeeps and trucks), in the flat and limitless expanse of the Compound's front parking lot, there erupted the long-awaited engagement. Something of Wild West proportions, marveled T.K. But not for long. The incoming rounds blistered the snow-pocked lot pavement everywhere, and a nearby group of jeeps was lacerated into metal-twisted oblivion, an explosion that sent T.K. and Raul Macon hurtling for cover behind a cement bunker suddenly metamorphosing into a dumpster bin enclosure.

Straining to see through the ensuing smoke, T.K. lost sight of the fenceline where the Feuer Bande was barricaded, and there was no sign of Mik. With a tidal wave might darkness suffused T.K.'s vision. He swam through a river of pain which in fact was still the befouled air. The earth heaved in tectonic dismemberment around him. For awhile he lost sight of Macon -- though Raul's voice continued to rasp out commands and curses at point blank range, allowing T.K. to follow in a belly crawl along the blackened pavement. Pathetically T.K. kept shouting back, fearing at any moment to lose desperately needed verbal contact.

It was the time for Judgment. All else had been unreal illusions ...

For some contemplative being, the picture unfolding was the epitome in all its mobile parts of a neo-masterpiece painting, perhaps titled *The Medulla Massacre*. The great canvas of this slice of forest life was blurred by Leonardo's *sfumato* brushwork and pallid hues languid with a creator's contrived obscuring. All the figures of this battlefield epic could now be seen by a distant voyeur as small parts of the greater whole. But how integrated with the whole could these figures hope to be?

Still the major figures contorted in agony by this unseen master shimmered with stark outlines, if not always colorful ones, through this veneer of smoke. Those in the foreground -- T.K., Macon, Camrack, "Rolfstein," Lacer and the emerging duo of Nils Mupreen and Brice Rampoul -- all vied to become the centerpiece of attention, or the fiery composition's focal point. Carrying their own backpacks of pilfered Medulla Agent ingredients now, Mupreen and Rampoul begged in a confused medley of hysteria to be allowed safe passage through the fracas -- with its multitudes of bodies scattered about like upset chess pieces -- to the waiting trucks of still fighting Puma regulars. It was a screaming plea ricocheting as shrapnel might across the tender tympanum of T.K. Keller's just barely functional hearing.

"Let them go!" Raul Macon shouted, fatally bayoneting a green uniformed C.I.D. figure in his way. With unparalleled combat ferocity, Macon's physique (in all its muscular energies channeled towards destruction) clearly dominated this battlefield composition. Lionesque, he moved with unsated fatalness, his killing anger now reaching its climax. With sword and gun in hands, Macon slaughtered and dismembered both Federal and Puma foes with a disinterested zeal, like a man axe-chopping wood repeatedly, inexorably, without end. Blood and body parts flew around him -- and T.K. as well -- until the inferno of all neo-techno hells opened around them, spawning this flaming mix of metal and flesh. The opposite of any baptismal blood bath, it was the desecration of a once human spirit rendered into a somatic bloody being, for this once and perhaps final time.

Warring alongside Macon, it dawned on young Sgt. Camrack that this double-agent of fatalities might have no real enemies except man himself. Camrack was stunned to see Macon alternating his kills between G.I.s and Pumas during his mad and bloodied rush towards the fence gates, and readied himself should Macon turn on him as well. Camrack saw instead Macon wrestling with the steroid-pumped replica of the C.I.A. deputy chief "Rolfstein," both having knocked the weapons from each other's hands and reducing bloodlust to bare-knuckled fundamentals. So stunned was Camrack by the incredible sight that he nearly inhaled a toxic cloud of *sfumato-gas* now unfurling like the breath of the late Li-Us god itself, or any other bio-toxin.

Though still adhering to his original plan, Camrack knew that, on a day bathed in darkness where once the sky appeared an unfathomable ivory cloud stretching into a space without beginning or end, things were happening too fast for the naked eye to really perceive. Another flailing soldier suddenly passed by, namely one severely wounded Sgt. Wayman Lacer, apparently more dead than alive in the crepuscular fumes. Somehow Camrack managed, cradling his rifle, to crouch low in a still steaming crater and avoid meeting the demonic sergeant whose body, in parted mid-section, revealed a mixture of human organs connected to techno-machinery, joined by synthetic parts spilling openly a garish green liquid. Even in the encroaching smog fumes, this smelled more rankly than real death itself.

But to the true omniscient eye there remained the convoluted fury of battle and all its enmeshed forms. Not to overlook the pathetic T.K. Keller still crawling towards the fenceline, knowing Mik's small boyish frame was silhouetted there like a dwarf scarecrow, his hands upraised against the spark-spitting chainlinks. "Hold on, Mik, hold on," Keller pantingly muttered, hoping that Lacer was somewhere in the immediate vicinity. Which he was, still battling with the very M.P.s he recently turned against, and feeding the finale of one mass confusion. Lacer worked his way to a row of untouched trucks and, through whatever now ultra-human strength, pulled the door completely off a three-quarter whose engine quickly sparked into droning action – then he held aloft the dreaded stave of his rifle, which glittered faintly in the now faux night.

"Here, Keller, here! ... Where's Macon?"

They would yet sunder this appalling sea of darkness, T.K. Keller hoped, no matter what. His own mortality was now as inconsequential to him as a bug's, though he continued fearing the worst. The three-quarter truck began to move inexorably forward despite the sounds of gunfire ringing it like a frying pan. An overhead burst of flares suddenly illuminated the battlefield's parameters with incredible brilliance, and now T.K. saw lucidly Mik still standing at the fenceline, along with the nearby struggling forms of Macon and "Rolfstein" locked yet in wrestling combat.

T.K. shouted, rolled over, and just evaded the tires of the oncoming truck, which now careened unstoppably around him. The flares' radiance continued to bathe the scarred terrain with miraculous light, so that distant mountains could be seen in the eerie and immobile background, a visitation that for an instant was prehistoric.

T.K. still cried out for Macon through the undiminished cacophony of battle dominating all. Time stopped, outlawed by a greater power. Only the indiscriminate movements of destruction reigned. "Rolfstein" and his formidable enemy continued their battering of one another, until Macon – in a burst of feverish hateful adrenalin – was able to gain supremacy and wield his considerable bulk into a crushing vise-grip around the C.I.A. man's body. With "Rolfstein" underneath him, Raul began repeatedly bashing the deputy's head against the earth and crying out a woman's oath-like name.

Only when Macon saw his prey's eyes turning a reptilian green did he stop his torrential primal attack. Only when he recognized something in those eyes – something so deeply and unsettling feminine – did he release his hold from "Rolfstein's" throat and abandon that lacerated wretch to the judgmental fates awaiting all.

"Get in the truck!" Keller was screaming. "Mik's there at the gate."

The spinning three-quarter abruptly halted just then, and its engine died with it. Macon leaped towards it, pushing out the slumped-over remains of Sgt. Wayman Lacer into the littered and unrecognizably razed parking lots. Then quickly he got the engine going just before the last overhead flare's illumination sputtered out as a sky candle would from the whoosh of an unseen Achilles blazing by.

"Get in yourself, T.K.," Macon said angrily. "Lacer's dead – or his engine's really totaled ..."

Without pausing, T.K. first pulled what was left of Lacer into the truck's rear and just had time to hop aboard himself as Macon gunned the vehicle straight ahead through a field of intermittent red, yellow, and blue explosions. Keller hugged his backpack with its weighty contents of Medulla Raze. No ride he ever took would equal this one. Behind him the Medulla Compound smoldered like a burnt mushroom in a napalm defoliated garden no spring would ever see again.

They were *free,* just about, and everything hostile allowed them to proceed remarkably enough, as if an unseen force had given that signal. As they sped bumpily along (with Macon yodeling madly behind the wheel), T.K. could see the sooty forms of Brice Rampoul and Nils Mupreen carrying their precious Medulla cargo and making it out first. T.K. could also detect straggling Puma guerrillas sighting the truck through high-powered binoculars as Macon exultantly transmitted on his walkie-talkie: "We're comin' through too, comrades, right behind Mupreen! We've got the goods – clear the gate! Open that mother wide, babes –"

As they passed through, Raul Macon viciously nailed down the brakes and T.K. lurched so far forward he nearly slammed his head against the cab. Clearing his head and looking up, T.K. was greeted by Mik's moon-round face as the boy climbed aboard. A rare moment of reunion's gladness surfaced for them, spoiled too soon by what next happened.

Seated in the truck, Macon was excitedly talking to some Feuer Bande members when Brice Rampoul approached. Macon flashed him an okay sign.

"Welcome back, comrade," said Rampoul. "This is from Tito and Canal Street." Then he raised his 9 millimeter pistol and shot Raul Macon at point blank range.

T.K. screamed. Crimson spray coated the truck's window almost simultaneously with the fired shot's eruption. That and the truck's engine revving and the three-quarter speeding away seemed to occur within a fraction of perceptible seconds.

No one stopped them. No one fired at their truck as it barreled like an otherworldly machine into the forest's clammy twilight.

The three-quarter ton truck had becom a rogue elephant, something almost driving itself pell-mell along the twisting German highway. Higher and higher the road ascended through the darkening mist, until T.K. realized they were deep into the Saar region's forested hills and low mountain ranges, where pocks of frozen snow still lingered like cemented reminders of a neo-Ice Age.

All through the bumpily uncomfortable ride T.K. bear-hugged small Mik for all he was worth, afraid any moment they'd be pitched out and away from the incredibly careening truck's rear. The engine's whine gunned unrelentingly into their ears, until it was a sound of conquering pain they almost became one with speeding along. Occasionally T.K. could hear the crackle of radio messages and static urgently building from Raul Macon's walkie-talkie up front.

For T.K. the most unsettling fact of all became the now oozing remains of Wayman Lacer spongily caking the rear truck cargo bed. Occasional moonlight glinted over this pulsing mass, revealing remnants of Lacer's internal organs – including his overlarge heart – but hardly any of the ultra-tech mechanisms once so abudantly present in the non-com's body. At one point T.K. screamed aloud from this troubling sight, as Mik whimpered besides him, and he wondered if this green stellar ooze would toxically contaminate them like liquid anthrax. It hardly mattered to him at this point.

By dawn, when the truck finally lurched to a crunching stop, T.K. could see that most of the foreign oozing mass had evaporated, along with Lacer's once gigantic heart.

Raul Macon descended unsteadily from the truck cab. In his yellowish eyes the night had not ended. Most of his field jacket was heavily imbued with his dark blood, its hue turning stiffly brown in the dawn's pale light. He'd been shot high on the chest, perhaps even at the left shoulder so drastically tilted downwards as he tentatively moved along, favoring it. The radio clipped to his side kept intermittently broadcasting traffic in German and English too garbled at times to understand.

"I knew it," Macon muttered, cursing and stumbling along. When T.K. asked if Macon was all right, no immediate answer came. But the high mountain air – so crisply cold and invigorating, plus the spectacular forested scene from this altitude – was all apparently that Raul Macon-May desired at the moment.

"I knew it," Macon kept repeating, his voice a sandpapered lament. "Well ... we've lost the bastards, anyway. Even the polizei don't want us, T.K. Not yet anyway."

"Why is that?" T.K. wondered, upholding his backpack as if gold was inside it. "After all, we've got it. The Medulla Raze."

"Who gives a rat's tail," Macon spat, holding his shoulder, finally letting T.K. examine it and wrap a portion of his shirt around the wound, which appeared enormous.

"Something's still in me," Macon had to admit. "It hurts like hell, kid."

They were both sitting now at the road's edge, which skirted a nearby cliff ridge not twenty yards behind them, marked only intermittently by reflective warning posts. T.K. unfastened his canteen and slowly let the water pour over Macon's face and mouth as little Mik stood by watching, a forlorn and poignant survivor, wishing he could help. Tears were in T.K.'s eyes. Macon shut his own, breathing heavily, his face averted. T.K.'s assault rifle was still slung like an inseparable body part over his right shoulder.

Slowly T.K. stood, then walked towards the cliff's edge. He could see the mass exodus of vehicles and marching refugees in the far distance. Tears still burgeoning in his eyes, he kneeled down before the great expanse beyond him, unsure whether he would pray silently or aloud. Impressively the stillness everywhere was overwhelming. Trembling, he unslung his rifle and held it – like an acolyte would an offering to a god unknown – horizontally and above his head for perhaps the longest minute of his life. Then gruntingly he could bear it no longer, and hurled the stave with all his might into the arboreal fastness below.

"Don't lose it on me, kid," Macon quietly said. He could hear Keller's now painful sobbing coming in starts and stops.

"You and Mik are gonna make it out. You promise me that, all right? Promise me that, T.K."

Eventually T.K. Keller nodded through his stifled weeping and stood up, eyes open, staring still at the forest's implacable majesty: something that had somehow always gotten the better of them. Then T.K. heard a startlingly familiar American voice coming loudly from Macon's radio:

"Hello, Raul Macon-May, wherever you are. Greetings, this is Sgt. Sheldon Camrack of the 76th Military Police Company in Forgrau, Germany. I hope you're able to hear this, brother. Please come in ..."

Macon made no effort to acknowledge or answer the radio transmission, though clearly he heard it, adjusting the volume.

Camrack's voice continued: "I just want to tell you that your daring guerrilla raid has apparently been successful, up to a point." Macon cursed, believing this a lie. "After all, Raul, you and your Puma buddies got away with enough Medulla to terrorize a great deal of the world into submission, as your co-conspirators also listening now know. The problem, Raul, is simply this. *Everything* was staged for your benefit. You were all but invited to hit the Compound. What you saw inside was a completely computerized light show. There are no alien somas such as PQ-31, no real Li-Us superbeing at all, and the Project Director, Herr Freunderstein, was only an actor!... What you witnessed, as I've said, was a deception completely fabricated by us – your friends in the United States Government, in association with its allies ..."

Camrack's deeply Southern voice dissolved into a long moment's laughter.

"It's unauthorized for me to be telling you this, Raul, but I'm doing it for your own good. It's too late now anyway. The media has splashed this event all over the newspapers, T.V.s, radios and computers worldwide, thanks to your actions. That media say that you, the Feuer Bande, successfully attacked our installation and effectively hauled off several pallets of Medulla Raze... The media say that alien beings actually do exist – and that they're holding world governments hostage to their demands and threats of imminent destruction ...! The media, Raul, say that you terrorist bad guys are a bunch of holy heroes out to save the world from galactic invaders the U.S. is helpless before – but I'm here to tell you otherwise. I'm here to tell you everything about the Medulla Project is a hoax, okay? I'm here to tell you there's *no* real Medulla Agent – *no* Raze – that it's a complete panacea as harmless as aspirin, Raul, when taken orally or anally! Just kid's candy, no side effects. And I'm here to tell you all that for your own good, so that you'll stop doing what the U.S. Government wants you to do: to be its scapegoat in this international witchhunt against innocent individuals worldwide, just so it can increase its black market imperialist policies of deceit in every country on the face of this once green earth ...

"Do you roger that, Commander Macon? Please acknowledge, over –"

Macon again cursed, then began laughing extensively despite his pain. From this laughter tears formed almost in his red-rimmed eyes. He knew Frenderstein had died for their sins.

"You're a lying brown-noser, Camrack," Macon finally said, but not into the radio. He suspected the root of all the world's problems was its tendency towards polymorphous perversities of the flesh (which had ailed the Canal Street whore Jari, one he now remembered with pangs), and shook his head. "What a something to die for."

Eventually Macon's walkie-talkie fizzled into an elongated static – then went dead.

"Did you hear all that, kid?" Macon asked as T.K. returned to kneel by his side. When Keller nodded, Macon laughed all the more. It was to him the greatest joke in the world, or cosmos. "That's Hollywood, baby," he added, coughing up blood.

"Hey, Raul."

"Open your backpack, kid, and stop blubbering on me ... Don't have much time left ... let's find out if that stuff's really safer then aspirin."

T.K. fumblingly did as told. Inside a hermetically sealed blue plastic case resembling a medical kit was prodded open by T.K.'s knife. There were several syringes, cotton swabs, needles, along with bottles labeled, among other things, *Medulla Agent.* Macon's eyes opened big-time when he glimpsed all this.

"It's a junkie's dream," Macon marveled.

"You're not really going to take this stuff, Raul?"

Macon indicated he had no choice, that he'd lost too much blood and would soon fatally lose consciousness. There was sadness on his sweating face now, and T.K. knew the proverbial die was cast. He filled one of the syringes and prepared the injection. Macon rolled up his sleeve, winked, and poised the needle himself above the proper vein before fully injecting the Medulla Agent into his bloodstream.

"I used to do this with Euro-hemp, T.K. Don't worry, I'm an old pro."

T.K. lowered his head, feeling an abjectness. Behind him Mik began speaking for the first time, in something that T.K. took as gibberish at first. But the alien words definitely shocked, for Mik had seemingly been near deaf-and-dumb for so long (especially following what Christina Alpreece had subjected him to) that this vocal moment was, indeed, miraculous. What Mik said resembled the sounds and cybernetic "words" of the destroyed alien soma – PQ 31 – back in the Medulla Compound, and T.K. felt a chill of foreboding overtake him – one at once frightful and otherwise. There was a strange look of new born joy on the boy's face, as if he'd recovered a lost innocence.

"I don't believe this," T.K. said.

Then, looking back down at the bloodied Raul Macon, T.K. witnessed another unusual metamorphosis in progress. Macon now appeared immured within a coma. His hair fell out quickly, his depilated skin turned an orange, green, then marble-white hue. His bleeding stopped, and his guerrilla fighter's garments fell off him in slithering bacon-like strips, revealing his now almost emaciated and genderless body.

The air smelled with a displeasing burst of napalmed aromas. T.K. realized he was seeing something like those Cranach creatures who once haunted the Medulla Compound's uniquely insulated territory, the Alpha Sphere, and wondered if Raul Macon's new incarnation – neither *dead* nor *alive* – was close to what the late Project Director termed "The Aleph Point," that nuclear juncture of consciousness where ultimate transcendental powers of inner-and-outer space were said to *energenetically* intersect – providing its subject with the most omniscient (or worthless?) powers in the Universe.

Yet – looking again at what remained of Raul Macon-May – T.K. sort of doubted it. Hours may have passed during this steadfast contemplation, and behind him boy Mik continued to babble his litany-like imprecations in the happiest manner imaginable. They hardly noticed the large ebony crow which alighted nearby on a lichen-thick rock. Cawing at them, the digital crow croaked "... Evermore –!" to Mik's prattle – T.K. was sure of it – before flying off with a portentous flap of wings.

Somewhat extraordinarily, T.K. Keller managed to control his dread long enough to realize he had to get back to Amsterdam with Lelica's boy Mik. T.K. yearned to see and make amends again with that buxom Dutch barmaid, and knew – thanks to Raul Macon – he could. The fact of the Medulla Raze would remain a secret buried deep within him. There atop a stark Teutonic hill in West Germany, T.K. Keller could sense a new day awakening, even if it would be governed from a long-distance by that invisible Cranach government which the earth's fate depended on – or so he had to believe.

Their descent back to the autobahn-like roadway took hours, and once there they were passed by others, on foot or in cars, hastening towards a destination they were loath to inform T.K. of. Some of the pitiful hiking Germans were refugees, he knew, from bad things happening around the country – and the world. T.K. could see the far horizon clouding over with great clouds of smoke, and what appeared to be a formation of air ships. In his exhausion he felt himself returning to an ambiguous state of being, wherein all he perceived seemed governed by something outside himself. Alternately walking and hitching rides for days, they finally reached a large lake of ice poised -- like an albino crater in the now treeless expanse of gutted wilderness, where all that remained were charred arboreal stumps with broken limbs pointing crookedly accusing fingers into the pale sky.

Above them over the lake T.K. saw the hovering and blue shapes of giant spacecraft hauling up the refugees with large dangling plank-ladders. He pulled Mik along into the bustling crowd streaming magnetically toward the ladders, and glancing up saw the Black faces of waiting crew stationed at the triangle-shaped entrances. He was told they would be going to a New America that existed somewhere in the distant regions of Space, and he was not afraid. There they would be reunited with a Oneness awaiting them, into a place of scintillating levitation courtesy of these supernatural magnetic physics, a final ascension delivering them from the ravaged face of a sodden earth.

POSTSCRIPT NOTES:

1. nu -- The 13th letter of the Greek alphabet.

2. nu -- *well? so? so what?* -- Yiddish

ISBN 1553698916